R

PRAISE FOR

Under the Same Sky

"A beautifully written, riveting novel that had me hooked from the opening sentence. Genevieve Graham is a remarkable talent."

—Madeline Hunter, *New York Times* bestselling author of *Dangerous in Diamonds*

"*Under the Same Sky* weaves together the lives of its two protagonists with such skill and poetry it's like entering a dream, one that will leave you both marveling and richly sated."

—Shana Abé, *New York Times* bestselling author of *The Time Weaver titles by Genevieve Graham*

UNDER THE SAME SKY

SOUND OF THE HEART

Sound of the Heart

GENEVIEVE GRAHAM

BERKLEY SENSATION, NEW YORK

THE BERKLEY PUBLISHING GROUP
Published by the Penguin Group
Penguin Group (USA) Inc.
375 Hudson Street, New York, New York 10014, USA
Penguin Group (Canada), 90 Eglinton Avenue East, Suite 700, Toronto, Ontario M4P 2Y3, Canada
(a division of Pearson Penguin Canada Inc.) • Penguin Books Ltd., 80 Strand, London WC2R 0RL,
England • Penguin Group Ireland, 25 St. Stephen's Green, Dublin 2, Ireland (a division of Penguin
Books Ltd.) • Penguin Group (Australia), 250 Camberwell Road, Camberwell, Victoria 3124, Australia
(a division of Pearson Australia Group Pty. Ltd.) • Penguin Books India Pvt. Ltd., 11 Community
Centre, Panchsheel Park, New Delhi—110 017, India • Penguin Group (NZ), 67 Apollo Drive,
Rosedale, Auckland 0632, New Zealand (a division of Pearson New Zealand Ltd.) • Penguin Books
(South Africa) (Pty.) Ltd., 24 Sturdee Avenue, Rosebank, Johannesburg 2196, South Africa

Penguin Books Ltd., Registered Offices: 80 Strand, London WC2R 0RL, England

This book is an original publication of The Berkley Publishing Group.

This is a work of fiction. Names, characters, places, and incidents either are the product of the author's
imagination or are used fictitiously, and any resemblance to actual persons, living or dead, business
establishments, events, or locales is entirely coincidental. The publisher does not have any control over
and does not assume any responsibility for author or third-party websites or their content.

*For Dwayne,
my real life hero.*

ACKNOWLEDGMENTS

I must start with thanking my brilliant editor, Wendy McCurdy. Without her insistence that I write the companion to *Under the Same Sky*, this book might never have come into being. And thank you to my exceptional, always gentlemanly agent, Jacques de Spoelberch, who asked me that day, "So do you think there's a story?" To which I, of course, replied that there definitely was. For sure. Then I ran around shrieking, tearing my hair out, praying for a story to fall out of the sky and land on my pages. Fortunately, Dougal arrived to save the day.

Thank you to all the friends and family who read my early drafts and assured me this novel was as good as the first one. And to those friends and family who haven't read it until now, thank you for supporting me blindly. Your belief in me means so much.

Thank you to my online friends and editing clients who have encouraged me all along this exciting process. And to the generous book bloggers and reviewers who helped a debut author reach further than I ever imagined I could.

Working with history allows me to meet passionate people who are often generous when asked to help. Without Scotland's Lawrence Clark, bushcraftventures.co.uk, I'm not sure how Dougal would have survived such a tight spot. Thanks, Lawrence.

Thank you Kaki Warner, Joanna Bourne, and Madeline Hunter, wonderful authors all, for taking me under your beautiful wings.

Thanks, Mom, for always believing I could do whatever I said I wanted to do.

Thank you to everyone who loved *Under the Same Sky* and recommended it to their friends. It's an honor I never dreamed possible.

Most of all, thank you to the patient, generous, wonderful love of my life, Dwayne.

And thank you to the loves of *our* life, Emily and Piper.

And Murphy the dog.

And the chickens.

PART 1

Dougal

CHAPTER 1

One of Many

Dougal was no stranger to the voices of the dying. He was a warrior, born and trained to kill. Death was simply part of his life. In the heat of battle, blood roared so ferociously through his head, he barely heard the sounds of men drawing their last breath.

But on this bloody morning in April 1746, one voice cut through the curtain of noise. The sound was small, almost buried beneath the misery, and yet he heard it, a voice he knew so well: his father's voice.

His father had known this would not go well. Earlier that morning, Dougal had looked into Duncan MacDonnell's liquid blue eyes, tearing from the cold, and had seen the knowledge. When Duncan gathered his sons to him for what would be the final time, there was defiance in the set of his bearded chin.

"I'm proud o' ye, my lads," his father had said. "An' I'm proud to be here wi' ye."

Dougal remembered the weight of his father's hand as it had

clapped on to his shoulder. Then the cannon had started up and the hand was gone, grabbing for pistol and sword.

When the battle began, the four had gone in together as they always did—Dougal, his brothers Andrew and Ciaran, and their father Duncan. Andrew always ran at Dougal's right flank, his father and their younger brother, Ciaran, at his left. The MacDonnell men fought in pairs. Dougal and Andrew had trained to fight side by side, covering each other's more vulnerable points. Together they were an invincible force. Since Ciaran was the youngest, he and their father fought together, Duncan taking Ciaran's weaker side. But when Dougal looked beside him sometime later, it was his father, not Andrew, next to him. The English had managed not only to decimate the Scottish army, as ragtag as it was, but to fracture his family's tiny battalion.

"Where are your brothers?" his father had hollered. They seemed to have vanished, swallowed up by the smoke-heavy mist.

Dougal glanced around and spotted Andrew, leaning in to take a swipe at a redcoat. Ciaran was a few steps back, watching, sword at half-mast. Andrew finished defending his younger brother, then swung around and yelled something Dougal couldn't hear. But in Dougal's mind Andrew's words were clear: *Kill or be killed, Ciaran! Fight, damn it!*

"There, Da!" Dougal yelled, pointing across the field. "Andrew's just saved Ciaran's arse again."

His father nodded shortly, his face haggard behind a shaggy beard. "They'll do. Let's you and I go then."

The two roared into the thick of things, black-haired demons with fury burning in their eyes.

But now the fire had been extinguished from his father's. One minute he was beside Dougal, cursing the English in furious Gaelic, hacking through them as if he swung an axe through trees. Then he was on his knees, gaping into the victorious expression of one of them. The soldier's bayonet was sunk deep in Duncan's chest. Duncan's filthy hands, emptied of their own weapons, clutched at the blade, heedless of its edge as it sliced through his fingers.

Dougal thrust his sword through the soldier's back, then fell to his knees at his father's side.

"Da?" he cried. "Da!"

Duncan's eyes had begun to glaze into an opaque stillness Dougal had seen too many times. Blood snaked from the corner of Duncan's mouth, but he tried to smile, pulling back his lips and showing teeth dark with blood.

"Proud of ye, son," he grunted.

"No, Da! Hold on!"

But Dougal knew, as his father knew. Nothing could be done for Duncan.

They were in an area to the side of the main field, slightly out of the range of the oncoming missiles of grapeshot and cannonball. Dougal dragged the anchor of his father's body out of the way, avoiding the incoming tide of foot soldiers. Duncan needed his son, needed *someone*, and everyone else was gone. Dougal hunched beside the shuddering body, bracing his father with one arm, gripping his sword defensively with the other. Just before he had to rise and fight, he heard his father's last breaths, a weak gasp, then a lifeless whistle as his lungs released air for the final time.

"No!" Dougal cried, rage and grief roaring like flames in his chest. His breath came in gasps as he set his father on the ground and bent over the still chest, forcing tears to stay within. There was no time for them now. "I fight for you, Father," he said, then leaned forward to kiss the clammy brow.

Turning away, Dougal threw himself into the battle like a man possessed. These men would pay. They would pay with their meaningless lives for the only one that had mattered. Dougal was a *ban-sidhe*, a whirling monster sick with rage, black eyes burning through a face smeared with filth and blood.

Such was his trance that he didn't notice the five sweat-soaked redcoats surrounding him until the black mouths of their muskets yawned at his head.

"'Allo, you scum-suckin' toad," one yelled over the battle noise, peering at Dougal through his sights. He took a moment to spit to the side and peruse the fallen bodies at Dougal's feet, then set his chin back to the handle and squinted. "We'll 'ave yer 'ead for all this mess, we will."

Dougal stood panting, his face twisted with fury, either hand clenched around the hilt of a different sword. He drew a blackened arm across his brow to clear his eyes of stinging sweat, lifting his upper lip in an instinctive display of teeth. "No' one of ye to pull the trigger? Go on then. Afraid I'll come back from the grave to haunt ye? Clever bastards, ye are. For I will. I will remember each of ye. I'll tear yer hearts through yer teeth while ye watch."

A cannonball ripped through the air twenty feet away, crashing through trees, men, mules, anything in its path. Muskets flashed, men shouted, but the nervous glance exchanged by a couple of the soldiers seemed more related to Dougal's threat than to the obvious physical one. They shuffled nervously and two muskets wavered, but at a grunt from the lead soldier, they snapped back into position.

The first soldier smiled and gave Dougal a knowing wink. "You ain't comin' back, mate. Where you're off to, they don't let you come back. Tell you what, though. We won't kill you just this minute. We'll 'ave a bit of fun with you first, right? And when we're done, I'm willing to wager you'll wish one of us 'ad shot you. An' then maybe we'll just take you wif us when we go 'ave a little visit with your mother and sisters, shall we?" He nodded at Dougal's two swords, dark with blood, held in readiness at the warrior's front and side. "Drop those, would you?"

"I won't," Dougal assured him.

The soldier shook his head with apparent disappointment, as if Dougal were an obstinate child requiring discipline. "Oh, you will." He jerked his chin toward a soldier behind Dougal, who, on cue, slammed his musket into the base of Dougal's skull.

When Dougal awoke, he lay on his stomach, unable to move. He opened his eyes but kept his head down, leaving his cheek to chill on a bed of mud. The air was still, its quiet engulfing the ringing in his ears. Battle sounds had ceased. It was done. The back of his head felt as if a horse's hoof had dug into it, with the weight of the beast behind it, and his eyes throbbed from the pressure. His shoulders ached. He tried to bring one palm to his forehead but discovered his hands were tied and bound behind his back. His feet were tied as well.

So, he thought. *My head isna the worst of my worries.*

He wasn't alone. He lay among others of his kind, all similarly trussed, most groaning with pain. From his vantage point, facedown in the dirt, Dougal didn't think any of them seemed too badly injured. That meant, he assumed, they were to become prisoners of the damn English dogs, slaves to their demeaning whims. From the furious Gaelic grunting going on around him, Dougal knew some of the men here would rather die than face that prospect. Rather slit their own throats than submit to English rule. But Dougal had other thoughts. He would survive, if only to make the English regret everything they had done to him. To his father. To his brothers.

Where were his brothers? Not here in this writhing mass of captives. He studied the group as closely as he could, checking each dirty face, listening for familiar voices, but found nothing of them.

Very carefully, trying to ignore the crushing agony at the back of his neck, Dougal turned his head so he faced the battlefield. As he'd thought, the fight was done. A pall of thick smoke still hung in the mist, stinking of sulphur and death. Wincing at the pain, he peeled his cheek from the wet ground so he could see farther. He narrowed his eyes, watching dark, red-tinged figures wander through the field. Occasionally the sharp crack of a musket cut through the fog. Putting the badly injured out of their misery, he figured. Maybe that was a blessing, to end the suffering. If they weren't hurt too badly, it appeared they ended up here on the ground, tied like a beast.

Dougal's gaze picked out two of the distant soldiers and followed their movements. They walked, stopped, then leaned down, jerked back up, and repeated the motion. Strangled sounds of men were cut suddenly short. Dougal shuddered and thought of his brothers again, this time with more urgency. *Please God*, he prayed. *Don't let them be lying injured on that smoke-shadowed moor. Not shot to pieces and still breathing.* Because those poor souls were being systematically dispatched by English bayonets.

"Wherever ye are, brothers, I go wi' ye in spirit," he murmured, then lost consciousness again.

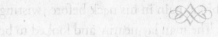

A Different Kind of March

Dougal's cheek still pressed against the mud when he awoke, numb from the cold. He was tired, always tired these days, but Dougal had never been a man to admit to that. He was frozen and half-starved, as they all were, and that weakness had contributed to a lot of the killings today. He kept his eyes closed, tempted to cry, but he lacked the strength.

Before they'd even stepped onto the frozen marshes of Culloden Moor, Dougal had known the Scots would suffer. He hadn't needed one of his damn dreams to tell him this battle would not go well. He and the other Highlanders had marched and practically starved for the past two months, and their plaids had been poor protection against the miserable late winter. None of the crofters they had passed on their travels had food to share. The whole of the Highlands was suffering. The men had gone down to London, up to Culloden, back and forth in the miserable winter and spring months, completely at the whim of their chiefs and Prince Charles himself.

Damn Prince Charles. Dougal had pride in his people, sure. But to throw thousands of them away just so one man could settle his well-dressed arse on a throne? Useless. Unforgivable. And if Dougal ever saw Charles, he'd tell him so to his bonny wee face.

"Hey," he heard from his right side a few feet away. "Help me, man."

Dougal consulted the stabbing pain in his neck before twisting to see the source of the voice. The man lay nearby and looked to be about the same age as he, with a dark complexion and straggling brown hair pasted to his face. Dougal didn't remember having seen him before, but there had been so many of them. What was one man out of thousands?

"Aye, sir. How do ye fare?" Dougal asked.

"Och, I've the most terrible itch on my nose. Ye dinna think ye could help me wi' that, could ye?"

Dougal stared at the man, whose expression was dead serious. For a moment, Dougal was speechless, then he burst into laughter, feeling his lip split with the effort and his head pound with renewed vigour. Laughter was an unexpected sound, and a few others glanced over to see what was up.

Still laughing, Dougal said, "We're the lot of us trussed like turkeys, probably set to be hangit, an' ye're fashed about a wee itch on yer nose?"

"Aye, I am," the man replied indignantly. "I canna reach it."

"No, I dinna suppose ye can," Dougal said, trying to stem his laughter. "An' how am I to manage it then?"

"I've no idea. But 'twould be a blessin' if ye'd figure it out."

Dougal snorted, then, with a flick of one black eyebrow, agreed to try. He rolled to his right side and used his heels to shove his own body, bit by bit, closer to the man. When he was a foot away, he spoke again.

"Bring yer damn neb here," Dougal said. "I canna reach farther." He wiggled his swollen fingers in illustration. They tingled with strangled circulation from within their rough bindings.

He heard the shuffling of a body behind his, then felt the strange pressure of the man's nose moving against his fingers. Dougal couldn't help himself. He started to giggle.

The man behind him moaned with relief. "Ye're a godsend, man," he said. "That was killin' me."

"*That* was killin' ye? Well, if that's all, then ye're better than most of us. That is one of the strangest things I've ever been asked to do," Dougal said, still smiling. "All done?"

"Aye, I am. Thanks very much."

The men rolled onto their stomachs, though Dougal would have greatly preferred to lie on his back. If only their hands had been tied in front. The man beside Dougal gave him a friendly smile and what would have to suffice for a nod.

"John Wallace," he said. "Yer servant, sir."

Dougal returned the smile. "Dougal MacDonnell. Good to meet ye as well."

There wasn't much to say, so the men sank into an uncomfortable doze while they waited to find out what would happen next. It was becoming more difficult for any of them to stay awake these days, weakened as they were. Now pain and—Dougal hated to accept the word—defeat weighed down every fibre in his body.

Dougal hadn't realised he had fallen asleep until he was jolted awake by a solid kick against his ribs. He grunted and rolled away, wide awake. But when he automatically reached for the offending boot, his bound arms permitted no such movement.

"Wake up, dog," a soldier snarled.

Dougal smothered the retort that pressed against his lips. It would do him no good here. He would wait. Bide his time. Beside him, John Wallace apparently came to the same conclusion. He snorted into consciousness, looked around, then dropped his face back down to the mud.

Someone grabbed Dougal's feet. He kicked and tried instinctively to yank them away, but his legs were held fast. He twisted as far as he could, then watched a soldier untie the ropes at his ankles. So they would be walking, would they? Fine. Anything was better than this, lying helpless as a lassie in a roomful of brawlers.

Other men's legs were being untied as well, and there were groans and mutterings as the Highlanders stumbled to their feet. Most of their hands were still bound, so the men were limited to shrugging and squirming to release cramped muscles.

They were a sorry lot, Dougal thought, watching the others rise and stretch as best they could. Especially when compared to the English soldiers, who were clean, fed, and glowing with victory. The Highlanders were filthy and bedraggled, covered head to barely covered feet by bruises and blood. He recognised a few men with whom he had walked on the road to hell, men who, like him, had left their families alone and unprotected while they'd gone off to war. That thought brought Dougal back to images of his family. Of his mother in particular. Dougal was fairly sure he was the only man in the family to have survived. So now she was alone out there, with no means of defence other than her dirk, which she carried all the time.

Be strong, Mother.

She was smart, so she might take to the woods. Then again, she might stay in the house, waiting for her men to return. They were big men, all of them, and she wouldn't have expected any of them to die.

No. That wasn't true. She'd known as well as they had. She'd packed their food and seen them off, then turned and ducked through the small door to the croft. She'd never shed a tear. Or if she had, it had been secret, falling within the refuge of her empty home.

What of his brothers? He knew, of course, the fate of his father. But what of Ciaran? And Andrew? He should have been with them. His back should have been against theirs, fighting as they'd been taught. But that damn fog, the cursed smoke. He'd lost them as soon as they'd started running, shrieking, onto the frozen moor.

John Wallace jostled him from one side and Dougal gave him a placid smile.

"What of it?" John asked.

"Eh?"

"I was sayin' I think we should leave," John suggested. "Just go. When the sons of bitches are lookin' elsewhere."

"Oh, that's a fine idea, John. I reckon they'd just let a wee slip of a man like yerself take a walk off into the trees wi'out too much notice. No, ye fool. They've plans to work us hard. Otherwise they'd have shot us by now."

John shrugged good-naturedly. "Worth a thought."

Dougal gestured with his chin toward a cluster of older men off by the trees, hunched and curled into themselves with resignation. "Those fellows willna fare well. Nor those." He switched his gaze to a couple of small boys standing together, studying the activity with owlish expressions. They were probably no more than thirteen or fourteen. Drummer boys, he imagined. Frightened lads who should have been home practicing with wooden swords, not facing the menacing glares of hardened English soldiers, ripe with victory. The boys' hands were untied, he noticed, as were those of some of the older men. The ropes were for bigger men, those who offered obvious threat to the soldiers.

"I'd think they're no' much use besides entertainment."

As if he'd been overheard, a couple of soldiers strode toward the

boys. Dougal saw them stiffen but set their slender shoulders in defiance, and the darker of the two stepped forward, placing himself as
a shield in front of the smaller one. The soldier stood head and
shoulders taller than the little Highlander, but Dougal wondered
which, when faced with death, would be braver. The soldier chuckled at whatever the boy had said, and Dougal heard the cold sound
from thirty feet away. The boy's jaw was clenched, and when the
soldier turned away, the boy spat at the receding red coat.

The soldier whirled and Dougal took an instinctive step toward
the youngsters. "You little pig turd," the soldier growled. "You'll
show a bit more respect, you will."

Using his momentum, the soldier ploughed his fist into the boy's
cheek. The slender body crumpled, and though his hands were still
tied behind him, Dougal stepped in as the soldier moved toward
the smaller boy.

"If it's a fight ye're after," Dougal said. "Might I offer my own
services? Surely ye'd no' want yer men to see ye crowin' o'er a couple
o' wee lads. Doesna seem so gallant when they're barely thirteen,
does it?"

"Sixteen," came a whisper, which Dougal ignored.

"You've fight left in you, 'ave you?" the soldier demanded with a
sneer. "Bloody Scots 'ave no idea when to quit." Needing no further
encouragement, he smashed one fist into Dougal's cheek, then
plunged the other upward, under Dougal's ribs. Dougal doubled over
as the breath whooshed out of him, then turned to the side and spat.

He straightened and glared at the soldier. "Better?" he asked, voice
gruff from lack of wind.

The soldier gave him a wide smile, his mouth a checkerboard of
missing teeth. "For now, my lad. But we'll talk later, shall we?"

Dougal slid his jaw one way, then the other, testing the extent
of the injury. The soldier hadn't had much of an arm, fortunately.

Good enough, but now Dougal knew what the man was made of. And at least he'd forgotten about the boys for now. Satisfied, he sniffed and started back toward John.

"I could have done just fine on my own, sir," came a whisper.

The boy still standing was slender and gaunt, large blue eyes huge in his sunken face. His blond hair raged wildly around his head, and Dougal had an urge to pat it down. To cut it off, even.

"Sure. I reckon ye could have. 'Twas only I've a fondness for gettin' hit," he teased. "It had been a couple of hours, I reckon, since the last one."

The boy, lips tight with pride, studied Dougal skeptically.

"Dinna fash," Dougal said. "They'll come back to hit ye soon enough. There's plenty hungerin' for a fight. An' they dinna seem to mind if it's a young lad, an' old man, or a big fellow wi' his hands tied. I'd keep well enough out o' reach, if 'twas me."

The small face seemed to relax a bit. "Thank ye, sir," he said. "I'll do that."

Dougal looked down at the fallen boy, just starting to push himself back to his feet. The side of his face where he had been hit was already swelling; the other side was black with fresh mud. How many times had Dougal taken part in boyhood brawls, gotten hit, then jumped back up again, eager for a rematch? He waited to see the boy's expression, nodded approval when he recognised the glare of defiance, then turned back toward John, who had come closer to watch.

"Very gallant," John said.

"Oh aye. I'm a real hero."

"Right. Well, then I'll stay by you. They'll hit ye first, I reckon."

"Ye're a smarter fellow than ye let on, sir," Dougal replied.

Within a half hour the crowd of men was shuffling along on the rough, drenched road to Inverness. Dougal's shoulders ached, the joints burned from the restraints on his wrists. His worn shoes scraped along the road so that little pebbles danced ahead of him like raindrops on a still loch.

God, he was tired of walking. Always walking. Or waiting. He wasn't sure which was worse. Either one allowed him to drift away in his mind, which could be either a good or a bad thing. Sometimes he used the time to think about easier times, to bring back memories and voices that made him smile. But more often his mind slid back to the sight of his father's dying eyes, and the sound of his voice. *"I'm proud of ye, son."*

He thought of Andrew. Two years younger than he, quiet and introspective but with a sharp mind. Andrew was the thinker of the three brothers. No, that wasn't right. Ciaran was the thinker, the one with promise, the one the family hoped to send to Europe to attend university someday. Andrew was the dreamer. Always sinking into places Dougal never saw. Always with that faraway look, as if he saw something beyond the sea. But when the situation demanded it, Andrew was just as quick as Dougal. Just as strong and skilled with his sword. They'd been more than brothers. Andrew was Dougal's best friend.

It didn't seem possible, imagining Andrew dead. Andrew was the most vibrant person he knew, empowered by a deep energy that never let him rest. He was almost as big as Dougal himself: easily over six feet. While Dougal's hair was jet black, Andrew's fell in brown waves. Dougal's eyes flashed a clear blue while Andrew's were a deep brown. Other than that, the two couldn't have been mistaken for anything but brothers.

Dougal tried to picture Andrew's body, motionless like all the rest, blood matting his hair and staining his kilt, his dark eyes forever closed. But he couldn't hold the image. It felt wrong. The thought that Andrew's corpse might be sprawled on that field of death was beyond Dougal's comprehension. He looked into the forest on either side of the parade of captives, peering deep into the spring branches. The slender trees glistened with promise of new life, but any buds were barely visible. It was too early for green. Still, Dougal looked for any sign of his brother, then snorted at his own idiocy. Even if Andrew had somehow survived, even if he had run for his life, he wouldn't be stupid enough to hang about and follow soldiers.

Go home, Dougal thought hard. *If you're out there, go home.*

He could almost visualise Ciaran going down. That seemed, though the thought broke his heart, almost feasible. Their younger brother was smaller-boned and almost feminine in his looks, but fierce from necessity. The way of the youngest, always chasing the older two. He stood up to everyone, wanting to prove he was more than just a bookish mind, but swordplay wasn't his strongest asset, and they all knew it. Ciaran should have been fighting with his father that day. That was how they'd always practiced.

Then again, Duncan was dead. He wouldn't have been much help.

For the thousandth time, Dougal sifted through his memories, wondering if there were anything he could have done to change the day's outcome. At least to have his brothers and father marching alongside him on this miserable road to incarceration, rather than headed for an English funeral pyre.

Hundreds of bodies burned. Thousands more limped along this road with him, the undead marching toward the unknown. The Highlanders had set off the year before with such confidence, building their numbers and their conviction with every step. The clans had come together for their Prince, and now they had died for the man. And where was this wonderful Prince? Gone. Some of the men in the crowd actually spoke of seeing him ride away. He'd cheered them on, ridden his beautiful white horse back to a safe distance, then turned tail when the loss became horribly obvious. Dougal shook his head with disgust and winced at the resultant pounding in his head.

There was nothing he could have done to save the others. He knew that. And yet he supposed his soul would always wonder.

CHAPTER 3

Talk of Brothers

Throughout their lives, Andrew and Dougal had heard each other's thoughts. The natural flow between the brothers wasn't something they discussed, and they never told anyone else about it. They talked as regular people talked, of course, but this was something deeper, and something entirely their own. They had no trouble finishing each other's sentences, or not speaking at all but knowing the words nonetheless. There were occasions when something needed doing, or emotions needed sharing, and they both knew. *God*, Dougal thought, swallowing a knot in his throat, *I will miss that most of all*.

Thinking of home made him look around again, and he wondered where they were headed. The sun was there somewhere. Just hidden. He squinted up into the gray, looking for a hint of brightness. Ah. There. He had been right. West to Inverness. That was the only nearby place he could think of big enough for all of them. Three hours' hike at least, with all these stumbling captives and their guards. His feet ached at the thought, his head even worse.

He'd been to Inverness once before, riding with his father and Andrew. It was a grand place, with more folk than he was used to seeing, though there had been even more at the Gathering two years prior to that. He smiled, despite the present situation, thinking of that week. So many of his clan and others, all coming together to celebrate . . . what? To celebrate life, he figured. To celebrate each other. The food, the music, the competitions—it had been an exciting time. And the lassies . . . oh, there was a thought to make any man smile. He could practically hear their sweet laughter even now.

Dougal loved the lassies. Fortunately, they were drawn to him like bears to honey. He knew he was handsome in their eyes. He was tall and strong, with midnight hair and a dusky complexion. His bright blue eyes twinkled with mischief, and the creases at their corners were testament to how he loved to laugh. The hill at the Gathering had been dotted with hundreds of tents and families, lit by campfires and whisky. And the lassies popped out of those tents, flirting with Dougal and Andrew, succumbing to their masculine charms with giggles and kisses.

Dougal rarely said no to an interested girl, but he'd never found one who could hold his attention for more than an hour or two. He wasn't sure what he was seeking, but he didn't consider it important to get married until he found that one. He had seen love in his parents' eyes when they looked at each other. He had also seen folks whose marriage consisted of passing each other in the doorway with barely a word, meeting up once in a while to breed. Dougal knew which he wanted and was in no rush.

When they had headed to battle almost a year past, there had been no one special in his life. Ciaran had a bonny wee thing at home, but then again, he was only sixteen. He was at the age when he thought he was in love as long as a girl fluttered her lashes at him. Dougal, being twenty, was of the opinion that a man was happiest without tethers. A brief dabble in the more enjoyable aspects of socialising, but nothing permanent. So he'd left no one behind.

He and John Wallace fell into step together, both of them tall with long strides.

"From where do ye come?" Dougal asked.

"By Urquhart, in Glenmoriston. My family has a wee cottage there."

"Well then," Dougal said. "We're practically neighbours. 'Tis a shame we've no' met afore this. I'm from Invergarry. My uncle is the MacDonnell. Iain MacDonnell."

"Is that so? I'm wi' the nephew o' the great MacDonnell, am I? Well. 'Tis an honour, sir. An' how did he fare today?"

Dougal exhaled loudly. "I reckon he fared as well as most o' the others. Though come to it, I'd say if I were a chief, I'd hope to die on the battlefield. I'd no' want to think what the *sassenachs* will do to a chief in their custody."

John said nothing, but wrinkled his nose and shook his head.

"Had ye family here today?" Dougal asked.

"Aye, I did." For a moment John's eyes lost their natural shine. He dropped his chin and watched the ground beneath his feet for four or five paces. "But I already lost two brothers at Prestonpans, so today 'twas only my da an' myself. An' he . . . well, suffice to say, he's no' with us on this fine day's walk."

They walked for a while in silence. Then Dougal said, "My da as well. I stood beside him as he fell. My brothers, well, I've no idea. But they're no' here."

John glanced over his shoulder. "Ye're sure, are ye? There's an awful lot of us here."

"I'm fair sure. They'd find me, or I them." He didn't bother mentioning that if Andrew had been among the prisoners, the brothers' minds would already have found each other.

They stopped after about an hour, shivering at the side of the road while their English captors sipped beer and ate bread and cheese. Dougal looked away. He wondered if they would feed them wherever they were going. He'd give just about anything for a crust of bread.

Someone else seemed to have the same urge, because at that moment a chorus of shouts broke out a few feet behind them. Dougal and John turned toward the sound and watched two soldiers drag one of the Highlanders into the middle of the road. The man was curled into a stubborn ball, hands at his mouth, chewing furiously.

"'e stole my bread!" one soldier said belligerently, jabbing his finger into the Scot's chest.

The accused kept chewing, then finally swallowed. He didn't say a word. Didn't have to. His sunken eyes wavered in the general direction of the soldier, but they were unfocused.

"That's thievery," the soldier said. He looked at the others. "Cap'n wouldn't want us to bring in a thief if'n we could help it, is my way of thinking." Two of the men grabbed the Highlander from behind and the soldier punched him hard in the gut. The prisoner collapsed onto his knees, gasping, then looked up with empty eyes.

"I was 'ungry, ye bastards," he said, his breathless voice a sob that twisted Dougal's heart. His own stomach growled in sympathy.

The soldiers hauled the fallen man to his feet and grabbed him under the arms. They half marched him, half dragged him into the frozen woods, then disappeared into the early spring foliage. When they emerged again, it was only the two soldiers. Dougal never saw the thief again.

Two hours later, Inverness loomed, larger and more forbidding with every labouring step. The ragged prisoners were herded into whatever spaces could be found in the city's gaols, cold rock cells that had already been emptied of English prisoners. Some of the Scots simply dropped where they stood. Dougal and John kept moving, hoping at the end of this there would, at least, be food. But Dougal's hopes were disappointed. No food or water was given. With nothing else to choose from, they leaned back against the stone walls of the gaol and did little else for two long days.

On the morning of the third day, they were visited by their captors, who turned away with disgust when they witnessed the suffering spread before them. They returned a few moments later, their noses shielded by cloth, and began by removing the corpses, bodies of starved and injured men whose wounds had never been treated. They proceeded through the masses of men, trying to collect names, but few of the prisoners could even speak, weak as they were. Through clouded eyes, Dougal stared at their backs as they left the cell, leaving the Scots alone again in freezing darkness.

That night they returned, having decided to give each prisoner half a pound of oatmeal per day along with a small serving of water. Dougal tried very hard to make the meagre portions last.

"Hardly a feast," John muttered.

"Ye'd expected one, did ye, my lord Wallace?" Dougal said, smiling at his new friend. "Wi' a side o' mutton perhaps? An' a dram to wash it down?"

John closed his eyes and drooped against the wall with a slow, lazy smile. "Aye, that's the thing," he said. "That's just the thing."

CHAPTER 4

Sentinel

Very little happened in the prison over the next couple of weeks. At first the men were too weak to say or do much, which was all right since their accommodations were tight. Some struck up conversations and new friendships, but they were often tentative. Though everyone there was a Jacobite, a supporter of Prince Charles's cause, they were not all of friendly clans. Forced together, they would have to make do. They were eventually given the bare essentials of medical supplies: water and bandages. Over the next month, some of the prisoners tended wounds that never healed. Those injuries festered and the men developed fevers until their teeth rattled with bone-deep tremors. Dougal watched helplessly, trying not to breathe in the stench as men around him turned inward, sliding away from the others, easing toward death. He wondered if they felt the actual disease take hold. He wondered if they could feel, with some kind of numb fascination, their existence hovering on the edge of death. And he wondered if they cared either way.

He had been close to death once, but he'd been young and lucky. He'd beaten the pox and been left with only a few tiny scars as evidence it had ever ravaged his body. That time in his life seemed like a dream, a dark night in which blurry shapes of his family hovered around him, disappeared, then returned, looming over his bedside like ghosts. He had thought he saw great beasts, thought his family was scheming to kill him, thought he would fall through the earth if he rolled in his bed—all lies his fever told his brain. He had recovered slowly but fully. Now he watched the brave men of Culloden rot until their hearts simply tired of battle. Cold, stiff bodies were taken every morning and the remaining group spread out a little more every time one of the corpses vacated a space. A little more food to share, a little more to drink. A little hole stabbed into each of their souls every time one of them died.

The prisoners were a mixed group of crofters and those who had existed closer to clan power. Dougal was one of the latter, having lived and worked on the land of his uncle, Iain MacDonnell, chief of Clan MacDonnell. He had enjoyed the lifestyle, the benefits of position. Now here he was, lumped in with every other poor soul whose chief had decided they would fight. And where were their chiefs now? Had they survived only to be executed?

Dougal fought his nature while he was imprisoned in Inverness. As he gained strength, every wasted muscle in his body lusted for action, demanded he break out and slay his captors. But only a fool would make enemies with the ones controlling both food and punishment. The prisoners were kept in the gaol for, he figured, just over a month. Then they were herded together and marched toward the Thames. At the port bobbed seven ancient transport ships, shadowed by their escort, the H.M.S. *Winchelsea*.

Dougal was one of about a hundred souls to board the *Thane of Fife*. The men, and even a few surviving women who had been captured alongside, were separated into groups and led one by one over the rickety gangways. Considering the unhealthy appearance of the prisoners as they boarded, in combination with the condition of the ships in which they would be jailed, Dougal reckoned there would be a lot fewer of them disembarking whenever they arrived at their destination, wherever that might be.

Dougal felt sick, waiting for his turn to step onto the creaking bridge leading from land to sea. It was more than anxiety over their destination that troubled him. Just the thought of vanishing into the black hold of one of the decrepit ships, rolling on the waves like stiffened cadavers, made him realise that while the Inverness prison had been bad, it couldn't compare to what was coming. The ships stank of death before the men even stepped on board. But he had no choice. He, along with all the others, was shepherded across the gangplank and locked into the bowels of the ships.

The two young drummer boys were on the same leaky ship as Dougal and John, looking even frailer than they had on that long walk from Culloden Moor. They moved like twin shadows, as if attached to each other by some invisible force, and they clearly didn't belong there, fragile creatures that they were. Like rabbits, they lived a wary existence, surrounded by large, starving men. They rarely joined in conversations with the others, but Dougal watched them, knew they listened and probably discussed their thoughts between themselves at a more private time.

The boys' reality was made painfully clear one day—at least Dougal *thought* it was day. In truth, he wasn't sure if it were day or night, because the light poking through holes in the old ship always seemed a dark gray of no consequence. It seemed to him that the mouldy boards containing the prisoners appeared a shade brighter when the men were given their daily rations, so Dougal assumed that marked morning. Each man received a small, dry bowl of oatmeal, a cup of ale John likened to piss, and occasionally a biscuit. They took this feast to their accustomed spots to eat in relative quiet. On this particular day, Dougal spied a couple of the men watching the boys with interest and muttering between themselves. Struan Grant, he mused. The other was Keith. He could never remember if Keith was the man's first or last name. It didn't matter much either way. The man was wiry and stooped, and his carcass would probably be tossed over the side soon enough.

Dougal knew what they were thinking. In fact, he knew what most men were thinking, whether he wanted to or not. Throughout his life Dougal had been able to hear the thoughts of some men, though he couldn't hear those of women, no matter how he tried. It was different from how he and Andrew always communicated, which was mutual. Listening in wasn't something he enjoyed doing. He usually tried to shut out what they were thinking, except when the thoughts might be of interest to him. For example, his odd talent was useful during card games, which was why he never played with Andrew. If he read the other players' thoughts, Andrew would read his, and that took away Dougal's edge.

Dougal had always been a defender of the underdog. He and Andrew both. Ciaran had often required their assistance, though he'd never asked for it. Their younger brother was smart, but not quite strong enough. So Dougal had always shared his own strength, stepped in when he was needed. These two boys were even slighter than Ciaran had been. Especially in their state of near starvation.

He heard the thoughts of Grant and Keith, though their voices were too low. The men were hungry and they saw an easy source with the boys. The young drummers were oblivious to the men's attention, distracted as they were by their own private conversation. The two customarily sat off to the edge, away from the rest of the prisoners, relatively close to where Dougal and John stayed. They kept to themselves, bothering no one. Dougal leaned forward, watching as the men approached the boys.

"What's amiss?" John asked, following Dougal's gaze.

Dougal jerked his chin toward the men. "Up to no good, them," he said.

John watched quietly from beside him. The boys had just noticed Grant and Keith and had risen to their feet. They stood with their bony fists on their hips, glaring up at the men with feigned bravery. The lads' eyes were huge, but their backs were straight. They wouldn't show their fear to anyone, and Dougal had never been able to read it in their thoughts. In fact, he couldn't read the boys at all.

Dougal stood and crossed his arms, still watching, standing just behind Grant and Keith.

"I'll have that bit o' bread an' thank ye for it," Grant was saying, holding out his hand for the dark-haired boy's portion.

"No ye'll no'," came the brave response.

Grant rolled his shoulders back. His voice dropped so it was less conciliatory. "I'll have that bit o' bread or ye'll no' have need of it."

The boys, standing side by side, pressed against each other for support. "Ye have yer own," said the light-haired lad, and took a cautious bite of his bread, eyes always on the man. Grant suddenly struck out and cuffed the boy's head, sending him sprawling. But the biscuit remained clutched in the small hand.

"Give it here," Keith demanded in his scratchy voice.

The blond lad shook his head, then bit into the biscuit again. Dougal wasn't sure if he'd done it belligerently or simply to ensure he at least had something to eat before Grant took it away, but it was poorly timed. Everything happened at once. The men moved toward the boys more quickly than Dougal had imagined they could, until the lads were backed against the ship's walls. Dougal stepped in between and eyed the men with a mixed expression of challenge and appeasement. And a hint of disappointment.

"Ye'd steal from children, would ye, Grant?" he asked.

"We're no' children," he heard from behind him.

He scowled over his shoulder at the boys. "Shut up, the both of ye."

"Step aside, MacDonnell," said Grant. "This doesna involve you. These lads have somethin' that belongs to us."

"Oh, aye?"

Grant stepped up to Dougal until they stood chest to chest. They were about the same size, so Dougal looked directly into the other man's narrowed eyes.

"Aye," Grant said. His breath rushed through a gaping hole that should have contained teeth, its heat brushing Dougal's face. Dougal, repulsed, took a half step back.

"Ye'll no' bother these boys for their supper," he said.

"An' ye'll no' tell us what to do," Keith said, his voice low.

"No, maybe not. But I'll tell ye what *not* to do," Dougal replied calmly, and waited.

There were no weapons aboard the ship. Those had been confiscated by the soldiers weeks before. But none of the men were strangers to fighting with the weapons given to them at birth. Dougal was ready. He had, after all, put himself in the middle. So when Grant twisted to the right, clenching a fist meant for Dougal's face, Dougal was there first with a short, direct shot to the man's gut. Grant groaned and bent reflexively, but straightened again, red-faced. Again Dougal was ready. When Grant's eyes were almost level with his own, he slammed his fist against the toothless jaw, snapping it to the side, knocking the man flat on his back.

Dougal was weary, weak, and hungry, like everyone else. He was sick of this putrid hold and her stinking cargo of Highlanders. No one on board was fit for fighting, but Dougal relished the sting as his knuckles split. The sharp pain was like a blast of mountain air, something he longed for with all of his soul. He spun sideways in time to slam into Keith, using his left this time: Dougal's stronger hand. A left to his gut, a right to his jaw, and the man's eyes rolled up in his head. He landed with a thud, his head bouncing against Grant's slack belly.

Dougal's blood sang until he felt dizzy. Oh, he had always loved a fight. Even in fun. It was something about the gut-clenching intensity, the primal urgency. He and Andrew had bloodied each other's noses constantly as boys, goading each other on until one or the other collapsed. Their mother had clicked her tongue in mock horror at her filthy sons and their father had nodded approval. His boys were well respected, as they should be. Even Ciaran, though he did his best to stay out of the limelight. Duncan's sons were nephews of the MacDonnell clan chief. They stood up for themselves and did their father proud.

As Dougal had grown older, he'd stepped into brawls, taking on the biggest men he could find, tossing smaller ones aside as if he were a bull surrounded by calves. It was as if the power of the fight fed his blood. He'd never pick a fight himself, but he wouldn't step away from one either. When he was old enough to sample larger quantities of drink, he found the fights came more often, but he lost some of the concentration he required. That bothered him. So he never allowed drinking to get out of hand after that.

War had been a good release for him. The Highlanders had fought in their time-honoured way, screeching as they ran from their hiding places among the trees, shooting pistols, then tossing them aside when they ran out of shot. They unsheathed their swords and sliced through the enemy, but when they were too close for blades, Dougal's fists had flown, quick, sharp, and hard as hammers.

Now he stood in the bowels of this rotting ship, panting, watching the two men slowly regain consciousness. It disappointed him that a short bout like this had worn him out. He stretched his neck from side to side, extending muscles that longed for more.

"We were fine."

The voice came from behind him, full of tremulous bravado. Young and cocky. Dougal turned toward the boys, who had peeled themselves away from the wall and now swayed on their feet, staring at him. They were smeared with weeks of grime, but even so, Dougal could see the light-haired fellow had a dark red bruise blooming on one cheek.

"Oh, aye. I kent ye were fine," he assured them and cocked his head toward the fallen men. "'Twas only I didna like the look o' that one. Didna want him comin' after *my* supper another time."

The boys nodded, seeming satisfied. Their honour wasn't going to be questioned then.

"Ye no' goin' to eat that?" Dougal asked, lifting his brow in question.

Both boys looked at the biscuits in their hands, as if surprised to see them there. They instinctively thrust the food into their mouths, then the blond stopped chewing. He frowned, pulled a small piece back out of his mouth, and held the morsel out for Dougal.

"Would ye have some yerself, sir?"

Dougal considered it. He was, after all, as hungry as anyone else. The boy swallowed.

"Nay, lad. I thank ye. I've had my supper." He turned back toward his regular spot where John sat, watching the proceedings.

"Lovely, that," John said with a nod. "Ye've a dead wicked temper. I'd best remember that."

"Aye, ye should."

"Decent of ye, helpin' out those lads. Poor fellows, barely old enough to leave their mother's teat."

"Oh, they're older than that. Only small. But quick, aye? Ye can see they're canny."

John pinched his thumb and finger against his scalp, grimaced, then flicked a small bug onto the floor between them. "They've no family, ye ken."

Dougal hadn't known that. He'd tried to get inside the boys' heads but had gleaned nothing. He thought maybe the two were so closely entwined with each other, they had no thoughts to spare for anyone else.

He ground the heel of his boot on the bug. "No? Like us then?"

John smiled. "I suppose. Only I've heard they never had family. Lived wild in the woods, the two of them."

They watched the boys for a while. "Handsome wee things," Dougal said, then grinned. "They'd best watch their arses around here."

"True enough," John said, digging for another mite. "The men are tiring of each other's company, I reckon."

The possibility prompted Dougal to move their places closer to where the boys stayed. So when it happened a couple of days later, neither Dougal nor John were overly surprised. Dougal had always slept light, his restless sleep disturbed by other men's voices wandering through his mind. When he heard the creaking of nearby boards beneath someone's feet, followed by a muffled cry, he was in a fighting crouch in the blink of an eye.

The men's hands were firmly clamped over the boys' mouths, pinning their struggling bodies to the floor. The rest of the ship writhed in its customary noisy discomfort, some sleeping, others resorting to whatever they could on which to hook their last threads of sanity. The craft moaned with her movements on the sea, with its captives, with its misery. Few heard the panicked cries of the two boys.

Dougal did. He was on his feet and shoving one man away before they were even aware of his presence. John awoke beside him and interrupted the second man's frenzied attempts to grab at the dark-haired lad. There wasn't much of a fight after that. The attackers were still lost in the fog of lust and attempted rape, the defenders blistering with righteous fury. The intended victims sat shaking, white as the stars they couldn't see.

In the morning when Dougal awoke, he held a crust of bread in his hand that he couldn't recall having seen before. A biscuit lay on the floor by John's hand as well. Dougal peered toward the boys, who were blissfully asleep, curled around each other like overgrown puppies.

A thank-you, he thought, and nodded to himself. He crunched into the bread, hard as the wood on which he lay, and felt the tiny morsels disintegrate on his tongue then travel down his gullet.

CHAPTER 5

Tilbury Fort

Dougal never did find out exactly where the stolen treasures came from, but he suspected the boys were more slippery than he'd thought. If they were, indeed, orphans who had lived as animals throughout their young lives, they would be well versed in the art of self-preservation. Dougal never mentioned the food to them, and they never said a word about it to him.

Attacks on the boys continued for a while. And every time, Dougal and John stood to their defence.

Throughout all of this, the floating prison on which they suffered hadn't travelled anywhere. The *Thane of Fife* was moored at Inverness harbour for weeks before the captain received orders. When the ship finally raised her sails, the prisoners felt the increased rise and fall of the sea. The previous nauseating motion felt inconsequential compared to this. Many of the men on the *Thane* were already ill; some feared typhus and stayed as far away from others as possible, trying to avoid contact with the contagious group. When the wind rose, the ship bucked and rolled, making the illness much worse. The stink rose with the tide, never quite washing out of the floors or walls. It mixed with the reek of urine and shit and rotted fish, mingled with sweat and disease. If the English had intended to win the war simply through torture, Dougal thought, all they would have had to do was pack their enemies onto these ships.

The *Thane of Fife* and two other ships unloaded their cargoes of over two hundred Highlanders on a misty morning in August, and a new contingent of red-coated soldiers marched the dismal group to their new home at Tilbury Fort. They left four ships rocking silently on the sea behind them, four disease-infested, floating coffins cradling more of Dougal's countrymen and kin.

The Highlanders shuffling along the road were, by then, mere shadows of the fierce warriors who had humiliated the English on the battlefields without fail—until Culloden. Their wild beards moved with lice, their eyes sank back into their heads and carried no trace of defiance. The fierce battle cries that had sent English armies fleeing in terror were reduced to helpless retching and coughing, mixed with moans of hunger.

Dougal knew he looked just as bad as the rest of them, but he had fared relatively well as far as his health. He hoped this march meant the end to the suffering was near, or at least that things would improve somewhat. He felt like a different man than the one he had been before, and not one he liked. He staggered on bare feet, which felt soft on the pebbled road, his legs were weak and unsure from their wasted time on the ship. He inhaled the fresh air, grateful they'd left the ship's stench behind, but otherwise uncaring. Occasionally he lost concentration and his mind wandered off. And when that happened, his mental defences came down, inviting in the pathetic thoughts of so many defeated men.

God, he was tired.

John limped beside Dougal. His heel had developed a sore that threatened never to recover, and the walking opened the weak skin further. Maybe the clean air would help. Dougal hoped so. He had seen men die of wounds like this, when a small cut swelled and went dark, when pus seeped out and clouded the air with the sweet stench of sickness. When it poisoned the man, fever took over. It seemed ironic that John could die of something like this after having survived everything else. And yet it was entirely possible, if the sickness in his foot climbed up his leg and grabbed hold of his heart.

As the prisoners passed under an archway, Dougal squinted and read the words "Tilbury Fort" etched into the stone. The prisoners were directed into a long, dark room, its stone walls cold as the blade of his sword in winter. The dank walls and clammy floor smelled of gunpowder, and from that Dougal surmised they were probably inside an unused weapons magazine.

The door slammed behind them, shutting out all light but a thin crack from the edge. The men stood still, waiting for their eyes to adjust. As the vague lines of wall and floor were defined, John sighed.

"Home, sweet home," he said.

Two days later, the prisoners were called into the rain in groups of twelve, where they followed orders and stood in the semblance of lines.

"Right," an officer said, his youthful voice ringing across the yard. He was a new arrival, Dougal reckoned. Young and straight-backed, his jacket was freshly cleaned, his proper white wig at odds with the dingy surroundings. "You men are filthy and sick," he declared. "We have orders to remedy both these situations as well as we might. You shall remove your clothing."

Dougal and John exchanged a glance, then shrugged and unwound the stiff wool of their plaids from around their bodies. It made a soft crackling noise as it was peeled off. The other prisoners did the same, muttering and moving awkwardly as the plaids fell solidly to the ground. The soldiers, faces twisted with disgust, carried the lice-ridden material and tossed it into a fire that burned beneath an overhang at the other end of the yard. Dougal, feeling nothing but dazed, watched the fire catch the edges of the plaids, taste the fouled material, then burst joyfully into flame.

The captives stood waiting, naked and shivering in the rain. Clutching his arms around his body for some hint of warmth, Dougal looked at the stooped bodies of so many beaten men, their bones obvious through mud-encrusted skin. The rain started to work on the dirt, beating away layers of the stuff, and the men used their hands to weakly scrub more of the filth away.

Dougal lifted his chin and closed his eyes, letting the rainwater pelt his face. Ignoring the men around him, he dropped his hands to his sides and let the moment carry him back to the Highlands, back to his home, back to the neighbouring loch that had been his sanctuary. Despite everything, he felt a smile rising within him, but a curt order from a soldier drove it back down.

The plaids were replaced by shirts and breeks. Dougal hated the breeks. He felt confined in every sense of the word. They chafed the insides of his thighs, they blocked any possible ventilation . . . and they forced him to pick a side. The Scots objected to the clothing, feebly demanding their traditional dress, but the soldiers informed them of a recent law passed in parliament. Plaids were no longer allowed. No tartans permitted at all in the kingdom. No tartans, no bagpipes, no dancing, no traditional songs, no weapons. Anything that represented Scotland had been outlawed. The penalty for going against any of these edicts was a severe beating, even death.

"So Scotland is gone," John muttered under his breath.

"No, John. She is only in hiding."

When the group's shock faded to mumbled complaints, each

man was led to a chair, where servant women sheared off most of their hair and beards, letting the greasy locks drop to the dirt. This, too, was thrown into the fire.

It was a strange sensation, the tickle of air and water against Dougal's shorn scalp. Rain washed over the bristles, running in rivers down his face and neck, making him almost giddy. He hadn't worn short hair since boyhood. Running his fingers curiously over the uneven tufts of black hair, he tried to visualise his appearance. He dug ragged nails into his scalp and scrubbed hard, enjoying the tingle and burn of his skin under the attention.

His cohorts looked completely different, their features clear for the first time since they'd gone to war. Now that John's hair stood up in sharp contrast to his white scalp, Dougal realised it was closer to a copper colour than brown. Where the beards had been, the men's sunken cheeks were a sickly white, darkened by blue-black bruises of exhaustion. They were a sorry lot, and Dougal was well aware that he looked almost as haggard. Almost, because he and John had occasionally enjoyed clandestine contributions of extra food provided by the two boys.

Dougal knew a few of the men in the makeshift prison. Two were from his clan, both older than he by about ten years. There were others from nearby lands with whom he'd had a passing acquaintance growing up. But he and John had struck up a friendship from the moment Dougal had scratched his friend's nose, and it suited them both. John was a friendly, cordial soul, just like Dougal, and both were comfortable in a fight, beating back whatever deluded fools thought to challenge them. They were also the ones who kept the men in fine spirits whenever possible, telling stories and encouraging others to do the same. Having spent months together by now, the stories were getting old, but there were ways to tell stories so they were always entertaining, and the two men were fine at that art. Dougal was convinced they would have made great friends in the outside world as well, had they been given the opportunity.

The young boys slowly emerged from within their cocoon, gaining confidence now that attacks on them dwindled. They began entering into conversations, offering glimpses of their past. John had heard correctly. They were orphans who had come from way up in the North, farther than any of the other men had ever been. When their families all died of an illness that somehow left the two of them unaffected, they set off at the age of ten, brothers in every way but birth.

They were smart, Dougal thought. Always listening, always alert, like the forest beasts with whom they'd spent their lives. The dark-haired lad, Joseph, was the louder, more assertive of the two. While both were reserved, Joseph was the one to bring up a story when it was called for, and to tell it with colour and flair.

The other boy, Aidan, could also tell a pretty tale, but tended to leave the talk to his friend. As he grew more sure of himself, Aidan contributed to the general good of the group in a unique manner. On some evenings, when spirits lagged more than usual, he sang to the men. His voice was sweet and high as a lassie's, soothing to the men, evoking bittersweet memories. More than one man, including Dougal, wiped precious moisture from his eyes when Aidan sang. Sometimes when Dougal watched the boys, he couldn't help remembering Andrew, and missed him so much he wondered if a heart could indeed break like the poets claimed.

Aidan was quicker than Joseph, both mentally and physically, with a lithe, slender form better suited to a rabbit than a Highlander. He wasn't strong, but then again, none of them were anymore. The boys had taken to sleeping close to Dougal and John for protection, and on nights when sleep eluded him, Dougal stayed awake and listened to the noises around him. Sometimes, since he couldn't hear inside the boys' thoughts, he eavesdropped on Aidan's habit of whispering in his sleep. The words were quiet, almost not there, but Dougal heard them, though he couldn't understand a single syllable. There was something haunted about the whispering, urgent but unintelligible. A secret the boy's dreams wanted to share.

At other times the boy reversed the roles, staying awake so he could listen to Dougal speak, though Dougal wasn't talking in his sleep. He encouraged Dougal's endless stories and asked questions just so the words could go on and on. It saddened Dougal, because it was as if his simple words somehow fed the boy's desperately lonely heart.

"What is it ye want to hear, boy? Why do ye bother me so?" Dougal teased one night.

"I dinna ken," Aidan said, blue eyes smiling. "I only want to hear more. More about yer family, aye? I canna remember much o' my own, but when ye talk, it helps me think o' them a bit."

Sometimes Dougal felt drained by the end of the day, and his stories ran dry. Even then, Aidan stayed beside him, asking questions, sometimes offering insight into Dougal's own thoughts. He was a very intelligent, perceptive boy, who always seemed to need . . . more. It seemed a shame he had been deprived of any sort of education besides the very basics.

One night, when Dougal's words faded away, Aidan asked a question that had been on Dougal's mind for weeks. "What do ye think will happen to us?"

They had been stuck in this place, doing nothing but aging. It was frustrating. The fact of their not knowing lengthened the stay interminably. "I've no idea," Dougal said. "But they'll have to think o' somethin'. We're only takin' up space as it is. Maybe they'll decide they've had enough an' simply let us go, aye?" He grinned and the boy snorted. "No, no, I reckon not."

"They wouldna just . . . kill us, would they?"

Dougal shrugged weakly. "I suppose it depends on who's in charge at the time. But no. I'd no' think they'd do that. Too many of us. They'd run out o' shot, most like."

Aidan shuddered. "I'll no' be here for that," he said quietly.

"No? An' why not? Have ye other plans?"

Dougal had expected Aidan to laugh, or at least to react with surprise, but he didn't. Instead, the boy studied Dougal's expression closely, as if trying to read his mind.

Dougal frowned. "What is it?"

Aidan took a deep breath, then made his decision. "Joseph an' I, we've found a way out," he whispered.

For a moment, Dougal simply stared, mouth hanging slightly open. Then he found his voice, but kept it low. "There's a way out?"

"Aye, but I wasna sure ye'd be fit for it. Ye must be fairly wee to manage it."

A thumping in Dougal's chest began, a sensation he had almost forgotten. Could it be hope? "Oh, dinna fash, lad. I can make myself small enough," he assured Aidan.

Aidan glanced toward John, who napped beside them. John seemed wearier these days, and had torn one sleeve from his tunic to wrap around the sore on his foot, which was getting worse. "And him?"

"Aye, he can, too. What is it, then?"

The blue of Aidan's gaze on his was intense, as if he tried to read the truth behind Dougal's lips. "It's secret."

"I'll no' tell a soul but John, aye? Ye ken it'll go no farther."

Very slowly, Aidan nodded. "When we go outdoors in the mornin', everyone walks, aye?"

Dougal nodded in encouragement. He pictured the prisoners, forced on their daily march, pacing around the area like the walking dead, gaunt and unaware.

"No one does much but walk," Aidan said softly, rolling his eyes as if he couldn't believe the stupidity of them all. "Walkin' an' some-times talkin', but mostly just walkin'. Like there's nothin' else they could be doin'. Well, Joseph an' I have been busy. We've no desire to live our lives out here. We found a spot, aye? A place in the wall that hasna fared so well as of late." Aidan held out his hands, palms down. His fingers were cut and stained with old blood, the nails shredded. He looked at Dougal. "Ye see my hands?"

"Aye, so?"

Aidan's grin was deliciously wicked, curled up on one side. "We've broke a hole through that wall."

Impossible. The wall loomed in Dougal's memory, a thick, solid fortification of stone and mortar that wrapped around the entire yard. He'd seen no possible opening. Dougal narrowed his eyes, regarding the boy skeptically. "Go on, lad. Dinna stop there, for God's sake."

"We've been at it for weeks, Joseph an' I. We pick at the rocks every day, then put them back in place so no one would be the wiser. Now we're just about done, an' we're goin' home."

Dougal was rarely at a loss for words, but this young lad held him mute. Dare he hope?

"Two, maybe three more days an' we'll be ready," Aidan was say-ing. "The guards dinna pay us much mind because we're wee, but you two lads are difficult to miss, aye? We'll have to be careful."

Dougal frowned. "Why wait for us then, lad? If ye an' Joseph can get away on yer own, ye'll be better off. You show me the spot an' in a week John an' I can catch ye up."

But Aidan shook his head. "Ye canna wait that long," he said. "The guards are talkin'. There's a Captain Eyre on his way, an' talk is he's charged wi' the keepin' of us. No one's sayin' more, but some-thin' will change soon, I reckon. I fear we mus' go afore he arrives."

That seemed sound enough reason to Dougal. He turned and jabbed at John's curled back, to wake him. John didn't open his eyes, but muttered something that suggested he considered Dougal to be the spawn of the devil.

"Come to yer senses, man," Dougal said. "We've business to attend."

John's eyes brightened. And by the time Dougal and Aidan told him the plan, he was wide awake.

CHAPTER 6

Little Pieces of Paper

The next day the men were led into the courtyard as usual. Dougal hung back with John, surreptitiously watching the boys. He had to admit they were skilled at hiding what they were doing. Not even one soldier looked in their direction. The other prisoners didn't pay attention to them either. He and John came as close to the boys as they could without making any obvious movements, and calmly observed the construction of their gateway to freedom.

"Fine lads, these," John muttered.

Dougal nodded, keeping his eyes on the unwary guards. "Two days, they reckon. Then we'll go."

"An' what shall we do first?" John mused.

Dougal frowned at him. "When?"

"When we're out of this cesspool. When we're free men again."

Dougal grinned and crossed his arms over his chest. "Oh, there are a great many things I'd like to do. An' to drink. But first off, I'd have myself a great, thick slice of meat. An' fresh bread."

John's expression was wistful. "Oh, I barely recall what that tastes like." He licked his lips and Dougal noticed he'd lost a tooth that had been there the day before. "My mam always had bread for me," John said. "She said no one could eat like I could."

Dougal chuckled. "She an' my mother could have compared."

An official-sounding shout cut through the yard, and the soldiers awoke from their stupors. Dougal saw Joseph and Aidan wander back to the group as the soldiers corralled the prisoners. John and Dougal stood with the rest, arms folded, watching a group of important-looking men stride across the yard toward them.

"That'd be Eyre," said a small voice. Joseph. He peered between the shoulders of the larger men like a curious blackbird. "He's the one in charge now."

Dougal had no idea how Joseph had known, but it was indeed Eyre. He was introduced to the men with much pomp, and the Highlanders watched, curious but wary. After having looked them over, Eyre straightened, jutting out a young chin freshly shaven that morning. Dougal's own beard had grown back in, and looking at the man's naked face made his own itch. Eyre gazed over the prisoners with a discerning eye.

"Through the generosity of His Majesty the King," he declared in a voice strong with confidence, "it has been determined that from the Jacobite rebels every twentieth man will be brought to trial for his part in the Uprising. He will be tried on behalf of the rest of the men contained here in this fort, as well as on behalf of those prisoners still contained on the ships tethered offshore."

The Highlanders exchanged puzzled glances. One man to stand and take the responsibility for twenty?

"And what's to do with the other nineteen?" called one of the Scots. The others kept quiet, waiting.

"The remaining prisoners will be transported to His Majesty's colonies."

That met with louder objections. The colonies were known to be a land dominated by beasts and savages who would be only too happy to feast on a Scotsman's flesh.

John turned to read Dougal's expression and Dougal gave him a one-sided shrug. "I'd rather face a wild animal than feel the hangman's noose 'round my neck."

"Sergeant!" Eyre shouted.

"Yes, sir! All prisoners will now be arranged in groups of twenty, and will draw lots."

Dougal's stomach tightened with anxiety. This was happening very quickly. Aidan had warned it would be soon, but today? Too soon by far. He glanced toward the boys. They had both gone white and were whispering madly to each other. This could foil their plans. This could change everything.

The soldier began reading names from a long list, and each man stepped forward to be put into a group of twenty. Dougal and John went together, and Joseph with them, the top of his spiky black hair just reaching Dougal's shoulder. But Aidan was directed twenty feet away and dropped into a different group, where he stood watching anxiously, looking very small.

Eyre spoke calmly, his voice assuming the confidence of a man given full authority and no blame. "Each man will draw a paper from the hat. White paper indicates transport. Each prisoner drawing a black paper will be sent to trial. Results will be listed beside each prisoner's name."

Dougal did a quick count, coming up with seventeen groups of twenty. Over three hundred starving men, all looking unusually alert, their stooped shoulders a little straighter now that a verdict was to be read. All the months of stagnancy, days and nights that never ended, and suddenly, in this one decision, their lives would be permanently changed.

A soldier passed along the lines of each group, checking names. Behind him came another, carrying a shiny-furred beaver hat, which he held over the men's heads. Once a prisoner's name was checked, he was instructed to reach inside and pull out a paper.

A black paper meant the man would remain in England and go to trial. Any man going to trial must automatically be found guilty. After all, each Scot had been dragged off a battlefield where they'd been killing English soldiers. The only way any of them would survive, Dougal thought, would be to turn evidence against their own.

A white paper meant the man would be sentenced to an existence in the colonies, however brief that might end up being.

One by one the men reached up and dug into the hat. Their expressions, for the most part, were either blank or shadowed by confusion, though relief did wash over some of them when they plucked a white paper from the hat. The first man to pull a black paper stared at it for a moment, then clutched it to his chest. He started chewing wildly on his lower lip, but said nothing. A friend leaned in and asked him something, but the man stared distractedly at the empty yard beyond, giving only a slight shake of his head to show he'd heard what the other had said.

The group on Dougal's other side quietened when a black paper was pulled. The recipient was an older man, probably a man of substance in his previous life. He stared at his sentence in silence, then the deep lines on his face wilted and he began to cry silently. After all this time, after suffering through everything, now he would die. Yes, he was promised a trial. But they all knew that meant he would die.

The beaver hat was passed along another group and Aidan waited, wide-eyed, for his turn.

"It's all right," Joseph called.

Aidan nodded back with a vague smile. "You as well, Joseph."

Both boys had turned seventeen sometime over their stay in Tilbury, and yet in this moment they both still seemed very young. Dougal tried to smile encouragement toward Aidan, standing thirty feet from them, but the boy glanced away. Dougal slapped Joseph on the shoulder.

"We will be fine," he assured him, hoping for all their sakes he was right. He peered down the line at the men, watching their expressions as they each pulled out a white slip of paper. The odds worsened with every sigh of relief. He and John stood at the back. He felt a little queasy, watching the hat come closer.

When it was Aidan's turn, all three watched the boy reach inside the hat. He pulled out the paper, keeping his eyes squeezed tight, but Joseph's happy cry urged them open.

"Ye're fine, Aidan! White! Ye're fine!"

Aidan stared at the little white square with a look of amazement, as if he'd never seen anything like it before in his entire life. Then he looked up at Joseph and smiled. His expression took Dougal by surprise—he hadn't seen that smile before. It was the kind that came from deep within, a relief that reached inside the boy's eyes and lit them up. He found himself staring at Aidan, remembering when he could smile like that. When his brothers smiled like that as well.

Two soldiers stood in front of Joseph now, and the first recorded his name. The other lifted the hat slightly out of reach and laughed at Joseph's efforts. Dougal stepped up and yanked the soldier's arm lower, giving him a glare that discouraged arguments. The soldiers were clearly in charge, but Dougal's expression glittered with warning. Scowling slightly, the soldier lowered the hat and let Joseph reach inside.

He was quick, dropping his hand in, whipping it back out,

watching closely. A white slip of paper fluttered between his fingers and he whooped before he could stop himself. He turned toward Aidan, whose smile was huge.

Two more men stood behind Joseph, then it was only Dougal and John. Dougal started to feel a glimmer of fear. Trying not to change expression, he let his gaze flicker toward his friend's face. John had the same thought, for his shadowed brown eyes were focused on Dougal's.

"If it should happen to be my lot," John said, "I'll be sorry to bid ye farewell." Then he grinned ruefully. "Then again, I should feel somewhat the same if it were you drawing that damn black ticket."

"It shallna be either of us, John," Dougal assured him. "I'm sorry for whoever it is, but I fear ye an' I will be huntin' bear in the colonies before too long."

But the black slip wasn't pulled by either of the men in front of them. It was down to Dougal and John.

"Together?" John suggested.

"Aye."

They dipped their hands into the beaver hat and Dougal felt the back of his friend's hand brush against his. He felt the tickle of paper against his fingertips and they pulled out the last two pieces of paper at the same time. Dougal felt a leap of relief, then a sickening plunge. John frowned at the black paper he held between his fingers. Joseph stepped up beside him and nudged his arm.

"It's only a trial," he said, though every man knew the chances of John being found not guilty were extremely slim. And John wasn't the kind of man to turn traitor.

John swallowed, then twisted a dark smile toward his friends. "Aye. It's only a trial. Like life, aye? An' we die at the end o' that, too."

What bothered Dougal the most, not that it mattered anymore, was that their plans for escape were so close to fruition, and John would never reap the rewards. The soldiers took him away immediately after that, clapping him in unnecessary irons, leading him to a different cell. John had joked that maybe he'd be fed better, and Dougal had nodded speechlessly as he watched his friend's receding form limp away.

Dougal was quiet that night, as were most of the men. They had lost seventeen of their men in one day, and not through the usual means of illness or starvation. They had stood by helplessly, watching their friends be led to their death. It was a cold feeling, one that reeked of guilt, and Dougal let it sink deep into him. Once again, as he'd known after Culloden, there was nothing he could have done, but the warrior in him craved release. Demanded revenge. Except he had nothing with which to fight.

The boys said very little that night, though they brought Dougal an extra helping of stew they'd found somewhere. Sometimes Dougal wondered where they found the food, but tonight he didn't bother thinking about it. The stew was cold and tasted like foul water, but he spooned it into his mouth without a word. Something hard had settled in Dougal's chest, making it difficult for him to breathe. He stared at the wall ahead of him while he ate, unsure of what he was feeling. He wondered if it could be resignation. He'd never swallowed that bitter taste before. If that was what giving up felt like, it was colder than the stew.

Joseph sidled up to him and hesitated before he spoke. Then his voice was so quiet Dougal almost missed the words. "We go tomorrow," he whispered. "We canna wait to see about John. I'm sorry, Dougal. Aidan an' I leave tomorrow, an' we'd like for ye to come as well."

Dougal swallowed, then nodded slowly. "I'm wi' ye. John'll no' come back."

Aidan sang for John that night. Sleep never came to Dougal.

CHAPTER 7

Beyond the Wall

It was difficult to predict how the rain might affect their escape attempt, but it would be a factor one way or the other. No miserable mist, this. It poured in sheets from the heavens, and the prisoners were unsure whether they would be going out for their regular breath of air. But the soldiers swung open the dark, heavy doors and ushered them outside.

Dougal raised his face to the endless gray overhead and swallowed the raindrops as they hit his cheeks and nose. He stood alone in the middle of the muddy yard, his feet like ice. The other men had avoided him all day, as if they feared he might be contagious. Catch whatever it was from Dougal MacDonnell and lose a friend. No. They left him alone.

The rain showed no prejudice. It pelted the English soldiers as well, sending them running for cover. They were supposed to keep their eyes on the prisoners, but why bother? The Scots weren't going anywhere. They hadn't in months. Why would this stormy day be any different?

The boys had moved smoothly to their accustomed space against the wall and were shifting rocks so slowly and casually Dougal wondered, when he took a moment to look over, if the job would ever be finished. But in time it was, and Aidan glanced over at him. The boy tilted his head slowly to the side in a deliberate invitation.

Dougal felt almost weak-kneed with anticipation. He could practically feel the grass beneath his feet, a sensation he hadn't felt in months. The blades would be cool and wet, quick with freedom.

How would this end? If they were caught, they'd be shot or hanged. Or at least flogged until they'd prefer death. If they survived, what then? In truth he had very little idea of where they were. Somewhere in northern England, he supposed. He and the boys would find a place and hide there until the danger was past. But if they were caught . . .

"I'm sorry ye're no' here, John," he muttered, then, for the benefit of any soldier watching, feigned disgust with the rain and slumped toward the boys.

They stood against the long stone wall, one facing the yard, one hidden from view. When Dougal approached, they didn't say a word, didn't nod or show any sign of having noticed him. They'd discussed it earlier, and though they'd put up a weak argument about his size and the measurements of the hole in the wall, he'd insisted they go first. He would be their shield. It would have been easier to block the view if he'd still worn the long length of his plaid, but of course that was long gone. So instead he stood, hands on his hips, facing the rest of the yard while the two boys silently removed the stones and squeezed through the opening. A low whistle informed him that they were safely through, and Dougal stepped backward, toward his escape.

His heart thundered, and he was glad of the rain because no one could see the rivers of sweat flowing down his ruddy face. Dougal glanced around, trying to appear bored, if anything, but always scouting for danger. Three soldiers huddled nearby under an over-hanging roof, standing out of the way of the cascading water, but they were talking together, paying no mind to their charges. There were two more close by, Dougal knew, but he hadn't seen them for a few minutes. Probably hiding from the weather.

This was the moment. No one was near, no one was looking. The other prisoners wandered around the edges of the yard, dulled to the rain and the misery of their lives. Dougal stepped back against the wall, hands behind him, and curled his fingers around the uneven line of stones. It had taken weeks of dedicated effort and many split fingernails for the boys to have accomplished this. The opening was narrow, as they'd warned. But he was sure he could manage. Slow or quick? He decided it would have to be slow. If he moved swiftly, he was sure to catch someone's eye. If his actions were hypnotic enough, any curious onlooker would get bored and look away.

Dougal slipped one leg through the hole in the rock. It was awk-ward, because the other side of the wall was lower than the yard. He held on to the wall so his body kept blocking the passage, then slowly, slowly lowered himself sideways and twisted his other leg through. At his feet, the boys crouched, piling rocks back into place with practiced ease, seeming to know exactly where each one fit. This was the trickiest part. It had to be done in a moment, so no one noticed the thin slice in the wall. That would buy them some time before the guards realised anyone had gone. While the boys worked, Dougal stared around him with disbelief.

Green. They had spent months in nothing but gray and brown. Green was the colour of life. Now it was the colour of freedom as well.

"Go," Joseph whispered. "I'll get the rest an' follow."

"I'll no' leave ye here," Aidan hissed.

Joseph fixed his friend with a dark glare, forbidding him to argue. "I'll be right there. I ken better than ye how these stones lie. Come on. Ye ken ye dinna run fast as I. Keep up wi' Dougal an' I'll meet ye beyond that tree there."

Aidan looked terrified at the prospect, but Dougal understood. One person was less likely to capture anyone's attention. He grabbed Aidan's arm and tugged him away. The land around them was mostly flat, the grass underfoot marshy from the downpour. Dougal aimed for a clump of tall grass, intending to wait for Joseph there. Aidan ran hard beside him, bare feet slapping through puddles. They had gone forty feet or so, and had just reached the hiding spot when they heard Joseph cry out. Dougal shoved Aidan hard so they both sprawled facedown on the long grass, chests heaving from the unfamiliar exercise.

The grass, as Dougal had imagined, was wet and cold on his cheek, and it smelled . . . of home.

Aidan squirmed under his hand. "Stay down, fool," Dougal whispered, burying his own head as deep into the grass as he could manage.

"Let go!" Joseph shouted. "Get yer filthy sassenach claws off—"

A shot rang out and Aidan uttered a small, choked gasp against the ground. Dougal held the boy's head down and slowly raised his own. He blinked away the rainwater that streamed over his forehead and tried to see.

Five soldiers. How they'd managed to spot wee Joseph through all that rain, Dougal would never know. But they'd come in force and shot him dead. The soldiers shoved aside the weakened rock wall and climbed through one at a time. They stepped over the small, lifeless body and peered around, clearly suspicious Joseph hadn't been alone.

"Dinna breathe, lad," Dougal whispered. "Else ye'll no' live past this moment."

Aidan lay still and mute beside him, and Dougal wondered if he had, in fact, stopped breathing. He kept his palm on the boy's back, holding him down, keeping him safe. The rain beat against their backs, cold and relentless as hammer strokes. Beneath his hand he felt a short jerk and shudder, then more rolling bumps as Aidan silently grieved.

CHAPTER 8

❦

On the Run

The rain was both a refuge and a nightmare. It fell in frozen sheets, forcing Dougal and Aidan to cup their hands around their eyes so they could scout the land. They lay motionless for ten horrible minutes, during which they saw the solid lump of Joseph's body on the ground by the wall's opening. One soldier stooped and hoisted Joseph onto his shoulder then carried him back into the prison. Half a dozen soldiers still milled around the broken wall, pointing and stomping in the mud with annoyance, but seemed unwilling to go chasing through the storm for anyone. The escapees stayed flat behind the tall grass, waiting.

Finally, just when Dougal feared he might get sucked into the mud if he didn't move, the soldiers turned back toward the yard, passing one by one through the hole. The last two glanced behind them, scanning the open field, but their eyes passed safely over the hidden Scots. Dougal blew out his breath and lowered his brow to the ground with relief.

"Where do we go now?" Aidan's voice was hushed, unsure.

Dougal took a moment before lifting his head again so he could look at the boy. When he did, he was struck by the fragility of the young, pale face. His blond hair was plastered onto his skin, muddy and wet, until it was close to Dougal's own black shade. Mud smeared his face but his lips were chalky white, hinting at blue. Any sparks were gone from Aidan's sad blue eyes. Dougal felt an impulse to grab the boy by his upper arms and shake him, shake the sense into him. *We're free, lad! We survived!* but instead he looked away. He was free, too, but by watching the boy, Dougal was drawn into the bone-deep misery threatening to suck the life from Aidan. Joseph was gone. John was gone. Andrew was gone.

But this was no time for grieving. Nor was it time to celebrate. It was time to concentrate on survival. Dougal shuffled up onto his elbows but kept low, wary of soldiers returning. He huffed out his breath and ran his hand over his face, wiping rain from his line of vision so he could survey the ground surrounding them. It was flat and marshy, providing little more than the occasional shrub or clump of grass as a hiding place. Beyond that, Dougal could see a flooded ditch, possibly a hundred feet across. It looked manmade, like a moat. Grass grew on the opposite side and a dark line of trees beckoned from beyond.

"Can ye swim?"

Aidan shook his head, his mouth pulled down at the corners.

"Well, I can," Dougal said. In fact, Dougal swam like a fish, as had his brothers. He loved the water. What he needed now was a way to get Aidan across with him. There would be little risk of being seen in the water even if a soldier deigned to come that far. The rain would dimple the surface until it was impossible to see much of anything. "Have ye a good grip?"

Aidan stared, mute, then slowly nodded.

"Good. Now . . ." Dougal glanced around, scouting the best route to the water. He pointed to a shrub, then more grass. "Ye must be quick, aye? First to there, then there. We'll get to the water bit by bit."

"We'll . . . swim?" Aidan asked, eyes wide. "But I'll drown."

"No, ye'll never. Ye'll hold me, is what ye'll do. Now go to that bush there. Now! Run!"

Aidan scampered across the marsh like the rabbit he so resembled. He crouched by the shrub, making himself almost invisible among the branches. Dougal skidded to a stop beside him a moment later, and through a zigzag journey between spots, they eventually ended up at the edge of the ditch. They lay flat again, looking down into the moat.

The water roared under the deluge, sparkling silver and black with the dancing rain. Dougal assessed the distance, factoring in his own dwindled strength and Aidan's added weight. It would be damn cold, too. But the challenge sparked something within him.

"Stay here," he said.

Aidan seemed more than happy to oblige. He stayed on the ground, watching with increasing panic as Dougal slipped over the edge and splashed quietly into the ditch. Curious about the depth, Dougal let himself sink then pushed up like a frog when his feet touched the murk at the bottom. Ten, maybe twelve feet, he estimated. Not too deep, but deep enough. His head broke the surface and he shook the hair out of his eyes. Aidan's white face stared down at him, mouth agape.

"Brr!" Dougal exclaimed. He grabbed a stray root to anchor himself in place, then grinned up at Aidan. "It feels wonderful to be alive, does it no'? Come on then."

"What? Me? In there?" The boy shook his head. "I canna go in there."

"Sure ye can. Ye'll ride on my back."

"No I won't."

"Come on." He held his hands up, curling his fingers in invitation.

"No."

Dougal peered down the waterway, but there was no bridge, no path, no other way. The opposite bank looked very far away, gray as mist through the storm.

"Right. Well, I'm goin'. Ye might as well head back then. This is the only way."

For a moment, Aidan looked as if he might cry. He did the same as Dougal had, glancing both ways along the water, then across to the other side, searching fruitlessly for any other option. Finally, he stared back at Dougal. He swallowed. "Dinna drop me."

Dougal smiled again. "Dinna let go. Come on now. We've no' got all day. Pull yerself over the edge an' I'll catch ye."

Aidan hesitated, then took a deep breath and inched forward, sliding on his belly through the mud. The boy had the courage of a lion, Dougal thought, and reached for the slender form as it came toward him. Aidan yelped as his body hit the cold water.

"Climb on board, lad. Here. Wrap yer arms round my neck, but dinna choke me. If ye do that, we'll the both of us sink like stones. All ye need do is hold on an' let me move. Right?"

Aidan nodded quickly, then did as Dougal said, clambering onto his back and hugging his neck.

"A wee bit looser, aye?" Dougal asked, his voice slightly hoarse. "Relax yer arms. Just hook yer hands together." He felt the pressure ease slightly around his neck and Aidan's weight settle against his back. When the balance seemed right, he shoved off the edge and started swimming toward the other shore.

The arm around his neck jerked tight until Dougal felt Aidan's face press against his own head. Every muscle in the boy's body shook and small peeps of terror escaped his lips.

"Stop that! Let go before ye drown us both, ye fool," Dougal growled, and the grip relaxed a little. "Ye've faced an entire army of cannon-firing sassenachs, and *now* ye panic? Trust me, lad. I'll get us there safe if ye'll let me."

Aidan's vibrations never stopped and his teeth chattered so loudly in Dougal's ear it sounded like a woodpecker at times, but at least they reached the other side still attached to each other. As soon as Dougal shoved him up and over the opposite bank, Aidan collapsed and vomited into the grass. Dougal stared at him, shaking his head, then collapsed beside him. Dougal's chest heaved with exertion. It had been farther than he'd thought, and he was weaker than he'd imagined, but he'd made it. They'd made it.

"Nothin' would have happened," he said, puffing through the words.

Aidan wiped his mouth, then glanced at Dougal. His blue-toned lips twisted into a sheepish attempt at a smile. "Aye, well, I've never swam before."

Dougal snorted. "Ye didna swim this time, either." He lay on his back, breathing hard for the next five minutes, letting his eyes close. He felt exhilarated with a temporary sense of freedom. When his heartbeat had slowed to a regular rhythm, he sat up, but not before he'd cast his eyes back across the water and checked for any witnesses. Satisfied, he turned to Aidan. "Right. Time to go," he said. "An' the next time I say ye will be fine, believe me, aye?"

The boy nodded, then lifted his eyebrows in an unexpected show of disdain. "If ye're right, I will."

With a chuckle, Dougal rose and led them toward the next concealing shrub. Their destination was a thin but promising forest. After leapfrogging carefully for a bit, Dougal decided they were out of range and sprinted into the dark shield of trees. Aidan ran at his heels, ducking under dripping branches when he reached the woods.

The forest was still but teeming with invisible life. Dougal felt its energy pulsing all around. Rain shushing on leaves had forced any animals into hiding, but he sensed them there. Their familiar, almost forgotten presence was so comforting that tears filled his eyes and blurred his vision. For so long he had been in the company of men and only men. His surroundings had been cold and hard, hungry for his soul. Here, cutting paths through these strange woods, climbing around fallen trees and tumbled rocks, he breathed in life. The deeper they went into the trees, the stronger he felt.

Aidan panted behind him, doggedly following his steps. Dougal slowed and eventually stopped in a small clearing sheltered and fenced by trees. He bent in half, wheezing in breaths and trying to slow his racing pulse. The rain had stopped, but water still pattered against wet, shiny leaves. He stood upright again and a drop landed on Dougal's nose, making him smile. He sat on the ground and leaned against an ancient oak, groaning as his legs finally rested. He had been so thrilled to taste freedom he had barely felt the burning in his muscles as he'd run. Now everything hurt.

Aidan sat nearby, curled into a ball at the point where a birch had split into three trunks. "I dinna think I've e'er been so tired," he said quietly.

Dougal watched him, saw the boy's eyelids had almost closed, saw the droop of his chin toward his chest. "It's been a long day, lad. Go to sleep." He met the boy's eyes. "Ye'll be safe. I'll keep watch."

"But you—"

"I'll sleep when ye're done."

Aidan gave him one last, weary smile, then closed his eyes. He was sound asleep before Dougal could say anything more.

Night closed in two hours later, and Aidan awoke, shivering. "Have a good sleep?"

"N-n-n-no," Aidan muttered, then moaned as he stretched out his legs.

"Come here, lad. It's too dark to find our way through the woods. We'll have to sleep here. I've dug in these leaves an' found a few not soaked through, but there's no' enough for a fire. We'll use what we can for a blanket."

Not that they could chance lighting a fire even if there was enough dry tinder to raise a spark. Neither of them dared send a smoke signal to any curious Englishmen. So there was little they could do besides move continuously or stay close together, feeding the other what little warmth they had. Dougal gave up trying to stay awake after a while, and the two of them nodded off, leaning back to back, pressing their sides against the biggest tree they could find.

It was the crows that woke them, distant but distinct, shattering the stillness with cries that sounded like screeching soldiers. Dougal and Aidan awoke at the same time, leaping to their feet so leaves showered off them.

"C-C-C-Christ," Dougal stuttered, shuddering with the cold.

Aidan hugged himself, then clicked his tongue with annoyance. "'Tis only c-c-corbies."

"Aye, well, it's good they woke us. The sun's up an' the fort will ken we've gone. Now that the storm's gone, they'll come after us. We've no time to waste."

"And if we run, we'll warm up," Aidan grumbled.

As if Dougal's mood had inspired it, the sun shone all day, drying their clothes and raising their spirits. They stuck to lesser used paths for miles, staying close to the line of the Thames, but far enough that they avoided any possible meetings. If they followed the Thames, Dougal realised, they'd eventually have to reach London.

At least from there he'd have some idea of where they were. They ran without stopping as often as they could, needing to put distance between themselves and Tilbury. Dougal was relieved to learn Joseph had been wrong. Aidan wasn't slow at all.

It took two days before the stench of London reached them. They smelled the city before they saw it, shadowed by a low black fug of coal smoke. It hung over the city like a sweaty cloud, sullenly independent of the rest of the sky. Sewage was the least of the odours. Beneath that the heavier, cloying tang of sickness was weighed down by the stink of rot, decaying flesh both animal and human. The city was a miasma of stink unimaginable to most, but it hardly bothered either Dougal or Aidan. They had lived among it on a smaller scale for months.

About a mile outside the city, Aidan and Dougal dropped onto their backs in a tall field of grass, trying to prepare themselves for whatever lay ahead. They were weak and close to starving, having eaten nothing but seeds and berries they'd found along the way. There was more traffic now; horses and buggies travelled the main road, and with them came the threat of highwaymen. Worse than these were the footpads, cold-blooded and desperate criminals who would butcher a person for the sake of a couple of shillings without the slightest tweak of conscience. Dougal was well aware that if he and Aidan ran into this kind of trouble, they might not be strong enough to fight back. Not that they had anything for the creatures to steal, but they wouldn't know that until they checked, would they?

"I'm so hungry I dinna feel it anymore," Aidan muttered, staring toward the city.

His voice was sad and weak. It had sounded that way ever since they'd lost Joseph. Dougal watched the boy's face, wishing there were something he could do. Grief was heavy in his own heart as well. He had liked Joseph. But seeing Aidan's agony only reminded him of how lost he felt without his own brother. So many needless deaths. It was a difficult enough life without having to battle continuous loss.

"We'll find food soon," Dougal assured him. "An' ye'll start to feel better. About everythin'. Aye," he said, seeing the doubt pool in Aidan's clear blue eyes. "Ye will. O'er time."

A bird called from far away, then another, and Dougal started to wonder if the sound was actually a bird, or rather someone screaming. London loomed before them, offering . . . what? What were they getting into? He'd visited Edinburgh a long time before, and it had been a big city with big-city troubles. But it hadn't carried this heavy layer of foreboding over it. Or maybe it was just that Dougal now saw threat in every shadow.

"Should we wait for dark before we go in?" Aidan asked.

Dougal shook his head. "I reckon we should see it in daylight first. We'll jus' go canny. Stay quiet like. Maybe we willna stay at all, only find a meal or two." He twisted his face in a comical expression of disgust. "I hope the food tastes better than it smells, aye?"

Aidan smiled vaguely. "I'm hungry enough to eat it either way."

CHAPTER 9

London

The cloud overhead was dark, but the city was darker. Dougal hadn't seen any soldiers in over a day, so he made the remainder of the walk easier by following the regular road into London. It bustled with activity, jingling and banging with horses and carriages that barged through without waiting for the travellers to move aside. More than once he and Aidan were splashed by the rush of narrow metal wheels bumping through mud puddles. Houses began popping up along the sides of the road, and Dougal shoved Aidan out of the way once, in time to avoid being hit by slop as it was dumped from an upstairs window. Coming into the actual city, the cobblestone road was thick with mud, and the gutters ran with all sorts of refuse. As they walked past the first few buildings, they had to step around a woman squatting in her skirts at the side of the street, concerned neither with modesty nor with the call for a chamber pot.

Aidan's eyes were huge, his grimace tight with distaste. He glanced toward Dougal. "The smell," he muttered.

"Breathe through yer mouth. The entire place is like a chamber pot ne'er emptied."

"An' it's so . . . loud."

Dougal nodded and grimaced as he stepped over something he thought might once have been a cat. Flesh seemed to move under a layer of maggots, and flies buzzed past Dougal's face, furious at having been disturbed.

"Aye. It is that. We'll keep goin'. Maybe it'll get better."

Aidan swallowed. "Or maybe it'll get worse."

Some of the tall stone buildings, for Dougal couldn't make himself see them as houses, leaned in a gentle slant over the road, looking precariously down as if curious. Their brickwork appeared to be dangerously loose, and chunks were missing here and there, leaving gaping black holes like missing teeth in their place. Children ran screaming through the street, their faces smeared with filth, shouting curses Dougal had never even considered using. And he wasn't usually particular about his wording.

A woman in a faded red gown, barely holding its shape over wide, bouncing hoops, spotted them and approached Dougal as if she knew him. She was probably young, he thought, but time had had its way with her, carving her down so she was thin as a branch from a silver birch tree, with skin almost the same hue as the bark. She wore a yellowed white wig and her lips were painted tomato red.

Aidan took a step back when she came close. "What's wrong wi' her?" he whispered, his expression horrified.

"Wrong?"

"Her face! What's wrong wi' her skin an' all?"

"I dinna ken," Dougal said. He'd never seen a woman dressed this way and it felt almost intimidating, the way she walked closer. What was it about her that spooked him? He stared openly, glued to her features by some grotesque fascination. She didn't seem to mind. In the moment before she touched his sleeve, he realised what it was and stepped away. Her eyes. Her eyes, outlined in thick black, were dead. He'd never seen dead eyes on a living woman. They were horrible to see.

She misread his expression. Instead of turning away, she drew closer, smiling conspiratorially. "Care for a little fun, my lad?" she purred.

Dougal was used to people with bad teeth, but this woman didn't have that problem. She had no teeth at all. He'd seen that with old women, but not one this young. It seemed to have affected her cheeks and chin. They rolled inward, making those dead eyes seem to pop out even more. She ran a long, pink tongue over her lips and flared her pinched nostrils as she looked him over appreciatively.

"Are you a big lad, then?" She studied Dougal from his head to his waist, taking in the lines and curves of his body. Her eyes started to show a little life, widening under fluttering lashes. "I imagine so, judging by those thumbs of yours."

Dougal blinked. He had no idea what she—Oh. Now he did. He stepped back again, shocked. He started to object, but she had already moved on to Aidan. Her fingers combed through his fair but filthy hair, which had grown long enough to reach just past his shoulders. The blond strands were heavy and dark with a need for soap. Aidan stared furiously at the ground, trying to ignore the woman's touch.

She sounded pleased. "And what have we here? I've not had a young man in a long, *long* time." She snorted, then looked skyward for a moment, remembering something. When she looked back at Aidan, her eyes were a bit unfocused. "They say I'm a good teacher."

"Go away," Aidan hissed. "I dinna need yer teachin'."

"Oh no?" the woman replied with a chortle. "You know how it all works, do you? Well, why don't you just come along then and show me."

"Go. Away."

Dougal took the woman's wrist gently between his thumb and forefinger and slid it off Aidan's bowed head. She turned her attention back to Dougal.

"Leave the lad," he said. "He's asked ye twice."

"And you, sir?"

"I am in search of a meal an' a bed. Jus' for me an' the boy."

Her eyebrows shot up and Dougal noticed they had been entirely shaved off. Only a thin pencil line marked her expression of surprise. "Oh? It's like that? Well! I wouldn't have taken you for the likes of that, but . . ."

"No," Dougal growled, his face suddenly burning. "That is not—"

"An' what if it is?" Aidan piped up. "'Tis none o' yer business, is it, lady?"

Dougal and the woman both stared at him, startled by his sudden outburst, then closed their mouths at the same time. The woman nodded slowly. The corners of her painted mouth were drawn down, one eyebrow raised.

"Fine, then," she said, though her tone suggested it wasn't the least bit fine. "Pardon me for intruding."

"Aye, an' ye *should* apologise," Aidan said, taking an uncustomary step in her direction. "Ye shouldna frighten folk to death wi' yer silly prattle."

Dougal stared at him. He'd never heard the boy talk this way. "Right," he said, shuffling Aidan away. "We'll go now. Em . . . good day to ye, ma'am."

Aidan was still glaring at the woman, his narrow chin raised. Dougal nudged his side, forcing him into the tide of humanity flowing down the street. He peeked at Aidan's expression, and was amused to see a hint of pride in the boy's handsome face.

"What was all that?" Dougal asked.

"What? Oh, that. Nothin'."

"Oh, aye? Ye bristled like a wee cat back there."

Aidan shrugged. "I didna like her much. An' I didna like what she was suggestin' is all."

"Oh, an' ye'd ken all about that, would ye? Livin', as ye did, in the woods an' all?"

"I ken enough," the boy replied coolly.

Dougal suspected the boy did know, had learned a lot over his time spent on the ship and in the fort. Life would be hard for a pretty boy like him, Dougal imagined.

"I'm so hungry," Aidan said quietly. "But we've no money."

They walked in silence, observing the deranged circus of London dance around them as they went. Through one of the open doors they passed floated the sweet smell of something cooked, something slightly charred perhaps. Dougal's mouth watered at the thought of meat spitting and crackling over a fire.

"What if ye—" He grimaced and stepped over a puddle, then turned his blue gaze toward Aidan. The boy sulked beside him, looking pathetic. "Would ye think to maybe sing for our suppers?"

"Eh?"

"If we were to go to a tavern, maybe, an' ye could sing while I pass the hat."

Aidan frowned, then gave a slow nod. "I imagine so—" He stopped walking and looked up at Dougal. "They'd feed us?"

Dougal shrugged. "Worth a try."

CHAPTER 10

Songs for Supper

There was no shortage of taverns along the street. Some welcomed visitors with hanging metal signs that squeaked when the wind gave them a shove, some were unmarked but seemed to bulge from within with noisy patrons. Dougal pulled one such door open and stepped inside a room boiling with rage. One corner of the place was engaged in an open brawl, while the rest of the place cheered it on. Aidan paused in the doorway, looking dubious.

"Let's try somewhere else," Dougal suggested.

The next tavern was quieter, and the sweet aroma of roasting meat wafted through the large room. Dougal's stomach cramped instinctively, demanding attention. He patted it with reassurance while he scanned the room for an empty table. No one paid any attention to the two travellers as they made their way toward the kitchen and claimed a small, wobbly table.

"Right," Dougal said. "Ye'll stand on this stool an' sing like ye do, an' I'll collect what I can, aye?"

Aidan looked unsure. He looked warily around the room, wide eyes darting over the dozens of faces. Dougal watched his reaction, suddenly realising his young friend had probably never seen anything like it before. He'd most likely seen small family gatherings many years before, and he'd seen more than his share of imprisoned men, but an amiable, voluntary group of men in a room like this was something entirely new.

"What should I sing?"

"Dinna ask me. I've no idea. I canna carry a tune, let alone remember the name of one."

"But—"

"Are ye hungry, lad?" Dougal asked. Aidan nodded, looking pained. "Then sing."

"But . . . what of soldiers? What if they come in? They'll—"

"We must eat, Aidan. Never ye mind about the soldiers. I'll keep watch."

The tavern buzzed with low chatter, punctuated by wheezing coughs from an old man in the corner, the clinking of cups and voices raised in an occasional burst of laughter or disagreement. Dougal gestured at the stool again, then moved toward the bar while Aidan climbed onto his little stage. An empty cup had been left unattended on the bar, and Dougal picked it up. For a moment, Aidan said nothing, only gazed thoughtfully around the room, as if searching for inspiration. He didn't look nervous, Dougal thought. Just pensive.

And then the boy started to sing. The room went immediately silent when Aidan's voice filled its worn stone walls. Every face turned his way. Dougal paused, too, taken aback as he always was by the sweet, sweet voice, like a bird greeting the spring. Aidan hadn't chosen one of the sad, dreary songs Dougal had heard him sing in the prison or the ship. Those were like dirges compared to this, though they'd seemed cheerful enough at the time.

Dougal had never had much of an appreciation for music, despite being easily swept up by battle drums and pipes. But he knew what this boy had was special. A gift that had been wasted on the cold darkness of their prison. Dougal gazed out over the rapt faces of men conditioned to the worst of the world, and he decided to use his own gift. He read their minds.

At first he heard nothing, only sensed a mutual sigh blowing through the room as they adjusted from their conversations to Aidan's melody. Then slowly, like creatures emerging from dens after a storm, he heard the men's appreciation rise into the thick tavern air. Memories of their childhood. Of love lost. Of someone dear for whom they longed. When the song ended, Dougal felt a distinct quaver of loss flit from the audience, a collective hand grasping out. They wanted more. They might even have *needed* more. Aidan held them in the palm of his small, pale hand.

"Don't stop now, lad," someone muttered.

Aidan smiled beatifically, gaunt cheeks colouring as the men banged cups on their tabletops, demanding his voice. "Keep singing?" he asked Dougal from the corner of his mouth.

"Aye! Sing 'til ye've no voice left. We'll eat well tonight, my lad."

Dougal edged between the tables, cup in hand, constantly flicking his eyes toward the door to check for incoming uniforms. The men at the tables frowned, not understanding and not appreciating this beggar at their table. One man reached out and shoved Dougal's cup away.

"Get your begging arse out in the street where it belongs," he snarled.

Dougal straightened, then realised the misunderstanding. He started to explain, but Aidan got there first.

"Good day, gentlemen. I'm pleased to sing for ye all, but it shames me to say that I mus' also beg for yer coin. My friend an' I havena had a meal in a very long time. If I dinna eat, I'll die before I remember how the next song goes."

There were a few grumbles, but before long, coins clattered in Dougal's cup. Aidan sang songs of love and longing, then, with a twinkle in his eye, switched to slightly bawdy songs that made the men laugh. Dougal laughed with them. One of the songs was in French, and Dougal watched the boy's expression soften, becoming wistful as he remembered the words, or maybe as he recalled the time in his life when he'd been taught. Dougal had to remind himself that he was working, when what he really wanted to do was sit and listen. When every song finished, there was more pounding on the tables and calls for drinks. After half a dozen songs, Aidan stopped for a drink himself, and the barkeep put an ale for each of them on the bar. He also brought them a plate of meat, bread, and cheese, and the two sat and ate like wild animals.

"God, this is good," Dougal said through a full mouth.

Aidan said nothing, just used his bread to mop up the sauce on his plate. When he'd swallowed that, he downed the rest of his beer and set down the cup. He grinned at Dougal, that beautiful grin Dougal had seen only a few times before, then let out an impressive belch.

"Well!" Dougal said, laughing. "Ye've a good voice for that as well!"

"Shall I sing more?"

"Aye, why not? Sing all ye can, an' maybe we'll sleep on a bed for a change."

"A bed?"

Dougal smiled. "Sure. It's been far too long since I've had a mattress beneath me."

Aidan fixed Dougal with a wide-eyed stare. "No' near as long as me. I've no' slept in a bed since I was wee. Maybe six years or so."

Dougal reached across the table and gripped Aidan's shoulder with one hand. "Then we shall sleep in a bed, lad. We shall start our new life off well, aye?"

"I'd better sing, then," Aidan replied, one eyebrow lifted. "So I can pay for all these things."

Dougal grinned, then held up his cup, still half full of ale. He thought the boy might need it more than he, to help his voice. "That'd be best. Here, take this."

Aidan sang for another half hour, persuading his listeners to laugh, then cry. Occasionally they joined in and Dougal watched Aidan purposefully lower his voice during those times, resting it briefly. Aye, he was a clever boy.

During one mournful song, Dougal thought about Joseph and sobered with sympathy. The lad had been Aidan's other half, and whenever Dougal saw Aidan's face pale or his step falter, he knew his thoughts were on Joseph. It would have been fine indeed, to have both Joseph and John with them on this voyage. But Fate had been cruel, as she usually was. They would manage, just the two of them. They would be fine.

At the end of the evening, the tavern owner rented them a room above the bar. Their drinks had been filled again and again, their plates always held more to eat. So well fed were they that when the evening ended and they headed to their room, it was almost impossible to believe the condition in which they had first arrived. Dougal followed the tavern owner upstairs and Aidan wandered behind, more than a bit disoriented by the drinks and the excitement.

They paid the man, and Dougal slipped him two extra coins along with the request that they not be disturbed. In particular by anyone in uniform. The tavern owner nodded then pocketed the money before turning and walking back down the corridor.

Dougal and Aidan closed the door behind them, then stood without speaking just inside the doorway of their small room. The floor vibrated and thumped beneath their feet because of the tavern's noisy patrons, but overall the room was neat and plain and perfectly ordinary. It was also entirely foreign to them both. The walls were surprisingly clean, especially when compared to how the building had appeared from the outside. Even if it hadn't been, neither man would ever again complain about dirt, not after everything they'd survived. In the centre of the room, its wooden headboard pushed against one wall, stood a large, neatly made bed covered by a black wool blanket. A chamber pot sat on the floor beside it. A chipped ceramic ewer and bowl, which the owner said he would come back to fill, waited on a small table along with a lit candle.

Dougal walked to the bed, sat on its edge with his elbows braced on his knees, and dropped his chin into his hands. Aidan leaned back against the door, watching. His eyelids drooped, only half open. A smile played with Dougal's lips, and he grinned at Aidan.

"We made it," he said softly.

Aidan chewed his bottom lip, then nodded. A tiny, very careful movement. "So far." He yawned and dropped his hands to his stomach, puffing out his cheeks like a squirrel's. "My belly doesna ken what to do wi' all this food. I feel like I might burst apart."

"Aye." Dougal smiled and patted his stomach. "'Tis a good feeling I've missed for far too long." He cocked his head toward the rest of the bed. "Seems big enough for the both of us. But if it's no', I'll take the floor. Ye were the one, after all, what sang for our suppers."

Aidan crawled onto the bed, lay still as a corpse on top of the blanket, and closed his eyes. "It's plenty big enough, Dougal."

Dougal blew out the candle and the weak yellow glow of the room was plunged into night. Aidan was right; there was enough room for him on the other side of the bed, so he lay back, hands linked behind his head. He waited for his eyes to focus, then stared at the blackened ceiling beams. He could hear the boy breathing softly beside him, and listened to hear the breaths come more slowly as he faded off to sleep. He knew Aidan's sounds. He'd slept beside him for months and found the near silence brought him comfort. When Aidan started to fall asleep, Dougal would listen for another sound: the urgent, incomprehensible whispers Dougal needed to understand.

Despite everything, Aidan didn't fall asleep as quickly as he usually did. They lay in the dark for a while before Aidan finally spoke. And then his voice was almost a whisper. Like the voice of a child.

"Where do ye think Joseph is now?"

Something in Dougal's heart twisted and he swallowed before answering. "Ye dinna mean what the soldiers—"

"No, no' his body. I dinna want to think of that. I mean the real Joseph. Where is he?"

"Did yer family no' take ye to kirk, lad? Did ye no' learn what will come after?"

Aidan shook his head silently in the dark.

"The Bible tells a great many stories of jus' that," Dougal mused. "But I dinna suppose ye've read that." Aidan still didn't speak, so Dougal continued. "I imagine Joseph's in heaven wi' the Lord lookin' o'er him. He'll be safe now, wi' the angels."

"Really? Ye believe that, Dougal?"

Dougal turned his head on the pillow and frowned at Aidan's dark profile. "Aye, I do. What other choice is there? I'd no' like to think it's no' true, after all."

"Aye," Aidan said, his voice almost a sigh. "For if there were no heaven, then what? Where would Joseph be now? Nowhere? Simply . . . gone? How could that be?"

Dougal felt such a pang in his chest at those words, he almost choked. The image of Andrew appeared in his mind and he hung on to it with everything he had. Andrew couldn't simply be gone, either. No. He felt sure he would have known somehow. He'd have felt . . . something. His dreams would have told him . . . something.

"There's a heaven, lad. An' Joseph's in it."

He could tell Aidan was crying, though there was no sound. The air felt thicker between them. It was as if the boy held his breath, not wanting to admit the tears. Dougal feared speaking in case his voice betrayed the same aching loss. Finally, Aidan took a deep breath and the mattress crackled as he wiped his eyes.

"I miss him somethin' terrible," he whispered.

"I know ye do."

"I hope he's all right."

Someone in the tavern roared, yelling something incoherent, and laughter rumbled through the floor. Dougal waited for the noise to die down.

"Aidan?"

"Aye?"

"He's all right now. An' I'll take care of ye from now on."

Aidan sniffed. "All right, Dougal."

The boy rolled onto his side, still silent, but Dougal felt the bed bump a little when Aidan held in his sobs. He considered leaving the room, giving him privacy, but didn't know where he could go. He wasn't up to visiting the tavern again. And what if Aidan needed him and couldn't find him?

Seventeen years old. A man, really, but still a child in so many ways. What would Dougal have done if this were Ciaran grieving beside him? Nothing. There was nothing he could do but move forward for them both. He turned onto his side, facing away from Aidan, and closed his eyes, pretending not to know.

Later that night Dougal awoke to Aidan's strange sleeping murmurs: soft, quick whispers that sounded urgent. He knew from other, less comfortable nights that the boy's eyes were snapping from side to side beneath his lids as if seeking escape, but Dougal didn't wake him. As a child, Dougal's mother had warned him about waking a sleeping person. Something about the sleeper losing part of his soul to the dream. But he did worry about the constant stream of fear flowing through Aidan's thoughts. He edged slightly closer so the back of his shirt touched the back of Aidan's. Just enough that the sleeping boy could feel his presence.

In that instant the whispering stopped, and Aidan's breathing slowed. Reassured, Dougal let sleep come and carry him away.

CHAPTER 11

Handed Down

Tap tap tap.

Dougal awoke, disoriented and thick with interrupted sleep, and pried open one eye. Ah. Now he remembered. The strange pressure beneath him, it was a mattress. He was upstairs, above the tavern. He was safe. He would never see Tilbury Fort again.

Tap tap tap.

He glared at the ceiling. How could it possibly be morning already? Damn. Now he needed the chamber pot. He stretched his legs, extending his toes as far as they could, and groaned softly. But it was so comfortable, just lying here, thinking about nothing. Maybe he could just sleep a little longer—

Tap tap tap.

If it weren't for the damn *tap tap tap*, that is.

Now fully awake, Dougal sat on the edge of the mattress and glanced around. A small rectangle beside the foot of the bed told him the room contained a window, but it was shuttered, keeping out the light and noise—or at least that's what it was supposed to do. Dougal rose and stretched, popping his shoulders and yawning widely as he walked toward the window. He tugged open the shutters and leaned out, becoming instantly acquainted with the source of the noise. Rain fell in a continuous mist, drenching the city, and when the water toppled off the roof, it landed right on his windowsill. Except this time it landed on the crown of his head instead.

Tap tap tap. Dougal didn't much mind. He was too curious about the city to be bothered by a little rain. The road outside the tavern door was a cesspool, trapping mud and slop as it drifted down the slight slope, but no one bothered to remove whatever was blocking the flow. The stink of the city slithered up the wall of the tavern, clawed around the edges of the window, and seized Dougal's nostrils. He paid it no mind.

He stared down at the busy road, bemused. People came and went, talking with each other then moving on, as they would in any other village. But this was no village. This was a busy swamp. And these people, for some reason Dougal couldn't fathom, seemed to have chosen to live this way. He didn't judge them. He figured people were entitled to live as they wished. But he was confused by it all. How could they be happy, raising their children in this pit? Not for him, this life. Dougal ached for the Highlands.

He glanced back toward the bed, where Aidan still slept soundly. In the moments after Dougal had risen, the boy had emerged from the tight cocoon of his sleep and now sprawled like a star across the empty place where Dougal had lain. Sleep took years from the boy's face and Dougal couldn't help staring. He was a beautiful lad, with soft lines to his face, long eyelashes touching bone white cheeks. Angelic, almost. What was an angel doing in this hell? From the beginning, Dougal had felt protective of Aidan and Joseph, simply because protecting the weak was in his nature. Now he felt a resur-

gence of his initial need to take care of the boy. Especially with
Joseph gone.

Aidan and Joseph had been best friends for six years, inseparable.
And before that? They'd grown together since they'd been bairns,
sharing families, meals, secrets.

Like Dougal with Andrew. Not that they'd been alone. They'd
had a good life, with everything they could ever have needed. Their
parents, unlike many he'd known, loved each other and showed
nothing but affection and respect for each other, and for their sons.
Their father taught them how to hunt, fight, survive. Their mother
gave them the other side of their education: the reading and writing
and arithmetic. Dougal had tried to raise some sort of interest in
what she taught, but it was lost on him. Not because he wasn't smart
enough. He knew he was, and he learned all that was required of
him. It was just that his body was constantly on the move, his mind
always seeking adventure, wanting to accomplish, not just sit and
learn.

Dougal and Andrew had been very close. He had always heard
Andrew's voice in his head, but there was more. When they'd sat
quietly together, or when they spoke without words, Dougal felt a
pressure, a direction, as if he were being led toward something. And
he was fairly sure Andrew felt the same way. Neither of them ever
mentioned this strange connection; it seemed too odd to discuss out
loud. The feeling was like something magical, and magic was not
always wise to discuss.

Even if they hadn't known each other's thoughts as clearly as if
the words had been spoken out loud, they would have been inseparable. Part of the reason Dougal had so much trouble believing
Andrew was dead was because somewhere, in a tiny place in his
mind, Dougal thought he could still hear him. He knew it could
be happening just because he had always been there and the

memory was as real as his presence had been, like a deep footprint in the mud, but he didn't think that was it.

He frowned, still staring at Aidan. A slight smile played over the boy's lips as he slept. What would it be like to sleep so deeply? Dougal never did. What did the boy dream of? Dougal closed his eyes and tried to relax his mind, dig into Aidan's unconscious thoughts, but there was nothing. As if a barrier existed, one Dougal couldn't breach. It was frustrating, because Dougal rarely had trouble reading most men's minds. He usually had more trouble blocking them out.

There was no need to wake the boy. There was nowhere they needed to be. But Dougal was restless. He felt a buzz in his veins, a need to move, to explore, to make things happen. How long had it been since he had walked without orders, letting his feet go where they would? He decided to come back later for Aidan. The boy needed sleep. He left quietly, went downstairs, and told the tavern owner to let Aidan know, if he asked, that he had gone out for a bit.

He stepped out a side door and emerged into a dark, narrow alleyway, walled on both sides by chipped bricks and falling mortar. Using the infinite gray of the sky, Dougal took in the scene, letting his eyes follow the lines of the walls as they climbed. The buildings looked as if someone had built them as quickly as they could, so they could move on to the next one. He saw no windows besides the one in their room, and other than the one through which he had just passed, Dougal could see no doors. Only brick, mud, and misery.

He stood in the doorway, trying to decide whether it was really worth wading out into the deepening puddles of muck. Probably not, he thought. But he couldn't just stand still.

He stepped around an open drain, shuddering when his foot flattened something he didn't want to identify. He moved more quickly after that, striding through the honeycomb of alleyways, following a vague hint of light that he hoped was the exit onto the main street. When he looked up, the walls over his head seemed to lean toward each other, as if weary of standing straight. A sinister mound loomed up from the ground and Dougal hopped to one side of the alley, then the other, to avoid whatever it was. He clutched at the blackened brick wall beside him when he lost his balance, then recoiled when his palm struck the cold, slimy stone.

Why would anyone choose to live this way? Like rats, he thought. Except rats probably had it better, because they seemed able to eat anything and still flourish. As if he had summoned the creature with his thoughts, an actual rat appeared a few feet away, waddling rapidly toward him, its profile black as the rest of the place. Dougal wished he had his knife, but he had no weapons. Hadn't had one in months. If he did have one, he could have made a meal out of the creature for both him and Aidan. The rat didn't slow in its approach and Dougal stood back, waiting for the vile thing to pass, which it did. It seemed unconcerned by the human presence. At least he hadn't sensed a meal, Dougal mused as he continued toward the street.

Finally Dougal burst into the relatively bright grayness of the street, and the noise, muffled before by the alleyway walls, struck him anew. Shouts and cries, people selling anything from boots to fruit. Young boys—or were they girls? it was impossible to tell through the grime on their bony faces—flitted like dragonflies from door to door, hovering, then darting away. The streets of London were no prettier today than they had been when they'd arrived. Would sunshine have been an improvement? Probably not.

A woman sat in her doorway, offering small bottles of clear liquid, and Dougal glanced at them with interest. He was thirsty.

"Gin, my love?" the woman asked. One swollen finger trembled when she pointed up at him, blinking milky white eyes. "Made it myself, I did. Sweeter than any of the other rubbish you'll find around here."

"Gin? Oh, I've no' the money for gin." He indicated his empty hands. "I've no' the money for anythin'."

The woman cackled, and Dougal noticed a vague hint of yellow in her skin. The woman had tasted her wares a little too often. "Nor have any of us, my lad. You'd best figure out a way to have some or you'll be dead as yon cat before nightfall."

Dougal turned his back on her and continued down the street. The mist was letting up but the air was still cold, to say nothing of the freezing mud under his feet. He shivered and clutched his arms over his chest, trying to preserve whatever heat he carried.

Despite what he'd told the old woman, he carried some money from Aidan's performance the night before, and wondered how best to spend it. Food? No. Aidan could provide that if he sang again.

"Damn!" he exclaimed, yanking his foot from something brown. "That's disgusting, that is."

Shoes. Maybe he should buy shoes. That would be fine. But necessary? No. Not a priority. Though if he were to cut his foot on something, then step in something worse, well that could end badly. Yes, shoes were on his list.

Shoddy stalls were set up along the side of the road, some nothing more than a few wares spread over a cloth, and Dougal perused each one as he walked. He stopped behind a small crowd, peering over their heads at a puppet show: two wooden-headed figures bobbing with disembodied voices, banging at each other with sticks. The audience laughed on cue and Dougal let the meaningless entertainment divert him for a moment.

He felt a tug on his breeks, slight enough it could have been a breeze, only it wasn't. Dougal's hand shot out and grabbed a tiny wrist just reaching for the paltry bag of coins at his waist. The wrist was attached to a bony arm, which led to a furious red face.

"Let go," the child hissed.

"So ye can take my money?"

The child, whose head reached no higher than Dougal's belly, stuck his other hand on his hip, hitching up a stained pair of breeks. Long black tendrils of hair covered most of his face, like algae on a rock. The boy's eyes were hard, and old.

"Because if you don't, I'll tell everyone you're an escaped prisoner."

That knocked Dougal back. He blinked. "What?"

The boy's lips puckered briefly, relaxed, then puckered again. He tilted his head to the side and regarded Dougal critically. "They'd all believe me, you know. Why, maybe you are, come to think of it. You're a filthy Scotsman, you are. These folk would be only too pleased to—"

"Enough, mouse turd," Dougal snarled. "Ye've a mouth on ye needs to be sewn shut. Ye need to learn yer craft better. Look at me. Look how I'm dressed. I've no money for ye. Get away." He shoved the bony wrist away, and the boy stumbled backward. The little face studied him a moment longer.

"Watch yourself, Scotsman," he warned through missing teeth, then spun and vanished into the growing crowd on the street.

Had he just been threatened by a six-year-old? Why yes, he had. That was a first. The most frightening thing was how quickly the boy had identified him, revealing just how easy it would be for Dougal to end up imprisoned again. Or worse.

The encounter gave Dougal a feeling of helplessness, a sensation he despised. He felt relatively confident that his strength would return soon, bolstered by air, movement, and food, but his fists would only take him so far. He decided what he needed to buy with his meagre cache of coins was a knife.

"Oy! That'll teach you!" came a cry, followed by a small grunt.

Dougal turned toward the voice, which was being joined by others. Some poor devil's hands and shaved head drooped from a pillory, set on a raised platform so onlookers could have easy access. Something red and slimy slid down the man's miserable face, hooking on his ear, then plopping onto the floor by his feet. Rotten tomato, Dougal thought, then figured at least that was better than an egg. As if on cue, a hard white missile flew through the air, just missing the man's head, whacking him instead on the side of the shoulder, where it split on impact and flooded the air with a sulphuric stench.

The onlookers issued a collective "Aww," when the stink hit them, and hands fanned uselessly in front of noses. Dougal kept walking, reading the man's crime with vague interest: THIEF was carved into a board by his feet. As Dougal left the area, more people moved in to take his place, their interest fed by the smell and the shouts.

People blustered on their way, regardless of Dougal, even though he stood a head taller than most of them. A scrawny, hunched woman, her scabbed face partially hidden by a shawl, shoved past Dougal, muttering obscenities. A skeletal woman dragged a screaming urchin by one ear.

Down a little farther he came upon a man selling a variety of swords and knives, their blades old and most likely dull. His wares were displayed on a slanted table set in front of a doorway. He had fashioned a kind of awning over the top, but rain still soaked the table, shining the metal of the knives, rinsing old blood and rust from the blades. Dougal paused, studying the sad collection. He wanted a weapon very badly, but these were rubbish. Old swords with chunks of metal broken from them in key spots, knives pocked with rust, others with broken hilts.

"What you looking for, man?" asked the salesman. He was short and stocky, with burly arms folded across his chest. He wore a dirty white shirt covered by an ancient green waistcoat, as if he'd dressed for a formal gathering but had done it all wrong.

"No' these," Dougal replied. He stood taller and folded his own arms. Staring down at the salesman, Dougal could hear the man's thoughts, dark and confrontational, as clear as if they were written on his forehead. A mean man, one who felt himself superior to the rest of the population, but he was also a man intent on making a sale. Dougal knew how to handle a man like this. "I couldna cut a branch wi' the likes o' these."

The man snorted. "So you're a man who knows his blades, are you?"

Dougal didn't bother to respond. Instead, he fingered the dull edge of a short sword lying on the side of the table. It was thick in both width and breadth, a powerful weapon in its day, but it was so worn he doubted he could ever get much of an edge on it, no matter how much he sharpened it. He frowned at the salesman, waiting.

Dougal's glare made the man uncomfortable. He shifted his feet and put his hands on his waist. "I've more in the back that might suit you," he offered. When Dougal said nothing, only deepened his frown, he hollered over his shoulder at his wife. The woman in question emerged from the building a few minutes later, weighted by a bag of swords and knives she'd slung over her shoulder. She was small and young, with black hair that hung listlessly from under a white kerchief. She laid the bag at her husband's feet with a clank of metal.

Dougal heard the rage in the man's thoughts, felt the tension in his head burning red with fury, but the anger didn't seem to be based on anything in particular. Every bit of it was focused on the woman.

"Not there, wife," the salesman roared. Filled with hate, this man. He pounded splayed fingers on the surface of the table. "Up here, stupid bitch. We don't need the customers to have to work for their purchase now, do we?" He shrugged at Dougal and gave him a sheepish smile. "Useless slut, she is. Don't know why I bother to keep her around at all."

She didn't look at him, only leaned over and grabbed the bag as if it were a stone. Metal shifted and scraped as she hefted the heavy sack up onto the table. Dougal caught a glimpse of the side of her face, blackened until the bruise had bled into her eye. Caught her a good one, he had. She felt Dougal's gaze and peeked up at him, her expression wretched. Black brow, black eyes, blackened heart. A Celt, he thought, like him.

"I thank ye, missus," Dougal said, reaching to help. "Here. Let me lift that. Heavy load, that."

"Ha. She'll manage. She does nothing else all day."

The girl kept her gaze down, but Dougal saw the hatred in her eyes. The salesman was a large, strong man, his wicked temper strung tight across the air. Smart girl, holding her tongue. She laid out the metal so he could look them over and Dougal shifted his attention to the new load of weapons lying before him, a dozen or so relatively newer pieces.

"Just picked those up the other day," the salesman assured him. "Haven't cleaned 'em up much yet."

Dougal looked from the new assortment to the old one and flicked an eyebrow at the man. The two piles looked very similar. "Cleaned them? Like ye cleaned those?"

The salesman stewed for a moment, torn between defending his wares and making a sale. Dougal could hear the man's conflicting

thoughts and picked up on a guilty secret, one he seemed to want
to keep from Dougal.

"These are no good," Dougal said.

"Em, Richard," she said. "Have ye the ones—"

Richard's thoughts went black with fury, filling Dougal's mind
with poison. "Shut your mouth!" the man shrieked. He stared hard
at her, and to her credit, the girl held his eyes with her own. Through
his anger, however, Dougal heard the man weighing the woman's
suggestion. "You don't speak," he said through his teeth. "I've told
you before, wife. You don't speak."

He returned his attention to Dougal, seeming to remember something. The girl looked away, folding her arms and shaking her head
with disgust. "I might have a few others to interest you, but
they're . . . older."

Dougal gave him a single nod that said, "Show me." Richard
turned expectantly toward the girl, and she rolled her eyes before
heading back into the house. When she returned, the bundle she
carried was far too heavy for her. It was wrapped in a faded plaid,
which she tried to keep hidden against her chest. Dougal was surprised to see the material; owning even a strip of tartan was against
the law these days.

"Right," Richard said as she shoved the others aside and set the
new blades on the table. He squinted at Dougal, looking wary.
"These are . . ." He coughed. "These are—"

"They're stolen from dead Scottish rebels," the girl declared, then
ducked as her husband swung toward her with an open palm. Still
bent low, she fixed Dougal with a black stare, daring him to touch
the metal.

He forced his eyes away from hers and leaned over the table,
examining the old blades before him. They were indeed swords and
dirks like the ones he knew so well. He tried to picture each one

hanging from the hip of a Highlander. Two long, thick swords with intricately worked basket hilts lay beside two shorter, more tarnished weapons with unprotected hilts. Where were their masters now? Two lethal broadswords protruded from either side of the pile. Not lethal enough, he thought grimly, though from the amount of dried blood that still painted the blades black, he thought they'd done their share. He shifted his attention to the dirks. Most of them were over a foot long, with handles worn to the shape of their owners' hands.

Something warm rose from the depths of Dougal's chest. His hand reached without hesitation toward a thick, brown-handled dirk. Its handle was slender but well worn, its blade still sharp. In the moment that his fingers touched the hilt, his vision went black, and his head filled with the roaring of blood. Very clearly, as if he stood right beside him, he heard Andrew's voice yelling, *"Ciaran!"*

He could see the dirk in his youngest brother's hand, see his grimy fingers clenched around the handle. In Dougal's memories, long before the war, Ciaran laughed. He looked over his shoulder as he raced Dougal through the woods, this same dirk in his belt, laughing as if he hadn't a care in the world. At that time, Dougal supposed, he hadn't. The memory was as real in his mind as was the dirk he now gripped in his hand.

"Ciaran," he whispered, closing his fingers around the hilt. He drew it toward himself and held the blade flat against his chest. *I'm so sorry, little brother.*

When he opened his eyes again, Richard and his wife were staring at him. He nodded. "This one," he said.

The man tried for a ridiculous price on Ciaran's blade, but Dougal shook his head.

"This is my brother's dirk," he said calmly. "I'll take it from ye with my thanks. I'll buy a second, though."

"*Take* that? As in . . . not pay for it? I don't think so, sir!" cried Richard.

Dougal's sneer was cold, unforgiving, his voice like ice. "I'll take it or the authorities will hear o' these blades. An' the tartan as well."

He heard the resultant panic in Richard's mind and leaned over to choose a second dirk. He would give it to Aidan. Or maybe he would give Ciaran's dirk to Aidan. He would decide later. Richard complained, but in the end he gave in. From beside him, the girl watched Dougal intently. Before he could leave, she reached swiftly under the table and brought out two leather belts. Her husband glared murderously at her, but she stared warily back, watching him as she handed Dougal the belts.

"We don't give to no charity," the man growled.

"The blades belong to this man," she answered, her Scots brogue thick. *From the North,* Dougal thought. What had brought the poor lass this far? "An' he canna carry them wi'out a belt."

With a brief nod, Dougal fastened both belts around his waist. He slid Ciaran's dirk into one holster and the other into the second belt.

"I thank ye, my lady," he said quietly. He glowered at the salesman and Richard's thoughts quietened. "Hear me, sir. I shall come back tomorrow an' the day after that, lookin' for this woman. Understand this. She shall come to nae harm for doin' me this service."

The man's nostrils flared, but he nodded once in understanding.

CHAPTER 12

Claiming Proof

Dougal didn't remember walking back to the inn. None of the noise, the sights, the activity woke any interest in his mind. He had no idea if it still rained and didn't care if it did. He was entirely focused on the thick blade of metal, heavy in his belt, heavier in his heart.

Ciaran. Ciaran was dead. He carried proof.

Somehow Dougal found the alley that led to the inn. Rusted hinges squealed as he shoved the door open and strode into the main tavern. He let the door slam behind him and sat at a table against the wall, saying nothing, just breathing and staring at the tabletop, swallowing back emotion.

He was vaguely aware of the tavern's keeper polishing the bar at the other side of the room. It was midmorning and the room was mostly empty of patrons. Dougal glanced up and nodded at the man, who poured and brought him a mug of ale. He put a coin in the man's hand, then sipped on the drink. It tasted less like ale than dirty water. But it was wet.

The dirk made a hollow shushing sound as he pulled it from his belt and laid it on the table before him. The tarnished silver called, and he followed, losing himself to the past. The morning of the battle came back, kept coming back, no matter how hard he tried to hold it away. How Ciaran's bright blue eyes, so like his own, had looked at him that miserable morning. How his little brother had quietly admitted, "I'm no' ready to die, Dougal."

How had he answered? He couldn't recall. Something intended to play down his brother's fears, he supposed. Like he had always done. Always the protector. Always the big brother. What had it been? Something like, *"We'll none of us die today."* Which had been a ridiculous thing to say.

Was it a lie when false reassurances were given? Was it a lie for Ciaran to accept his reply, even though they had all known with certainty that some would die that day? And if so, was it his lie or Ciaran's? The thought that the final words he'd ever uttered to his youngest brother might have been a lie twisted like an eel through his chest.

Lifting the mug to his lips, Dougal was startled to find it empty already. He looked back toward the tavern owner, but his gaze caught on the small form of Aidan two tables away, sitting alone, holding his own drink. Aidan's wide blue eyes watched Dougal, but he said nothing. It was as if he understood Dougal didn't want company. He stayed where he was, offering support and friendship, but only if it were desired. Dougal tilted his head with invitation and slid the dirk back into his belt. Aidan shoved back his stool, picked up his own mug, and joined Dougal at his table. The barkeep brought another drink for Dougal, and none of the men spoke.

The door swung open and the frenzied noises of London crushed the quiet. Dougal, jolted back to the moment, unbuckled one of the belts he wore and handed it across the table to Aidan. It was the second belt, since Dougal had decided to keep Ciaran's blade for himself. It seemed right. A penance of sorts perhaps, a reminder certainly.

"Might be a bit big for ye, but there's a dirk in the side there—oh, watch that. Aye. Got that for ye this mornin'."

Aidan nodded thanks and buckled the belt around his hips, then slid his new dirk from its sheath. He thumbed the edge critically, then examined the hilt, taking care to avoid Dougal's eyes. Eventually he slid it back into his belt and cupped his hands around his mug. He stared into it, saying nothing, letting Dougal have his quiet.

For some reason, Aidan's presence calmed Dougal, took the pressure off his heart. After a moment he sat up straighter and pulled Ciaran's dirk back out of its sheath. He laid it on the table between them, and both men stared at it. Aidan looked up, questioning.

Dougal frowned. "My brother, Ciaran. That's his dirk."

"Ciaran?" Aidan asked, his eyes widening. "That's yer youngest brother, aye? Is he here, then? I thought ye said he—"

Dougal shook his head. "Nay. No' here. No' anywheres. I bought this dirk from a man who'd stolen it from the dead at Culloden."

Aidan's jaw dropped. "Stolen from—" His words dwindled and his face lost all colour.

Dougal nodded when Aidan silently asked permission to touch the knife. The smooth handle settled into Aidan's palm, and he slid a curious thumb over the blade. Dougal watched the boy's hands, remembering other fingers that had gripped that hilt. Longer fingers with a darker hue to their skin. Narrow, like Aidan's, but thicker and stronger. Unlike Dougal and Andrew, Ciaran hadn't been built like a warrior, but he had been bigger than Aidan. Aidan's hands were small. Delicate even. Like a woman's, though he would never say such a thing to the boy.

"My brother was only a year older than ye are," Dougal said softly.

Aidan's eyes met his, then flicked away. "I'm sorry, Dougal."

Dougal took the dirk back and held it in his own hand. *Ciaran!* he heard in his head. Andrew's voice again, yelling with desperation. *Ciaran!*

It wasn't as if it were a shock. Dougal had assumed they were all dead. He knew about his father, of course. Now he knew about Ciaran. What of Andrew? Would he ever know?

"What else did ye see out there? On the street, I mean," Aidan asked, glancing toward the door, which was just slamming shut again.

Dougal clicked his tongue and shook his head with irritation. "It's a horrible place, this. Loud and filthy, full o' criminals an' whores. I've no wish to stay any longer."

"No, nor do I. But . . . what did ye see?"

Dougal recognised a hint of eagerness in the boy's tone. So he was curious, he thought. Not surprising. "Did ye want to go out?" he asked, hiding a smile. "Take a wee keek? Go on then."

Aidan shook his head. "No' on my own, thanks. I was only wonderin' is all."

With an internal sigh, Dougal realised he should have woken Aidan before going out earlier. Now he'd have to go again. Sure, the lad said it was of no consequence, but what young man wouldn't be interested in the excitement of London? Dougal scraped his chair back and rose to his feet.

"Let's go."

"Oh, there's no need. I—"

"Come on then," Dougal said, and turned toward the door. He heard Aidan follow, and pulled open the side door into the alleyway. "I must warn ye, it's a wee bit dark at first. This leads to the street. Stay close. There are, well, dinna step in the centre bit, aye?"

The rain had, thank the blessed Christ, stopped. Remnants still dripped from the tattered roofs, but the sky had lightened and a suggestion of warmth filtered into the air. Dougal stepped into the putrid alley and heard Aidan grunt with disgust as he avoided something. When they eventually emerged into the main thoroughfare, Dougal noticed more hawkers setting up with the brief hope of sunshine. They slammed tables together and organised their wares for any interested browsers. A woman hung ribbons from a pole, another set out bread. A boy tugged a wagon behind him, jugs clanging together as he walked.

"What's that?" Dougal asked.

The boy looked at him as if he were an idiot. "'At's milk, is what it is."

"Fresh?"

"Sure," the boy answered quickly. "Milked 'em this morning."

"Really? Where's yer farm? Yer kine?"

"Near enough," the boy said.

Dougal picked up a jug, popped the cork, and sniffed. Sour as his old grandmother, as they say.

"Pah!" he exclaimed. "Foul-mouthed brat. That's a week old, that is."

"Then don't buy any," the boy said with a belligerent snarl, and walked away, tugging his wagon behind him.

Aidan giggled.

"Funny?"

"Sure," Aidan said. "The lad should learn his business better. He should sell it as sour milk an' he'd do jus' fine."

Dougal grinned. "Come an' see all this. These folks will sell anythin'."

He led Aidan through the growing number of stalls and paused at the puppet show. Aidan was captivated by the spectacle, laughing and clapping when one of the silly things did something.

"Oh, that's brilliant!" he exclaimed at one point, treating Dougal to one of his rare, sunshine smiles.

"It is?" Dougal asked, scratching his head. "I didna hear—"

"Oh, ye see, it's all a joke, aye? They look as if they're discussing the weather, but it's no' just that. See there, that's a duke, an' the other's a crofter, an' they're discussing taxes, but the duke's no smarter than the shoon on his feet. An' the crofter, well, he's gettin' the silly man to agree to his terms though he has no idea—"

Dougal glanced at the stage, then back at Aidan, surprised. He knew the lad was intelligent, but hadn't had occasion to see this side of him. He watched the show while Aidan laughed and pointed out things the puppets had done or said, and Dougal found himself appreciating the spectacle. After a while they moved on, and Aidan headed toward a stall offering books. He picked up a large brown book, covered in worn calfskin, and slid his fingers over the soft cover. Then he opened the book and smiled wistfully.

"I wonder what the story is," he mused.

"Ye dinna read?" Dougal asked. He checked the front cover. "Well, that's as well, for that one's a dull story."

"An' how is it ye ken that?" Aidan demanded, looking shocked. "Ye can read it?"

"Aye, I can."

Dougal flipped through three or four books, eventually coming upon one he remembered from years before.

"Ye'll like this. I'll read it to ye." He handed a book to Aidan, who clutched the treasure against his chest. "*Robinson Crusoe.* Have ye heard of it?"

Aidan shook his head. His eyes were wide. "What is it about?"

Dougal pulled out the small purse of coins he had slid into his shirt that morning and peered inside. Not much left. Should he spend it on a book, or could he remember the story well enough without it? Aidan held the book in both hands, caressing the cover with dirty thumbs, as if it were a religious object.

"How much?"

"Tenpence, sir," the woman behind the table said.

"I've six," Dougal countered.

She squinted at him, looking dubious. "'At's not ten, is it?"

"No, but it's more than what ye have so far."

She glared at him, calculating. The streets weren't yet crowded after the downpour, though more people would come. Dougal was right, though. She hadn't made a lot of sales so far that day.

"Eight," she said.

"I said I have six."

She huffed through a flattened nose. "Fine then. 'And it over."

Dougal dug into the purse and fished around for sixpence, no more. In fact, he had little more than that anyway. He handed the money to her and nodded at Aidan.

"It's yours now."

"Thank ye," Aidan said, looking confused. "But I canna read."

"I said as I'd read it to ye, did I no'? Anyhow, ye need no' thank me. It was yer own money we jus' spent."

"Still," Aidan said. He looked up at him and smiled. "It feels like a gift. I havena been given a gift in a very long time. Thank ye."

Something so little, Dougal thought. Yet it meant so much. The boy carried, at least for now, an expression of happiness that had been absent for too long. Seeing him like this lifted a weight from Dougal's own spirit, urged a smile to his lips. The sun peeked through the clouds in that moment and Dougal seized it as a sign of hope and freedom. A sign that their new life began today. He dropped his hand to Ciaran's dirk at his belt and squeezed the handle.

"Ye're welcome, my friend," he said. "We'll read it as we head home, aye?"

"Home? We're goin' to Scotland?" Aidan asked, his expression hopeful.

"Aye. That'd be best. We canna live here, among these sassenachs, can we? An' we're still too close to the fort for my likin'."

Aidan glanced at the people jostling around them, bumping into each other without offering apologies, slapping their children and each other. "Aye," he agreed. "We'll to the Highlands."

Despite this declaration, they decided to spend the rest of the day and that evening in London. Aidan repeated the previous night's performance, providing the coins they'd need to hold them through their voyage. It would take months to get home, but this small amount would at least give them a start. After collecting Aidan's pay, Dougal claimed the same table they'd taken the night before, leaned back against the cool stone wall, and listened to the boy sing.

It would be too bad when the boy's voice finally changed. It was lovely to hear it as it was. But it would happen soon. Dougal never outwardly questioned the fact that Aidan was taking a long time to grow into a man. Not even a hint of a beard had sprouted on his fine-boned jaw. But he'd known a few boys like that, boys who didn't mature until eighteen or so. No need to rush anything.

Aidan sang for two hours, delighting the patrons, filling Dougal's little purse and their bellies. When at last he climbed down from the stool for the final time, he looked tired, but pleased.

"Will ye read to me tonight, Dougal?" he asked.

Dougal wasn't surprised. Aidan had clung to the book all day and laid it carefully on the table while he was singing. But it was too late to read. Dougal hated to disappoint the boy, but he didn't have a choice.

"We havena any light in our room, lad. Only the wee candle and it's nearly done," Dougal reminded him. "I'll read on the road, aye?"

The boy looked crestfallen, but nodded, and they went to bed.

Dougal let himself sleep a little longer the next morning. Well, not really sleep. He couldn't do that. Never had, really. But he lay on his back, hands linked behind his head like a pillow, and stared at the ceiling. He needed to put together some kind of plan. Where should they go? How would they live? It would have to be on their own—he didn't want anyone turning them in to the English. He didn't think Aidan would mind it being just the two of them. He seemed to enjoy the quiet. It would be as if they were brothers. Both of them needed that.

Dougal sighed with frustration. He wasn't a planner. He didn't think about things; he did them.

"Ye think almos' as loud as ye snore," Aidan mumbled. "What is it?"

Dougal grinned. Aidan was faced the opposite way and couldn't have seen that he was awake. So maybe he did, indeed, think loudly.

"Nothin'. But I canna sleep. An' I dinna snore."

Aidan rolled onto his back and blinked at Dougal. Sleep weighted the boy's eyelids, his golden hair was mussed. He had fallen asleep in his clothes, and the dirty fabric emphasised his pale skin. Unexpected morning sun sliced through the narrow window, brightening the pillow. He looked very young.

"Why no'?" he asked.

Dougal shrugged.

"Fine," Aidan said, matching his shrug. "Let's go." He sat up, then reached for the book, lying on the floor by his side. He frowned at Dougal. "But when we stop, ye'll read, aye?" Dougal nodded and

Aidan tucked the book inside his shirt so it was safe, then slid his feet off the bed.

"Ye look a mess," Dougal told him.

"Do I? Well, thank ye very much, sir. On the other hand, ye look ready to meet the king," Aidan snapped.

"We could use a wash, aye?"

"We can stop at a river," Aidan suggested. "Get the stink off us."

An unaccustomed warmth to the day gave a lift to their feet as they stepped onto the still-mucky street. The heat cooked up the street odours so it was impossible not to notice, but Dougal and Aidan were happy. It was a fine day. They were going home.

"Watch out!" someone cried, and from the corner of his eye Dougal saw a brick tumbling from the shoddy building beside them. He shoved Aidan out of the way and the brick smacked into a murky puddle, but missed them both.

Aidan, recovering from his surprise, bowed elegantly at Dougal. "I thank ye, sir."

Dougal grinned. "My pleasure, my lord."

All Dougal wanted was to leave this city far behind him. He tired of the grating English voices, the depravity of the place. Far in the distance, the shadow of the Highlands beckoned. He couldn't see her yet, but she called her sons and he intended to answer. He longed for the clear blue lakes to freeze his blood, the wind to burn his ears. He looked forward to the ache in his atrophied thighs as he climbed unforgiving rock faces. Just thinking about home made his heart sing.

They followed the main road out of London, keeping an eye open for soldiers and criminals, both equal threats. After an hour or so they ran out of discussion topics, so they walked in silence until Aidan started to sing. Dougal walked happily beside him, listening to songs he'd always known, sung in Aidan's beautiful tones. Sometimes, though he knew he had no talent, Dougal sang along. Aidan never objected to Dougal's singing, which he thought was quite generous.

"What's that?" Aidan asked suddenly, his step faltering. He frowned at the road before them.

Dougal squinted into the sun. "A body."

Their pace slowed as they neared the lump by the side of the road, wrapped in a long black cape. Flies buzzed around the form, lifting and settling so Dougal and Aidan had to wave their hands to keep the things out of their faces. Dougal leaned down to investigate.

It was the body of a man. A small, hatless man in his fifties, perhaps. He was curled on his side and had obviously bled to death through a slice in his abdomen. A horrible way to go, Dougal thought. From the look of the man's shredded waistcoat, the cut wasn't very large, so it would have taken a while for his life to seep out onto the road. Dougal frowned, then tugged the heavy cape off the body. The robbery must have been interrupted, or there would have been nothing left of the man other than that with which he had been born. But this was a perfectly good cape and would fit young Aidan. He handed it to the boy, who grinned.

"That'll be fine for when we reach the hills," he said.

"And for the rain when it comes again," Dougal agreed. He scratched his head, studying the body. "Ye need shoes, Aidan. An' a new tunic as well."

"Do I?"

"Aye. Yers are no' fit for a beggar."

And with that, he pulled off the shoes and shirt of the man and handed them to Aidan. The boy rolled the shirt into the cape and set it on the ground, then inspected the shoes, peering suspiciously into the toe.

"There's no mice in there," Dougal assured him. "I've only jus' pulled them off the poor wretch's feet."

Aidan shrugged, then sat and tugged the shoes on. "A little big," he said.

"Room to grow," Dougal assured him.

Aidan grinned. "'Tis a funny feelin' no' bein' able to wiggle my toes in the mud. I wish I'd had these in that city."

"Ah well. Ye'll have them for the next one."

"We'll ne'er find shoon big enough for yer feet," Aidan said.

"Probably no'," Dougal agreed. "Are ye no' goin' to put on the new tunic?"

Aidan shook his head and bent to pick up the bundle of clothing. "Later. After I wash. I'm fine for now."

They turned back to the road, leaving the mostly naked corpse to bake in the sun.

Having no sporran in which to store food or other small things, both men's shirts bulged with the items they carried. When the sun reached the top of the sky, Dougal pulled bread and cheese from within and began to eat while he walked. The cheese was warm from his skin, soft on his tongue. He handed a chunk to Aidan, who popped it into his mouth and grunted with appreciation. They would eat sparingly, since they had no idea when they might come across more food. But they wouldn't starve. No. Dougal promised himself he would never starve again.

The road was a long, uninterrupted one, with fields on both sides and very few trees, which stood far back from the road like a distant army. There were no birds or animals on the road, since they kept a safe distance, enjoying a relative security in the shadows of the woods. It was hot under the sun, but a lovely breeze riffled through Dougal's hair. The winds were changing.

CHAPTER 13

A New Existence

Scotland had changed since Dougal had offered his life for hers. She was no longer the sweet but hardy refuge, the place where families could disappear into the glens and forget about other people in other worlds. She was now a hostile playground for English soldiers. Dougal and Aidan passed families on the road, people put out of their homes, mothers leading emaciated children toward the unknown. Many of their homes had been burned to the ground, their men killed either in battle or in plain view of their wives and children. Slaughtered carcasses of cattle lay like putrid boulders across the open spaces; thousands more driven south and sold. It seemed everywhere they went, they met up with Highlanders who had decided it wasn't worth the risk and were escaping to Ireland and other havens.

Dougal and Aidan never knew what had happened to the family whose tiny croft finally became their home. Aidan discovered it by the aptly named Birks of Aberfeldy, nestled within a thick forest of birch. The building was empty, stripped of people and almost every-thing else. Inside it reeked of mould and rot, but it didn't appear the owners had met with a violent end. It seemed they had simply packed up and moved away, carrying whatever possessions they could.

The cabin was tiny, but it had a roof and four walls. There had been animals, as evidenced by the rotted hay in the back room, but they were gone as well. A low wooden wall divided the front room from the rear, the latter for the nonexistent livestock. The sweet, stale reek of pig still clung to the timber.

The first thing they did was remove all the old straw and sweep the dirt floor with a broom they found in the yard. Someday maybe the back room would house a pig again—even a cow. But for now it would stand empty, or would be used to store furs or food they managed to catch.

The roof needed new thatch and Dougal set about collecting branches and dried grass to ensure it was weather-safe before winter. A small but neat pile of peat squares, just like those used to complete the walls, leaned against the stone foundation of the croft. Aidan shared the task of carrying them inside and coaxing a small fire from its damp fibres. They kept the smoke and noise to a minimum, always wary of discovery.

It was a challenge, keeping quiet while he cut trees, but Dougal needed to cut wood to make furniture. Everything from before had been made poorly and threatened to collapse under their weight. He was an able woodworker, had always enjoyed working with his hands. It wasn't difficult for Dougal to produce a table and a couple of stools where the two would sit when they could. Beds weren't a priority, since they were used to sleeping wherever they could find a place to lie down, but eventually he produced two small bed frames and Aidan pulled together soft branches for their mattresses.

A stream nearby, perhaps thirty feet across, poured clean, cool water over a series of cascading falls. The water was deep near their croft, but it rushed noisily over a small rapids, gurgling and splashing as it raced toward a dramatic waterfall, half a mile away. The noise of the water helped mask the sounds Dougal made cutting wood.

Dougal loved living by the stream. He spent long periods of time in the freezing water, forcing his naked body to stay under the surface for as long as he could. He considered it a personal challenge. As if it proved he was still able to win a battle—even if it was only against the power of nature.

Aidan liked the water as well, though he couldn't swim and didn't go in when Dougal did. They went fishing together, or washed clothes in the current, but he never took his clothes off in front of Dougal. He never had. Dougal didn't judge him for it, only wondered. He must have some reason for guarding his privacy. Dougal wondered if he was hiding a hideous scar or birthmark of some kind, but he never pressed the issue. It didn't bother Dougal. Everyone had their own way of doing things, including him.

Aidan visited the stream almost every day. After the first shy request, Dougal stayed respectfully away. The two were content in their new home, sharing the duties of hunting, fishing, and trapping as well as cooking and cleaning, though Aidan was by far the better cook. Or perhaps it was just that Dougal was not a good cook by anyone's standards. The boy worked hard and carried things that appeared far too heavy for his slender arms, but he never complained. At night Dougal read to him until the light gave out. Aidan couldn't get enough of the stories. Dougal read *Robinson Crusoe* in its entirety three times, and Aidan still begged for more.

"I'll no' read it again, Aidan. Ye ken the whole thing in yer mind as it is. We'll have to find a way to get another book to read."

"Something good. Like *Crusoe*."

"Aye. Like that. But there's no one about who has books, is there? So it'll be a while."

Aidan looked disappointed, as he did every time they had this conversation. He hunched over a long stick he was carving into a bow, his lips tight with frustration.

"How about I teach ye to read?" Dougal asked one night.

Aidan stared at him, still as a nervous squirrel. "I'd never be able to read."

"Why no'? Ye're halfway smart anyhow," Dougal teased.

Aidan snorted. "Smarter than ye are by far."

"Then why can ye no' learn to read?"

A fragrant curl of smoke rose from the peat fire, elusive as Aidan's thoughts, which Dougal had never been able to read. This was easy, though. Aidan was afraid of failure. The very idea made Dougal shake his head with wonder. There were so many things to be afraid of in this life, and sometimes failure could be lethal. But not in this case.

"Ah well. If ye're scairt—"

"I'm no' scairt," Aidan growled.

"No?"

"No."

Dougal put his hand on the book and slid it across the table to Aidan. Aidan glared at him, then at *Robinson Crusoe*. Slowly, the crease between his brows softened as his eyes focused on the words and letters. He licked his lips with anticipation, as if he wanted to devour the entire book in one gulp.

"Ye can teach me this? Really?"

Dougal shrugged. "I can try."

"Tonight then," Aidan demanded.

He had a temper like a whip, Dougal had discovered. He was

particular about small things, and extremely suspicious of strangers. He was fine with children and animals, but usually stood back and observed adults from a distance.

Dougal was entirely the opposite. He was a social creature who liked nothing better than to make people laugh. Well, that and a good fight. He really enjoyed fighting.

Aidan was the smarter of the two of them. Dougal had realised that right off the start. In the beginning of their friendship, Aidan had been shy to offer opinions, seeming unsure of himself around Dougal's intimidating bulk, but as they grew close, Aidan opened up, speaking his mind to the extent that Dougal turned to him for advice on many things. He began to rely on the boy almost as much as the boy relied on him.

It was more than that, though. Aidan wasn't simply a help and a partner in survival. He was a friend. He listened and empathised and laughed at things Dougal hadn't mentioned to other men, fearing they'd be considered silly. Aidan never made Dougal feel self-conscious. In return, Dougal was the same kind of friend for Aidan. He learned about Aidan's tenuous existence as an orphan, his decision to join the army, and his kindred friendship with Joseph. They mourned their losses together, and each man understood the other's pain, though they were unique.

Autumn arrived with a chill they'd both forgotten, but knew like an old habit. Dougal felled a couple of elk, and after hanging and salting the meat, he and Aidan fashioned the hides into cloaks and boots. Aidan was a trapper, but also an amazing archer. He brought in smaller game and presented Dougal with rabbit fur mitts, the most comfortable thing Dougal had ever felt against his skin.

It was a difficult winter, but Dougal had cut plenty of wood in advance, so they kept warm and ate when they could, hunkering down in furs when the snow got too deep. When spring returned, melting the jagged icicles until a small moat circled the croft, the men stepped out into the sun and welcomed the green.

Dougal was the hunter, but Aidan was the one with the gift for setting effective traps. So there were times when Dougal sat back and did other things while Aidan went to check and empty traps. One day in April, Dougal decided this was one of those times. Rain hadn't fallen for almost a week, and he wanted to climb onto the roof and settle it after the winter had played havoc with the thatch.

It was heavy work and a welcome distraction. The air was crisp and clean, but instead of snow, Dougal could smell sprouting grass, trees anxious to leaf out. The fragrance brought back memories of spring in his family's home. How he and Andrew had cut the garden dirt, soft after the winter had gone, and Ciaran came behind to seed. He remembered the joy of stepping onto grass instead of snow, leaving their shoes outside the door as they dashed outside, barefoot, playing some game or other. Their house had been larger than this one, with two bedrooms behind the main room. Their roof had been sturdy and the walls thick. A far cry from this little shack. Dougal thought about his uncle Iain's castle, almost surely destroyed by now. Prince Charles himself had stopped in there before they had gone to Culloden. That would have been an attractive target for the English, no doubt.

Culloden. The images came back as soon as the thought hit his consciousness, taking the sun of spring and smearing it with the sounds and smells of battle, the mortal screams of men. He'd seen terror and madness in so many eyes, seen his own hands crusted with the blood of fathers, husbands, sons. With the blood of his own father.

Strange how men always fought. And even stranger that Dougal, a lover of people, loved to fight. He flexed his knuckles, taking a moment from his work to consider the irony. Aidan would appreciate that. He leaned into the roof, jerking the squares of peat back into position.

An unfamiliar sound from within the trees grabbed his attention and he froze. Like a bird's call, but not quite. He listened, but the sound didn't come again, so he shrugged and reached toward another peat square.

There. Not a bird. A shout of panic. A sound that stopped Dougal's heart. Aidan.

He dropped from the roof and was running before he'd caught his balance, vaulting over a fallen tree and shoving aside lichen-slick branches as he ran.

"No!" came a scream, a high, furious sound that tore at Dougal. If they hurt Aidan, if anyone laid a hand on that boy, he'd tear their hearts out while they still beat.

"I'm comin'!" he roared, tearing through the trees until he burst into a small clearing. He had expected to see red coats and English muskets, but was surprised to be met by the dark tartans of four Highlanders, filthy and haggard. Like bears come from their winter slumber, looking for anything to satisfy their hunger.

He saw a flash of golden hair partially hidden behind one of the men, and Dougal slammed into the first Highlander, a dark man almost as tall as he. He knocked him unconscious with one solid blow to the face. The second came at him and Dougal thrust his dirk into the man's belly and yanked straight up. His attacker fell like a stone.

Aidan was screaming like a wild animal, pinned to the ground, his long, bare legs kicking madly.

Then came an anguished cry that Dougal had only heard once before, when Joseph had been killed. The two Highlanders knelt over Aidan's struggling body and Dougal grabbed the first with both hands. He gripped the man's arms and threw him across the clearing. The last man ignored Dougal, intent on the wriggling body beneath him. Dougal drove his dirk into the man's kidneys. The body of the man collapsed on top of a weeping Aidan.

"There, lad," Dougal said. "It's over. It's over. Sons o' bitches won't—"

He stopped. He had shoved the body off Aidan and the boy was rolled into a ball, most of the clothing stripped from his body.

Except it wasn't Aidan. It couldn't have been.

The stricken face turned toward Dougal, blue eyes pleading, tears streaming down the filthy, bruised face of an angel.

"Aidan?" Dougal's voice was a whisper.

"I'm sorry, Dougal."

Aidan sat up, trying to cover his body, but failing. And Dougal saw what had been hidden for all that time. The body of a woman.

CHAPTER 14

Explanations

He had covered her with his shirt and led her home.

He had left the croft when she needed to clean herself up.

He had come back an hour later, but made sure to knock first. It was the very first time he'd ever knocked on that door.

And now he sat, staring at the fireplace, saying nothing. He felt numb. And incredibly stupid. He couldn't get his thoughts to flow. Every time he tried to think of something, the realisation came back: *Aidan's a woman.*

For nearly two years he had spent almost all his time with her. He had slept beside her, for God's sake! He had told her everything about himself and she had—Damn. She had said so much, but never that. Why? Why had she kept it from him? Why had this whole thing been a sham? He felt ridiculous and frustrated and angry all at once. And he felt a loss as well. Aidan was gone.

"Dougal?" The familiar voice was timid. The voice of a stranger.

Dougal had pulled his stool close to the fire, away from the table where she now sat. He knew she could see his profile, but he didn't turn to look at her. He didn't respond at all, just continued to stare at the fire. Was it because he was angry? Not entirely. It was just— he felt lost.

"Please, Dougal," she said. "Please talk wi' me."

He swallowed hard and turned his head away so she couldn't see his expression. He was afraid for a moment that he might cry, and he wasn't even sure why.

"Dougal? Please?"

He turned back toward the fire and dropped his face into his hands, scrubbing them over his cheeks as if to wake them from this bad dream.

"Why?" he finally asked.

He heard her pick up the stool and walk to the fireplace, then set it down beside his, but he didn't look up.

She sat in silence for a few moments, then the truth began to trickle from her lips. Her voice was hushed but calm. As if she spoke in a dream.

"I have been a lad to everyone for so long. Ye must understand. I *had* to be a lad. A lassie canna fight in battles. A lassie canna spend months in a prison wi' great, huge, hairy men an' come out in one piece. A lassie canna do any of these things. But a lad can. An' I did."

Dougal rubbed his hands over his face again, then cradled his chin in his palms. "But why?"

She sighed. "It happened a long time ago. An' it was for the best. Ye see, it was my mam who made me into a lad."

Dougal dropped one of his hands and peered sideways at her. Her clothes had been torn, so she still wore his shirt, which covered her to her knees. She had wrapped the cape of the dead man on the road around herself as well, for modesty's sake. It felt strange, knowing she had to do that.

"Yer mam?" Dougal asked skeptically.

She nodded, but looked away. "I'm no' my father's daughter, aye? My real da, the one I should have had, was killed the year before I was born." Her hands, folded neatly on her lap, suddenly clenched into fists. Such small hands. *Aidan always had such small hands.* "The neighbour man forced himself on my mother before the stones were cooled o'er her husband's body. She got wi' child an' nearly died when I was born. The man came back when I was nine. She saw him comin' an' ran to find me an' Joseph. She hid me in the shed an' bid Joseph cut all my hair an' give me his plaid."

Aidan's chin quivered. "She didna want him near me. She tol' him he'd sired a lad." Her fists unclenched and she clutched her kneecaps, then finally met Dougal's eyes. "He forced himself on my mam again. I heard her screamin' an' Joseph an' I ran to help, but he'd raped her an' beat her to bloody an' then he turned on us. I remember him grabbin' my chin an' sayin' 'Ye're a bonny lad,' an' I was afraid he didna believe it. I should have kept quiet. But my mam was cryin' an' I tol' him to get away from her. He slapped me hard enough that I fell over, an' Joseph . . ." She swallowed, watching Dougal's reaction. "Joseph stabbed him." She snapped her fingers. "Killed him jus' like that."

And she had watched Joseph die outside the prison, trying to help her escape again. Dougal started to understand the terrible pain she had felt when he'd died.

"My mam yelled at us to run, to hide, to ne'er come back. We did. We ran. An' we hid on our own for a month. But we were only nine or ten. We wanted to go home. An' when we did, we found them all long dead. Ye see, they did die o' the illness. But we didna get sick because we weren't there."

Now it was Aidan's turn to rub her hands over her face. She pressed her fingers against her temples and closed her eyes, and

Dougal wondered if she were trying to forget it all, like he did with the battles. She dropped her hands back to her lap and looked at Dougal again.

"We kept up that I was a lad. It seemed safer. We met folk, an' they assumed I was a lad. I was treated like one, an' we never worried about my bein' attacked like my mother had been. It all worked so well until the day we were ordered to march. I had no idea how to shoot. My mam had never taught me that. I had only ever used my bow, an' that just for hunting. Oh, an' my dirk, but I'd never had cause to use it in a fight. When they decided we were goin' to fight, Joseph an' I had to learn from the men, but they didna trust us wi' weapons. So we were the drummers. That suited me fine."

It was the same voice, the same mannerisms Dougal had seen all along, but everything was different.

"But why could ye no' tell me?" he asked. "Did ye no' trust me, either?"

She tilted her head, regarding him with such regret. "Oh, Dougal. So many times I wanted to tell ye. I didna want to live wi' this secret forever. But I was afraid ye'd hate me, or tell me to leave. I thought maybe if I could only keep ye thinkin' I was a lad, I could stay wi' ye." She paused and her eyes filled with tears. "Oh, I so wanted to stay wi' ye, Dougal."

Their eyes met and held. Dougal couldn't pull away. A thousand thoughts flew through his mind in that moment, but the one that held his attention the tightest was what an amazing feat she had managed, carrying this act out for so long in the midst of such conditions. She was watching him but had stopped speaking. It was his turn. They both knew he could end their entire friendship in this moment if he wanted. It was all in his hands.

Why was he so hurt? Why did he want to scream? Trust. He had trusted her. "Ye lied to me."

She shook her head. "I never did. I may have twisted a few things to make it work better, but I never lied. Except for my name, an' even then—" She smiled sadly, remembering. "I think it was Joseph who introduced me to ye. I never said my name."

All the familiar lines of her face seemed different now, and yet it explained so much. He understood why he had been captivated, watching her sleep in the past. Why her voice had soothed every man in those horrible places. She was beautiful. She had always been beautiful, but he had looked away from that. She was a lad, and she was his friend. And now?

"What's yer name then?"

She smiled. It was a bright, beautiful smile that filled her eyes though they spilled over with tears, and he forgave her everything. "Glenna. My name is Glenna. An' that's the first time I've been able to say so in almost eight years."

"Glenna," he mused, testing the name on his tongue. It felt good there.

She reached toward his arm, but he pulled away.

"No," he muttered, sitting up straight. "I'm no' quite ready for that."

She nodded and looked into her lap. "I am sorry. Truly."

"Aye, I ken that. It's only . . . well, it's a bit of a shock, isn't it? Safe to say ye're no' the man I thought ye were." He offered a small smile, meant to put them both at ease.

"But I am still the *person* I was, Dougal. An' the way ye an' I are, well, it's no' changed. I'll still be a lad, if ye like. I'll work as hard as I ever have. Harder, if it helps ye to forgive me."

He shook his head. "Ye work plenty hard enough, Ai—Glenna. No need for that. It will only take me some time, I think. I look at ye an' ye seem like someone I've never known, but someone I've always known. Does that make sense?"

She nodded, eyes full of hope.

"I suppose it's a blessin' I found out now. I didna spend the rest o' my life no' knowing."

"An' I'm so glad I dinna have to hide it anymore," she admitted. "Everythin' became a habit, but still. It will be easier on me now at least."

She reached for his arm again, and this time he didn't move away when her fingertips rested on the taut muscle of his forearm.

"Still friends?" she asked.

"I'd be yer friend anyhow, *Glenna*. It wouldna matter if ye were a lad or a lass. Aye, ye're stuck wi' me. An' I'm sorry if this is a problem, but I, well, I really *am* a lad."

"I'm well aware o' that, Dougal," she said quietly, then stood and walked across the room, clutching the cape around her.

"I'm an oaf," he blurted out, getting to his feet. "I didna think to ask ye—are ye well? Did they hurt ye?"

"No," she replied, shaking her head. "I'll only need to mend my breeks is all."

"Yer breeks . . . ye'll still dress like that then? Like a lad?"

"Aye, I will. No need to change that, is there?"

Dougal thought there probably *was* a need for that, but he wasn't going to be the one to say so. Aidan/Glenna had worn either a kilt or breeks ever since the first day they'd met, and Dougal had never looked twice. But now . . . She was a beautiful woman. He was going to have enough trouble dealing with that without having to worry about the look of her backside or the slender outline of each individual leg.

She heard his hesitation. "Dougal? Is that a problem for ye?"

"No," he said, doing his best to sound offended. "Why should it be?"

She squinted at him, probing, but his expression gave nothing away. "Fine then," she said. "I'll just do my mending an' get back to the traps later. I canna very well go out in naught but yer shirt, can I?"

Dougal said nothing. He felt a sudden urge to go fishing. "I'll be back later wi' supper," he said, and left.

CHAPTER 15

Sharing the Water

It took some getting used to, but Dougal was determined that it should work. That he wouldn't lose the friendship, the closeness he and Aidan had developed. Their connection had become essential to him. Glenna would mean just as much to him as Aidan had, he decided. It was just that he felt he needed to approach her differently now, talk about different topics, and he was running out of things to say that sounded halfway intelligent. He missed Aidan. He missed talking about nothing under the stars, never worrying about what to say. Now it was as if he always wanted to impress Glenna with something.

Glenna put a stop to it one morning a week later. She'd disappeared into the woods, following her trapline, and hadn't told Dougal where she was headed. Why would she after all? He hadn't been there. He'd been in the stream, washing. When he'd returned, she was gone. The house felt hollow without her in it.

"Glenna?"

She wasn't in the house, nor anywhere nearby. His heart started to thunder with unfamiliar panic. Where was she? What if something had happened to her? Why hadn't he been with her, protecting her? He growled with self-disgust, chastising himself for being so irresponsible. What if the men from the other day returned hungry again, looking for revenge and finding a tasty little morsel?

He ran toward the clearing where he'd discovered who she really was, hoping to find her, but also praying she wasn't there. He burst through the trees, panting, and took in the scene.

"Glenna?"

She wasn't there. He retraced his steps, then realised she had probably gone out to check her traps. He dug carefully on the side of the path they'd cut, knowing where she always left the traps. He found the first one. Empty. His chest loosened with relief. *Yes.* He would find her now. Watching the path for traps, he followed the line. They were sometimes hidden deeper than he thought and could be difficult to find. Once he barely yanked his foot out of harm's way. She wouldn't be happy if he messed up her traps, he thought wryly. He ducked under branches and slapped at midges, his eyes darting constantly, searching for her.

Then he heard her. That nightingale voice, singing something low and sad, a lullaby she thought she sang only to herself. He leaned against the thick trunk of an oak, hidden from view, and watched her work. She leaned over a trap, setting to her work with her normal efficient manner, cutting the carcass from its noose and tying it to her belt. She moved like a man, only smoother. Fluid, he thought. Like a strong, capable deer. He liked observing her when she didn't know he was there.

"What are ye watchin'?" she asked, her gaze still on the trap she was resetting. Dougal jumped but didn't speak. "Dougal," she said, standing upright. She rested her fists on her hips and tilted her head, giving him a look that made him feel as he had twenty-odd years before, when his mother called him on something he'd done. "I asked what ye were watchin'."

He stepped out of his apparently poor place of concealment and walked toward her. She grinned at him. "How ye manage to be such a skilled hunter, I'll ne'er understand," she said. "I could hear ye breathin' a mile away."

"Ye've the ears of a squirrel," he grumbled.

She nodded, then returned to her earlier line of questioning. "What were ye doin' there?"

"I came to see . . . I was worried that . . . I thought maybe . . ." He winced, realising how pathetic he sounded. He leaned down to pluck a tiny purple flower from the grass and snapped the bloom between his fingers.

"You were worried? About me? Since when? After all ye've seen me do, ye'd ken that most of the time I'm just fine on my own, thank ye very much." She glared at him. "I'm no' delicate flower, Dougal MacDonnell." She gestured toward the torn flower between his fingers. "I'm no' shrinkin' violet, either. If I'm a flower at all, I'm maybe . . ." She paused and grabbed the crushed flower from Dougal's grip. "Maybe I'm a thistle. Ye'd best not squeeze me too hard." She slid her knife back into its sheath, keeping shrewd eyes on him. "Ye know what? I'm sick o' this, Dougal. O' the way ye treat me these days. *I'm* no different, but ye are. What is it wi' ye? Why do ye sneak around behind me all the time, watchin'? Why can ye no' be yerself anymore?"

He shrugged. "I've no idea."

"Ye'd best just say it," she demanded. "For if ye dinna speak yer mind, this will never ease between us, an' it will end badly."

"I canna say what I am thinkin', because I dinna ken what it is."

"Ye do."

"I don't."

She shoved his shoulder and he stepped obligingly back. She came closer and pushed him again, harder this time. He frowned and his backward movement was less.

"That's right," she said. Her eyes glittered with anger. "I'm askin' ye to be the man ye were. The man ye are now isna worth a pot to piss in. Ye dinna speak of anythin' worthwhile, ye dinna laugh, ye dinna do anythin'! Ye're dull as a stone!" She shoved him hard again. This time he tripped back, then stepped forward and grabbed her wrist, holding it in place.

"Don't do this," he said, almost pleading.

In response, she slapped his face with the hand he wasn't holding. He shook his head to clear the sting, then grabbed that wrist as well. She leaned toward him, trying to put her face in front of his, but he was a foot taller. She hissed up at him through bared teeth.

"Do somethin', Dougal MacDonnell. Dinna turn into some ninny. Do somethin'."

"I dinna have to do anythin'. I've no need to prove myself."

"Oh no? Then why is it ye're spendin' so much time talkin' of things that dinna matter? Why do ye try to do more than ye did before? Is it because I'm so wee, now that I'm a lass? Because I'm so small an' weak an' helpless? Ye need to show me what a big man ye are? Is that it?"

"No . . ." he said, but his voice lacked conviction.

She pressed even closer to him. Her voice lowered to a dangerous level, almost a whisper. Almost the sound he'd heard her make in her sleep. "Do ye think I canna take care o' myself anymore? Is that why ye came out here jus' now? Well, I can do jus' fine on my own, sir. I heard ye comin', an' I'd hear that lot if they came within a mile o' me."

Dougal felt the air buzzing between them, felt the pulse hammering in her wrists beneath his fingertips. Her eyes were furious, glowering at him like blue flames, challenging him. When she had been Aidan, they had never fought. Never had occasion to disagree, because everything had been so easy. What was it now?

"What do ye want?" he demanded. "What do ye want me to do?"

"Anythin'! Just be the Dougal ye were, man. Dinna tend to me as if I were a child. I'm still me. Why aren't you still you? Do something, Dougal. Do something!"

So he kissed her. He dropped her wrists and seized the sides of her face, bringing her lips to his. She pulled instinctively away, but he held on, kissing her mouth, slightly open with surprise. He touched the skin he had longed to touch ever since he'd first found out the truth about her. It was warm, hot even, because she was angry. He felt his own face warm as he sank into the kiss.

She was so small, just like she'd said. Despite what she claimed, the bones he held between his hands were so wee, so delicate, fitting into the palms of his hands like she was made to be there. He slid one hand down her back so it rested on her waist and pulled her snug against him. He felt her body adjust, felt her muscles bunch up in response. Yes! Yes, this was what he'd been wanting. His blood sang, tingling his fingers, dancing in his lips—

And she bit him. He yelped and stepped back, rubbing his lower lip.

"What—" he cried, but she was there first.

"What was *that*?" she shrieked, sounding out of breath. Now it was her own hands clutching her face, her fingertips digging into bright red cheeks. "Ye jus' think ye can . . . Ye grab me an' . . . I canna *believe* ye'd—" She exhaled quickly and spun away, heading back toward her trapline. "Ninny," she muttered.

"Oh no, ye don't," Dougal said, finally roused. A ninny? She'd see he was no ninny. "Ye canna dare me as such, then spurn me. I'll no' have it."

"Spurn ye? *Spurn* ye?" she hissed at him. "Is that what ye think this is? Ye think ye can—Och!" Her fingers went to her hair, gripping the roots of it so the long blond locks popped out from between her fingers. She held her head tight, as if afraid it might explode. Even standing like this, angrier than he'd ever seen her, he admired her. Maybe even more. Falling from between her fingers, her hair was smooth and golden, shining with sunlight since she'd washed it that morning. He had traded for some lye soap in the nearby village, and she'd been ecstatic after she'd cleaned herself with it. He had thought she was beautiful before, but now, furious and flushed, he thought he'd never seen anything quite so magnificent. "I said for ye to do somethin', but I didna mean—"

"Aye, ye did," he said, his mouth quirking up in a smile. She tightened her lips and shook her head slowly, but without much conviction. Her eyes darted to the right, then the left, like she was thinking, looking for words.

But Dougal now knew. What he wanted more than anything in the world was to repeat his performance, hold her and kiss her until neither could breathe. But he held back. It was up to her now. She'd asked for him to do something, and he had.

"Right. I'm goin' for a swim," he said, and walked away.

CHAPTER 16

Sound of the Heart

He tried to look nonchalant. As if this were something he did every day. Smiling to himself, he relived what had just happened. Well. Even if she hadn't wanted that, *he* had. And now he could go on with his days, knowing what it felt like to kiss her.

Except . . . his step faltered. Except he'd still have to live with her if she hadn't liked it. That could be tricky. Nothing he couldn't handle, though, he was sure. Almost sure. He kicked a pebble down the path in front of him, frowning. What had he done? Surely they would work this out somehow. She wouldn't just leave, would she? Certainly not. She might be strong, but not that strong.

He pulled the image of her back into his mind, the one where her cheeks blazed red and her eyes glinted like freshly sharpened daggers. That was grand. He could do with upsetting her more often if she were to react that way every time.

He slipped off his breeks and tunic and waded into the freezing stream, feeling everything below his waist pull tight in reaction to the cold. He shivered but pressed forward, needing to cool his emotions. Something smooth tickled past his ankle and he wished he'd brought his fishing pole. At least she'd left the lye soap on the big rock where they always stepped into the water. He grabbed it and scoured the soap over his chest and belly, scrubbing the dirt from his skin. The stream was never deep enough that the surface went over his head, but the bottom dropped suddenly in one spot so the water covered most of his shoulders. The rushing water took what it could of the lye and dirt while Dougal raked soapy fingers through his mass of black waves. He plunged under again, using his fingers like claws to rinse the soap from his hair. Then he burst through the surface, grinning and swiping hair from his face. He loved the shock of the cold water. Made him feel alive.

A sound from the shore distracted him, and he blinked water from his eyes. Glenna sat on the big boulder, calmly tossing pebbles into the water and studying him. He wasn't surprised to see her there, and didn't pretend that he was. Whether she were pleased or not, Glenna never walked away from a discussion that needed to be had. He tossed her the slippery soap and she caught it deftly, setting it beside her on the boulder. She hopped down to rinse the suds from her hands, and scooped a handful of pebbles into her hand while she was there. Climbing back onto the boulder, she lobbed one of the little stones. It landed with a neat plop beside his head. Exactly where, he knew, she'd intended for it to land.

"What do ye think about at night, Dougal?" she asked, tossing another pebble into the water. It landed six feet away from him.

He shrugged. "No' much."

"Do ye think of me?"

Dougal rubbed his hands over his wet face, hiding a grin. "What a question," he replied, emerging with a straight face.

"Do ye?"

"Ye're a cheeky lass, askin' questions like that. What do ye think of?"

"No. I asked first."

"So ye did." He stroked his jaw and gazed skyward, toward where the sun glinted through treetops, on its way down. His beard needed a trim. He hadn't shaved in two days. He started wading casually toward shore, needing his dirk for the operation. With every calculated step he revealed more of his body, confident now. He was in good shape. They had eaten well and worked hard since coming to this place, and he felt like himself. He knew he looked good, and he wasn't shy to use whatever weapons he had in this battle.

The water had just reached the level of his navel when she slid off the boulder, looking suspicious. "What are ye doin', Dougal?"

"I need my dirk," he said.

"Stop," she ordered. "Catch." She yanked his dirk from his belt, then tossed it in a gentle arc toward him. He caught it by the handle and nodded thanks. Just for fun, he took another step forward, feigning innocence.

"Dougal!" she cried. "Turn around an' go deep."

"When, my dear Glenna, did ye become such a prude? Ye spent months wi' the hairiest, most naked men alive, ye saw all there is to see, an' suddenly ye're shy wi' me?"

She frowned, arms crossed, then looked toward the trees as if something fascinating was going on in there.

He wanted to laugh. He hadn't been wrong after all. He just had to figure out a way to help her see that he was right. She was, after all, only seventeen. She knew little about love. Neither did Dougal. But having reached the ripe old age of twenty-one, he did have a fair amount of experience with women. He was more than willing to teach.

"What do ye think of, Dougal?" she repeated quietly.

And one thing he knew about women was that they liked to talk. Dougal could talk.

"Not much," he admitted. "I think about the day, I suppose. What we've done. Sometimes I think on my family, but mostly not." He tucked up his chin and dragged the dirk along his throat and under his jaw.

She watched him dip the blade in the water, then scratch at his cheeks, sucking in his upper lip so he could clear the moustache from under his nose. "Why do ye ask?"

"It's the only time we don't speak," she replied with a shrug. "From the moment we're awake in the morn, we talk all the time. Then there are those moments just before ye fall asleep, aye? After ye're done readin' to me? An' those are the moments when I think the most. So I just wondered if ye were the same."

She was right, of course. Because he did think before falling asleep. He just didn't want to talk about the things he sometimes saw.

"Aye, that's the same wi' me. What is it ye think of?" he asked.

"Oh, everythin'," she said, exhaling so her breath puffed up the short fringe on her forehead. "I think about Joseph a lot. About how we were, an' I think about the last time I saw him, crumpled on the dirt like that." She hesitated, letting herself think a bit. Dougal said nothing. She had started this conversation, so she most likely had more to say. "I remember a lot of the battles, too. I remember all about Culloden. On those nights I practically smell the stink of the gunpowder as I fall asleep. I think that smell is maybe burnt into my nostrils."

She looked straight at him, blinking as if hypnotised. "But I think of good things, too. I think of the fun Joseph an' I used to have before all this happened. An' now I think about how much I enjoy bein' wi' you, Dougal. How I've never laughed so much or felt safer. How much our friendship means to me. I dinna ken what

I'd do wi'out ye," she said quietly, and from twenty feet away Dougal saw her eyes shine with tears. "I feel as if I've known ye forever an' I'd be lost on my own. So . . . so when ye kissed me . . ."

She shoved the heels of her hands against her eyes to keep the tears at bay, then sniffed. When she glanced back toward him, Dougal saw the reddened skin where she'd pressed. He felt an urge to comfort her, but didn't move.

Her voice was choked. "I canna lose ye, Dougal. I'm afraid that if we become more than friends, I'll lose that. Ye've acted a complete fool of late, an' ye had me right pissed at ye. But the thing is . . . well, the thing is I—Oh. Never mind."

Dougal cleared his throat. "Look away, lass," he said, and splashed out of the water. He lowered his tunic over his body and as it clung to his wet skin, he wished, as he always did, that he had his plaid. Then he wouldn't have had to worry about a shirt at all. He supposed he could have only put on the wretched breeks and forgotten about the shirt, but at this point that might make things even more awkward with Glenna. He tugged on the breeks, belted them, and slid the dirk into its sheath.

She was looking into her lap, toying with the pebbles on one palm. Her head was tilted and a soft veil of golden hair fell across her face. He was struck again by how angelic she appeared, then fought the urge to tuck the loose hair behind her ear so he could see her perfect features. His Glenna. She was a challenge. Skittish as a fawn, with the teeth of a wolf.

"Look," he said, taking a casual step toward her. "I've had friends my whole life. Folk I've laughed with, fought with, oh, done most everythin' with. My brother Andrew was always my closest friend. And now it's you. Ever since we first struck up a conversation, I've felt as if I'd known ye forever. Even wi' yer secret, well, ye knew I was hurt that ye didna tell me sooner. But I understand it now."

Dougal was a talker. Loved words and innuendos and games. But right now he wasn't tempted to tease. He felt a need to say it like it really was. Make everything clear. He lowered his voice so its tone was gentle. "Glenna, I understand what ye're sayin' to me. I do. And I feel as ye do. I'm unhappy when I'm no' wi' ye. But aye, I admit it. Knowing ye're a lassie changes how I look at ye. Ye're lovely."

"But I'm no' Aidan, am I?" she said softly. She was frowning, offering him a challenge.

He ignored it. "Why must ye be Aidan? I loved Aidan as a friend. Very much. But wi' Glenna it would be different. It would be more."

She swallowed. "I'm afraid, Dougal."

Go canny, lad. She's the fawn at the moment, but could tear your heart out in a breath. He took the five remaining steps until he stood directly in front of her and, with a monumental effort, kept his hands resting on his hips. His voice was calm. As if he soothed one of the horses at his uncle's stables. "I'll never hurt ye, Glenna. Whether ye decide ye want me or no', I'll never hurt ye."

A tear trickled from the corner of one of her eyes and tumbled down her cheek. "Oh, Dougal."

He leaned forward and set one hand on either side of her, bracing himself against the boulder. This brought them face to face, and he was suddenly very pleased he had shaved, though he hadn't done a great job at it. She didn't shy away, but he saw the panic in her eyes. Her breathing got faster; he felt it on his cheeks. Her smooth white complexion was flushed and her eyes probed his. Anchoring his hands securely on the rock, Dougal touched her lips with his. She didn't move, but when he drew away, her eyes were closed. So he did it again. This time he felt her lips move against his, experimenting. He laid one palm on her cheek, gentle, gentle, as if she were a babe.

His hand drifted down her neck, over the curve of her shoulder, and started down her arm. His other hand moved to her waist.

"Come here, lass," he breathed into her ear, and she sighed. He felt something give within her; the walls she had so carefully built around her heart began to crumble. Dougal would be the one to catch the stones as they fell. She wrapped her slender arms around his neck and kissed him a little harder. He put one of his hands on her cheek, gently stroking the line of her jaw with his thumb, and the woman in her responded to his touch, leaning against his hand, uttering a small purr of pleasure when he kissed beneath her ear.

He guided her body closer, until it pressed against his, and his fingers returned to their slide down the contours of her sides. As they travelled toward her waist, his thumbs brushed the sides of her breasts and she gasped, jerking a little with surprise. She almost pulled away, but he held her tight and did it again. This time she shuddered against him and the sensation made his pulse jump. Her kisses dove deeper, and she breathed more heavily. He responded, letting his hunger take over.

"God, Glenna," he murmured against her lips. He reached down until he cupped her bottom in his hands, then lifted her from the boulder, kissing all the while. She wrapped her legs around his waist so he could carry her more easily, and when she shifted against his hips, the sensation made him dizzy.

He carried her to a place where they'd often sat on pleasant days, a soft bed of grass atop a granite outcropping. The view of the Highlands from the spot was magnificent, falling in shadowed peaks for hundreds of miles. But neither of them noticed. She watched him through heavy lids as he laid her on the grass, then he settled onto his hands and knees, poised above her, wondering what to do next.

CHAPTER 17

A Lad No Longer

Kissing and touching was one thing. He'd done that with a great many willing lassies over the years. But going any further than that was always a question. Some had bargained with him: would he marry them if they agreed to make love with him? No. He had sufficed with the more innocent contact, and made do. Others had welcomed him to their beds, but afterward, though he left with a smile on his face, he often carried a feeling of indifference as far as the girl was concerned.

Neither was the case here. Clearly, Glenna was as roused as he. She waited beneath him now, eyes closed, chest rising and falling with excitement and, probably, fear. If he made love to Glenna, there was no going back. She wouldn't ask about marriage. Their partnership was one that would never require confirmation of that sort. But it would change their bond. There would be no indifference between them, ever.

She opened her eyes and they softened as they met his, blue as the sky, deep as the ocean. *Love me,* they said to him. For the first time, he heard her voice as clearly in his mind as if she'd said the words out loud. *Love me, please.*

"Ye're sure?" he asked quietly. If she asked him to stop, he would, though he thought he would probably explode at the least breath of wind.

She nodded and whispered, "Aye, I am."

His stomach rolled with anticipation. She sat up and took a deep breath, then offered him a tremulous smile. "Ye'll have to help me out," she said quietly. "I'm new at this, aye?"

"Glenna." He kissed her again, then turned his concentration to her tunic. Fighting the urge to rip the worn, flimsy material off her, he gently tugged her tunic out of her breeks. She giggled suddenly and slammed her hands down onto the tunic.

"Tickles," she said.

"Oh, does it?" he asked, matching her grin, then adding a little spice. "Just ye wait."

He pried her hands from her stomach and placed them at her sides, though he could see she had trouble keeping them there. Every fibre in her body was taut. He leaned down to kiss her again, and found that while he did it to reassure her, it did the same for him. She seemed to gain strength from the kiss. Maybe she sensed his own nervousness and wanted, as usual, to help.

The material skimmed her belly and Dougal leaned down to kiss it. Her skin was white as snow under the rough fabric, and it jumped at his touch. He cursed the fact that he'd done only a haphazard job on shaving; his whiskers would scrape her perfect skin. But she didn't complain. Instead, she giggled, only this time her voice was a little less confident. She was questioning now, without saying a word, and he wanted to give her all the right answers. The material strained a bit against his fingers as she took a deep breath, readying herself. As she might for battle, he thought wryly.

"Dinna be afraid, Glenna," he said. "I want only to love ye, to give ye pleasure."

She sniffed quickly and nodded. "I'm fine," she managed.

Best to just dive right in, he decided. He pulled the tunic up, trying not to stare, but failing miserably.

"God, Glenna," he said. He put his hand behind her neck and pulled the material over her head, then dropped it on the ground at their side.

"What?" she asked, her voice like a small child's.

He stared at her perfect body, marveling at all she had hidden for the past two years. Her breasts were small, which had been useful for her disguise, but they were by no means insubstantial. Her stomach lay flat, rising quickly with her nervous breathing. The arcs of her hipbones were visible above the waist of her breeks, fragile and strong all at once.

She eyed him without moving, watching his reaction. He caught her gaze and grinned, aware his smile might resemble that of a wolf at that particular moment.

"Ye're no laddie, Glenna."

She chuckled, then shivered. "I'm cold," she said.

"Aye," he replied, looking pointedly at her breasts. "I can see that. No' for long, though." He got to his feet and removed his own tunic in one quick motion, dropping it beside hers. Then he dropped back down to his hands and knees so he could kiss her some more.

That's when he noticed how her expression had changed. Her blue eyes were wide with curiosity as they flicked over the contours of his chest. He waited, letting her see or touch, letting her do whatever she wanted to do. If she wanted to see, he would show her.

Anything she wanted, he would give her. God, she was beautiful. The lines of her face were softening with this new expression. Her eyes seemed darker, her lips were partially open. Could it possibly be that she felt the same way as he did? He watched the corners of her lips curve gently upward and she blinked at him, looking something akin to guilty.

It was his turn to ask. "What?"

Her fingertips touched the dark skin of his chest and goose bumps rose like wildfire over his body. "Ye're no lassie," she said.

He roared with laughter and dug his lips into her neck again. She had seen him without a shirt so many times and had never reacted this way. He was delighted.

"Those are very cold fingers," he said, then pressed his hand against the back of hers so her palm lay flat against his skin.

"I can feel yer heartbeat," she said quietly. "Under my hand."

He dug beneath her and wound his arm around her waist. Lifting her from the ground, he pulled her against him, kissing her all the while. Her breasts were cold, pressing against his chest with a sweet urgency he had hardly dared hope for. The difference in temperatures between their skins was one of the most exquisite sensations he had ever felt.

Still holding her against him with one hand, he reached to the side and grabbed their discarded shirts. He bundled them into a makeshift pillow, then set it on the ground behind her. "Lay yer head down," he murmured, and she did.

Dougal's body screamed for release, but his mind was wholly occupied with devouring Glenna. He knelt beside her and ran his fingers over her body as if she were a musical instrument and he searched for the right notes. He found a spot on her lower belly that made her jump, then kissed her there. When he caressed her breasts, she gasped and stared at him as the sensation raced through her.

Her eyes were wide and searching, but he just smiled. She bit her lip, then lay back and let him do what he wanted.

What he wanted was to be gentle, to trace the lines of her with his fingertips until she shivered uncontrollably, but there was only so much he could restrain. He straddled her and leaned down, kissing upward from the centre of her belly, and tasting each breast in turn. She made a small whimpering sound and he froze.

"Does it hurt?" he asked. "Are ye all right?"

"No, no," she said, her words coming in gasps. "No' so much hurt . . . I'm . . . Do it again."

This time she held his head against her chest and moaned as his lips closed over her. His head buzzed when she raked her fingers through his damp black hair.

"God, Dougal," she whispered and he chuckled against her skin, now warm and damp from his kisses.

With his lips still at her breast, his hands slid to her hips, then to the tie of her breeks. Her hands suddenly caught his and he met her gaze.

"Ye'll no' hurt me?" she asked.

"No' on purpose," he said. "But—the first time a lassie makes love, it can hurt."

"Oh?" Her eyes went round again and beneath his hands he felt fear clench in her belly.

"Only for a moment. Then . . . then it shouldna hurt."

She swallowed, then nodded and worked the tie of her breeks. "I can take those off."

"It's all right. I want to," he assured her.

It struck him that this small act was intensely erotic, removing a woman's breeks. Before Glenna, he hadn't ever seen a woman dressed in anything but gowns, and he'd become fairly adept at helping them to remove those. This was something new. He pulled the knot loose and began to slide the worn brown wool down her hips. He followed the line of the material with his thumbs, tracing her hipbones until he revealed her lower body. He pressed his fingertips against the blond, coarse hairs and she relaxed again. His breeks joined hers beside them and it was her turn to stare.

"What?" he asked, flushing slightly. "Ye've seen it before."

"I havena seen it do *that* before."

"No?" He chuckled. "Well, I canna help it. I want to be inside ye more than anythin' in the world."

She bit her lip. "I'm frightened."

"Aye, I ken ye are. But I've promised, haven't I? I'll hold ye close. Trust me."

One large knee worked its way between her thighs and he settled on top of her, balancing his weight on his elbows so as not to crush her. She still trembled under him and he wondered if she could feel his own tremor. He felt dizzy with anticipation. He kissed her breasts, her neck, her lips, anywhere he could reach, and she kissed him back. Her fingers explored him, grabbing the muscles of his arms, skimming over the lines of his chest. At some point he felt the tension in her legs loosen and slowly, slowly, trying not to spook her, he shifted positions and pressed her thighs apart.

He held her gaze, asking. She looked back at him, small face so trusting beneath his. She nodded.

"Dinna be afraid," he said, then pressed himself between her legs. She stiffened immediately, and he met opposition from within. He kissed her again, soothing, reassuring, then pushed hard.

He tried to ignore the cry of pain he shoved out of her. He tried to disregard the taste of salty tears on her cheeks he knew he had put there. Instead he concentrated on the feel of her around him; not only from within, but in the solid press of her thighs against his body, the cut of her fingernails as they dug like claws into his back.

Eventually the little sounds she was making changed, softening into something more like curiosity than pain. He dared himself to look in her eyes and discovered she wasn't even looking at him. Her eyes were skyward. He stopped moving.

"Glenna?"

She jerked her gaze from the sky. "Aye?"

"Are ye all right?"

"Aye, I reckon I am. Are we done?"

He frowned. "No' quite." He propped himself up on one elbow and peered at her. "Are ye no' enjoyin' yerself then?"

She shrugged. "Well, it doesna hurt now, if that's what ye mean."

"No, that is no' what I mean. Does it feel good to ye?"

This time it was she who frowned. "It feels . . . odd. I reckon I'm still thinkin' on that first bit. It's no' like that every time, is it?"

"No. Only the once. Glenna?"

"Aye?"

"Forget that first bit. Look at me. Am I who ye want?"

Her eyes grew dark, like very deep lochs. "Oh aye, Dougal."

"Then let me love ye proper. Forget that part an' think of how it feels now."

He moved slowly and her eyes started to close. He sank his lips into her neck, feeling her pulse, quick and light under his tongue.

"Does that feel good to ye, Dougal?"

"Oh, aye."

She relaxed under him. He could tell the moment when she decided to stop thinking and instead enjoy the sensations as they presented themselves. Now it was his turn to think rather than feel. How to bring her pleasure? He wanted her to love this, to feel the exhilaration he felt. He wanted her to want more. He certainly did not intend for this to be their one and only time. He tried varying his speed depending on the little purring noises she issued, then realised he couldn't stand thinking anymore.

He closed his eyes as a familiar, delicious rumble began deep within him, taking hold and growing, wave after wave, taking possession of his mind and body.

"Glenna," he whispered, and surrendered.

And somewhere in the back of his mind he heard another sound: Glenna's voice, calling to him, crying out.

When he opened his eyes at last, she was watching him, her face relaxed into a sweet, peaceful expression. She closed her eyes and started to drift off to sleep, but he gathered her up against him first, turned her back to his chest, and pulled her tight against his body. She was soft and pliable in his arms, as if unwilling to argue. He wrapped an arm over her, stuck his nose in the golden tangle of her hair, and fell asleep.

CHAPTER 18

Dougal's Secret

The most beautiful sounds Dougal had ever heard filled their croft. When Glenna wasn't singing, she laughed, and when she laughed, he couldn't stop his own from bubbling over. And the relief he felt was almost as wonderful. He had known all along there was something between them. A connection that went beyond friendship. And now here they were, lovers as well as friends, their days and nights filled with each other.

He hadn't been wrong, approaching her like that. Now there were no more nights of silence. Their beds were pushed together so they fell asleep in each other's arms, sometimes mid-sentence. They awoke in the barely lit hours, nudging each other by accident or on purpose, making love whenever the feeling came upon them.

And she no longer whispered in her sleep. She had shed her secrets, let them out of her head and given them to him.

When they weren't loving or laughing, they worked together at making their secret life in the Highlands successful. Life wasn't safe in Scotland anymore. Not only did the English still wander the Highlands, ridding the land of Scots, but Glenna and Dougal were escaped convicts. They had to stay hidden from any wandering troops and were always on the lookout.

They did the best with what they had. They fished, hunted, and trapped side by side. Glenna was a skilled archer, and Dougal delighted in watching her take down a deer with one perfectly aimed arrow.

Every now and then they made the trip to a nearby town to trade in furs and come back with necessities. In the beginning they had hidden beneath hoods, skulking in the streets. Then one day Glenna traded for a plain homespun dress. She brought it home and slipped it on, then tied the long fall of her hair back. It took Dougal back a step, seeing her dressed like that, and she seemed equally shocked, but it made visiting town a lot easier. When they were alone, she usually still wore breeks because she complained the dress was heavy and bulky, but whenever they went to town, she was every bit the beautiful, but typically dressed lady.

No one was looking for an escaped Scottish prisoner who wore a dress.

Dougal shaved his thick black beard almost every day, and cut his hair until it no longer covered his face unless the wind pushed it there. The ends reached to his shoulders but no farther, and he combed it back into a tail, tying it with a leather cord like he had as a boy. He wanted to look as presentable as she did when they went into town.

In the twilight, in the flickering dimness of an oil lamp, he taught her to read. She was frustrated at first, demanding perfection from herself from the beginning, but he moved slowly, with infinite patience. She wanted this, and Dougal was determined to give her everything she wanted. He brought new books home from almost every trading mission.

When they reached the end of one of their tethers, they would either stop for the night or move on to something new. Dougal dug in his memory for the lessons his mother had so earnestly tried to teach, and was able to unearth lessons in mathematics, history, and geography. Glenna was a sponge, soaking up everything he had to offer. There were times she nearly wore him out with her thirst for learning, but he never discouraged it. Every bit of information he taught her opened a new window into her fascinating mind and he reveled in her determination.

Glenna sang to him almost every night. Sometimes after they made love, he was aware of her watching him fall asleep. She leaned on her elbow and toyed with the strands of his hair while singing something sweet as honey, just for him. He felt her there, though his eyes were closed. It was as if her diminutive presence cushioned him, kept him safe, as ridiculous as that might sound. Her fingers were strong, their tips small and calloused, and he kissed each one separately, listening to her giggle.

But deep in his heart, which was almost entirely filled with her, he struggled with an unspoken secret. Every time she looked at him, her eyes so trusting, her own secrets all told, he got closer to telling her what no one else knew. About the things he heard in his head that he shouldn't hear. He'd never shared the secret with anyone.

One night after they'd made love, she snuggled her back against his side and sighed deeply, resting her cheek on his arm as if it were a pillow. He imagined her feathery eyelashes touching her cheeks and kissed the back of her neck.

"Ye dinna believe in the kirk, do ye?" he asked.

"In the kirk? Why? What made ye think of that?"

"It's only I want to ask somethin' that has to do wi' believin' what ye canna see."

"Oh?" She rolled back so that she faced the ceiling, and gave him a bemused smile. "Believin' what ye canna see is easy for me."

"Is it? Why's that?"

"Because, my wee fool, I canna see how much ye love me, but I believe it."

He grinned. "Ah. I'm the fool, aye? Well, perhaps ye're right, *mo ghràidh*. For ye're wise—most of the time."

She nudged him with her elbow. "Tell me this thing. What is it I canna see, Dougal?"

He propped himself up onto one elbow so that he gazed down into her face. She lay relaxed, her expression curious. She made him feel safe, and that made him marvel.

"I've never told a soul this," he said, then paused, still waiting to hear her laugh at him, doubt him, ignore this most precious of secrets.

"Tell me," she whispered.

"It's something that I . . . Well, it's something I've done since I was a young lad. Ye'll say I'm—"

"Dinna think of what I'll say, Dougal. Just say it."

"All right. Here it is then. Laugh if ye must. Since I was wee, I've been able to hear what some men think."

She frowned and gave a little shrug. "Aye? So? It's easy to tell what a man's thinking."

"No. No' like that. No' like ye think. I dinna read a man's expression an' figure it out from there. No. I hear what's kept inside their heads. Andrew could do it as well, I think."

The frown still creased her brow and he dragged a golden strand of hair across it. "If that's so," she asked, "then why is it ye didna ken I was a woman?"

"Because I canna read women's minds."

She lifted her eyebrows and the wrinkles disappeared. "Do ye do it all the time?"

"The voices come to me whether I want them or no'. Sometimes I listen, sometimes I try not to."

A few moments of silence passed while she ingested his secret, then she looked away, staring instead at the wooden beam of their home. When she looked in his eyes again, he thought he detected sadness in them.

"That must be a chore," she said, then brightened. "Then again, it might be a help as well."

"Aye. It can go either way."

She didn't move for a second and Dougal peered closely at her in the darkness. She stared back at him, her eyes open wide, unblinking, her face a mask of intensity.

"What is it?" he asked.

She continued to stare at him, saying nothing.

"Glenna?" he demanded. "Are ye all right? Are ye angry? Did I say somethin' to upset ye?"

She huffed and grinned. "All right then. I was just makin' sure."

"Of what?"

"That you couldna read my thoughts. I dinna want ye in my head all the time."

He laughed and ducked his head down so he could nuzzle her neck. "Why no'? Ye're in mine all the time." She giggled. "What were ye thinkin' of anyway?"

"I was thinkin' how much I'd like to go huntin' tomorrow, fetch us some venison."

Dougal shook his head, smiling. "I make love to ye, I tell ye my deepest secret, and ye think of aught but huntin'?"

He saw the white of her smile in the dark. "I only wanted to think of something ye'd no' be able to guess." She took one of his ears between her fingers and began to massage it in the way he couldn't resist. "Can ye read what I'm thinkin' now?"

"No, Glenna, I told ye, I canna—"

Her other hand skimmed over his chest, moving downward until she could press it firmly between his legs.

"How about now?"

He breathed deeply and kissed her waiting lips. "Oh, aye. I read ye well."

Days, months, and years passed, their lives as simple as those of any other couple in the Highlands, aside from the fact that they were outlaws and therefore needed to remain invisible. Dougal was constantly amazed at how she made him feel, how she filled him with such contentment, whether they kept busy around the home or simply sat by the fire, doing something quiet like mending or sharpening blades. He had thought his life before had been happy, before war had taken it away. But it was nothing to this new existence, this sense of knowing. Of understanding that he had found what he'd been lacking all along.

She was everything he needed: a companion, a confidante, and a lover with a hunger equal to his own. He still missed his family; he wished he could introduce her to them. Andrew would have loved her. He'd have said she was far too good for Dougal, but Dougal would have known he was joking.

His mind drifted to Andrew fairly often, reluctantly following that bittersweet path. Of anyone in the world, Andrew would appreciate the life Dougal had now. If only he could have lived long enough to experience his own love. If only he could have lost himself to a woman as Dougal had. The thought made Dougal chuckle. How would their silent conversations go then? Maybe it was better he couldn't share those thoughts. As much as he was proud of Glenna, wanted to show her off, there were certain aspects to their relationship that no one but they should see.

Glenna seemed just as happy as he felt. Her smile became a sight so familiar to him he couldn't imagine living without it. As long as he had Glenna, everything would be all right.

CHAPTER 19

The Hunt Begins

The winter of 1756 had been brief and violent, as if it had handed out a severe punishment, then relaxed with satisfaction, witnessing the devastation it had wrought. Hunters and hunted were famished when mid-February arrived, and fortunately it was warm enough for Dougal and Glenna to hunt again. Ice and snow still claimed most of the land and the few tufts of stubborn grass poking through were dry and brown. Deer were scarce. Dougal and Glenna spent all morning scouring the woods for spoor, though they knew any prey they found would be emaciated.

At last they found a small pile beside their trail, still slightly warm, and hope began to stir in the hunters' hungry bellies. The track led to a treeless outcropping, the granite slick and black underfoot. Dougal was surefooted as the wiliest of deer, but even he had trouble keeping his feet under him when they passed by the edge of a sheer cliff. Below they heard the rush of rapids, swollen by the beginnings of spring thaw.

Glenna led, creeping away from the precipice, her gaze rapt. When she stopped, so did Dougal, ignoring the urge to tug affectionately on the single flaxen braid falling down her back. Instead, he followed her line of vision and caught sight of the deer.

The beast stood no more than twenty feet away, upwind from where Dougal and Glenna stood, almost hidden among the skeletons of leafless trees. Young, with only two small points to his antlers, the buck had plainly eaten even more poorly than Dougal and Glenna lately. The angled mounds of his shoulder bones protruded under the mangy coat, the hard prominence of his rib cage was clearly visible, his round black nose was dry, and his neck arched with a distant memory of health.

The deer's long lips flapped at small piles of unmelted snow as if hoping to find some trace of sustenance buried within. Dougal slowly reached behind his back to slide his bow from his shoulder, but Glenna was there first. Silent as the cloudless sky, she had already nocked the arrow, a look of fierce concentration claiming her expression. Her shoulders were taut, strong right arm hitched back, fingers hooked on the string. She squinted, closing her left eye and focusing on the target. Dougal's gaze flickered from her to the deer, heard the almost imperceptible twang of the release, then the subtle thud as the arrow struck home.

The sorry buck collapsed, half into the mud, half into the porous crystals of a black-crusted snowdrift. The beast lay still, without even one jerking muscle. Clean through the heart, then. Her skill always impressed Dougal. He'd never seen her miss.

Glenna shrugged. "Poor fellow did better by my arrow than he might have by other means."

"True enough," Dougal said, nodding. "He was starvin' worse than we are."

She shouldered her bow and they walked toward the motionless brown shape. Halfway there, Dougal stopped short, startled by an unfamiliar *click!* from within the trees. Glenna stood still beside him and glanced inquiringly up. He peered through the woods around them, but saw nothing move. He supposed it could have just been a lump of melted snow crashing through the brittle limbs.

"Ye heard nothin'?" he asked.

She shrugged again. "No."

Slightly reassured, he nodded and unsheathed his dirk, then went to gather up the deer. He crouched beside the animal's mangy coat and rested his fingers on the neck, feeling for a pulse, finding none. He tugged the arrow from the animal's side, absently noting the weak resistance of the heart muscles as it released. Glenna's aim was absolutely perfect, he thought, smiling to himself.

Dougal swiped the broad arrowhead against his breeks, cleaning the blood from its tip, then straightened, handing the arrow to Glenna. But what he saw in her expression froze the blood in his veins. The sun was sinking, its pale orange rays surrounding her like a halo. She stood stiff as rock, save the rapid flit of her eyes.

Behind and beside her stood five red-coated soldiers, faces partially hidden by the open-mouthed barrels of their muskets. The soldiers looked almost as scruffy as did they, but were much better armed. Dougal stood to his full height so that he towered over them, and took a protective step toward Glenna.

The muskets immediately transferred their attention onto him as was his intent. Dougal looked at Glenna, trying to hold her eyes on his. She was trembling, her eyes wild with panic.

This will be fine, his expression tried to tell her. *We will be all right.*

A shudder ran through her and Dougal knew she saw again the life they had escaped back at Tilbury, a decade ago.

I'm here. I'll keep ye safe, he tried to tell her, but she looked away.

She knew. Just like his brothers had on that bloody April morning. He had assured them they would live, and they had died. They had known despite what he'd said, but he'd said it anyway.

"This here's the king's property," announced one soldier, jerking Dougal's gaze from Glenna. "And you'll be coming with us as well."

"Why's that?" Dougal asked.

"You're poachers, you are."

"No' poachers," Dougal replied, folding his arms across his chest. "This land isna English, 'tis still Scotland, the last time I checked, and—" He stopped abruptly, feeling foolish. Of course it was English. There was no Scotland anymore.

"Good of you to feed the king li' this," another soldier said, stooping to lift the slack-jawed head of the deer. He examined the slender neck, then dropped the head to the dirt. "His Majesty's army is hungry." He grinned, showing dark, tobacco-stained teeth, which would shortly be tearing into Glenna's catch.

Dougal wasn't sure what to do. They were plainly outnumbered. He had to protect Glenna. Fortunately, the soldiers solved his dilemma when one of the soldiers grabbed at her, attempting to cup her chin in his hand. Dougal lunged at him without thinking, grabbed the man, and rolled him to the ground. He slugged the soldier's face and heard the fine jawbone crack under his fist. He pulled his arm back to strike again but hunched forward when a boot connected with his kidney. Rolling off the first soldier, who now lay moaning and gripping his face in the mud behind him, Dougal seized the offending boot and yanked the second man to the ground. They rolled over each other, sliding down the slippery granite floor, grasping at any kind of purchase while still concentrating on the fight.

The soldier managed to slam his fist into Dougal's nose, hard enough that his head snapped back on his neck. For a moment he saw stars and a wave of nausea caught in his belly. He gasped in air and forced himself back to the fight, but by now the soldier had climbed on top of him and was pressing the long barrel of his musket across Dougal's throat, leaning hard so that there was no more air to grab. Stars began to reemerge in his vision.

"Dougal!" Glenna screamed.

He couldn't see her, but he heard her terror, and from that he garnered enough strength to roll his legs under the man's belly and kick up, sending him flying. Grasping at his throat and wheezing hard, Dougal struggled to his knees, forcing the bruised muscles to open, to allow in air. He took a moment to glance toward Glenna and saw two soldiers had her arms pinned behind her back. For the time being they weren't hurting her, only watching Dougal battle the other three. She struggled against them, but she wasn't going anywhere.

They couldn't go back to prison. Couldn't. It would kill her, and quite possibly kill him as well. He couldn't allow it.

The stunned soldier had gotten back to his feet and returned to Dougal. One hand clenched the hilt of a light English sword, tarnished blade almost black in the fading light. The other hand was an angry fist. The soldier's eyes flickered to just behind Dougal's head and a smile lifted one corner of his mouth.

"Dougal!" Glenna shrieked, this time with urgency. Dougal's blade was halfway out of its sheath when everything went black.

CHAPTER 20

After the Fall

When he awoke, his body was screaming for air. Solid weight held him down, a strangling pressure, crushing his chest. His heart leapt into action, pumping panic through his system, forcing fire from his lungs. He clawed through the force, trying not to see the lights that danced in the darkness behind his eyes. *So close, so close*—he burst through the surface of the freezing river, gasping, sputtering, inhaling every bit of air he could find.

And then he was under again, his feet flailing beneath him, kicking out, searching for something solid. They were numb and it took a great effort to make them kick, to make his arms paddle.

The river took pity and shoved him up just long enough so he could scrabble around, gasping, trying to fix his position. Harsh white foam hit the rocks on the edge of the river, like spit on sharp black teeth. Twenty feet away, now fifteen, closer, closer . . .

The water sucked at him, dragging him under, popping him up again, carrying him downstream and building speed. Dougal was helpless, riding the current, grabbing ineffectively at boulders that poked through the shallower sections. He was weakening, losing the battle to stay afloat. But his hands and feet took over, grasping for rocks, searching for the stony bed of the stream.

He felt a jarring impact of granite against his knee, the edge slicing deeply enough the pain cut through the numbness. He grabbed for the sharp edge, felt the slick rock slip through his fingers. His arm reached for the brief opportunity and the rock dug into his chest. The current shoved at him again, pulverising his grip on the rock, forcing him to let go, and his body was suddenly flying through the water, floating, then sinking, floating again, drawing closer to the inevitable drop of the approaching falls.

Dougal's mind calmly informed him that the falls would kill him. The bottom was, more than likely, lined by more boulders, their edges whittled to blades by centuries of relentless water. But there was nothing he could do. His body spun as the current grew more urgent, so that his legs went first and he stared helplessly over his toes. His feet rose straight up, as if his body were a plank of pine, up and over his head. Then the water closed over him, and for the first time in his life, Dougal gave up.

CHAPTER 21

Existing in the Dark

What tied him down? His hands were bound—no. They weren't bound. They weren't held at all, but heavy, numb with cold, weighted by his own defeat. Slowly, slowly, awareness began to bloom in his waterlogged mind, like a seeping wound onto linen.

He didn't move at first, keeping his eyes closed while he tried to locate his limbs. One arm extended over his head, as if he raised it in greeting. The other was pinned beneath him, squeezed by a collection of various-sized rocks, most of them rounded by age. And his legs, well, they were there, somewhere, though he felt no evidence of them.

The cold. He had to move. If he stayed in this frigid river, he would be dead before nightfall. He pried open his eyes, but it felt like a foreign act, as if he'd never opened them in his life. His lids were swollen, banged, and bruised. He tried again, urging the light to come, disregarding the sensation of scraping sand over his eyes until finally he could see his surroundings.

He lay on his side and saw he had landed, by some trick of God, with his face angled off a flat rock, like a pillow. And because of that rock, he thought, he was alive.

Huh. Was that a good thing or bad?

The back of his head was splashed repeatedly by waves. Concentrating hard on controlling the limbs he couldn't feel, he pushed with his lower arm, finding balance with his hand, then shoved upward, needing to get his head out of the water. The moment he did, his brain exploded, firing flames through the backs of his eyes and ears, stealing sound from his mouth. Farther down, his neck seized into a vicious cramp, holding him hostage until he was able to wiggle out of it. He lowered his waving hand from above his head and reached for the spot where the pain seemed to start. Gingerly, he touched the large, hard swelling pressing up from under his hair. When he pulled his hand away, his palm was bloody. At least the cold water would keep down the swelling. But that bump. How had he—

In a breath it came rushing back: the fight, the soldier's grin, Glenna's cry—oh, Glenna!

Get out o' the water, clumsy eegit, he told himself and began to drag his body through the boulders, toward the promise of dry spring grass. As he pulled, twisting his body in whatever direction it needed to go, he became aware of other injuries, most likely cuts and bruises suffered during his fall, but also his throbbing nose from the earlier fight. The lump behind his neck was a constant dagger sunken through his brain.

He slithered from the water, barely registering how the boulders tapered off, becoming smaller rocks, then pebbles, scraping his belly. His fingertips were raw, leaving a watery trail of blood as he passed, but he hardly noticed. Instead, he cringed as blood poured back into his numbed feet, howled as surges of liquid fire burned through the sleeping limbs.

He dragged himself four or five feet beyond the reach of the river, then stopped and let his cheek fall onto the pebbles. He shook from the cold, sweating from exertion and pain, and his eyes burned, begging to close again. So he let them. What did it matter where he was, or what might happen? Why had God even brought him through this ordeal? He wished He hadn't.

Because Dougal wanted to die. In his mind he saw the soldiers with Glenna, saw how her expression must have appeared as they heaved his senseless body over the edge. She was no longer a girl in boy's clothing, but a beautiful, vital woman, now prisoner to five soldiers.

"God, Glenna," he moaned.

Something in his chest caught fire, a pulsing burn that forced tears from his eyes. The sobs came from deep within, rocking his frame, shuddering through his torn chest and bruised throat. *I'm here. I'll keep ye safe*, he had tried to tell her. And she had looked away. She had known even then he would let her down. That he would allow the enemy to take her, as they had taken everyone else in his life. His mother and father, brothers, friends . . . Everyone he had sworn to protect was gone. Assurances and promises made and broken, that's all he had brought to this world.

But for some reason, he was still alive. Somewhere in his memory his mother told him, *"There is a reason for everythin', my lad. There is a reason you are here."* He could think of only one reason. With the life he still had, he would find Glenna. She could still be alive, and he was the only person on earth who cared enough to save her.

Dougal needed to get warm. He would be useless to Glenna if he froze to death. He patted the soaked sheath at his side, relieved his dirk had miraculously remained with him throughout the wet journey, then eased up onto his feet. Wobbling slightly, he aimed for the sparse forest twenty feet away.

Lighting a fire was second nature to Dougal. First he had to find a protected area where he could sleep if he hoped to survive the night. Not so much from animals, because he knew the slightest noise would wake him. No, predators were not a big threat. But the frigid water that had soaked into his bones, the winter air that threatened to freeze him from the outside in, that was a problem. He found a small clearing fenced by fallen trees, and knelt on the cold, wet ground. Shaking so hard he couldn't yet control his individual fingers, he made his hands into shovels and scooped together a small nest of rocks. He laid strips of birch bark on top, then added a handful of curled, dry moss he'd pulled off a tree. Then he went in search of a fire starter.

Near the base of another birch tree grew a strange white fungus, protruding like a horse's hoof from the papery bark. Dougal cut off a large chunk with his dirk and managed to control his hands enough that he could curl back the tough outer layer, revealing its ochre-coloured flesh. He stretched the inner part of the fungus over a boulder, then struck it hard with the handle of his dirk until the flesh began to flatten under his blows. The skin of his knuckles, already split from the earlier conflict, opened again. Before long, fresh blood painted spidery trails over the thick bones of his wrist. But the movement was welcome to Dougal, despite the pain. He needed to feel as if he were accomplishing something again. As if he were alive. The repetitive pounding woke the rest of his blood as well, stoking heat in the veins that had cooled in the river.

He hammered the belly of the fungus into a flat strip with the consistency of leather, then tore it down the middle and gently scraped it with his knife so the tiny fibres curled into a soft tangle. He pressed the material flat on a small granite rock with his thumb, letting the frayed edge extend over the corner, then struck the rock with the back of his dirk blade again and again. Bright orange sparks shot into the air until at last a tiny ember caught onto the hairs of the flattened fungus.

Dougal puffed gently on the light, encouraging it, giving it enough strength that when he held it against the small nest of dried moss and bark, it finally lit. Tentative tongues of heat licked the tinder. Dougal crouched as low as he could, breathing life into the flames and gradually feeding twigs into the fire.

His face glowing golden in the flames, he held his fingers as close to the fire as he could, then did the same with his feet. When at last he was warm, when the quaking throughout his body had ceased, he cut down a few small branches and laid them over his body, hoping for any possible insulation. Eventually, curled tightly into a ball, Dougal drifted to sleep.

He rarely saw his dreams. But on this night, lying in the moment between sleep and wakefulness, he saw his mother's face as he'd last seen it, lined by years on the farm, bravely set in a smile as she saw her men off to battle. What of her? Did she yet live? Did she wonder what had happened to them all?

In his dream he searched for a way home, a way to the life that once was clean and clear and fragrant with heather. His laughter rolled through his brain along with that of his brothers, his mother and father. And the sweet, sweet giggles of Glenna. She was there, too. They laughed and danced—then all at once were gone and he sat alone in a black corner of their home, hearing nothing but the sound of his heart.

And from within the cracked shell of his dream he heard a familiar voice. It was calm, sweet, almost teasing, and it seemed to pass through his mother's lips, though her image had disappeared with the others.

Don't look back. It's all gone.

"Mother?" he whispered in his dream.

Gone.

Consciousness cut through the murk like a talon on the soft

underbelly of a rabbit. He fought it, needing to hold the dream just a moment longer, needing to hear more. But, like everything else, it was gone.

He forced himself to sit up, groaning as his body reminded him of his recent adventure. Glancing across to the river, he noticed the water was calmer here, settling in from the runoff of the falls. Weak beams of setting sun played off the water, painting red gold arcs and shadows. Glenna would have loved it. Would have been in awe of the colours. Would have tucked her arm into his and nuzzled against his side. *Beautiful, isn't it, Dougal?*

He frowned up at the cliff on the far side of the river. He had no memory of going over, so he must have been unconscious at the time then managed to float downstream. He gave a weak snort, imagining himself drifting face up, sprawled like a star. Some sort of feeble joke God had played on him, keeping him alive. Why bother?

A bat flitted over the surface of the stream, followed by two more dancing shadows dipping and teasing the water, searching the early spring night for an evening meal. Dougal was hungry, too, and shivering from the cold, which led to thoughts of the deer they had slain. The shaggy carcass was probably slung over the shoulders of one of the soldiers, sorry head lolling behind the man's back. And behind that followed Glenna, prisoner again.

If she yet lived, where would they take her? Where was the closest prison? Maybe Stirling?

She would hate it. She would need air and open spaces, finches and scrawny deer. She would need his snoring to wake her in the middle of the night and the pathetic meals he served when he attempted to cook. Only he knew how she liked the back of her neck scratched and that she preferred honey in her oats.

How could he exist without her?

CHAPTER 22

Finding the Road

Dougal awoke in the morning, smothered by fog, his muscles cramped into near paralysis. The tiny fire by his feet had long since gone out, leaving only a pile of charred twigs and stones as evidence of his passing. He had eventually curled within the negligible shelter of a rotted-out tree trunk, which had provided no heat and even less comfort. Though it was a mild one, it was still February, and he knew he was in danger of never moving again. He was freezing and starving, he hurt all over, and he was thoroughly miserable.

Glenna. She was the first thought in every one of his days—why should today be any different? Where was she? Was she alive? Had they harmed her? The thought made his hollow stomach clench. He saw again the panic in her pale blue eyes and hated himself for it. She shouldn't have been there, hunting alongside him. She should have been at home, doing something a woman normally did. Cooking. Cleaning. Then she would have been safe, would have—

That was ridiculous. Glenna wasn't that kind of woman. That was one of the reasons he loved her with all his heart.

He had to find her. He struggled to brace his feet underneath him, but his legs seemed unwilling to cooperate. Still sitting, he straightened his knees and yowled as the muscles cramped, then scrubbed his fists furiously over his thighs, carefully avoiding the bruised patches, until eventually the muscles loosened. His chest bore a long gash from the boulder in the river, the rock that had offered safety then ripped it away. The blood had dried the night before, along with numerous other ugly cuts, though a few opened up in his hands when he moved them. From gripping at the passing rocks, he realised. The bruises on his knuckles would have come from when he'd broken that soldier's jaw. How had he not broken his own head on the way over?

Leaning heavily against the slimy log at his back, he groaned and stood, slowly uncurling his back one vertebra at a time, then reached his arms toward the sky and looked up into the gray. Every muscle felt as if it had been pounded over and over by a smithy's hammer. Flexing his fingers brought nothing but pain, but it was a familiar pain and didn't bother him much.

He needed food. That was imperative. Without something in his belly, he'd never heal enough to follow her. He staggered toward the river, squatted, and sank his hands into the freezing water, then drank long and deep, trying to temporarily fill those empty spaces inside his belly with water. Then, because he needed something to awaken him from his daze, he splashed his face and hair. He shivered convulsively, then stood and shook purposefully, like a dog.

The movement stung, and he looked down at his chest to see a fresh red bloom of blood spreading under his shredded tunic. With a grimace, he tugged at his shirt, but it had fastened to the healing wound overnight. He gently peeled it away, thread by thread, revealing an ugly, fairly deep gash that would need mending before he could go any farther. He looked at his palms and saw the cuts on the insides of his fingers, red and swollen. Yes, his injuries would need attention.

Naked spring branches stretched over his head. Bearing them, protruding from the winter-killed earth, were the silver white trunks of birch. Their papery bark, stippled and striped by the elements, was patched by clumps of black and gray that resembled poorly healed sores. Dougal stumbled through the trees, bracing his hands against the damp wood, then searched the lower sections until he found what he needed. Using his dirk, he carved soft, fat lumps of white fungus from the birch, and laid them on the forest floor. He cut the top of each one into a square, then peeled back the top layer and gently spread them across the gash on his chest, and the one on his left thigh. The fungus clung to his skin, offering a cool respite from the burn.

He stayed within the shelter of the trees, seeking whatever meagre protection he could find from the breeze off the river, and stopped beside the sturdy trunk of a willow, already beginning to spread light green shoots off its branches. Dougal cut one of the shoots and stuck the cut end into his mouth, chewing on it. The bitter liquid made his mouth flood with saliva, and he swallowed it all down, knowing the plant would give him some small bit of pain relief.

If the shore hadn't sloped downward, it might have been difficult to see in which direction he should head. The river had carried him far from his landing place, wherever that had been, so he had no landmarks with which to judge his location. He stepped gingerly over algae-coated logs, using his bare feet like claws as he moved away from the rocky shore. When at last he reached the grass, he scouted for a deer trail and found it, meandering vaguely through the winter-stripped trees.

He would find better food soon, but for now he had to make do. He squatted beside a clump of juniper and plucked some fat blue berries from between the needles. They were bitter when he squashed them in his back teeth, but they were something. A little farther on in his travels he found a series of rosebushes and chewed on a few of the hips. The energy they gave him outweighed the bland taste. He tucked as many as he could find inside his shirt for later.

The woods along the river were quiet, the only sound coming from the soft crunching of his feet when they sank into melting patches of snow. He walked without thinking, his plan simply to follow the line of the water until he found someplace recognisable. The constant walking kept the circulation flowing in his legs and feet, but he had to stop occasionally when the pain from his injuries overtook him. At the end of a day, and sometimes midday if the pain was too bad, he lit a small fire to warm and partially dry himself, then set off again.

It was three days before he found any sign of another human being, and that was in the form of a splintered wagon wheel, half submerged in a slushy puddle. The rough path on which it had met its demise eventually led to a kind of road, stretches of thin brown interspersed with rocks and early spring green. Dougal stepped from within the protection of the trees and gazed down the road, looking . . . for what? If he'd expected Glenna to emerge, to run down the road with her distinctive spring, he would be waiting an eternity. There was no movement as far as he could see; only the slight tremble of branches in the breeze gave away the fact that the panorama wasn't simply a painting. Far beyond the trees, farther than the road dared stretch, were the misted mountains of the Highlands. Dougal felt a twist in his gut when he realised he might never see them again. He'd felt the same regret when he and his family had set off to war. Even now the mountains were only shadows. Maybe they were nothing more than a trick of light through the clouds.

Maybe he would come back one day. With Glenna.

He took a deep breath, then let it out, turning to his right and setting his path toward what he hoped was Stirling. He didn't think it would be far now, since the road was better travelled here. His feet were worn and tired, but the skin was tough as deer hide, so he barely felt the pebbles as he came across them. A drink of something other than river water would be welcome, he thought, swallowing reflexively.

About an hour later, Dougal met up with the first person he'd seen in days. Before he laid eyes on the man, however, Dougal heard him. The fool threw himself onto Dougal from the side of the road, wheezing with exertion. Sidestepping neatly, Dougal turned and felled the man with a solid blow to his gut. The man moaned, crumpled to his knees, and Dougal knelt beside him.

"Hello, sir. Is there somethin' ye'd be needin'?"

The man growled through blackened teeth; the air around him stank of rot. Dougal recoiled and stepped away. He turned his back on the man and continued down the road, then called back over his shoulder.

"If ye were lookin' for coin, ye struck the wrong traveller. If ye were lookin' for an easy kill, again, ye picked the wrong one. Mark yer prey better, man." He paused and turned back, chuckling a bit. The man still sat despondently at the side of the road. "Or maybe ye should—"

He didn't hear the second attacker, or the third. So the first had been a decoy, and Dougal had fallen for it. The oldest trick there was, and he had swallowed the bait. *Stupid, stupid,* Dougal berated himself, struggling against the man who held his arms behind his back. The other man was short and wiry, and not appropriate for the task, which was to punch Dougal until he couldn't fight back. He did land a few good punches, which saved the entire scene from being laughable. On the whole, Dougal seemed to be in less pain than his attacker.

"Give us your money, mountain man," the little pugilist demanded, panting between punches. He hit Dougal's rib, and Dougal grunted.

"Have I no' just told yer mate that—ugh—I've nae money wi' me? Oof. Here. Stop that."

Tiring of the game, Dougal lowered his chin to his chest and reared back until he felt the back of his head connect with his captor's nose. The nose made a satisfying crunching sound, accompanied by a howl, and Dougal's arms were suddenly released. Once free, Dougal took no time before returning the little man's attack.

"Damn Scotsman broke my nose," the one behind him moaned, sounding distinctly nasal. "Kill him, Smit!"

Smit made a noise that Dougal supposed was meant as agreement, but the threat was absurd. Dougal flicked one eyebrow sardonically at Smit then brought his fist in a perfect arc under the man's chin. The narrow head snapped back and the wiry body flew a few feet backward.

The stubborn man with the broken nose was back, and he came at Dougal, brandishing a long dirk in one hand.

"Ye dinna want to fight me wi' that," Dougal muttered. "Silly sod."

"I'll kill you!" the man cried.

He was taller than Smit, and broader, but lacked a certain amount of coordination. It could have been the injury, but Dougal thought he had a weakness about him to begin with. A bit of a limp. The man lunged at Dougal with the knife and Dougal spun to the side, avoiding the thrust and gripping the man's hand, clutched tight on the hilt. He squeezed the fingers in an iron grip until the man gasped, unable to hold on any longer. The knife dropped to the pebbled ground with a soft thud.

Dougal glared at his attacker, now hunched over and panting, blood draining in viscous strings from his nose. The sunken eyes narrowed, then darted between Dougal and the fallen weapon.

Dougal shook his head slowly. "Leave it there, man, an' ye might live to rob another poor soul."

Dougal turned away again, but he already knew what was about to happen, and it made him angry. He heard a grunt and three footfalls as the bloodied man attacked from the rear. Dougal grabbed his own dirk, spun to face the man, and planted his dirk squarely under the man's rib cage. There was a yowl of disbelief, then a pathetic snuffling noise, and the man fell in a lump at Dougal's feet.

"I said I'd nothin' in my pocket, sir." Dougal bent and yanked his dirk from the twitching body, then wiped the bloodied blade on his breeks and slid it back into his belt. He straightened. "What I'd forgot to mention is I've nothin' to lose, either."

He glared at the other footpads, who were out of commission, rolling in misery farther down the road. Glancing one last time at the dead man, Dougal shook his head with disgust, then continued on his way.

A little farther down the road, Dougal stiffened, hearing hoofbeats approach from behind. After so long hiding in the woods, the clopping hooves shot panic through his bloodstream. Two horses, he thought, and automatically stepped to the side, keeping his face turned from the road. But the horses stopped, reining in on either side of Dougal until he was trapped between them.

"What the—"

"What have you to say on the charge of murder, sir?" one of the horsemen asked. With a sinking heart, Dougal registered the English soldier's cultured accent.

He frowned. "I say it is an unpleasant thing."

He was rewarded with a tight grimace Dougal thought was meant to be a smile. "And what have you to say on the charge that you murdered a man, just up the road?"

"I have naught to say. The man died while I defended myself."

"That's not what his mates had to say."

"Well, o' course they wouldna say that. But—"

"You are coming with us," the second soldier said from his perch, then slid off the saddle. "Hands in front, please."

Dougal was too surprised to argue. Staring in disbelief, he lifted his hands until they were held prayer-like in front of his chest. The soldier wrapped a length of rope around Dougal's wrists and tugged tight.

"What evidence have ye?" Dougal asked. "The word of a couple of footpads?"

The soldier gave him a wry grin. "Aye. Theirs over yours. And I'd rather arrest you than bother with both of them. At least you can walk. Don't worry. You'll get your trial."

The soldier mounted and leaned his legs into the animal's sides. The horse walked obediently, tugging Dougal along behind. He called out, demanding they stop, but they paid no attention. He yanked on the rope, but the horse pulled back, and it was stronger. In the end, all Dougal could do was try to keep up, and hope their destination was nearby.

It was, in fact, a very long hour away, one consisting of awkward falls and slips, moments when Dougal couldn't maintain his footing and was dragged until he could regain it. He was bruised and battered when they finally arrived at a small fort where he was to be incarcerated, and his wrists were rubbed raw. The horses stopped in front of a dark building and the soldiers dismounted. Without a word, they half carried Dougal into the building and dropped him on the floor of a cell.

It had been a very long time since Dougal had been in a prison of any type, other than his own self-inflicted one. He rested on his knees for a moment, staring at the four stone walls, letting his eyes travel from the muck at his feet to the ancient rafters overhead. The air smelled of mildew and worse, and the stink seemed to be closing in on him. There was no cot, only a blanket tossed in the corner, and a chamber pot.

He staggered to his feet and paced from one end of his cell to the other, counting three steps each way. When he could bear the pain and exhaustion no more, he slid down the cold, damp wall. He sat on the blanket while a hint of sunlight from the front room slowly faded to black. Then he laid his elbows over his knees, sank his head into his arms, and fell asleep.

CHAPTER 23

A Dead Man's Suggestion

In what he assumed was morning, Dougal awoke to the jingle of keys in the door and it creaked open a sliver. It was hard to tell in the dark, but from the size and speed of the form, he thought it was a boy, crouched low. Whoever it was slid a plate of dark liquid into Dougal's cell, then vanished. The plate's contents smelled like something long dead, and a few lonely lumps within hinted at meat. Dougal was hungry, so he ate.

The cell door opened again later on, and by the flicker of an oil lantern he saw the shadowed features of one of the arresting soldiers along with two others, and a man dressed in an officer's uniform. They regarded the prisoner without saying a word, then turned inward to discuss something Dougal couldn't hear. He considered asking what was happening, but decided, on a rare whim, to keep his mouth shut. Nor did he try to hear the men's thoughts, as he knew he could have. He was too tired to bother. He would learn the outcome soon enough. The lesser men listened and gave slight bows of assent to their leader before all four turned to stare at Dougal again. After a moment, the cell door creaked closed and he heard no more.

Dougal was captive within the darkness. He had become accustomed to the dank smell and the heavy, unmoving air, but couldn't relax within the sensation of those stone walls closing in on him. From where he sat, on a blanket at the end of the cell, he could easily reach the opposing walls, and decided he felt safer when he braced his hands against them. As if he could prevent them from squeezing further. So he shoved his palms against the stone for as long as his arms could bear it.

He wasn't a man known for patience. He tired of holding up the walls. He paced like a wild beast in a cage, then sat, tugging at the frayed threads of his coat for want of something to do. He called out a few times, demanding attention, but his voice fell short in the blackness, and he heard nothing but a cold, deep silence in reply. He wondered if they might have forgotten him.

Near the end of the day, two of the men from the earlier visit, including the officer, came again, this time with two other strangers. They carried two lanterns with them, burning slow golden flames, which illuminated Dougal's visitors just enough to hint at faces. This time the men stepped into the cell—or at least two of them did. There wasn't enough room for all of them, and these two barely squeezed inside. Dougal was sitting when they arrived, and he remained where he was, glaring up at them, wondering if they warranted his standing.

"Filthy dog," one of the men muttered. "Waste of our time."

"Get up," the leader said. Dougal gritted his teeth, and rose slowly to his feet. Here to decide a sentence outside of the courts, were they? He wouldn't go easily. No, he knew what they could do, and he knew what he could do. Suddenly alert, his muscles buzzed with energy and his mind threw out ideas of how to shove through the men and escape. There would be no noose for Dougal Mac-Donnell.

The men stared back at him, saying nothing for a moment. Then the senior officer frowned and turned back toward one of the others standing in the doorway. "You're sure?" he asked.

"Aye, sir," came a voice. "I ken him well enough. Ye'd do best to watch yer step, sir, but ye'll no' find a better warrior."

Dougal frowned. "I ken that voice," he said softly, trying to remember. Shapes and shadows swirled in his head as he fought to match voice with face. Then the answer came, and Dougal shook his head. "But it belongs to a dead man."

"My friends would argue that," came the response. Dougal heard a distinct chuckle in the man's thoughts and shook his head with disbelief. "For I eat more than most of them."

There was a shuffling at the entrance to the cell and the two men slid back out into the hallway. A third man entered, and Dougal stared, waiting for the flames to bring him a face. It was the smile that lit first, and Dougal's heart jumped.

"John? My God." He stared, slack-jawed. "John Wallace? How in hell did ye—I never thought—"

His exclamations were lost in the wool-clad shoulder of the friend he thought he had lost so long before at Tilbury. The friend with the small black piece of paper. John had limped off with the soldiers the day before young Joseph was killed, the day before Dougal and Glenna had escaped. So much had happened since then. A lifetime of happenings. Ten years.

"I kent I'd see ye again someday, MacDonnell."

"Ye kent more than I, then. I thought I'd no' see ye on this earth again." Dougal's voice was cheery, but he was suddenly on guard, trying to read John's thoughts. If John knew who he was, then wouldn't these men take him back into custody? Not only for the murder of the footpad, but for escape from Tilbury as well. Perhaps there *was* a noose in his future.

John noticed him stiffen and gave him a reassuring smile. "Ye're among friends, Dougal. While ye've been away, the world has changed yet again. Now the English want us for a different reason."

Dougal made an enquiring noise.

"War is afoot in Europe and in the colonies."

"Nothin' new in that. Damn English tryin' to rule the world as always."

"Well, aye, an' this time the English are fallin' behind. Would it make ye laugh, my old friend, to know they are assembling a large regiment of Highlanders to fight for them?"

Something stirred in Dougal's memory, thoughts of a dream he'd banished, sending a shudder down his spine. "Oh, aye?" he asked skeptically. "Highlanders to fight for the sassenachs? I'm no' laughin', John. Under whose command?"

John chewed on the inside of his cheek, savouring the moment. "Archibald Montgomerie. We're takin' ship to the colonies to fight the damn French."

Dougal knew of Montgomerie, though he'd never met the man. Well respected was how he remembered him. But this made no sense. Montgomerie would never willingly work for the English. "No."

"Aye. We're to be"—John stuck out his chest proudly—"Montgomerie's Highlanders."

Dougal shook his head, trying to sort through all this. "So . . . Highland Scots will now fight *for* George? What sort of joke is that?"

"A brilliant one, my friend. The English ken they canna win wi'out us. It also gives 'em somethin' to do wi' all the wanderin'

Scots wi'out homes. An' after all, it's a joke that should bring ye relief, if no' laughter, for it'll save ye from the gallows."

"So? What's to do?" muttered one of the men in the dark hallway. "Is the beggar comin' wi' us or no'?"

John put a hand on Dougal's shoulder and grinned. His teeth shone yellow in the lamplight. Dougal kept his own expression hidden. "If ever I kent a man bent on raisin' a sword, it'd be this one," John said, watching Dougal's expression. "What of it? Would ye care to trade yer trousers for a plaid an' join a fight, my friend?"

He supposed it should have been an easy decision. Dougal had been a warrior without a battle for too long, and the choice he was being offered was either to fight or to hang. Fight with his countrymen again? Aye, that he could do. Fight alongside the English army? Stand for the king whose long-ago cause had stolen everything from Dougal, as well as from the rest of Scotland? John was asking him to fight with the very men who had taken Glenna from him, when all he wanted was to slit each separate English throat. The thought came to him that he'd rather die than stand with them.

"I'll hang, thanks. I'm no' English dog."

"Dougal, man. I ken what ye're thinkin', only it's none so bad as ye'd think. We're still Scots, no' English. We're only fightin' the French this time."

"I need time to think."

"What's there to think on? Fight for George or die."

"John," he said, lowering his voice. "How can ye do this? How can ye take up arms wi' the English? Does it no' bother ye?"

John's hand dropped from Dougal's shoulder. "Ye ken me better than that, ol' friend. But there comes a time in a man's life when he must face what *has* happened an' see what *will* happen. They destroyed us, Dougal. There is no Scotland anymore. There is only

England, an' her army will as soon hang yer sorry arse. Will ye die wi'out need? Is there nothin' in yer life ye still want to accomplish?"

Dougal swallowed. He wasn't sure.

John tried a different direction, clearly exasperated. "Will ye allow them to kill another of us?"

Dougal felt ill. This was a gift, an opportunity. A chance not only to survive, but to fight again. But everything in him screamed defiance. *Let them hang me. I'll no' bow down to the pigs. They killed my family. They stole my Glenna.*

But . . . what if she still lived? What if Glenna existed somewhere, waiting for him to find her? He couldn't abandon her, couldn't throw his life away if she still needed it. He had promised to keep her safe. He couldn't very well do that if he no longer breathed.

Pride was one thing, and he knew he had a lot of that. Probably too much. But common sense? That had never been his strength.

"I hate this," Dougal muttered.

John closed his eyes and nodded, but said nothing. Something curled in Dougal's stomach, shooting a flush through his cheeks, and he felt suddenly ashamed. Of course John hated it as well. Who was Dougal to imagine himself morally superior to his friend?

"Fight beside me, Dougal," John said quietly, shuffling slightly forward so the light caught his eyes. "I'm in no hurry to lose a friend again so soon."

Dougal felt deflated. "I need time, John."

Dougal didn't rise when John returned the next morning, but he watched him slide down the cool stone wall and settle beside him. Neither spoke for a bit. It was John who broke the silence, as it always had been in the past, so long before.

"They will hang ye," he said. "They'd rather do that than send ye overseas. Ye're too valuable as a soldier to waste ye as a slave."

Dougal frowned. "What's that mean?"

"Means they're only shipping the weak an' the women o'er. The men they're either puttin' in the army or in the noose."

"What are ye talkin' about, John? Shippin' who where?"

John shrugged. "They're still arrestin' Scots whene'er they can, aye? Clearin' out the Highlands, they call it. But they've no room for them all. So they're sent to the colonies, mostly, an' sold into service."

Dougal sat up straighter. "Have they shipped out many women from here?"

"Oh aye. Half a dozen were sent last week, poor souls." He shook his head. "Believe me, Dougal. You an' I have the better choice."

"Did you see these women?" Dougal demanded.

John frowned. "Aye," he said slowly, puzzled. "Why do ye ask?"

"Was there one small? Golden haired? Fights like a wee wildcat?"

John tilted his head, looking thoughtfully toward the ceiling of the cell. He stroked his chin. "I only saw them the once. I—"

"Think," Dougal growled.

John frowned at him, baffled. Then his expression softened as he figured out Dougal's urgency. "She was yours?"

Dougal nodded once, but didn't bother going into the fact that the feisty golden-haired lassie in question was also the boy, Aidan, from their prison. John returned to his thoughts, then sat abruptly taller and smiled. "Aye. I remember her now. Small as a boy, dressed like one as well."

Dougal thought his heart might stop. He could picture her standing in the courtyard in her breeks, afraid, but revealing nothing. She had endured prison before. She knew what she would have to do to survive. But being bound and sent on one of those godforsaken ships like the one on which they'd first been imprisoned? And if she withstood that, how would she deal with being someone's slave? Oh, Glenna.

"Ye said Montgomerie's goin' that way?"

John nodded and Dougal stood, mind made up. "I'll go wi' the damn English army."

John's shoulders relaxed and he got to his feet. He clapped Dougal on his shoulder again. "Come along. Ye'll need a wash first off, for ye stink somethin' awful. Then we'll find ye somethin' to eat, shall we?" He stared at Dougal a moment, then nodded again. "All will be fine, Dougal. Ye'll see."

"Stop wastin' time, John. Get me out of this hole."

In Dougal's tortured mind he had thought there was nothing left for him to lose but his pride. He'd wavered, late in the pitch-black hours, not sure his pride was worth the cost of his life. Now everything had changed. Now he had hope. Glenna still lived. It was possible that he could someday find her again, and that, well, that made life worth living. Exhaling hard, blowing the last remnants of prison stink from his nose, he followed John out of the cell and into the gray light of day.

CHAPTER 24

Montgomerie's Highlanders

Montgomerie's Highlanders did more than rescue Dougal from prison and hanging. Ironically, being a part of the hated English army, though stationed among the Scots, restored what still remained of his dignity. Being needed reminded him of who he was, both mentally and physically.

The troop of Highlanders were the only ones permitted to wear tartan after an English law forbade it. After having been trapped in breeks for far too long, Dougal reveled in the opportunity to roll himself in the twelve yards of rough wool the army provided, dyed in the midnight navy and green of the Black Watch. And though the red, gold-buttoned jacket felt morally wrong for him to wear, every morning he shrugged into it and tugged on the long patterned hose. He grew accustomed to shoes again.

Dougal shared lodgings with John and ten other men, sleeping like rocks in their bunks at night. As an added boost to the Scots, they awoke every morning to the skirl of the pipes echoing off the fort's stone walls. While the English had spent the last few years smothering any remaining Scottish pride, now they did what they could to encourage it. The ancient instrument, as well as the Scots' traditional clothing and weapons, had been resurrected from banishment because of its ability to stir the Highlanders' blood.

They sat around a long table in their room, having breakfast before beginning their daily grind of military exercises. John bent over his bowl, shoveling oatmeal into his mouth. He gave Dougal a sidelong glance. "Yer oatmeal's better than this, my friend. Hamish canna cook to save his arse."

Dougal tilted his head and nodded thanks. "Ye might be the first to ever say anythin' nice about my cookin'."

John looked surprised. "Oh no. I wasna sayin' anythin' nice. Yer oatmeal's no' good enough to feed to a pig. It's only what Hamish makes is worse."

"Ah," Dougal said with a chuckle. "That sounds more like it."

When they were finished, Dougal washed his hands, face, and knees, as was expected, then combed his long black hair and tied it into a club at the back of his neck. Then he and the others belted their plaids, holstered their weapons, filed outside, and lined up for exercises.

Once they were on the field, however, the Scots trained as the English wanted. Dougal defied the training at first, hating the disciplined English style of fighting. But he had no choice other than to fall in line. The men drilled twice a day, learning and practicing until the captain's commands were second nature. Over time the lighter-weight carbine musket in Dougal's hands came to feel as if it had always been there. The despised bayonet became an extension of his own arm. He felt as if he could march in his sleep.

In the beginning of his service with Montgomerie's Highlanders, Dougal fought the urge to feel physically beaten, though he would never admit it. He wasn't yet thirty, but his body ached with past injuries. More than that, his mind had been dulled by grief. He feared his heart, burdened by hopelessness, barely beat. But he wasn't the sort to lie down and die. Instead, he steeled himself and pushed harder than ever, demanding excellence from his body.

When they weren't polishing their soldiering skills, the men were usually busy with camp chores or sentry duty. Occasionally they were put to heavier labour, such as constructing roads and buildings. Dougal was happy to work every minute of the day. Happy to keep so busy he had no time to think of Glenna and what could possibly be happening with her.

But when the exhausted men took off their jackets, unraveled their plaids, and peeled off sweat-soaked stockings before falling into their bunks at the end of the day, she was in his head, waiting. His fingertips tingled with the need to trace the lines of her face. Her laughter trilled like a bird's song, her singing filled his head, though sometimes he had to listen hard so he could hear her over the snoring, farting group of men. Thinking of Glenna was an agonising memory he craved, a sweet torture he hated. Even her scent still dwelled in Dougal's mind.

Other men here had lost their families as well. Occasionally one of them would wax romantic about something his wife had once said, another might sit a little prouder when he discussed the height of his eldest boy the last time he'd seen him. When Dougal concentrated on a man's face, if the timing was right and he cared to listen, he could hear echoes of memories in the man's mind, half-remembered emotions that tethered him to the past.

Dougal didn't carry simple memories that would fade over time. For better or worse, he heard the voices, the words, the laughter as if they all still occurred. Though it was painful to hear, Andrew's voice was sometimes so clear it was as if he stood at his shoulder. At other times it seemed so far away it almost wasn't there. He dreamed of the voices of the rest of his family, remembered happier times. Glenna's voice was as clear to him as it had been in their little croft at Aberfeldy, asking if he would like some stew, would he like a swim, would he like to come to bed soon? He held on to the sound, needing to keep it safe, though he hadn't been able to do the same for her. But while this odd trick of his mind gave him strength, it also haunted him. She was gone, but his strange ability kept the pain as sharp as it had ever been.

The voices surrounding him now were commonplace, and soothing for that reason. The men's thoughts, on the whole, were regular, uninteresting, which made everything easier. He had spent years without the simple company of men after his escape from Tilbury, living in blissful peace with Glenna. But Dougal was comfortable among men, and he was a sociable sort. The brogues around him varied, but for the most part they were thick and broad, voices from the North, from parts of the Highlands Dougal had never travelled. There were some from his area as well, but the only man he knew well was John.

Dougal's mind had tuned to John's since they'd rekindled their friendship. He tried to block his friend's thoughts so he didn't feel as if he intruded, but sometimes it was unavoidable. When John exercised, his mind was blank, honed on targets. But when he set aside his weapons and took quiet time for himself at the end of the day, Dougal saw the pain John hid behind humour.

John's natural cheerfulness masked the scars he bore from grieving for his brothers and father. But nothing could hide the open wound that still seeped memories of his Mairi. She had been a camp follower, slain at the battlefield years before. John had seen the soldier slit her throat and drop her seizing body to the ground. He had run to her and dropped to his knees, rocking her in his arms in that brief moment between this world and the next, wishing it were his blood instead of hers that rivered down his arm.

Then he had plunged back into battle, slaughtering Englishmen in the hopes that he might diminish his own pain. But it had done no good.

"How is it ye come to be here, John? On this earth, I mean," Dougal asked one night as they sat outside their barracks.

"Oh, t'would take more than a mere hangin' to rid the world of me," his friend replied, nodding sagely. "But in truth, 'tis a good story, that. I stood in front of the judge, bonnet in hand, and told him I was guilty of everythin' they said. What choice did I have? They asked did I have anythin' more to tell them, did I ken any other Jacobites I should tell them about, that sort of rubbish, but I played dumb. Anyhow, I was ill, aye? From my foot, ye recall?"

"I do."

"It got worse by the minute, that damn foot. Hurt like hell. By some gift of God, I was graced wi' a judge none so keen to hang me. A fine gentleman. I was let off with a sound thrashing that had me abed for three days, an' when I woke, the doctor was tendin' my foot as well. He was better than most, I suppose, for I've barely a limp anymore."

"No, ye march wi' the best."

"Pah!" John exclaimed. "I march better than they do. An' I shoot a damn sight better than ye do, MacDonnell."

"No' for long," Dougal assured him, then made good on that by pushing himself harder than ever so he could match John's prowess.

As a result, the two won the attention of their lieutenant, Alexander Campbell, who recommended them to the posts of grenadiers. Only the biggest and strongest of the warriors were promoted to this level. Along with regular musketry, they trained with grenades and took part in specialised assault missions, combining stealth with strength.

Dougal's life, though routine, was driven by an urgency he couldn't control. He felt helpless, stuck in training while Glenna suffered somewhere. Or at least he hoped she was still alive. As if it might help him get to her sooner, he bullied the rest of the men, demanding they work harder, accomplish more despite their grumblings. It seemed the only way to make himself useful.

April brought a new sense of excitement to the fort. The troops marched to Greenock to board one of the huge man-of-war ships bobbing at the docks, then headed to Ireland. There they were to meet with Fraser's Highlanders, a company similar to their own but headed farther north.

Mist shimmered on the men's tartans as they marched and the spring chill squeezed through the layers until their skin stuck to the wool. It would be colder still on board, Dougal knew. Cold and dank and miserable. God, he hated boats. As much as he loved to swim, he couldn't abide the claustrophobic feeling he got while he was aboard what he considered to be a floating coffin. It didn't matter that when they travelled, the sea and air around them would be infinite. He still felt trapped.

Memories of another ship didn't help. Dougal's step faltered when the triple masts poked out of the fog, their sails folded neatly beneath. His eyes took in the activity on board, the shining deck, and the hatch doors leading to the unknown. Except he knew the unknown. Knew the mouldy-paneled walls that separated the wretched inhabitants of the hold from the depths of the sea, remembered the smear of it against his fingers when he tried to catch his balance. It wasn't cannon or muskets, nor was it the shrieking bloodiness of battlefields that froze Dougal's blood. As he looked into the murky waves of the harbour, he fought back terror at the mere idea of stepping back inside a ship.

"It's no' the same," John said wryly, seeing Dougal's ashen complexion when they reached the docks. "Ye canna smell them from here, as ye could the others."

Dougal's nostrils flared at the memory. "I'll recall that stink for the rest o' my days." He circled his shoulders, easing the tension in his back. "Aye, ye're right. An' this is only a short trip."

"An' we'll no' be shoved into the bowels of the ship, either."

Dougal's teeth clenched involuntarily, but John was right. The hold was reserved for supplies this time, for food, weapons, and extra sails, among other things. This time the men hung in hammocks in the Lower Deck, and swung to sleep between the imposing ranks of thirty-two-pounder cannons.

They crossed the channel and trained for two months in Ireland. It wasn't yet the colonies, but at least it was some sort of change, progress. There they exercised alongside Fraser's Highlanders. They were all Scots, wearing the English version of Highlander dress, marching in ordered English rows, and following commands issued by former enemies. It was almost as if they were a different people altogether. But in the evenings coats were shed, bare toes were warmed by fires, and the air hummed with stories of home in the Scottish Highlands.

Over time Dougal settled into an uneasy truce with the reality of who was in charge of this army. He barely managed to contain a sneer when ordered by a distinctly English accent, but he did what was required so he could hunt for Glenna.

Then it was time to go. Dougal felt the tension in the air, heard the thoughts of men who looked forward to adventure, or at least to a break in the monotonous training. His mind also filled with other men's anxiety and their fear that they might never return.

But over it all, or rather bubbling beneath it, was the knowledge that Dougal was finally getting closer to Glenna. He had no idea where in the colonies she might be, and he knew it was a vast land. He had no idea if he would ever find her at all. But just knowing he would be on the right side of the Atlantic energised him, helped him past his fear of yet another ship.

On the first of July they boarded their floating barracks and headed toward the colonies. Despite the rolling floor and salt-thick air, Dougal was relieved. He was among the majority who had tired of training. He craved the opportunity to test his newly developed skills in the colonies. The ships, ten in all, were escorted by three Royal Navy ships: *The Falkland*, *The Enterprise*, and *The Stork*, and twenty supply ships followed. Fraser's Highlanders sailed alongside, but at one point Dougal's ship turned toward the Charleston harbour, while the other battalion and half the supply ships continued north to Halifax.

The voyage took eight weeks, but it wasn't much of a hardship. The late summer weather was calm, other than two or three wicked storms that threatened to capsize some of the smaller ships. Most of the men were in high spirits throughout the journey, and there were many nights during which songs and stories floated up into a clear, star-filled sky.

CHAPTER 25

❦

The Colonies

Charleston's port was never quiet, but when the soldiers and their supplies landed and threw their heavy ropes across, tying onto huge metal cleats, the docks swarmed like a disturbed anthill. The folk of the city crowded as close as they could, peddling wares, gawking at the men now crossing the gangplank. The soldiers, having been surrounded by relative quiet for the eight weeks aboard ship, were taken aback at first, but Dougal's blood raced at the thought of dry land. He could hardly wait to join the noise. *Glenna,* he thought. *I'm here, Glenna.*

There was jostling going on behind him, he assumed, but the grenadiers were put at the head of the line, as they would be put at the head of the troops when the shooting began. John gallantly gestured then followed Dougal as he stepped onto the gangplank. The ocean beneath the platform foamed and splattered against the dock, as if the black depths celebrated their arrival. The air, humid but warm, lifted the coal black hair from his brow and dropped it gently back, settling like a cushion against his skin after the cutting wind of the ship.

Off to the side Dougal saw a well-rounded, red-haired woman whose flashing dark eyes focused on him. He wiggled his eyebrows and gave her a short bow before glancing to the other side.

"Very bonny," John commented from behind him.

"Oh aye, but after two months alone wi' these lads, I imagine anythin' in a gown might seem that way."

John pounded him on the shoulder. "Ye're no gentleman, Mr. MacDonnell."

"I am so. She didna hear me at all. An' look. I canna please them all." He lifted his chin so John saw another woman on the other side of the plank, ebony hair spilling over a well-displayed pair of breasts, red lips still puckered after she'd blown a kiss in their direction.

"I think that one's for me, sir."

"Oh?"

"Aye. See that?"

The woman wiggled her fingers in their general direction, then cupped her hands under her breasts, showing off her wares. Both men burst out laughing and she grinned.

"Look there," John said, rubbing at his beard. "That tavern wi' the flag out front. 'Tis callin' my name. Can ye hear it?"

Dougal grinned. "Ah, I do. Let's go have a well-earned dram, my friend."

The gangplank sloped down toward the dock and Dougal took long steps, letting gravity pull him toward the bustling crowd. The port was crowded with buildings, but in the background, late summer leaves glistened in welcome, and Dougal sensed this might be a good place to be. Two other grenadiers walked before him, thumbs stuck in their belts as they happily stepped foot on dry land. Dougal followed, grinning when he felt the dirt crunch beneath his feet.

"Dougal."

At the whispered sound his knees almost buckled and he felt dizzy, as if the impact of the voice had spun him around, then dropped him. As if the ground beneath him rolled. His skin practically vibrated, and for a moment he couldn't focus on anything, seeing only the smeared colours of the town's chaos.

"MacDonnell?" John grabbed the back of Dougal's arms, jerking him into the present. "Christ, man, have ye lost yer land legs already?"

Dougal struggled to regain his feet, shaking his head as if to rid it of the noise within. He put his fingers to his temples and breathed deeply, though the stink of the port made that somewhat unpleasant. He shrugged out of John's grasp.

"I'm fine," he told his friend, wondering if he truly were.

What was that voice? Who? And why now? He listened hard, but there were no more utterings, nothing strange in the sounds around him now. Just people calling out, dogs barking, doors slamming, bridles ringing cheerily as horses passed. Had he really heard it? Was there anyone there?

"I need a drink is all," he said.

The tavern filled quickly with soldiers celebrating their arrival. The volume rose, washing away the haunting memory of the voice. He was back in the world of the living, in the midst of drinking, singing, cursing, laughing men, and as was his wont, it wasn't long before Dougal was the centre of it all. The stories he had told the prisoners so long before came bubbling back to the surface, taken up by John whenever Dougal needed a break.

And when the stories wound down, Dougal worked his way around the room, speaking with strangers, asking if they'd seen a small blond slave woman, an angel called Glenna. No one could offer anything.

Ever since Dougal had first discovered too much alcohol limited his fighting capabilities, he had avoided overdoing it. He had never been a heavy drinker to begin with, and, being such a big man, a few drinks weren't enough to slow him down, but he knew his limit. John was not as disciplined. Dougal watched his friend's eyes start to shine after three quickly swallowed drinks, noticed that through the ginger beard, John's cheeks flushed as he downed a couple more. He started to sing, joining in when others danced a jig along with a fiddler's music.

When John threw back his head and laughed at something he'd heard, the movement threw off his balance, and he tripped backward until he ran into Dougal's table. He turned slowly, comically, giving Dougal a wide, amiable grin, then slammed both palms onto the table.

"My friend," he said, slipping over the words. "Are ye no' a dancer? I imagine ye'd do a fine jig, wi' those long gams o' yers an' all."

The sweet, burning scent of rum dominated John's words, as if he'd collected the air of the tavern, syphoned it through a funnel, and now poured it over Dougal's face.

Dougal grinned. "Will ye sit awhile, John? Maybe until the floor stops movin' beneath yer feet? Even the best o' dancers need to rest at times."

John pondered the suggestion, his eyes sliding in and out of focus. His smile softened into the loose-lipped grimace of an imbecile, then he nodded and plopped down beside Dougal. They sat at a table along with three other grenadiers, enjoying the company of some of Charleston's finest ladies. These were not like the women back home, whose sweet flirtations and harmless suggestions felt like a game. The women here were bold, used to selling what others desired, and entirely comfortable with draping their scantily clad bodies over soldiers' laps.

They alternated between the men's attentions, teasing one, then moving to the next as if waiting for the bids to begin. A tall, slant-eyed brunette with what Dougal considered an adorable pout appeared to claim him, refusing to budge when the women shifted places again. She distracted him from the others at the table, monop-olising him with questions, batting her lashes in a well-practiced manner. She introduced herself as Clara and her friend as Rose.

"You're all from Scotland? Ooh. That's a wild place, ain't it?" she asked, stretching the word "wild" into one long, sensual syllable.

He shrugged. "I've no idea compared to here. Maybe it is."

"Did you come here to kill off the Frenchies?"

"Aye, that's the plan," he replied, chuckling when her fingertips tickled under his chin.

She leaned forward and burrowed her lips against his hair, teth-ered behind his neck into a windblown club. Her warm breath tick-led his ear. "I tell you what, soldier. I sure could use a night with a big man like you," she murmured, just loud enough for Dougal to hear over the crowd.

Dougal grinned. "Oh, ye could, could ye?"

She sat straighter on his lap and smiled, her eyes half-closed at the idea. How long had it been since Glenna had disappeared? Since she had last regarded him with an expression similar to this one? Six months maybe? Dougal studied the woman, trying to compare the smooth line of her lips to the ones he had kissed so often. He laid his hand against her cheek and caressed the soft skin with his thumb.

"Ye're a bonny thing, Clara," he told her. "But I'm a mar-ried man."

The woman popped her pout back into place. "And where's she? I don't see her here. Tell you what, if she's any kind of good woman, she'd want you to be kept happy while you're out here fighting for our country, don't you think? It's a man's God given right is what it is."

Dougal looked in the woman's painted face, saw the weary lines around her eyes, and prayed to God that Glenna hadn't been forced into this kind of slavery. He knew it was possible. Many of the women here worked because they chose the life. Others had no choice.

"Clara," he said quietly, praying she would give him the answer he sought. "Ye dinna ken a wee golden-haired lassie named Glenna, do ye? She'd have come a-ship from Scotland a few months ago."

"I know a Glenna, sure, but she ain't fair, and that's a fact. The Glenna I know is darker than you even."

Relief tingled in his chest, though he had no right to it. So this one prostitute didn't know Glenna. That meant nothing. But it was a start.

Across the table from Dougal, John half slumped in his chair with Rose perched on his knee. Her legs were propped on John's lap, bare skin clearly visible from her narrow ankles to halfway up the creamy white of her thighs. John's hand rested just above her knee, his dark fingers making slight depressions in her flesh. His grip could have been desire, Dougal thought, or it could have been that he was simply trying to maintain his balance through a cloud of alcohol.

Rose, sensing Dougal's gaze, winked at him while she squeezed John's drooping face against her bosom. There was no mistaking her intentions. No spring lambs, these two. She wasn't pretty, Dougal thought, though she still had most of her teeth. Her blond hair was nothing like the shining white of Glenna's locks and she was tall enough that she would have dwarfed Glenna. The thought of her petite form came clearly to his mind, and he swallowed grief that tasted like bile.

"Oh, aye, we're off to war on the morrow," John declared, his words gently slurred. His expression was so sombre Dougal was tempted to laugh. "'Twould be such a kindness if ye were to care for me this eve."

"Your friend seems to be stayin'," Clara said, raising her carefully painted eyebrows with suggestion.

"So he does," Dougal replied, watching John nuzzle into Rose's neck.

"Rose lives real near me. Maybe we should take the two of them home, make sure they make it all right, you know?" She blinked prettily over big brown eyes. "These streets can be dangerous for a lady on her own."

Dougal squinted at her, fighting the desire to feel a woman beneath and around him. Clara's hands were soft but firm as they massaged his shoulders, then caressed his linen-clad arms. The need for release was more than simply physical, yet Dougal couldn't imagine following through. Memories flooded his thoughts, images of Glenna's soft curl of hair on his pillow, the crease in her brow and slightly parted lips when they were deep in their lovemaking. Her voice came as clearly to him as it always did, reminding him that she loved him, that she loved only him. And he knew that he could never love another woman.

"No' tonight, my dear," he said.

She stood and swept his hand away, uttering "Pah!" with thinly veiled disgust. After one last hopeful glance, she headed off to the bar and other potential prey.

That was when the door to the tavern swung open, ushering in a warm draft that temporarily cut through the haze of smoke. The volume in the room dropped, and Dougal sat up straighter to see who had come in. He recognised their captain's booming voice at once and watched the short, stocky man stride around tables, growling at his men as he always did.

"Get off yer ass, ye louse-covered sod. Else ye'll be on the receivin' end o' my boot."

Dougal kicked John under the table but got no response out of the dozing man. He kicked him again, harder. John sat up with a splutter, blinking and trying to focus.

"Wh-what's this, MacDonnell?" he demanded.

Dougal nodded toward another table nearby. "Captain's on his way, John. Ye'd best drop yer plans for this eve."

John looked from the approaching captain to Rose, then tilted his head. His smile, which had been rich with alcohol and anticipation, melted into a childish sulk. Rose rolled her eyes and scowled at Dougal, as if it were his fault. Dougal, quietly relieved he wouldn't have to dig his friend out from some awkward situation later on, shrugged and stood to go. Rose left to join Clara, who was already chatting with likelier customers.

"Come on, ol' man," Dougal said, offering his friend a hand up. He nodded at the captain as he led John outside, and the older man returned the greeting. Dougal smiled. He could tell the officer knew John was drunk, and on any other night he expected John—as well as a number of others in the same situation—would be punished. But this was their first night in the colonies. It was a night for celebration, and even the strictest of officers understood that.

CHAPTER 26

Into the Woods

The army spent the night in Charleston, wherever they could find lodging. The city didn't open their arms to the soldiers, providing them instead with only the most basic of lodging. Those soldiers who didn't warm a woman's bed or curl up in a hayloft headed past the city's centre and onto an open field. Dougal and John ended up there as well, stretched out in a six-man tent with another soldier.

Early morning sunshine baked the side of the tent, warming the little shelter until it was too stifling to tolerate. Dougal hadn't slept well as a result of John's inebriated snores, but stepped from the tent and stretched, cheered by the sounds of morning. He made his way out to a campfire, started and tended by sentries during the night, and joined others for breakfast. An hour later all the men were awake and lined up for roll call.

"Ye dinna look quite yerself," Dougal said to John.

John sniffed, then spat to the side. "I'll do," he muttered.

The camp was dismantled, the battalions reassembled, and the marching began. Montgomerie's Highlanders were to be stationed in the Carolinas, their first assignment to protect settlers from ongoing Indian raids. Dougal was looking forward to the change of pace. It wasn't what he considered to be real battle, but at least it was something that felt more familiar than constant drills. But their destination always seemed to be hundreds of miles away, through thick, smothering forests roped by branches and roots, waterways that soaked through the men's plaids, rocks determined to tear through black leather shoes. The forests were so crowded they rarely found flat enough areas in which to set up their hundreds of tents, so the Highlanders resorted to the ancient way of sleeping, rolling up in their plaids at the gnarled feet of trees.

In the morning, they washed in any available water they could find, combing their hair and shaving with razors or dirks. Their weapons and uniforms were always cleaned the night before so that when they awoke, they slipped into the cleanest shirts they had, wrapped on their plaids, and set their bonnets at the particular angle required by protocol. It didn't seem to matter where they were, the British army required a ridiculous standard of presentation. It seemed an awful waste of time to Dougal, but he had to agree that he and his cohorts did smell better than they had when they'd marched together before Culloden.

When they weren't breathing in the miasma of swamps and battling tangles of forests, the soldiers cut roads so their supply wagons could follow, and built small strategic forts by waterways or portages. The humidity of the land was such that the Scots spent more time wiping their brows than speaking.

"Ye must have delicious blood, my friend," Dougal said to John.

The day was sweltering, waking the hunger in swarms of ravenous mosquitoes. Dougal was fortunate in that the creatures seemed less enamoured by his blood than they were with others'. John suffered greatly, his neck swelling on one side until it looked twice as large as it should have. His fingers constantly scratched until the bites opened and bled, providing him with no relief.

"Aye, well," John grumbled. "I'm miserable with these devils. Miserable! They've come straight from hell, they have. An' they can go right back."

Fighting the back woods of the colonies was a never-ending drudgery, a constant state of slogging through life. For variety, Dougal and the others occasionally disappeared into the woods, which teemed with wildlife. The army provided no more than the daily rations of bread, potatoes, dried peas, mutton, or beef, but the forests and rivers easily gave up the rest. Despite the generous hunting, it soon became clear the land didn't welcome them any more than the people had.

"MacClanach doesna fare well," John muttered one day, stooping beneath the heavy branch of a water oak.

Dougal glanced over. MacClanach did indeed look poorly. He was one of the grenadiers, tall and fiery haired, big enough to intimidate most enemy soldiers. But he had wasted away, caught by the sickness that had grabbed so many of them. It had started with twenty men ill, but seemed ten times that now.

MacClanach looked like so many of the others had before they had given up the fight. But he was a stubborn bugger, not about to lie around complaining when he should be working. Over the past two days his skin had taken on a pasty white tinge that looked almost green in the right light, and it was always slick with sweat, night or day. Dougal saw him stumble and reach for a tree for support, but the tree in MacClanach's mind wasn't really there. He collapsed and made a halfhearted grunt when he landed. One of the others went to help him up and Dougal saw the big man try to wave help away, then resign himself to the need for assistance.

"Two days for the poor bugger," Dougal guessed.

John nodded and slapped irritably at a mosquito scouting for an open patch of skin on his neck. "I'll be dead from these devil creatures long before then."

Occasionally the army came upon the remains of homes and farms that had been plagued by Indian attacks. Sometimes all they left behind was burnt debris and smoking corpses. It was at times like these that Dougal had trouble with his rage. Yes, he had joined the 77th Highlanders voluntarily, but it had been for the ulterior motive of searching for Glenna. Walking through these devastated places, seeing the death all around, brought back so many horrors he'd seen in his homeland. Everything there had been caused by the English, and now he fought for the English army. And he hated himself every day for that. Here the Highlanders were called upon to get the Indians under control and defend the white settlements. It weighed on Dougal that the English had come across the sea and were now dedicated to controlling the native people here, as they had in Scotland. And now Dougal was a part of all that.

Dougal had seen Indians before, since some travelled with the Highlanders as scouts, guiding them through the thick forests. But those were calm, curious men, more interested in the army's coin than in their scalps. These marauders, though he'd never seen one with his own eyes, were obviously vicious. Their attacks, or at least the evidence of them, left a clear message that white men were not welcome in this land.

The men took turns as sentries. Those on duty were stationed around the camp, alert and silent. Their Indian guides had warned that they were never alone, and they should be prepared for anything. They thought they had been, but woke one morning to the awful discovery that they had underestimated the enemy. At some point during the night, five soldiers had been silently removed from the camp. Their bodies were found not far away, their heads scalped, their throats slit.

"Which did they do first?" John asked in a hushed voice.

"God, I hope the throats," Dougal said, rubbing his own in sympathy for the dead men.

"That means they'd have done the scalpin' after the lads were dead. Who does that to a dead body? What kind of man thinks that way?"

"Men we'd do best to avoid," Dougal replied. His eyes scanned the forest, looking for anything that didn't belong. Except that wouldn't help him, he thought. The Indians were a part of the woods and would have blended as well as the trees within. The realisation sent a thrill of fear up his spine, but his Highlander blood boiled with anger for his fallen comrades.

John evidently felt it as well. "I'll no' stand by an' let them slaughter us like hogs," he said, his hand resting on the hilt of the sword on his left hip.

Two days later, Dougal, exhausted and craving sleep, took his turn as sentry. He sat near the campfire outside his tent, using the fire for light because clouds blocked the moon. Settling on a supply box, he took out his dirk and started engraving his initials on his powder horn, feeling comfortably lethargic.

Dougal loved this time of night. As much as he enjoyed the company of men and the raucous laughter in taverns, he also loved the quiet. He closed his eyes for a moment, ingesting the tiny nighttime sounds of the forest. A cricket chirped nearby, louder than the thousands singing in the woods. There was a short scuffle he identified as an owl dipping low to pluck a scurrying meal from the undergrowth. The quiet hiss of a breeze through brittle autumn leaves reminded Dougal of home, and he missed it with a physical ache. All those times he and Andrew had slept beneath the stars, dreaming of battle, of saving Scotland from the plague of sassenachs . . . all empty dreams, but they'd been done under a full sky forever painted with promise in Dougal's mind. Their father had shown them how to follow stars if they were ever lost; their mother had taught them the legends behind the constellations.

But there were no stars tonight. It was peaceful and calm, and yet . . . something in the air kept distracting his attention from the carving in his hands. A twig snapped and Dougal looked up sharply, peering into the darkness, emptying his mind to hear whatever thoughts flitted through the air. He could make out no words, no distinct thoughts.

But there was something. A message he wasn't supposed to understand. He stared at the jumping silhouettes of trees and tents, lit by scattered campfires. Nothing else moved, no further sounds came from the darkness. For a moment he wondered if the vague voices he heard actually belonged to the forest creatures themselves. Maybe he'd only heard one of the other men relieving himself in the woods. Dougal cleared his throat and tried to return his concentration to his carving.

His hand cramped from the intricate work and he paused to rest it. When he yawned, his jaw clicked, and he caught himself staring at nothing. So, so tired. He closed his eyes, then rested his face on his hands. It would be so easy, he mused, just to fall asleep for a few minutes. The sounds, words, and voices that swam through his head were soothing, quiet. But if he slept, would he wake in time? He knew he couldn't give in, couldn't chance endangering the others, but oh, the thought was appealing.

"Dougal."

He shot to his feet, eyes wide. It was the voice he had waited so long to hear again, half hoping, half fearing its tones.

Every hair on Dougal's body stood erect, his nerves sizzled. His mind tuned to the babble of voices and he understood. Not sooth-ing at all. Secret. Coming from within the trees. He slid two fingers into his mouth and whistled softly to the other sentries. Two short blows. Dougal sensed the quick response of his cohorts, saw them stand to attention by their separate fires.

Dougal took five silent steps backward, his eyes trained on the forest, then crouched by the opening of his tent.

"Up, lads," he said quietly. "We've guests."

CHAPTER 27

Voices in the Forest

John had just crawled from the tent when Dougal became aware of the quiet shushing of feet through the long, cool grass. The thoughts came louder now, still unintelligible, but their meaning was clear. A spark exploded in the campfire and for an instant Dougal saw the whites of a dozen Indians' eyes as they emerged from the forest. Their faces and bodies were painted to blend with the darkness, their long black hair ribboned with equally black feathers. They had crept close to the camp in utter silence and hadn't counted on being detected, so when one appeared a few feet before Dougal, he yelped with surprise, then shrieked a stream of unintelligible orders to his fellows.

Dougal acted without thinking, swinging his sword in an arc so that it sliced across the man's belly, drawing blood. The Indian roared, seeming to gain strength from the cut. Injured or not, he seemed unconcerned about the dark red seeping down his belly. One of his hands held an ax over his head, and the arm supporting it was roped with muscle. He bared his teeth then lunged toward

Dougal, eyes wide and flickering with the flames of the campfire. Dougal swiped again with his sword, using his superior reach to fend off the wicked strike, and managed to jar the ax from the man's grip. It fell to the ground and the Indian hopped backward, avoiding the sword. Without missing a beat, he charged Dougal and bowled him over. The two rolled on the ground, both grunting with effort, both stretching their fingers around the other's neck.

The Indian straddled him, jamming his thumbs into Dougal's throat until stars flew and the man's face blurred in Dougal's vision. The Indian glared down at him, teeth clenched, sweat beading on his forehead as he pressed. Air became harder to find and Dougal's struggles weakened. Suddenly the Indian let go and replaced his hands with one knee, pinning his weakened foe and closing off Dougal's airway. Through vision gone red, Dougal saw the shape of the man as he reached to the side, grabbing a large granite rock with both hands and holding it, poised over his head.

Dougal closed his eyes, gasping like a fish, waiting for the strike. But John was there first, discharging his pistol before the granite reached its target. Dougal shoved the dead Indian to the side and scrambled to his feet. He nodded to John, then the two ran to see what was happening elsewhere.

The other Indians had raced back into the woods, finding safety in the dark. A group of soldiers took chase, shooting as they ran, but were left in the Indians' wake. They returned to camp empty-handed.

John and Dougal stared at the corpse of the man John had slain. The pistol had blown a hole in his chest, just beneath a necklace of what looked to Dougal like the nails of the claw of a bear: long, curved, and the colour of cream. There was no red wool jacket to soak in the blood, no white linen shirt to stain, because the man wore nothing but a loincloth, leggings, and the feathers in his hair.

Dougal squatted beside the body and examined the necklace, then studied the man's face. So this was an Indian warrior. A celebrated one, if this necklace were any indication. About the same age as Dougal. The man's face wasn't so different from his own: strong-boned, lean, with full lips and dark lashes, though for the Indian they were now forever closed.

John stood beside him, looking down. "What is it?" he asked.

"Oh, I was only thinkin' that if no' for the ocean, this could have been me."

"What? Dead?"

"Aye, dead, but also livin' rough like him, maybe even dressin' like him."

John chuckled. "The ocean an' perhaps a few other things. The man's a savage."

"So they say. But what makes him so different from me? Would I no' have done the same thing he did? When the English took our land, did we no' fell them wi'out hesitation? An' I'd do it again in a moment, as would you, I reckon. So what makes me better than this poor fellow?"

John squatted beside him and studied the body. "Well," he said slowly, "for one thing, ye're no' dead."

Dougal eyed him sideways.

"All right, Plato," John said. "I suppose ye're right. The English say we're much like these Indians, wi' their clans an' all. An' this land is no' so very different from where I grew up. So when ye—"

They were interrupted by the appearance of more soldiers approaching from beyond their tent. The newcomers stopped when they saw the fallen Indian.

"Ye've another one, have ye, MacDonnell? That makes four, I reckon," said one, puffing his chest with bravado. "They'll think again afore they attack us, aye? These savages are none so fierce."

Dougal frowned up at him. "Ye fought one yerself, did ye, Hamish?"

"Well, no," Hamish admitted, looking to the side. "But Stewart here saw—"

"Then ye'll no' ken the truth o' the matter."

Hamish paused. "Maybe no'. But I like the look o' that wee bauble around his neck. Here. Let's have a look."

He squatted beside Dougal and John and stretched his fingers toward the necklace, but Dougal stopped him with a quick elbow jab. "Dinna touch that."

"Oy!" Hamish rubbed the spot on his chest where Dougal had struck. He glared at Dougal, then spoke slowly, as if to a child. "Right then. If it's yer kill, ye can have the thing. I only wished to see it."

"It's no' mine," Dougal said. "If spoils go to the victor, then it's John's."

John reached for the necklace and held the string, still around the brave's neck, in the palm of his hand. His thumb caressed the smooth white claws. He looked from the dead man to the forest, then to Dougal.

"What think ye of returnin' this man to his fellows?"

The others looked at him, confused.

"It's only, well, these men are warriors. They ken battle an' death, an' from what I heard, they have strong beliefs about what happens after they die. So I reckon we have a choice. I could take the man's trophy as my own an' show any interested Indians that we've the power to kill as well as they do. Or we could return the man to his family, wi' the necklace still 'round his neck. A sign o' respect, I reckon, wouldna go amiss."

Dougal nodded, a slow smile creeping over his face.

"We've seen the scalpin'," John continued. "We've seen what they did to our own dead. Should we do the same?"

"Aye, we should," Hamish huffed. "Else they'll think we've no' heart in us."

One of his companions shifted, then sniffed and gazed into the starless sky. "I agree wi' John," he said. "Maybe they'd be less inclined to come after us if we give the man his dignity."

"Dignity?" sputtered Hamish. "This is war, lads! The savages would skin us as quick as a rabbit, an' here we consider their honour above ours?"

"No' above ours," Dougal said. "But it shows we *have* honour." He turned to John. "So what will ye do?"

"We'll leave the man to his necklace an' carry him to the forest."

Hamish snorted. "The captain willna be pleased."

"Maybe no'." He looked pointedly at Hamish. "Maybe he'll no' even ken this man has died if we do it quietly."

The men exchanged glances, silently debating their next move. Then Dougal stood and removed his jacket. He dropped it on top of the ruined chest, then leaned down to take hold of the strong copper shoulders. It would have been easier to toss him over his shoulder, but then the Indian's blood would have painted Dougal's shirt. John took the man's feet and the others moved in, both to help lift the dead weight and to shield them from view. While the bulk of the camp was busy tending to their wounded, Dougal and the others carried the body into the woods. They brought him to a low-lying area they hadn't visited before, crowded with birch that glowed in the night, and propped him up against a tree for his friends to find.

Hamish grunted. "Aye, well, I reckon this is better than if the others found him wi' no hair."

"Aye, they're plenty vexed as it is. They dinna need more cause."

The small group turned back toward their camp, saying nothing more. A damp chill gripped the air as the sky cleared, unveiling the stars. Dougal shrugged back into his jacket and noted vaguely that the dead Indian's body had fed almost no warmth into the wool. Despite the coat, Dougal shivered.

In the end, four Indians were killed, including John's, so the official count was three. Two soldiers had been injured, one of them seriously. He would be sent to the hospital in the morning, where he would be fed, tended, and charged two shillings per day.

With all the excitement, no one returned to sleep, though it could have been no later than three or four o'clock. Dougal wandered away from the others, picking his way along a rough trail until he could see a small stream twinkling under the moon. Ever since he'd been a wee lad, he'd gone to water when he needed to escape, to think, to renew his spirit. He needed water almost as much as he needed air to breathe. Now he cupped his hands and splashed his face, gasping at the welcome shock of it. He did it twice more, then sat back on the shore, stretching his long legs before him and leaning against the rigid bark of an oak. He stared at the silver water racing past and wiggled his bare toes. Of the few things Dougal treasured at the end of the day, taking off his shoes was one of his favourites.

The river sounded loud from where he rested, loud and soothing, blocking out the rest of the world. Dougal closed his eyes and imagined standing in rushing water to his waist, feeling it push and pull against his body.

"Who are you?" he asked silently.

Who was it that knew his name? Who knew exactly when to call for him? Why did the sound send blood roaring through him? Questions pulsed in his mind, but he kept them to the simplest. He had always known the silent thoughts he heard in others' minds were real. But this voice was something he didn't understand.

"Why do ye call to me?"

There was no answer, but Dougal hadn't expected one. He breathed deeply, letting his mind drift, not quite sleeping, not quite awake. It was at this stage that his mind usually played with him, bringing him the voices of his loved ones, intriguing him with thoughts from strangers. But not tonight. Tonight the steady beating of his heart provided rhythm beneath the melody of the stream, and nothing else. The silence felt warm. It felt welcome, like an embrace.

And to Dougal's mind, it brought safety, reassurance. He imagined his mother, her arms wrapped protectively around her eldest son while he tried so hard to be brave, to be the man he needed to grow into. His mind brought him the bittersweet images of his father, Andrew, Ciaran, and he almost felt the heat of their presence as they stood by him, their sturdy hands pressed against his arms and back as if to share once again the lives the English had stolen from them.

Leaves shimmered overhead, shushing like an unexpected ripple in the stream, and shifting his thoughts to another dreamed reunion. He thought of Glenna. Of how her arms slipped around his chest, pulling him toward her so they pressed together, their hearts almost touching through the welcoming pillow of her breasts. Of how he would sink his weight onto her, taste her neck, inhale the sweet fragrance that was hers alone, and feel as if he'd come home. God, how he longed for those arms, for that neck, for the balm of her whispers.

The embrace he felt in the air, if it were possible, tightened. Glenna held him fast, squeezing tears from his eyes. If he could have, Dougal would have disappeared willingly into the fibres of the invisible blanket, let the imagined limbs of all his lost ones carry him wherever they desired. The silence brought peace. The silence brought love.

"Dougal."

The word was a breath, a whisper. It vanished before he could trap it, slipping through his thoughts like a curling ribbon of smoke, and Dougal was left alone. The embrace opened, the spell released him, and the night air stole the warmth he had cherished.

CHAPTER 28

Stories Told Blindly

It was peculiar, Dougal reflected for the thousandth time, how familiar and yet how strange this army was to him. The Highlanders, as always, were strong and proud, willing to follow orders that sent them through the sunken quagmires of the Carolinas, north into the frozen wilderness of Pennyslvania, New York, and farther still.

On one hand, their dedication reminded him of how the clans had marched stubbornly through the Highlands, defending their lands, their traditions, and the ancient name of Stuart.

On the other hand, the shiny buttons that adorned Dougal's bright red jacket and the leather shoes that wrapped his feet prevented his feeling entirely a part of this army. The organised marches, when the roads were wide enough to accommodate them, were foreign; the barked orders lacked the passion and pride that had always been projected by the clan chiefs. It never felt right to Dougal, fighting for the English.

He had come to accept it was better than rotting within the icy confines of a prison cell or hanging from the end of a rope. That didn't mean he didn't hate himself for it. Did being here make him a coward? Perhaps. A realist? More probably. There was nothing he could do to change what he'd become. He heard his bitterness in the sharp lash of his tongue when he struck out at one of the others, and felt self-hatred hardening him from the outside in.

But somewhere deep inside, Dougal's heart still beat as it always had. He dreamed of freedom, of laughter, of Glenna. And Dougal clung to that desperate pulse.

General John Forbes led the men to Pennsylvania, toward Fort Duquesne. Positioned at the mouth of the Ohio River, Duquesne was a major shipping port with a trading store that did a good business with the French and the Indians. Despite repeated attacks and hundreds of lost soldiers, the English had been unable to win it from the French. Forbes's orders were to change the status quo.

"Nothin' but swamp," Dougal muttered to John, yanking his foot from a sucking clump of grass.

"Aye, but the king feels it should be *our* swamp."

The mud thickened and crackled underfoot as time crawled toward November. The men pulled their hose almost to their knees and covered their faces with their plaids when the wind set in. When they moved against Fort Duquesne this time, the French surprised them by lighting explosives in the fort's powder magazine. The explosion destroyed the entire eastern wall, the barracks, and a stable. Poor reward for the British troops. But the men made the best of the situation, celebrating around the roaring flames while they warmed their bodies and cooked their suppers.

It was natural, Dougal supposed, that the troops would divide into small groups of like-minded men. He and John, for example, spent most of their time with the other grenadiers, the larger, more dangerous men, since they had the most in common in terms of their work. There were others he spoke with, others he had nothing to do with, and others he purposefully ignored. The last group was made up mostly of disgruntled soldiers, men who carried a permanent snarl and muttered curses that worsened over time. One of those was Hamish, the man who, so long ago, had objected to John's proposal to return the Indian he had slain to the woods for his kin to discover. Dougal caught the glares Hamish had shot at John and was surprised by their intensity. More and more he noticed Hamish pulling others aside, talking in private, then glancing back at John as if he intended nothing less than murder.

"Wee Hamish doesna seem overly fond of ye, does he?" Dougal asked John one day as they sliced through heavy growth, cutting a new road for the army to follow.

John wiped his arm across his face and shrugged. "So I've seen. I've no idea why, do you?"

"Shall we ask?"

John shrugged again, always the easy fellow. "It wouldna hurt to know what it is I've done to piss him off."

But they didn't have to bring up the subject, because Hamish took things a step further that night. John and Dougal had taken their meals aside, lighting a small fire separate from the others. They were worn out from the heavy work that day, since it had been the grenadiers' turn to work on the road, and both men were more content in their own quiet company.

"Too good for the likes of us, are ye?" came Hamish's voice when he tracked them down.

Dougal's smile quirked when he looked at John, who rolled his eyes.

"Go away, Hamish," Dougal muttered, chewing a piece of meat, still hot off the fire.

"Oh, that's it, is it? The two of ye, so high an' mighty, so brave an' powerful, doin' as ye please."

John blinked. "What in God's name are ye talkin' about?"

"Oh, like ye dinna already ken that. How the two of ye, an' the rest of the damn grenadiers, ye march around like gods, all full o' mighty, tellin' the rest of us what to do."

John and Dougal exchanged a puzzled glance. "What is it we're supposed to have said?" Dougal asked.

Hamish pointed an angry finger at Dougal. "Dinna try to corner me, MacDonnell. Ye're just as bad as this one. Well, I'm tired of it."

"Of what?" they asked in unison.

Hamish narrowed his glare, aiming the worst of it at John. "Ye're a stuck-up arse wi' yer witty tongue an' yer judgin' eyes on the rest of us, makin' sure we do as we're bid. We're no' here for ye to laugh at, are we, Mr. Wallace? Ye wi' yer—"

Sensing John's rising ire, which rose slowly at the best of times, Dougal stood up before John could. He stepped in Hamish's face and frowned down at him. "What is wrong wi' ye, Hamish? John's done nothin', an' you—"

"And *you*! Ye think ye can stand before me, yerself a *murderer* an' all, an'—"

Dougal couldn't prevent the quick reflex that shoved Hamish away. He was tired, he was sick of the little man's bickering and whining, and he was incensed that his personal history was being announced in front of everyone else. When Hamish stumbled, Dougal was there, glaring down, eyeing him as he scuttled backward.

And still the words spewed from Hamish's mouth. "Ye see? There ye go again, throwin' around yer unnatural size, usin' braw to try an' intimidate me, but I—"

"Do ye have no idea when to stop?" John demanded, standing beside Dougal. "Come on, man. None of us here wants to fight, do we? I ken I don't, an' neither does he," he said, making a point of restraining Dougal's arm.

Dougal seethed. Despite John's attempt to defuse the situation, he would have been more than happy to leap into the fray. His muscles, wasted too long on building roads, and hefting weapons and supplies, were primed to go. His fists bunched and he raised them, savouring the power that swelled through him.

John must have noticed, for he intervened, shifting his bulk between the two men. "None of us is lookin' for charges to be laid against us for a needless fight. We're here to do a job, Hamish. If ye dinna like the two of us, that's too bad—an' rather poor judgement. We're no' bad fellows if ye take the time to know us. But make no mistake. We're here for the army, no' to make friends. We work together, an' no one says we must enjoy that. Ye go yer way, we'll go ours. Never ye mind what we do or say."

Hamish backed up farther, then scrambled to his feet, still glaring. "I'll no' forget this, MacDonnell. Do ye hear? Ye dinna shove a man before his friends an' walk away from it."

God, Dougal wanted to jump on him, throttle some sense into the idiot, but John wisely stayed between the two of them. Hamish walked backward a few more steps, watching the two men as if he were memorising their features, then turned and headed back to the main fire. Dougal and John watched him go, their expressions still confused.

"Did I miss somethin'?" John asked.

Dougal shrugged and scratched his head. "I've no idea. But I think we should step around the man for now. He seems a bit mad."

"He does at that." John shook his head as if to clear it, then grinned. "Well, that was inconvenient. I hope my dinner's no' cold."

The next few days passed without event, though Hamish never missed an opportunity to hiss a warning, or make some kind of rude gesture. When he lost his mind one night over drink, he was punished for it, and afterward told everyone repeatedly it was Dougal's fault, though Dougal had been nowhere near. Fortunately, the men who had shared Hamish's company of late had also sensed a change in the man's demeanour, and had started to drift away, leaving Hamish to stew in his own juices.

The days were too busy to be spent worrying about petty disagreements, and usually the nights were too short, stolen by deep sleep. Life went on with the army, marching into one mission after another, whether it was helping to keep the peace between neighbouring Indian tribes and white settlers, or planning major raids against the French. After the devastation at Fort Duquesne, they built a new fort, bigger than the last. Then they were ordered farther north, into the wilds of New York, where they eventually chased the French from Fort Ticonderoga. Again, they built another fort.

Dougal was a man conflicted. Though he fought and worked with indefatigable strength, everything they did felt relatively meaningless to him. The misery of marching, chopping, hunting, and eventually curling gratefully into damp, rough blankets at night seemed endless. None of it made any sense. It was his duty, and as was his way, he acted beyond what was expected of him. He led the men with a bravado he didn't feel.

And every time they met up with anyone, he asked about Glenna.

When the guns roared, something in his mind hardened, and he heard nothing but commands, saw only targets. His aim was always perfect, his intuition without flaw. The others followed, staying relatively safe in his wake. But in his heart he became more defeated by the day. Instead of celebrating victories, he blamed himself for any man lost, adding to the heavy toll that already weighed down his spirit. His family, his woman, now his men.

Ironically, Dougal maintained his sanity by listening to the voices in his head that no one else could hear. That fact would have, more than likely, labeled him as insane among other folk. But Dougal held on to those voices. When he heard his family, nothing else mattered.

On winter nights, after days spent plodding through the wilderness, Dougal huddled with other frozen Scots and shivered by the tiny stove in their barracks. Though he listened and told stories, laughing and commiserating in turn, his mind and heart were always somewhere else. His cheeks often burned with frostbite and his mittened hands occasionally lost all feeling, but Dougal was warmed by Glenna's song in his ear, never there, always present. When he could face no more blood, yet was forced to polish his musket for another day of slaughter, he heard his brothers' teasing laughter.

Men died through the winter. Scotland's winters had been hard, but their chill had somehow felt more manageable. Or perhaps it was just that when the ice and snow got too bad, he could come back inside, sit by the fire with Glenna, and create their own warmth. Here, far from the familiar mountains of home, the men fought the cold with all they could, but their adversary always seemed better armed. It claimed casualties and left bodies in its wake, bodies that would have to wait for the softer spring earth before they could be buried.

If the winter didn't kill men, it changed them. Their characters, already hardened by fighting years of impossible battles, grew brittle in the cold, like shells around an egg. Cracks began in some, lengthening over time. When the cracks became unmanageable, the shell fell completely apart. Such was Hamish's fate. Dougal watched the man's irrational hatred, now deeply rooted in his disturbed soul, grow thick and inflexible as an ancient oak. Hamish was locked away repeatedly, put in solitary confinement to try and break him of his hysterical ravings, but nothing helped. He became useless as a soldier, his mind too busy spouting nonsense to concentrate on the task at hand. He was hauled up in front of a committee of senior officers and the decision was made to release him from the army. When they reached the next town, Hamish was handed over to the local officials and confined to a prison cell.

The army continued without him, growing slimmer by the week as men died or deserted, defeated by the cold. They were back in Virginia when the season finally passed and green began sprouting around them, encouraging the men to emerge from woolen cocoons and breathe in optimism. Spring brought more than burials. It brought hunting and green leaves and warmth on better days. It was more pleasant marching and training when one wasn't forced to trek through crunching drifts of snow, feeling the cut of the wind as it sliced unprotected skin. Spring offered hope, though what hope a soldier could find, Dougal wasn't sure. Hope they would survive? Hope they would go home soon? Hope to die and forget all this?

There were times, like now, when nothing demanded his attention. Occasionally he welcomed the rest. But idleness summoned the voices Dougal sometimes couldn't bear to hear. Now he sat, leaning heavily against the wall, staring between his knees. He watched an early spring beetle meander between his feet, swaying and pausing as if whisky had gotten the best of him.

"Where are ye, Glenna?" he asked softly.

The beetle toddled away and Dougal squinted critically at its random wanderings. It should have stayed with him, he thought, away from the stomping of boots.

Dougal closed his eyes. He had backed himself into a secluded section of the courtyard, where he often did, needing a place to himself. If he were given the freedom to choose his ideal place, it would have consisted of cool, clear water, tonic to his soul, but there was none available at the garrison but the stuff in buckets.

A wind swept through the yard, lifting Dougal's hair, ruffling the heavy layers of tartan draped over his bent knees. If there had been water, it would have been frosted white by the wind. The trees nearby would be shushing, making oak leaves dance on their precarious stems. He breathed in another gust and let a smile tickle his expression. The wind was Dougal's substitute for water.

A sergeant bellowed at his men across the yard; two soldiers wandered nearby, their conversation bobbing just above the surface of Dougal's thoughts. Not enough to touch or disturb him. A ragged melody played from faraway bagpipes, a memory fluttering in the wind.

CHAPTER 29

A Voice on the Battlefield

Dougal was a warrior, and he knew he was a good one. He had been born to fight, to follow the hunter's instinct and chase victory at any cost. When he shouldered his musket and heard the commanding officer's voice, Dougal fell into the scene, losing all sense of where he was. Everything seemed to slow, the sounds of men and guns fading into a muffled cacophony that served as a background to his slow, steady heartbeats. He felt no fear, only a sense of calm determination. Now he turned toward a telltale red kerchief fluttering in the distance and fired. A hundred yards away an oak splintered, severed by a cannon's blast. Dougal heard it crack and pop as it fell, followed by cries of men stumbling to get out of the reach of its falling branches.

"Dougal."

The voice hit him between the eyes, the impact leaving him dizzy. He granted himself the luxury of looking away from the fight for a breath, trying to find the voice, but it was gone. In its place, however, he felt a pressure. A push. Dougal wheeled to the right, following the urge, and squinted across the gray field. A brief flash of red under a black tricorne. *Good God.* The voice was right. Dougal pointed and fired. The man toppled from the lower branch of an old maple, his cry disappearing into the fog. Another shot rang out and Dougal turned toward the source, finding and dispatching it instantly. He felt pressure in his mind again, like a warm hand guiding his own. He raised his rifle, letting the voice lead him to one target, the next, and the next, like a magnet to iron.

When the battle was done, the 77th lauded as victorious, Dougal walked from the bloodied field on feet that felt light. Everything around him seemed unreal. The voices of men, which always sounded muffled in his ears after artillery fire, were almost silent; his cohorts' bright uniforms were nothing more than shades of gray. When he inhaled, the cutting smoke that hung in the air didn't seem as harsh. The world was a different place.

He knew that voice. And he knew only one man who had been that intuitive about finding hidden targets.

Andrew. Andrew Adam James MacDonnell.

Dougal had been on the battlefield, and yet he hadn't been in charge of his aim. Andrew, his beloved brother, hadn't been there, and yet he had.

That night, as Dougal settled into his bedroll, his mind was with his brother. As much as Dougal never questioned the impossible voices running like an unstoppable force through his mind, he didn't believe in communicating with the dead. He had never heard voices from those no longer alive.

And that meant Andrew still lived.

The treasured sound of his voice was rare, and it was nothing more than the simple whisper of Dougal's name. But the syllables were more precious than gold, more nourishing than any feast. He thought back over the months and years spent on this continent, and realised the frequency and clarity of the whispers had everything to do with geography. In the Carolinas he could almost swear Andrew stood beside him, his voice a familiar deep timbre, not a faraway whisper.

So Dougal would go to the Carolinas. He would find Andrew. There was no question in his mind. He would have to leave the army, only wondered how soon he could do it. There was talk of their travelling north to Halifax for the winter, and if that happened, Dougal would escape before then. He couldn't afford to go any farther north. The roads Dougal had worked so hard to build would be off limits to him once he had deserted, but he would have to use them whenever he could, whenever there was no other traffic to avoid. He was well aware of the danger he would face. As a deserter he was committing a capital offense. He would be a criminal in the eyes of just about anyone.

The very idea would have been unthinkable to Dougal even a few months ago. Then he had been nothing but a soldier. English army or not, Dougal was a soldier, and proud of it. Now he started to play with the idea of leaving the army, making plans. He would finally escape the clutches of the damn English. And he was on his way to finding another who had evaded their grasp.

Andrew. Just thinking of his brother lightened Dougal's heart. So much had changed since the last time he'd seen Andrew, almost a decade past. What would Andrew's life be like? What would he be like as a man, after all he had survived? Dougal knew he himself was no longer the man he'd been before they'd set off to battle. He was hard now, compared to the jolly lad from before. He cared less about people, because he had made it so. After all the losses in his life, Dougal had become convinced that to make a friend was almost to read him—or her—a death sentence.

But not his brother. Andrew had survived. He wondered if Andrew had any idea Dougal was alive. Oh, what a reunion theirs would be! Dougal ran different scenarios through his head, passing the time, trying to envision the joy of that moment. *I'm comin' for ye, Andrew. We'll laugh together soon.*

PART 2

Glenna

CHAPTER 30

On Her Own

If she'd had a choice, Glenna would have chosen death.

She plodded behind the soldiers, wrists bound, reliving the last time she'd been captured. That had been another lifetime, before her days and nights and heart had filled with Dougal. Now she was Glenna, not Aidan. Everything was different. She was afraid to think of what might await her wherever they were taking her.

Dougal. They'd killed him. The knowledge was cold and sharp and black in her, something she couldn't yet touch. She knew that cliff where they'd thrown him, knew the impossible rapids in the river where he would have landed. The bastard had hit him hard from behind and Dougal had fallen to the dirt like a stone. She'd wrestled against the man holding her, screaming, kicking out at him, needing to rush to Dougal's side, but two of the soldiers dragged his senseless body to the edge before she could do anything. Rolled him over the sharp corner of the cliff, gave him a shove with one foot for good measure. At least he'd never seen it coming. She was glad of that. Being unaware would have made it an easier death.

Glenna had died in that moment with him. Crumpled on the ground, spared no pain. Maybe he was up in that heaven of his, watching her right now. She couldn't remember if Christians had any power from beyond the living. Could he take care of her from there?

No. She was on her own. No one would come for her. No one would care.

The soldiers hadn't tried anything yet, but she was ready. They'd taken her dirk, left her quiver of arrows in the early spring mud. Thought she was nothing but a helpless woman. But Glenna knew men and had fought them off plenty of times in the past. She might not have a dirk anymore, but she had teeth. She had nails and elbows and knees. She would manage. And Dougal would be proud of her, wherever he was. He'd taught her there was a weapon in everything. All she had to do was find it. And if she could see nothing, she could still use her mind, her words.

She didn't see any sort of sign indicating the name of the place when they arrived, but it was some kind of fort. A large courtyard surrounded by buildings of different descriptions. Some of them she thought were probably barracks, others would be storage rooms and offices. She was shoved through a small door and briefly saw the profiles of five other people inside before it slammed shut behind her. As the light was snuffed out, her courage went with it, stolen by the familiar terror of a stale and musty cell. Glenna squinted at the outlines of the other prisoners while her eyes adjusted to the lack of light. A small cluster of women sat on the floor, leaning against two of the walls.

One of them spoke right away. "Who're you?" she demanded.

"Lorna, dear. Now, now. That's no way to say a hello, is it? Come on in, dearie. Have a seat here."

Glenna stepped warily into the darkness, running her fingers along one cool wall as she went. Though the floor was probably filthy, Glenna was exhausted, her legs ready to collapse. She slid down the wall beside the others.

"Glenna," she said quietly. "I'm Glenna."

"Lovely, that. I'm Nessa, and these here—"

"We don't get much food, missy. Ye'll no' be takin' any o' mine."

Glenna wasn't in the mood. "I'll eat what I need, no more, no less."

"No, ye'll—"

"Lorna! Enough!" It was another voice chipping in. "Pay her no mind, Glenna. Ye'll need to get yer rest now."

Glenna closed her eyes and hung her head onto her chest, feeling the chill of the cell wheedle into her bones, feeling the darkness tighten around her chest. *Oh, Dougal. If only I had been there for you. If only I hadn't downed that deer. If only . . .* Her throat was thick with sobs now that she had the time to sit, to think, to understand. But she didn't cry. Her head already ached, and crying would do it no good.

She was startled when a couple of cool fingers pressed something against her hand. Bread?

"Here ye are," said a kind voice.

Glenna had forgotten how hungry she was. She'd been starving before they'd gone hunting, then had nothing over the past three or four hours. Every step had lulled her further into a trance of disbelief, and her body's physical messages didn't seem to matter after a while. But now that she held the woman's meagre offering, her whole body began to shake. She bit into the edge of the bread's sharp crust, cutting her gum, but she didn't care. The morsel melted in her mouth and travelled down to the pit of her stomach, soothing the cramping within. It was just a little bit, but it was something.

"Thank ye, Nessa," she whispered. "I havena eaten in a while."

"I'll wager ye've no' slept, either. Lay yer head, lass. There's nothin' here for ye to stay awake for."

Glenna let Nessa guide her cheek onto her lap, then closed her eyes under the woman's soft touch. A mother, Glenna guessed. The woman knew how to care for someone in pain. And Glenna hurt all over, inside and out. She gave in to the tears, though she kept them quiet under the woman's caresses, and fell asleep.

In the morning the latch on the door was thrown open, sunlight flooded the room, and a guard entered, waving them all to their feet. Glenna battled her heavy eyelids, forcing them open while the other women shuffled past her.

"That's it," the guard said. "Move along now. Right. Ah. You'd be the new girl then." Glenna kept her eyes on her feet and followed the women toward the outside. The guard grabbed her arm and jerked her toward him, forcing her eyes to meet his. He was a small man and carried a belligerence that could only come from someone holding power in the form of a gun. She said nothing, and his grip tightened. "That's right." His voice oozed and his eyes wandered over her face, then farther down. He pulled her closer, until they were practically nose to nose, and spoke through teeth so rotted the smell almost choked her. "You'll remember who's boss here, will you?"

"Leave her, Sergeant," one of the women said, tugging Glenna's arm from his grasp.

The man's smile never changed, but a slight frown darkened his small, close-set eyes. "For now," he said. He gave Glenna a wink, and she knew what he was.

The pebbles in the yard crunched under Glenna's feet, and she shielded her eyes with her hand, slightly chilled by the cool sweat that had bubbled up on her when the guard's fingers bruised her arm. His grip had been nothing special, but a threat nonetheless. Her reaction to it had been different from when she'd been grabbed the day before—God, was it only yesterday?—because then she'd been consumed by what was happening to Dougal. She hadn't cared what they did to her. If only they'd get off him, leave him be. She and Dougal had done nothing wrong but need food for their bellies. But the bloody English soldiers hadn't cared what she'd wanted. They'd killed the man she loved, then dragged her away without a look back, as if they were simply returning to work after dumping the refuse in the filthy streets of London.

But she knew the look in this guard's eyes, and now had no one to focus on but herself, since she need not worry about poor, dead Dougal. She blinked away the thought, taking care not to envision his body at the bottom of that cliff. Now she was on her own and realised she couldn't remember a time when she hadn't had someone to look after her. First dear Joseph, then Dougal. Things would be different now. She knew how to fight and could be tougher than anyone expected, but she was still small and most likely couldn't manage this one guard on her own. Avoidance would have to be key.

And perhaps Nessa. In the sunlight Glenna could finally make out the faces of the other women, also dirty but less bruised than she was, moving confidently into the yard as if they had spent some time getting used to the routine. Nessa wasn't the oldest and looked to be maybe in her forties, her hair almost pure white, her eyes, though tired, still stubbornly alive with intelligence and heart. The mother hen, Glenna thought, though there was an older lady there as well. Glenna couldn't remember most of the other names, but she spotted Lorna right off. Scrawny, weathered, her dry yellow hair pulled back from what might once have been a pretty face. Now it was twisted with suspicion and animosity. Like a dog beaten too often, quick to snap.

"Come along, Glenna," Nessa called cheerfully. "We'll walk a bit then take breakfast." She gave Glenna a wry smile. "Maybe we'll get a bucket an' wash ye a bit, shall we?"

She had been right in her initial impression of Nessa Drummond. Her new friend opened up right away, as if she felt it important to get the truth out in the open. She was a mother of five daughters and three sons. She thought maybe a couple of her daughters still lived, but she had no idea. Her husband was gone as well. She assumed he and their sons had all died at Culloden.

"They didna all die there," Glenna said quietly, hardly knowing how to answer a woman who braved such unthinkable grief. "I was there as well. So many dead, so much . . ." She stopped for a moment, unable to bear either the pain in herself or in the older woman's expression. "But there were thousands of us kept alive for whatever reason, kept in prison. I lived among them. Maybe they're still there."

Nessa smiled sadly and nodded, but never asked if Glenna had known anyone in particular. That, to Glenna, meant Nessa had given up. It was natural for Glenna to want to offer words of hope, but she didn't after that. The woman's nod indicated she neither expected nor wanted platitudes from anyone.

"That is Bonnie," said Nessa, indicating a quiet, mousy woman with a pinched expression. "She doesna speak much, but means well enough. Lost a husband and two sons at Prestonpans and Culloden, then was taken from her farm along wi' her daughters, but she hasna seen them since."

Nessa tilted her head slightly to the right. "Beside her is my friend Aline. She'll no' talk of what brings her here, so I dinna ask. She's a good woman, is Aline. Hates the English wi' every breath, but smart enough no' to show it. Aline kens her way around the healin' arts, she does. She helps here when she can, ministerin' to the injured an' even to the sick sometimes."

Nessa strode purposefully toward a particular guard, smiling as if the man were a neighbour, no less. Her silver curls, which Glenna could now see were darkened slightly by the occasional patch of stubborn brown, were swept back from her face, falling in a full tail down her neck and back. She calmly asked the man for something with which she could help Glenna wash, then followed the guard to a small room where the two women were left alone with a bucket of water and cloths. The water was lukewarm and far from clean, but it was water. Glenna took off her trousers and shirt, gratefully wiping the grime from her face and body.

"They're bringin' ye a gown," Nessa said. She went to the door, peered outside, and nodded, thanking the guard. She returned, carrying a folded dress. "This should fit ye fine."

Glenna had no argument with pulling the dress on. Her old clothes were so dirty they made her itch. The gown was loose around her waist and chest, but relatively clean.

"Thank ye, Nessa, for tendin' me so well."

Nessa smiled. "I'm glad to do it, child. We're all of us here together, aye?" She frowned. "Oh, speakin' o' which, think nothin' of Lorna. She's a cranky ol' sow, but more talk than bite. I've no idea of her story, but she seems the type to have been angry her whole life. I advise ye to keep yer distance just to avoid her spite. Ye canna make Lorna smile. It's no' possible."

"Nessa?" The voice was quiet, tentative, and yet Glenna whirled around, immediately defensive.

"Oh, Brenda, my love. Come in, dearie." Nessa shot Glenna an unreadable glance and Glenna decided to wait and see what it meant. A pretty, dark-haired girl, not yet in her twenties from what Glenna could guess, stepped like a mouse into the room, eyes wide.

"I couldna find ye," she said quietly.

"I'm only here, hen. Come an' say hallo to Glenna, aye?"

Brenda glanced around, as if expecting the walls to jump out at her, then slid quickly to Nessa's side. Her smile was wary. "Hallo, Glenna. I hope ye slept fine last night."

Glenna smiled back. "Well enough, thank ye."

Brenda crouched by Nessa's feet, then sat, apparently planning to stay in place. Nessa's smile was gentle, almost apologetic. She spoke to Brenda but her eyes held Glenna's.

"There now," she said. "Ye're fine, aye?"

Brenda nodded quickly, but Glenna couldn't help noticing how the girl rocked in place, staring straight at the floor as if hypnotised.

"What did ye see, Brenda, my love?"

"Sergeant Jennings," she whispered.

Nessa flicked her eyebrows at Glenna, communicating silently. "There now, pet. We've spoken of Jennings. All ye must do is keep yer eyes down an' give the man a curtsy, then walk around. He only needs to think he's the king is all. Costs ye nothin' to do that."

Brenda nodded again, still rocking. Nessa shrugged at Glenna. "Shall we find some breakfast then, Brenda? A wee spot o' parritch wouldna go amiss."

Staying in Nessa's shadow for the first two days seemed the wisest course of action, and from that vantage point Glenna quickly decided her place among the women, instinctively following their lead when it came to the fort and its guards. Lorna and Nessa seemed to have been there the longest, and they all knew the ins and outs of the place. They were kept relatively busy, cleaning up after the soldiers when necessary, working in the kitchen, sewing and doing odd jobs. Occasionally Aline was called away when an injury happened.

At other times the women were left to themselves. Glenna adopted one spot along the wall, on the other side of the women's cell, where she'd sit and think by herself. It was the only time she had enough alone space around her that she could grieve and talk with Dougal. In a hidden gesture of rebellion, she used a rusted nail she'd found to carve their names into the bottom of a post, large enough that she could read it from a few paces away. *Glenna loves Dougal.* She cut the letters carefully and cleanly and read them to herself every time she walked near.

"For you, my love," she whispered and kissed her fingers, then set them on the letters. "Ye're only gone in the flesh. I feel ye wi' me still. Never leave."

CHAPTER 31

Teaching a Lesson in Humility

Less than a month passed before Sergeant Jennings came to their cell, bearing news. "You ladies are shipping out tomorrow," he informed them.

Glenna and the others exchanged puzzled glances.

"How's that?" Lorna demanded, her usual snarl unsure.

"You are to go to the colonies, work for folk out there."

Glenna studied the sergeant's expression, searching for a better explanation. His eyes shifted slightly in her direction, then flicked away.

"Work?" Glenna asked.

"They call it indentured servitude," he said, his words cold and emotionless. "The folks in the colonies require workers. You are criminals. Therefore, you shall work for them."

There was no need to argue the question of their being criminals. They were criminals based on their nationality, and there was nothing any of them could do to contest that. They were indeed guilty of being Scottish. Glenna's stomach clenched, and she felt suddenly dizzy as the ramifications of what he'd just said came to her. She couldn't get on a ship again. The memory of the only other ship she'd known came to her and the reek hit her like a punch. She choked, clutching the wall to keep her balance. No one noticed. They were still asking questions of Jennings, but he had no more answers to share.

"Have we a choice?" Nessa asked wryly.

Sergeant Jennings snorted. "No. You go or you hang. Look," he said, looking slightly sympathetic and gesturing vaguely around the empty walls of their cell. "It can't be worse than here. Look at how you live. Like animals. The six of you are dirty and half-starved. At least there you'd have something different."

No one agreed with him, but no one disagreed, either. In truth, he was right. Glenna would go mad if she had to live here much longer. It reminded her far too much of the cold stone walls of Tilbury Fort. There at least she'd had Joseph, Dougal, and John as companions. Here she had only these women with whom to live, and she had never had to do that before. Glenna's whole life had been spent in the company of boys and men, never women. She didn't understand them and they didn't seem to understand her, either. And though there were male prisoners here as well, they were not permitted to mix. It was a strange feeling, not fitting in with one's own sex.

What could it be like, living in the colonies? More of the same? No. The sergeant had mentioned work, and here they did practically nothing. Work of what kind she didn't know, but Jennings might be right. Work anywhere might be better than existing in this miserable island of nothing.

Later that night, Glenna stepped outside the cell, tired of listening to the women and their silly talk that went nowhere. For an

hour or so, she sat in the cool evening air by the carving of their
names, knees bent within the circle of her arms, staring up at the
wash of stars. Their light was uninterrupted by even one cloud and
its brilliance flooded the yard. The moon was practically full, and
the thought made her sad. She loved full moons, loved what they
did to her: helping her see the magic in everything around her, making her laugh at things she didn't usually see as particularly funny.
More than that, she loved what they did to Dougal, prompting him
to puff like a cockerel, strutting as if to impress her. She chuckled.
As if he'd ever needed to do that. There was no one in Glenna's heart
but him, never would be.

God, she loved him. She caught her breath, surprised by the
unbidden jerk to her heart. She loved his eyes, those lips, the strength
of those always warm hands. His heart had owned her from the first
time they'd spoken, when she'd still been Aidan, and all she'd ever
wanted was to be near him. Her Dougal had a heart so big she had
always feared she'd never completely fill it. But he filled hers until
it overflowed, making her into a person almost worthy of him. She
still loved him now that he was dead, though she felt incomplete.
Sometimes the sensation of loss was so intense it was as if someone
had reached within her and yanked out whatever she needed to move
forward. It was more than her heart. It was . . . more.

She sighed and dropped her chin, staring at the dark gray homespun of her dress and plucking at its rough fibres. The material was
worn and stained, but stubbornly surviving. Glenna was so tired of
fighting. Every heartbeat prompted her forward, though her body
wanted to collapse, roll into a ball, and leave life behind. What was
the point of continuing if all life ever brought was pain and strife?
She tried not to cry these days. She didn't want to appear weak. Not
around the other women, not around Jennings. But oh, it hurt.
Sometimes during the day she could almost forget about him, dis-

tracted by whatever inane job the soldiers assigned to her. But he was usually there somewhere, watching, his bright blue eyes always interested in whatever she did. For all those years he'd watched her, and it had always been a thrill to know she fascinated him as much as he did her.

No, there was no one in Glenna's world but Dougal. And that meant there was no one left. She ran her thumb lovingly over the carving of his name and stared up at the sky, letting tears trickle down her cheeks, but she didn't make a sound.

That's how she was sitting when she heard a whimper. She frowned and peered around the yard, but saw nothing out of the ordinary. The place was dark, the only light coming from a few flickering lanterns hanging on the walls. She heard it again, but this time the sound formed words.

"No, please," she heard. A tiny sob, afraid to be released, unable to be contained. And not something Glenna could ignore. "Please don't."

She wiped her cheeks and got silently to her feet, then crept toward the pitiful sound, taking care to stay out of the spill of moonlight. The voice was coming from the other side of the armoury, a long gray building suffused with the stink of gunpowder. Glenna slid her hand along the wall until she reached its corner, then glanced behind and around her, making sure she was the only one to have heard the sounds. Then, very slowly, she edged her face around the corner and peered toward the sound.

It was Brenda, the young, nervous girl Glenna thought was a bit mad. She could only tell by her voice, because she couldn't see the girl's face. It was hidden behind the bulk of Sergeant Jennings, who was stripped down to breeches and shirt. He had her pressed against the wall and the tips of her fingers curled around his arms, gripping defensively. His voice was a low growl from where Glenna stood, the hungry noise of a predator, proud of his catch.

An involuntary shudder passed through Glenna. No, she didn't understand women. But she understood men, and she understood what it was like to be on the wrong side of a man's violent intentions.

Fortunately, Jennings appeared to relish the foreplay, terrifying Brenda with low threats while she squirmed under his grip. He hadn't yet gotten far enough in the proceedings that Glenna couldn't do something about it. The stone wall felt wet against Glenna's palm. She wondered absently if it was slick from dew, then realised it was only her own sweat. She stared at Jennings, chewing her lip as she did so. When she'd first arrived, she had felt beaten, vulnerable, and lost, too intimidated to take him on. Now that she knew him better, she knew she could kill him if required. If she did this thing, she would have to do it right. Dougal had shown her how.

Then again, if she killed him, she wouldn't have to worry about the colonies. She'd hang.

On the other hand, if she only injured him, he could accuse her, resulting in a similar punishment. How could she disable a man but leave him unable to talk about it?

Glenna smiled, remembering another lesson Dougal had taught her. A quick, effective lesson in humiliation. Granted, it had been easier to practice when Dougal wore his loose breeks, or his kilt, or nothing at all. Glenna watched Jennings's sturdy body before her, seeing how his breeks clung to his body. It required very little imagination. She squinted a bit, studying her quarry, then crept closer, staying purposefully out of Brenda's view. She didn't want the silly girl to give away the game. Glenna was going to have to move very quickly and with great precision when she did this.

She stopped a foot away from Jennings, breathing as quietly as possible. Not that it mattered. The man's hoarse voice never stopped spouting vile suggestions. In order to do this right, Glenna needed him to face her. She closed her eyes and pictured Dougal, wishing he could hear her, wherever he was. *Help me wi' this, would ye?*

She took a breath for courage and dove in, tapping Jennings on the shoulder. "Pardon me, Sergeant."

Everything happened very quickly after that. Jennings spun in place, eyes wide. Glenna swung her hand up hard between the man's tight breeks and squeezed. He made a high-pitched, squealing sound and his eyes bugged out. Glenna felt his weight sag against her hand, but she didn't let him collapse. Not yet. Instead, trying not to breathe through her nose, she brought her face close to his.

"Ye have no right to interfere wi' this woman or any other, Sergeant."

"I'll see you hang," he wheezed, then convulsed slightly as she tightened her grip. Oh, what a weakness these men had. *Thank ye, Dougal, my love.*

"I dinna think so, my lad. Rather embarrassin', this, is it no'? Ye'd have a time trying to explain how a wee thing like me"—she released her hold and he fell helplessly to the ground—"brought ye to yer knees. Wouldna look good on ye, Jennings. I canna see ye gettin' any type of promotion wi' this on yer record."

Jennings, on all fours in the dirt, glared at her. His eyes still leaked tears, his pale face was slick with sweat. In his eyes swam pure hatred, and she was suddenly relieved they'd be sailing the next day.

She held out a hand to Brenda, and the girl was instantly pressed against her side, thankfully mute. "I'll just take the lass back to our warm, inviting cell, shall I? An' we'll all forget this ever happened. After all, we're on a ship in the mornin'. We'll no' be able to get ye in any trouble then. Come, Brenda, let's to bed."

CHAPTER 32

Back to the Sea

In the morning Brenda offered half of her breakfast to Glenna. "*Taing*, Glenna," she whispered.

Glenna shook her head. "Ye're welcome, but there's no need for that. I'm only glad I could help."

"Please," Brenda insisted, pressing the offering into Glenna's hand.

After they'd eaten, the prisoners were taken into the yard, where they bunched together like cattle going to market. Brenda clung to Nessa's arm, hiding behind her whenever possible, and Nessa continued to smile at the others in an attempt to ease the fears of everyone, including herself. Bonnie hugged herself, as she often did, but only her eyes moved, sliding warily from side to side and taking in the activity around them. Glenna changed her mind. Not cattle, she decided, but deer. Frightened, confused, cornered, and helpless.

No one made any speeches or informed the prisoners about what was going on. The soldiers seemed to know, though, for they barely spoke as they went about their business. Eventually the prisoners, men and women alike, were sorted into lines. The women were kept together, which was a kind of relief, though it did nothing to expel the worry clinging to their nerves. Nessa did her best to reassure the others, telling them all would be well, but only Brenda seemed to be listening. Except Glenna couldn't tell if the girl really was listening, because her scared, flickering eyes seemed everywhere at once.

The women stayed together, keeping pace with the men as they marched for hours toward port. The cries of circling, diving gulls, their arched wings startlingly white against a clear blue sky, were the first clue that they were drawing near. Then the air changed, becoming thicker with its essence of saltwater and fish. When Glenna smelled the sea, bile rose in her throat. Her heart raced when she spied the masts looming ahead, like fragile crucifixes rolling on an endless sea. They reminded her of a graveyard, and she fought the urge to bolt. The soldiers wouldn't be patient on a day like this. They would kill any prisoners attempting escape.

But the ship terrified her to the soles of her ragged shoes. Some might breathe in the heavy salt air, find adventure in its scent, but Glenna smelled hell. The prison ship she'd survived with Dougal had stunk of the defeated, its floors and walls covered with the muddy waste of prisoners. Under that filth, beneath the slippery floorboards on which they'd tried to maintain their balance for so many months, the stream of salt air had constantly flowed, a reminder that even if she had been able to escape the morass of starving, dying pariahs, there was nowhere she could go.

When the ships came into view, rolling over a sea laced by white-tipped waves, a mixed reaction bubbled among the prisoners. Fear was prevalent: fear of the unknown, or at least of the little known. Rumours had flown about the colonies, about how they were inhabitable for civilized folk, how they were overrun by cannibalistic savages and wild beasts, all of whom waited hungrily on the shores for fresh meat from overseas. Glenna tried to imagine it in a different light. Out of necessity, she started to picture this wildness, to see the hidden glens and forests, and the image of Aberfeldy came to mind, bringing with it bittersweet memories of her life with Dougal.

She didn't think she was afraid of the new world. Because of her life in the woods with Joseph, then later with Dougal, she knew more than most people did about how to stay alive in the wild. She sensed opportunity. All she would have to do was get her lay of the land, then escape whatever this indentured service was. Then she'd be all right. She'd survive. She'd build a life after that.

But to get there, she would have to step on deck, then submit to the inevitable plunge into the hold. It was like asking her to go back to the men who had killed Dougal and ask them to do it again.

Aline came alongside Glenna and they walked awhile without speaking. Aline was a little taller than Glenna and probably in her late forties. She seemed a smart woman, but one who held secrets very tightly to her chest. Well, who didn't these days? It was only that while many of the others mourned all they had lost, seeking support and sympathy, Aline kept quiet. Glenna liked her company, as she liked Nessa's, though she always preferred to be alone.

The prisoners followed the road down a slope, headed toward the docks, and Glenna fought the lump in her throat. She would not cry. Would *not*. But oh, how her feet ached to turn the other way and run. Every muscle bunched, wanting to go, to slither through the others and vanish into the familiar blackness of trees and rocks.

"Ye've been to sea afore, I reckon," Aline said.

Glenna glanced at her, startled. "Aye, I have. How do ye ken that?"

"Yer face says so. I've been there as well. I ken what it is ye dinna wish to see again."

They walked without speaking for a few more paces, the road crackling beneath the worn feet of dozens of prisoners. Over a hundred men and women, Glenna guessed. Half of the number who had been onboard the other prison ship, but that didn't mean it would be any better. The ships ahead of her looked slightly smaller than the other one, though that could have been her imagination.

"They'd catch ye an' hang ye if ye ran, aye? Ye'd no' get far."

Glenna snorted, impressed at how well Aline could read her thoughts. Her mind flickered with a long-ago memory of Dougal, confessing to her that he could hear the thoughts of men. Ah, Dougal. "I wonder if a noose would be preferable to that ship."

"No. I dinna suppose it is." Aline frowned and shook her head, observing Glenna closely. "I'd ne'er choose certain death over a possible chance at life. Never."

Glenna frowned at her, curious about this sudden philosophical discussion. "An' ye've had occasion to choose before now?"

"I have."

Questions pressed against Glenna's lips, but she held them back. If Aline wished to share, she would. In her own time. It wasn't as if Glenna had told any of them about her life, either. All they knew about her was that Dougal, whom she called her husband, was dead, and she'd been arrested after felling a deer. Nothing more.

Aline swallowed noticeably beside her, readying herself to spit words she obviously despised.

"Ye needn't say more," Glenna assured her. "I've stories I've no wish to share, like you."

"'Tis only . . ." Aline shrugged and stared straight ahead. "There have been times when I suppose death would have been a better option. It would certainly have meant less pain for me in the end. But the whole time I kept thinkin' there must be a reason for it all. I promised myself I would survive and discover it." She chewed on her lower lip then took a breath. "I was on my own in our cottage, ye see. Two years past or so. My menfolk all gone, my daughters, thank God, off and married. The soldiers . . . well, I believe there were five or six o' them came calling."

Glenna closed her eyes, suddenly nauseous. She tried to compare any of her horrors to the one Aline now shared and found her complaints paled. She said nothing.

Aline's gaze travelled far away, beyond the bobbing masts. She swallowed, remembering. "Took me a good while to heal. There was no one about to tend me, so I made do. I kept thinkin' there had to be a reason I wasna dead. They could have killed me the whole time, but they only—" She dropped her gaze and took another deep breath, sounding tired. "Well, they tried to kill my spirit, callin' me Prince Charles's whore an' all, but I wouldna let them do it."

She took Glenna's hand in hers, linking their fingers as they walked. "Ye see, I believe the spirit is the only part of a person that canna be taken. Not unless it is given. And I will never give that away. No' to them, no' to anyone."

A tear slid down Glenna's cheek. Aline glanced at her, then away, back toward the sea. "I dinna tell ye this to make ye sorry for me, Glenna. But when we are in the black o' that ship and all the folk around us are sick an' dyin' an' moanin' for death, I want ye to keep my thought in yer head. Yer man was killed, but ye were not. There is a reason, an' if ye let them take yer fight from ye, ye've let them win, an' ye've lost yer reason."

Glenna sniffed quietly. "Have ye found yer reason, Aline?"

She shrugged. "Could be it was just now, savin' ye from a hangin'. Could be it was any o' those men I helped to heal at the fort. Could be it is yet to come. Or it could be all o' those things."

Glenna shook her head, considering the possibilities. "I couldna be as strong as all that."

"Aye, ye could. I heard what ye did for wee Brenda at the fort. She's a wee slip of a lass. If Jennings had done what ye prevented, well . . . She's already lost half her mind as it is, poor thing."

"But this ship—"

"Ye've reason, Glenna. Ye must believe ye've reason enough to survive this journey an' make it in the colonies. Ye'll ken when the time comes, an' then ye'll be glad ye fought back."

The ship's hold was worse than she remembered, and the journey farther. The worst part of it, in Glenna's mind, was that their hands were shackled the entire way. She didn't understand the need for that. What could they possibly do that would necessitate using chains? But the wrists of even the smallest of them clinked together the entire way, a constant reminder that they were no more than cargo.

Food was provided once every two weeks, and those who couldn't eat slowly enough fell easy prey to illness when meagre portions ran out. The darkness hid any idea of day or night, but when they took their mandatory daily walk about the deck, they gratefully absorbed the reminder that life existed outside of the ship, though it mostly appeared as a flat, endless horizon.

Aline and Glenna rarely talked about their pasts, but they did talk more. Glenna understood. Aline was the kind who didn't usually share personal memories, but had done so only because she felt it would help Glenna. There was no need to dwell on history. Glenna had been starved for intelligent conversation ever since Dougal's demise, and she found it with Aline. If Glenna mentioned a book she'd read with Dougal, Aline usually knew of it, though she'd never learned to read. Her mother had died when Aline was born, and her aunt had raised her. Aline and Glenna discussed the books they recalled and occasionally shared the stories with the others. If Glenna wanted to philosophise at all, Aline was more than willing to take up the opposing side. Bit by bit, the women learned more about each other, and Glenna eventually shared her story. Aline was delighted to hear about Glenna's masquerade as a boy.

"How canny of ye!" she exclaimed.

Glenna had frowned. "It wasna my idea. My mother—"

"Oh aye, but ye could have dropped the costume later. Instead, ye survived as a whole other person. So ye've been more than one person all along, Glenna. How wonderful."

Glenna still didn't see it that way, but enjoyed Aline's optimistic attitude about everything. After three months at sea, she was afraid, suddenly, of leaving the boat and leaving their friendship behind.

"Will we be separated, do ye suppose, when we land?"

Aline's expression sobered at that. "Aye, I think maybe so."

Glenna took her hands. "I want ye to know that ye're my first lady friend. Aye," she said, grinning at Aline's expression. "My very first. An' ye'll always be dear to me. If we are to be separated, I will carry ye wi' me, for I shall need yer strength, I reckon. Ye shall always have mine as well."

The older woman blinked quickly. "That means so much to me, Glenna. Thank ye. Ye'll be wi' me as well, my dear. An' who knows? Maybe we'll no' be far from each other after all."

On the morning they landed at the port in Virginia, Glenna felt ill with anxiety. Though she could see nothing new in the darkness of the hold, the sounds over their heads were clear. The deck pounded with activity and voices were raised, calling out, she assumed, to someone on shore. Everything in her life was about to change again, and it was, as usual, something over which she had no control.

All six of the women had survived the journey, though both Bonnie and Brenda were practically mute with exhaustion and hunger by the journey's end. A blanket of misery wrapped around them all, but the slightest chance of hope raised their spirits. As the soldiers came to retrieve the prisoners, the women held hands, then kissed each other's cheeks and squinted against the light of day as they headed wordlessly up to the deck.

CHAPTER 33

Another Role to Play

The port was noisy, a strange sight to see after so long spent in the dark. It would have been more of a shock had the sun been out, but the morning was swathed in gray by a stubborn fog. It closed over the port so only bits and pieces of dock and buildings could be seen from the ship, as if it kept secrets to itself. The deck of the ship was busy as well, the hustle of sailors tying the ship down and stowing away sails. The gangplank had been lowered, and both soldiers and seamen worked together, transferring cargo to the docks.

The women were led to a large barrel of water in a corner of the deck and were told to wash their faces and manage their hair, make themselves presentable in public. It was the first time in months anyone had worried about appearance above survival, and the women were quick to run fingers through their matted hair and piece together tattered gowns. There was no mirror on board, so the women were each other's critics. Glenna waited for the others to finish before she cleaned herself. The cool water felt good on her skin, and though it smelled nothing like the clear stream water back in Aberfeldy, it seemed relatively fresh, so someone had apparently brought it from the dock that morning. When she was done, she pulled out the tie in her hair, resettled it as best she could into a roll at the back of her neck, then joined a similarly clean Nessa at the rail.

"Quite a place, isn't it?"

The other women nodded. Beside them, Brenda spoke for the first time in days. "I dinna like it."

Nessa put one arm around the girl and squeezed her against her side. "There now, child. Ye canna say ye dinna like it if ye dinna try it first. Like tastin' a new food, aye? Ye'll be fine here."

"Will ye stay wi' me?"

Nessa exchanged a quick glance with Aline, then looked back at Brenda. "I think not, hen. I dinna ken for sure, but I imagine they'll send us to different places."

Glenna didn't think the girl could have gotten any paler, but she did in that moment. And she stopped speaking again.

"Right!" they heard, and turned as one toward the speaker, a large man in uniform, addressing them from the higher deck. "You will be taken down in small groups and will say nothing. Nothing. Do you hear? Any speaking will result in a severe flogging."

His audience was so weak Glenna doubted any of them could survive a flogging, so they did nothing but nod.

"Yes. Good. Now. Ladies first, shall we?" He gave the women a short bow and gestured, indicating they should accompany two wigged soldiers. Aline was the first of them to step onto the gang-plank, followed closely by Brenda and Bonnie. Nessa held Brenda's hand as they crossed over the water. Glenna and Lorna were the last two to cross.

The activity was even more bewildering once they were on the ground, caught up in the middle of it. Passersby jostled past, dogs sniffed and barked, people scurried by, carrying baskets and cases of whatever. Glenna and the other women faced the first soldier, whose eyes quickly passed over them as if evaluating goods of some kind. Then he stepped forward and grabbed Glenna by one arm. She stumbled forward, her chains cutting the calloused skin of her wrists.

"Up there," the soldier ordered, indicating a raised platform.

Glenna frowned at him. "Why?"

"Weren't you told *not* to speak? Get up there, woman."

Glenna glanced back at her friends, who shrugged, looking helpless. Clearly no one, as usual, knew what was going on. With no other choice, Glenna stepped onto the platform where a bald, portly man waited. He flicked a cursory smile at her, then turned his attention to a growing crowd of onlookers.

"Ah. Yes. Quite right. Here we have the prize of *The Edinburgh,* a sweet young thing, maybe twenty years old. Quiet, agreeable, and as you can see . . ." He turned back and, in one quick motion, tugged up the side of her skirt to reveal a strong thigh. Glenna gasped and slammed her shackles at the man's hands, but he was quick. Evidently he'd done this before. He grinned and muttered, "Keep quiet, girly. It's not worth a thrashing." He returned to his audience. "As you can see from those pretty legs, she's no weakling. I wager she's a good worker, if you know what I mean." He beamed and pointedly winked at the crowd. "So let's start the bidding. What do I hear?"

Glenna could do nothing but gape as numbers were thrown at the man, along with questions.

"Is she a virgin?"

"Wha—" Glenna's objection was met by a sharp jab of the man's elbow, rendering her speechless.

"I feel certain she is," the man said, nodding at the caller. There were scatterings of laughter around the crowd.

"Pah! A looker like that ain't no virgin!" someone called.

"Who cares?" shouted another.

"Does it matter?" asked the auctioneer. He nodded to an assistant, a burly, bearded man who had materialised behind Glenna. The assistant gripped Glenna's hands while the auctioneer grabbed her bodice, tearing it straight down and to the side, revealing all. Glenna shrieked and wrestled with her captor, trying to free her hands, but she was helpless in his grip. An appreciative murmur rose from the crowd and numbers started flying more quickly at the auctioneer.

Tears surged down Glenna's face and fell, unobstructed, onto her bare skin as she struggled against her captors. She could hear the women behind her, the sweet, pathetic moaning of Brenda as she realised it would be her turn soon. Nessa's voice, outwardly calm, vibrated with a trill of fear.

"Does she read?" The question cut through the noise in a deep bass tone.

The little round man turned to Glenna, frowning. "Nod or shake your head. Can you read?" Glenna nodded and the man turned back to the crowd. "She reads."

The same commanding voice bellowed out a new figure, silencing the other bidders. Glenna was tugged off the platform just as Lorna was brought on. It was the first time Glenna had ever seen Lorna look vulnerable, and as much as she disliked the woman, she hated the sight of her weakness even more.

The soldier finally undid the chains on Glenna's wrists as she was handed over to her new master. Money changed hands. The man didn't look her in the eye, only stepped back and draped a heavy black cloak over her shoulders, covering the ruined remains of her gown. She turned, looking for the owner of the cloak, and met the cool gaze of a solid, serious-looking man. He was middle-aged, his

eyes maybe a foot higher than her own. He wore a black wig under
a tricorne, an austere black waistcoat, and when she looked down,
she saw the buckles on his shoes were a good, polished silver. A man
of money had just purchased her. She didn't know how she felt about
that.

She spun around when she heard a yelp and saw Lorna, stripped
similarly to how she had been. The woman had a weather-worn,
cynical face, with eyes hard as rock. But her body was lush and
young. Voices were raised again and Glenna watched three of the
bidders call hard against each other. The eventual high bidder was
a large woman who shuffled proprietarily through the crowd, revealing a copper red crown of curls and a dark green satin gown. Most
of her breasts were revealed, bubbling over her bodice, and as subtle
as the large beauty mark painted on her chin. Glenna met Lorna's
eyes as they both realised Lorna's future, and thought she had never
seen so much loss of spirit happen all at once. It was Aline's voice
that returned to her then, her tireless need to continue on for whatever reason. *Just survive*, she thought as loudly as she could, then
turned away as Lorna was pulled off the platform and deposited into
her new master's hands.

Glenna glanced up at her own master—that was going to be a
hard concept for her to accept—and didn't see the same sort of
threat. The man was watching the platform where Brenda now stood,
shaking so hard she looked as if she might collapse. Glenna couldn't
bear the thought of what was coming. Bids came quickly and loudly,
men wanting to bring home this young treasure who quite possibly
was a virgin.

"Please, sir," Glenna whispered. Her master glanced down
quickly, surprised to hear her voice. "She's just a girl, sir. If ye were
to bring her wi' ye, she'd work hard. If only she could walk from
this wi' her gown still intact—"

"She doesn't look strong," the man said, dismissing her. He had an accent, sharp and almost guttural. "I need strong."

"Oh, but—"

His eyes swiveled to glare down at her, black as the darkest night in winter and just as threatening. She stared back, completely confused, and while they were held in this moment, the crowd cheered again. Brenda screamed, then bawled like a naked babe before dozens of hungry men. The same redheaded woman was back. She'd left Lorna with her man in the back and now came with eyes gleaming to claim this promise of treasure. Brenda's eyes, white with terror, darted desperately over the crowd, hoping for rescue. There was none. Her slender back disappeared amid the throng and Glenna choked back her grief.

Somewhere in the town, a bell chimed ten o'clock. The man beside her glared impatiently at the remaining women.

"This one looks strong," the man muttered, and called out immediately when Aline came to the platform. His bid was high enough that everyone around him hushed and Aline was led directly to him, her gown in one secure piece.

"This is enough. Come. Do not speak."

CHAPTER 34

The Student Teaches

The women clasped hands and Glenna inwardly celebrated having Aline with her. It could have been so much worse for both of them, and now Glenna had someone she could believe in. A friend. They exchanged a glance of such intense relief they both almost laughed. Without a word, they followed the man to his fine black carriage, led by a matching pair of impatient bay horses, and climbed inside.

They sat on one side of the carriage, the man on the other. He fell asleep in almost the first moment when they'd settled themselves on the tapestried cushions. The countryside raced by the carriage windows in a blur while the women gawked with amazement. The fog was fading quickly, and now all they could see was the green and gold of oaks, birches, and maples as they raced past. After riding the rise and fall of the infinitely black sea for so long and sitting in a miserable heap within the damp cold walls of the fort before that, the autumn colours of the New World were almost overwhelming.

After a half hour or so, the women leaned back in their seats and glanced nervously at each other, unsure whether or not they were allowed to speak yet.

"What do ye think?" Glenna whispered.

Aline shrugged. "I've no idea." She snuck a glance at the man opposite them. "Seems well enough, I suppose."

The thought brought the faces of the others back to Glenna, the realisation of how close she'd come to living her life on her back.

"If ye pray, ye'd best do so for wee Brenda. An' Lorna as well."

By now Glenna was used to her friend saying what she'd been thinking. "An' we've no idea of the others."

"Nessa will be fine," Aline said, though she looked dubious. "But Bonnie . . ." The words drifted unfinished through cracks around the windows and were sucked away into the fiery autumnal trees.

The trees in Aberfeldy would be golden by now as well. The oaks would be bathed in cloaks of red and yellow, dropping their leaves on the little home she and Dougal had left behind. As the carriage rolled farther into the countryside, Glenna brought the images of the little cabin to her mind, picturing the furniture Dougal had crafted, the bed with its finely carved wood posts, the thick mattress he had bought for her birthday. They'd never actually known her real birthdate, so Dougal had decided it for her. He'd come to her on the most beautiful autumn afternoon she'd ever seen, his arms full of goldenrods and sedum, his eyes dancing as he wished her a happy birthday. He'd decided the perfection of the day was due to the fact that it marked Glenna's arrival on earth. She had giggled and cried and he had gathered her up against him, kissing the salty tears from her cheeks, telling her he loved her and always would.

Do you still, Dougal? Is there love where you are?

The women settled into the uneven rhythm of the carriage, lulled by the hoofbeats always ten feet away. Without needing to say another word, they fell asleep.

Glenna awoke sometime later. The sun was past the midway point, so it was early afternoon. They'd probably slept the better part of three hours. As awkward and uncomfortable as these quarters were, they were a huge improvement upon the ship. And the air, clean and fresh, smelled more like grass than salt. It was a comfort Glenna had almost forgotten. She leaned over and nudged Aline from her nap.

The man sitting across from them still hadn't spoken, but was awake. He sat upright, glaring at his surroundings as if they had somehow offended him. His wig had been removed and set on the bench beside him, the black and gray hair beneath combed severely back from a well-defined widow's peak. During the journey he had unbuttoned the silver buttons of his waistcoat, and when he finally seemed to notice the women, he did them up again. He studied Glenna and Aline with a look bordering on disapproval, but Glenna wasn't offended. It seemed to be his regular expression. She offered a tentative smile, inviting conversation. Aline kept quiet. He narrowed his eyes at Glenna and at one point he looked as if he might speak, opening his mouth slightly and squinting with thought. Then he thought better of it, snapping his mouth shut and looking back outside. At a loss, she turned her head and looked out her own window.

Eventually they slowed, and the voice of the driver rang across the pebbled drive of a vast courtyard. Both women leaned forward, curious, then sat abruptly back, eyes wide with amazement. The house they approached was more than a house. It appeared to be a plantation of some kind, and its red brick face was more vivid than any house Glenna had seen before. When the horses pulled them to the front of the magnificent home, the carriage was welcomed by the main building, but more outbuildings stood behind, waiting to be introduced. When they stopped, Glenna stared at the huge, ornate door, freshly painted white, then counted three floors, with twenty white-framed windows in all.

The man cleared his throat and they turned expectantly toward him. "Stay here," was all he said, then he climbed through the carriage door when it was opened by a small, smartly dressed black slave.

Other than some of the deckhands, Glenna had never before seen a dark-skinned person. And to see one dressed in such finery was startling to say the least. With his wig firmly back in place, the new master stalked directly to the front door while Glenna and Aline watched. The little black slave, topped with a clean white, ribboned wig, closed the door carefully, nodded briefly at the driver, and the carriage moved on.

No more than five minutes down a small lane, the carriage stopped by a modest building, this one constructed of wood. They were greeted by a squat, round woman, her ebony skin a sharp contrast to the white cap she wore, which strained to hold in her curly black hair. The woman tilted her head to the side and folded her arms over a massive chest. She nodded slowly, taking in the two dazed faces staring through the carriage windows.

"Y'all be the new girls. Come now. We'll clean you up."

Glenna stared at the woman, mouth slightly open. She was mesmerised by the low, easy sound of her voice, the way the Southern words rolled through her lips.

The woman's eyes bulged slightly and she raised her voice a few notes higher. "What is it, child? Y'all gonna sit there all bloomin' day an' stare, or is you comin' inside so's I can dig you up somethin' to eat?"

Glenna shook off her daze and followed Aline out of the carriage. The woman ushered them into the house, and they stopped just inside, looking around at the sparse but clean furniture. The wooden boards underfoot were smooth from wear, but Glenna didn't see any dirt or dust. She wasn't used to standing on a wooden floor, since any home she'd had in Scotland was over a dirt floor, and felt suddenly as if she trespassed.

The woman noticed Glenna's discomfort and nodded. "Dat's right. We keep this house clean as a whistle. Y'all keep your nasty dirt outside the house." A wide wooden rocking chair creaked as the woman lowered herself onto it. She started to rock, back and forth, while she looked up at them, linking pudgy fingers on her lap.

"I'm Bess. This here is where we eat. You, me, an' some more. They all out harvestin'. You might see 'em later afore dey falls dead asleep. Which one of you be the teacher?"

Aline and Glenna weren't prepared for the question. They said nothing, and the woman sighed, exasperated. "Which one of you can read?"

"I can," Glenna said.

"Good. So you's the teacher. Massuh Schmidt gots eight little angels." She gave Glenna a wink. "He wants them all readin' an' writin' an' talkin' English good as can be."

She turned to Aline and eyed her top to bottom, hands braced on her broad hips. She nodded. "An' you'd be for the fields. Massuh wanted two whiteys to keep each other quiet an' share a room. Didn't figure it'd do to mix with us darkies," she said with a chuckle. "Good to see he found a strong one. I ain't got no use for no babes out in them fields."

She stared at them a little longer, big eyes narrowed. "You'll be hungry. Made some cornbread an' kept it for you. Sausage, too." Glenna swallowed reflexively and Bess's wide mouth smiled. "You ain't had nothin' to eat in a long time, I don't figure. Come along then. Y'all done found yourself a good place to live. Y'all are gonna work hard, that for sure. But here we always gots a bed and food."

Her face instantly hardened. "An' we don't mess with no fools. Any trouble out of y'all an' you'll feel it on your backside for a long, long time. You understand me, my little white lambs?"

They nodded quickly.

"Good. Now come sit your pretty selves an' we'll find you somethin' to fatten you up. Don't look like you ate much on dat ship. Den you'll need to wash up an' get some of that stink offa you."

Bess appeared to be telling the truth. So far, it didn't seem like such a bad life. The cornbread was delicious, the milk warm and thick. Bess showed them their house, four walls containing nothing but two narrow beds, and left them while she tended to someone or something. The women sat on the edge of the beds and stared at each other.

"Soft bed," Aline said. She sighed and pressed one palm into the mattress. "I reckon I've no' seen a bed in, oh, maybe six months. An' it were none so clean as this."

Glenna lay down, closing her eyes as her head sank into the cotton-covered straw. "God, I'm weary." She draped one forearm over her eyes and quietly wept, giving in to the exhaustion, the relief, the confusion, the grief. Neither woman spoke, and both soon melted into sleep.

Too soon, Bess appeared in their room, bellowing for them to get up. A tall, lean black woman had come with Bess, expressionless and plodding, and after shaking her head and sniffing with disapproval, had taken Aline away with her. Bess led Glenna to the main house, then in through the servants' entrance in the back. They took a quick right into a large, sun-drenched room where beams of dust sparkled over two rows of chairs with desks. A larger chair and table were positioned at the front of the room. *My desk,* she thought with amazement. Closer to the door stood a plush, red velvet armchair, looking out of place, and Glenna wondered at its presence.

Bess introduced her to the room. "This be the schoolin' room. Now step inside, that's right, and wait here, quiet-like. I'll get the mistress."

Glenna stared around the room, transfixed not only by the clean, bright space, but also by the very idea of what she was about to do. Teach? When she'd first met Dougal, the closest she'd come to reading was staring with a kind of lust at a book someone else held. He had taught her, one word at a time, and she'd surprised even herself with how quickly she'd picked it up, though he'd laughed at her every time she mentioned that. *Ye've always been smart as a whip,* he'd said. *Ye just dinna believe it yerself.* After reading worked its way into her brain, feeding her hungry mind, there was no stopping her. She'd been a thorn in Dougal's side, begging him for more books every time they'd gone to town. The books he'd first read to her were later read through her own lips while he lay content beside her. Sometimes when they lay in bed at night, her pillow propped as close to the candle as she could manage, he'd rest his hand on her belly and she'd pick up the cue, absently massaging the tired, muscular forearm as she read. She remembered that solid arm, those beloved calloused fingers, so clearly. As if he were there with her. As if she could turn right this moment and smile up at him. *Look at me, Dougal! I'm a teacher!*

But there was no one there, no one with whom she could share the indescribable thrill racing through her. And when the diminutive mistress of the manor, the regal Frau Ursula Schmidt, swept into the room, salmon-coloured skirts swishing along the shiny, wood-planked floor, Glenna wasn't about to admit this was her first occasion to fill the role.

Frau Schmidt wasted no time getting to know Glenna before she rattled off a list of everything she required from her children's new teacher. "Everysing vill be English," she ordered. "No German. You understand?" Glenna nodded. She didn't know any German, so that was a good thing. "Ze children vill learn reading, writing, arithmetic, sewing, music—you know music, *ja*?"

"I sing, ma'am."

"Do you? Sing now. Show me." She waved one hand impatiently, gesturing for Glenna to go ahead, then sank into the armchair. Ah, thought Glenna. The mistress's chair for when she wanted to look in on lessons. The thought made her heart flip a little. What if she couldn't do this? What if the woman discovered what a fraud she was?

Then again, they'd only asked if she could read, not if she could teach. Glenna took a deep breath and listened hard for Dougal's encouragement. She was here and she had been placed in a very comfortable position, while some of the other women faced hellish lives Glenna tried not to imagine. She could do this. She would succeed and make Dougal proud, wherever he was.

The frau raised one thin brown eyebrow, waiting. Her lips were pursed, chin lifted so she could focus completely on Glenna. The tight expression was critical, Glenna could see, but curious.

Fortunately, Glenna's gift for singing was one thing she'd never questioned. Glenna had sung on demand before, though that had been either in taverns, on slave ships, in prisons, or in Dougal's bed. She took a moment, trying to recall something decent she could present to this woman. An old hymn came to mind, one she'd heard on the journey across, and she filled the velvet-curtained room with her nightingale voice.

For the beauty of the earth
For the glory of the skies,
For the love which from our birth
Over and around us lies.

Lord of all, to Thee we raise,
This our hymn of grateful praise.

Mistress Schmidt stared. Her hands, folded in her lap, were almost hidden within her voluminous skirts. "Is there more? Sing more!" she demanded.

For the beauty of each hour,
Of the day and of the night,
Hill and vale, and tree and flower,
Sun and moon, and stars of light.
Lord of all, to Thee we raise,
This our hymn of grateful praise.

The woman's expression softened while Glenna sang, her eyes closed. "Ah," she said, her voice like a sigh. "My husband has brought me a bird. But zis is lovely. My children vill sing like zis, *ja*?" Glenna bit her lip, but the woman chuckled. "*Nein*. I know zis is not what you can do. But it vould be nice." She frowned, thinking. "Maybe Clara can do zis. Ve shall see." She got to her feet and stepped toward Glenna. The women were almost on eye level, though Frau Schmidt was perhaps a finger shorter. "And now you shall meet ze children."

A black servant girl who had stood waiting in the doorway now disappeared, reappearing moments later with a gaggle of well-dressed ducklings in tow, uniformed either in sharp waistcoats and breeks or in pinafores, the little girls' blond curls tied back from shining faces with white bows. They were quiet and respectful while being introduced to their new teacher, but Glenna watched carefully, looking for telltale signs of devilry among them. Out of eight, she thought three might be the "angels" Bess had mentioned.

Once again, Glenna changed identities. To these children, she wasn't Glenna the Scot or Glenna the prisoner. And she certainly wasn't Aidan, the waif in the woods. She was Miss Glenna, the teacher. To their parents, she was Glenna the Servant. All strange new costumes for her to wear, but Glenna had always been a chameleon. Stepping into roles had shaped her life. She slipped into her designated black gown, along with a white apron and matching cap, sat the children down for three hours every morning, and did what was expected of her.

For lessons, she drew on memories from their little home in Aberfeldy, remembering the precious hours spent with Dougal, hunched over a flickering candle and learning numbers, or nestled in front of the hearth fire while she plagued him with questions about the world. He had even taught her a little French, but that was mostly when he'd curled up around her in their bed, speaking lovely sounds into her ear. They weren't suitable words for a schoolroom.

She sang with the children, teaching them hymns Frau Schmidt requested. Once in a while she taught bittersweet songs she remembered from the Highlands, their melodies as sad and lonely as she often felt. In the beginning Ursula had been unsure about the introduction of strange Gaelic sounds into their household, but the music was so intoxicating that eventually she encouraged more.

CHAPTER 35

A Reason

In the afternoons Glenna joined the other slaves in the fields, eternally grateful to Dougal for everything he'd taught her. Fieldwork was backbreaking and endless, leaving the workers beyond exhausted by the time they finally staggered back to their beds. Tobacco leaves were gathered, then parceled together and placed on five-foot poles. Those hung in an open barn that reeked like overpoweringly sweet tea, drying so they could be pressed into hogsheads, huge barrels that transported the harvest to England. The smell of the leaves seeped into the slaves' clothes, their hair, their skin, so deeply woven into them they stopped noticing after a while.

Aline suffered every day in the fields along with dozens of others, working side by side with the black slaves. They all laboured hard, but Aline faltered. The unfamiliar heat and the relentless, steamy air sucked her strength. Lifting and carrying strained her back and legs so she could barely walk on some days. In the beginning she smiled bravely, assuring Glenna she was all right, but after a few weeks the smile faded, as did the light in her eyes. Eventually she was too tired to speak at all at night, though no one spoke during the day and she had initially craved Glenna's words.

Then there was an accident, and everything changed. Glenna was working in the fields one afternoon when a panting house slave ran to her. The girl explained, hiccuping as she tried to catch her breath, that two of the children had been playing near a dry well, and one had fallen in. Glenna raced back with her and peered down into the black tunnel of the well. The air wasn't fresh, coming as it did from the long unused pit, but it was cool, a relief after the fiery fields. She could see nothing, and her fingers felt only slick rock, bringing her back to days on the ships, nights in the cells. Her heart raced at the memories, but when she saw Frau Schmidt pacing, helplessly watching, her hands twisting with the anguish of not knowing, she knew it was up to her.

The well yawned up at her, offering nothing, and she feared she didn't have the strength in her heart to voluntarily climb over the edge. Then she heard a tiny whimper from the bottom, a sound that so pitifully echoed her own fear of being trapped in the dark. It wasn't as if Glenna even made up her mind. She just tied her skirt behind her back and used the rope dangling down the well to lower herself to the child.

"Hallo, lad," she called, trying to sound cheerful as she descended into the chilled shaft. "Did ye have a wee tumble then? I bet that was frightening. Well, dinna fash yerself, love. Miss Glenna's coming."

The cries rose now that the child knew there was hope, and she heard weak splashes as the child looked up, trying to see her. "I fell, Miss Glenna!"

"Aye, sweetheart. Rest there. I'm almost to ye. We'll have ye right as rain shortly. I think Cook has fresh biscuits for ye, too."

"My arm hurts. And I'm c-c-cold!"

She could tell from his voice and the hollow echo bouncing off the water below that she was almost there. Her feet touched wetness, and she shuddered as she sank mid-thigh into chilled, stagnant water. When she could finally stand, the floor was slick underfoot and she unwrapped the rope carefully, reaching for the sides and trying to find her balance in the darkness.

"A wee bit dark down here, is it no'?"

"I don't like the dark," the little boy sobbed.

It was one of the youngest boys, four-year-old Jürgen, who had fallen. She reached for him, squatting beside the trembling body and gathering him to her. The water lapped up against her chest, soaking her through, but she didn't move as he wailed against her. She did what she could to soothe him while she gently felt for injuries. Glenna could tell straightaway that he was not only scratched and bruised as an apple, but had a badly broken arm. Through some miracle, the boy must have fallen feetfirst, ricocheting off the walls. The water, as disgusting as it was, had saved his life.

"There now, lad. Ye've banged yer arm, have ye? Let's be very careful now. I'll tie ye, and Josh an' Peter will tug ye up to the sunshine again, all right?"

The child shook with terror and pain. Glenna tried to calm him, knowing every one of his sobs jarred his arm, making it worse. She carefully wrapped the rope around and under his body, then called up from deep in the well, and two strong black slaves began to gently hoist up the rope.

She waited at the bottom, blinking up as Jürgen was eased toward the circle of blue light overhead. Wisps of clouds skittered past, white and uncaring, perhaps providing a moment's break for the slaves in the fields. Glenna squatted where Jürgen had landed, knowing it would be a while before they returned for her. Their priority would be the little boy. He would be carried to bed, fawned over, made as comfortable as possible, and only then would they remember her, shivering in the hole. She lifted her chin so she could keep staring at the sky, letting the back of her head slide along the mysterious coating lining the well.

After a life spent in the forests with nothing but wild beasts to fear, she now seemed literally to drop from one prison to the next. Would she never be free to roam on her own again? Was Dougal free, wherever he was?

"Y'all still dere?" she heard.

"I'm still here, Bess," Glenna replied. "Where else would I be?"

"Takin' yo' time outta the sun, dat it? I'm tellin' ya, you white girls will do jus' about anythin' to get outta the sun." She chuckled and Glenna smiled at the low, fat sound. "We'll have you back to the livin' in a moment. Hang tight. Good work with that boy. The mistress is happier 'an a lark, she is, flappin' around the poor boy. He'll be gettin' treats for the rest of his life, seems like."

Eventually the rope was dropped again and Glenna, not much heavier than the little boy, was pulled up. She helped when she could, poking her fingers into little crevasses along the route, bearing some of her own weight. The circle of light over her head grew with every tug and she held her breath, waiting to feel the sunshine again. She had forgotten how the dark could creep into her, like the cold, and take hold of her spirit.

Jürgen was in bed when she arrived in his room, the covers pulled up to his pale little chin, and a messenger had been sent to bring the doctor. The child alternated between being inconsolable and being eerily silent. Something had to be done, and there was no way to know when the doctor might arrive. Glenna went to her mistress and dipped a curtsy, slightly nervous about what she was going to suggest. Though she fared better than most through her teaching position, slaves were often treated as less than human. How would the woman feel about the offer of a slave's medical help?

"If ye'll permit, ma'am, the servant Aline is well studied in healin'. She'd do well for the lad."

Ursula, chewing single-mindedly on short nails, glanced sharply at her. "Then get her! Get her now! *Schnell!*"

Aline's eyes were wide as she was led into the manor, taking in the grandeur, the ornamental decor, the aromas seeping through the air from the kitchen. Glenna led her upstairs to the boy's bedroom, talking to her about what was going on. When they entered the room, she was still staring blankly around, seeing the mistress for the first time, though she'd lived there for weeks.

"Aline," Glenna hissed and jerked on her arm.

"Oh! I'm sorry!" her friend whispered back. "I've no' been inside such a place in, well, ever. It's only such a shock."

"Aye, well, ye must concentrate now. The lad needs ye."

As soon as Glenna reminded her of her purpose, Aline snapped back into place. The little black house slave Glenna had come to know as Margaret stood nearby, waiting to fetch whatever Aline asked for. When she had everything assembled, Aline paused, fiddling with her fingers and glancing around for inspiration.

Her eyes lit on the table in the hallway outside Jürgen's door. "Whisky, if ye please."

"For my little *liebchen*? He's only a baby!" Ursula cried.

"Aye, I'm afraid so, ma'am. He'll no' do well with this wi'out a wee bit of help. Have ye any laudanum in the house?"

They managed to find some and a tiny portion was given, which the patient immediately threw up. Aline frowned, but nodded. "Maybe that's enough then," she mumbled.

When she was set, she gazed down at the patient, a calm, motherly smile on her sunburned face. Jürgen stared up at her, big eyes unblinking.

"Right then, sweet lad. I'm goin' to fix ye up proper, but ye willna like it one bit."

From the minute Aline set her fingers on the break, Jürgen lost consciousness, making the process easier on both the patient and the women around his bed. She did what she could to heal his other complaints, and the boy, after much maternal worrying and spoiling, eventually made a full recovery. As a result, Aline was promoted to house servant, a position much kinder than her previous one.

At the end of her first week in this role, Aline squeezed Glenna against her. "Maybe this is yer reason for bein', my friend. An' if it is, I thank God for ye." Glenna frowned, confused, and Aline explained, "Ye've saved my life, sure as the sun will rise on the morrow. I'd have been dead in another week out there. I've no' the strength for such work. But here, well, I can clean. I can tend folk. I've always cleaned an' tended, have I no'? So I thank ye for this, my dear Glenna."

The idea was strange, that Glenna had helped someone survive. She had done the same for Brenda, backed into the dark corner of the fort with Sergeant Jennings. Before that, Glenna had considered herself to be somewhat of a harbinger of death. Joseph and Dougal, the two people she cared for more than anything in the world, had both been killed trying to protect her. For Glenna to be the protector felt completely foreign.

But over the next two years, she settled more easily into that frame of mind. She came to care deeply for the children, tending to them as if they were her own. And she was content with that. As much as she would have loved to have held a tiny version of Dougal in her arms, she was grateful it had never come to be. A babe never would have survived her tumultuous life. If it had, it most likely would have been taken from her and sold. She'd heard about families separated and sold piecemeal to the highest bidders. She couldn't have borne that, to lose Dougal twice.

Aline's life continued to improve. She was the one sent to New Windsor when supplies needed buying, and it was there that she met another transplanted Scotsman and fell in love. Alan Cunningham was a free man with a small farm closer to the river. It took him a year, but at the end of it, he made his way to the Schmidts' plantation, dressed in his best suit, purchased Aline's contract, and asked for her hand in marriage.

As happy as she was for her friend, Glenna was surprised at how quickly Herr Schmidt had accepted the farmer's coin. It had been done with no negotiations of any kind. The rapid conclusion of the deal seemed odd. But Herr Schmidt was difficult to figure out at the best of times.

After Aline left, Glenna took over many of her duties, meaning she no longer had to work in the hated fields. Now she taught in the mornings, and on some afternoons she rode into New Windsor with Herr Schmidt, doing errands while he stopped in at his favourite tavern.

Going to town was something Glenna never quite got comfortable with. Though it was cleaner by far than London, with that city's foul streets and air, it was more crowded than she liked, the pace faster than that to which she had become accustomed. Still, it was a taste of freedom she'd almost forgotten, having lived so sedately in the Schmidt household. She didn't speak to anyone more than was needed for transactions, but listened, filling her hungry mind with the happenings of the day. She heard stories of Indian conflicts, of missing slaves, of a prominent man whose home had recently burned to the ground with him inside. The popular story behind

that was it had been set by an escaped slave. Though the relationship between masters and slaves wasn't something usually discussed
in public, Glenna heard enough to know she had indeed been saved
from a terrible fate.

Recently, however, Herr Schmidt had become short with her. In
fact, he was curt with everyone, including his wife. He had no time
at all for the children. And when they set out for town, which they
did more often lately, he seemed barely to remember Glenna was
there. On the drive in he was quiet, his eyes bright, but most of their
return trips were darkened by his scowl of obvious frustration. He
began to drink heavily. On some mornings fumes from the night
before seeped from his skin, filling the air around him with a stale
tang. At first Glenna wondered if the reason for this change in per-
sonality could be a mistress, but tossed the thought aside. Herr
Schmidt, thank God, was not a womanizer. He was a man of business and efficiency, most likely moved to marital relations for the
sole purpose of procreation.

Glenna never stepped inside the tavern, with its impressive white
brick front and faded black roof. Except for the lack of outbuildings,
the tavern was almost the same size as the Schmidts' plantation
house, and she was cautious, but curious. Few women ever went in,
so she limited herself to peeking through one of the large, green-
framed windows and observing the dozen or more men inside, seated
at round tables.

She studied her master through the window, then marveled at
her naïveté. Gambling. Of course. She should have been quicker to
recognise the greed and desperation glowing in Schmidt's dark German eyes. That explained a lot, like the disappearance of various
decorative items from the house. Among other things, she'd noticed
his fine collection of snuffboxes had grown smaller, and now she
understood. Ursula obviously had no idea of her husband's habit.

He barely looked at his wife now, a fact that had the woman tied in knots. She constantly begged Glenna to fix her hair in the latest fashion or sew something alluring to attract his gaze again.

One warm but breezy day in September, Glenna finished her shopping and headed up the main walkway toward the tavern. When daylight hours waned, she usually waited outside the door for him to emerge. She gave a brief but dismissive smile to a couple of men standing outside the door, combining it with a steely glare designed to warn them off. It seemed to work, because they returned to their conversation, disregarding her altogether. Glenna tucked a bolt of soft pink material under one arm and shrugged her basket higher on her other shoulder, then pressed her face against the window.

Her timing was perfect. Through the grimy pane of glass she saw Herr Schmidt had just completed what he'd been doing. He stood back from the table, his impressive height seeming a little less this afternoon. He glared down his narrow nose, listening intently to one of the men. He gave the fellow a quick nod, then another and spun on his heel. Glenna ducked out of the way as he shoved through the door, jamming his tricorne onto a mussed black wig. He strode toward their waiting carriage, his expression flushed with anger, never once giving Glenna a glance. She scurried behind and settled on the bench opposite, waiting.

When he spoke, it was without any emotion. "You shall pack when we get home, and you shall return here."

Glenna blinked, confused, and fought the sensation of the floor of the carriage falling from under her. Herr Schmidt stared out the window, his eyes anywhere but on her.

"What?"

"You will not live at our house anymore."

Panic surged through her, popping up in little beads across her brow. What did this mean? "But what did I—"

"You did nothing." He sighed and closed his eyes, uttering a sound of defeat Glenna had heard before, but only in her own heart. When he finally looked at her, his eyes were softer, and she recognised regret. "It is a question of money, *du Ärmste.*"

She didn't know much German, though the children had taught her some during their lessons, but she recognised this phrase as one of sympathy. That did nothing to calm her panic.

"Money?"

"Yes. This man, this tavern owner. Herr Frank Hill. I owe him more than I should. He will wait no longer. He knows people I do not want to anger, Fräulein Glenna. I will not put my family in danger."

"But . . ." Her voice trailed off as she took in what he'd said. She swallowed hard. "So ye lost me in a dice game? What does that mean?"

His face had been dark that morning, tight and gaunt as a result of too much whisky the night before. Now his mood was even darker. Angry, frustrated, sick with himself, he snapped, "It means you have nothing to say. You have a new home."

CHAPTER 36

Frank Hill

Once again, Glenna's life changed. As Herr Schmidt had said, when they reached the plantation, she and her things were packed into the carriage and sent immediately back to New Windsor. She wasn't given the opportunity to say good-bye to Ursula or the children and wondered vaguely how Herr Schmidt might explain this to his family.

She wanted to sleep as the carriage jogged and bounced for two more hours, but she couldn't. Her mind raced. What now? This new life, belonging to a tavern owner, would be entirely different from how she had lived, enjoying the staid, safe environment of the Schmidts' plantation. It was safe to assume there would be no mathematics lessons or singing of hymns within the tavern's white brick walls.

She rubbed her hands nervously, staring out the window as the line of storefronts and houses materialised again. The building looked different than it had hours earlier. Yes, it was nighttime now, but it was more than the beams of yellow light spilling through the windows, lighting the walkway by the road. Something about the windows. As if their bland, apathetic gaze from the afternoon had sharpened, spotting her, and now leered with a hungry malice.

The population of the town, faces barely lit by the occasional lantern, watched as Glenna's carriage pulled to a stop outside the tavern, but no one helped her get out or escorted her into the building. Frank Hill, the wealthiest man in New Windsor, sent no servants to assist her. So once the driver had dropped her small bag from the back of the carriage and driven back in the direction of the Schmidt home, she stood alone, staring up at the establishment.

Slinging her bag over her shoulder, Glenna stepped up to the front door. It swung open just as she was reaching for the latch, and two obviously inebriated men tumbled out, laughing as they staggered toward the road. Glenna watched them go, stomach churning. A tavern was no place for a lady, and after living in the Schmidts' fine home for so long, that's what she considered herself to be these days. Taking a breath for courage, she stepped inside.

The massive room was bright as day, and loud. Lanterns illuminated the red and gray bricks that dotted the walls like a stone-hard patchwork quilt. The floor was painted dark brown, but was well scuffed, with lighter paths leading to preferred tables over the years. Dominating the room was a long oak bar, shining with polish. Behind it stretched a marked-up old mirror, its reflection further brightening the place.

She turned quickly at a burst of laughter from her right, then spun again at the sound of raised voices by the bar. The place was more crowded at night than it had been earlier, and she noticed again that this was not a place frequented by female patrons.

But there were women. Half a dozen painted women whose husky laughter danced like smoke up to the grime-darkened rafters. Did this mean—

Glenna didn't wait to find out. Being caught escaping the idea of whoring seemed better than possibly living that life. She'd gladly hang, given the alternative. She whirled, reaching for the door, but it was blocked by a man who stood a few inches taller than Glenna. His arms were folded across a fine linen shirt, and silver curls, unencumbered by a hat, were greased flat against his head. His gray eyes almost matched his hair, meaning the only splash of colour on his face was the thick black moustache, curled at both ends.

"Well, now," he said. "Here she is."

"Excuse me," she replied, reaching past him for the door. "I'm just leavin'."

He shook his head and twisted one end of his moustache between thumb and forefinger. A tight little smile curled under his moustache. "I think not. I tell you what. Don't know if you've noticed, but ain't too many ladies coming in here unless they's looking for work."

"I'm no' looking for work, sir. Please excuse me."

He continued as if she hadn't spoken. He stuck one finger in his ear and wiggled it, then flicked something invisible to the floor. "And all them ladies work for me. So that must mean you've come here to work for me."

She frowned, uneasy. The man smirked at her in the strangest manner, as if his mind ticked with calculations. She wasn't sure if she should be concerned, but her instincts were on alert.

"I'll ask ye again, sir—"

"You are, I believe, Miss Glenna. Schmidt sent you over."

That stopped her. She lifted her chin, riding a swell of anxiety. "I am."

"Well, then. The name's Frank Hill. I imagine you know that name well enough. Let's go on in and get better acquainted." He held out one arm, indicating a door cut in one of the tavern walls.

Glenna took a discreet breath and headed toward the room that he'd indicated. She stepped inside and he latched the door behind her, then leaned against it, arms crossed again. Gone was the cheerful atmosphere of the tavern. Now she stood in a dark office dominated by a huge, ornate desk and chair. Back a little farther she could see the man's bedroom. The dim profile of his bed was a warning as clear as any battle cry she'd heard in Scotland.

"I seen you around," he said, barely nodding. She saw the glimmer of his teeth in the dark and couldn't help thinking of the nasty black and white badgers she'd trapped back home. "And when Friedrich got a little down on his luck, I knew precisely how I'd get to see you more often." He took a step toward her and she took one back, edging around the desk. His smile was slow, carnal. "You know you belong to me now, right?"

Glenna's heart raced, thrumming inside her chest. She had to get out. This was bad. "I belong to no one, sir. I ken I'm to work here, but I dinna belong to you."

"Ah, so that's how it's gonna be. I see. Well, the thing is, I do own you. I own everything from your pretty blond head to your tiny little feet and everything in between." He held his open hands parallel to the slender line of her waist. "You're *all* mine now." He closed in until she was backed against the wall.

She felt the edge of a doorframe and tried to slip out of reach, but he was fast, and stronger than he appeared. He grabbed her upper arms and threw her onto the bed in the back room, then slapped her face hard when she struggled. She flailed against his restraining hands, kicking uselessly against him as he straddled her. Too strong, too fast. *No!* she screamed in her mind, and heard her own voice spewing furious Gaelic syllables that did nothing to stop him.

She was so focused on wriggling out from under him that she barely noticed him working at her skirt. It wasn't until his sticky palm gripped her thigh and he dug his fingers into the muscle that she understood how much danger she was really in. She had always been protected from this before, had always managed to escape. But this was too close. *No no no! Too much!*

She pressed her thighs tightly together, growling and kicking, determined to wear him down, but he was stronger. He forced her legs apart and she could do nothing but shriek when he forced himself through. He moved urgently, brutally, with the detachment of a hunter, grunting with short, determined sounds. She kept fighting, screaming, working against sobs that rocked through her, but she could do nothing against him. She felt useless, helpless, weak. *Oh, Dougal! I'm so sorry!*

Eventually, Frank Hill rolled off. He left Glenna partially dead inside, though the greater part of her boiled with fury. Vibrations built up from deep within her, and she knew that despite what he had just done, she absolutely wouldn't allow this man to defeat her. Beside her, Frank lay contentedly, his chest rising and falling slowly as he breathed. A contented man. Eyes still closed, he raised one hand and lowered it again so his palm lay flat, proprietary, on one covered breast. That was too much.

"Damn ye an' yer useless wee pintle, ye fuckin' load o' sow shite!" she shrieked, shoving his hand from her chest as if it were a snake. She rolled to one side, trying to ignore the wetness oozing between her legs when she moved. He still wore his perfect white linen shirt and Glenna grabbed the collar with both hands, tearing the seam. She brought her face to his and glared down at him. "Ye'll no' touch me again," she said, spraying his face with spit, "or ye'll suffer for it."

"Is that right?" He chuckled, and in one instant had her pinned beneath him again. He was heavy, his weight squeezed her stays against her ribs. She panicked anew, afraid she'd soon be unable to breathe. "Well, my dear Glenna," he said, sliding his hand beneath her skirt again. He squeezed, and though his grip was low on her body, tears forced from her eyes. "I don't think so. As a matter of fact, I don't appear to be suffering one little bit."

She went limp and his tone changed to something that strove for comforting. "That's my girl," he said, bringing his hand back up and sliding it down her cheek. "You'll get used to me. As long as you understand that I . . ." He grinned suddenly, a wide, victorious flash of teeth. "I *own* you."

"Never," she whispered, sucking in a sob.

He tucked strands of her hair back, clearing her face so he could touch her cheeks, her brow, her chin, her eyebrows, her ears. His voice changed again, becoming conversational. "Ah, Glenna. I've wanted you for a while now, and I mean for us to get along. You'll see. I can be good to you. My wife used to understand that. She understood it long enough that she got her fat fingers so thick with jewels she can barely lift another cake to her big mouth. Smart girl, that one. She got so fat I won't touch her with a ten-foot pole. But you, Glenna, you can make me happy."

"No, I can't."

"I've just proved it, missy," he said with a self-satisfied chuckle. "I'm very happy right now."

Glenna turned her head away, wishing the pillow would suck her inside it. "Go away," she managed.

"Worn out already? Well, I suppose you've travelled a fair bit today. Sure. I'll leave you to rest. But I'll be back later, don't you worry." He climbed off the bed and stooped to pull on his trousers, smiling at her the whole time. His voice returned to business. "I'm glad you're here, Glenna. You and I are going to do just fine, but there are rules. Even for you." He buttoned his trousers as he spoke, then wiggled one foot into a shoe. "The moment we stop being friends, well, that's when I introduce you to the other gentlemen here. That's the way it works." He strode confidently to the side of the bed and gazed down at her, keeping his thumbs tucked in his waistband. "You see, my dear, I am the talk of the town. Everyone knows Frank Hill. Everyone wants to be like Frank Hill. Everyone wants what Frank Hill has."

She watched him from the corner of one eye, hating how fragile she felt. Rape was one thing, as repulsive and horrifying a reality as it was. But the idea of being owned by this creature was unthinkable. She would find a way to be the one thing Frank Hill did *not* want. The one thing *nobody* wanted. And if she could kill Frank Hill, all the better.

"Yes, ma'am. It's all about reputation. The more people hear about the famous Frank Hill, the more they talk, the more they come to my establishment and spend their hard-earned money. Soon I'll have no need of my pig of a wife or her money-grabbing family." He had the other shoe on and now smoothed back his slick gray hair. Glenna had the impression he was no longer speaking to her at all. "She won't have a thing to say once this place is mine."

He glanced into a mirror and tweaked his moustache. When he was satisfied, he turned back. "I'll give you a little time to get used to all this. It might be a while before I'm back. Then I'll bring something to eat. Suit you, Glenna?"

If only murder were possible through thoughts. "Nothin' about this suits me, ye bastard."

His smile hardened again. "I will be back soon."

CHAPTER 37

The Cost of Freedom

At first, she'd paced the room, banging on the door and walls, demanding release. No one came. She'd attacked his desk, hoping to discover a weapon of some kind, but it was securely locked. On its surface there was nothing but scraps of paper, a couple of worn quills and ink. She could do nothing. With no other options, she sat on the edge of the bed, alternating between crying, staring, and planning revenge, fueling her anger with memories of his body against hers. No man was allowed to do what he had done. No man but Dougal. This man would pay. He would suffer, just as she'd warned him he would suffer.

Despite what he'd said, Frank did not come back soon. She listened to the rising and falling volume outside the locked door and judged it was two days before he returned. By then she was brittle from hunger and thirst. The windowless room had become an oven, and she had been forced to undress to her shift.

So when he returned, she could do nothing but stare at him,

drained of food and water and any kind of fight. She curled on her side, hugging her knees to her chest.

"Glenna! Glad to see you're awake. Hungry?"

She closed her eyes. He would feed her. If he truly wanted her as he said he did, he wouldn't let her die.

The mattress sagged when he sat. He leaned over and kissed the cheek he could see. God, she was thirsty. She fought the urge to lick her lips, then gave in. *Please give me water.*

The cup was inches away, closer, closer, then blessedly pressed to her lips. He poured a small, precious sip into her mouth and she choked, both from the angle and from the fact that it wasn't water at all. She sputtered, craving the wet, flinching at the bite.

"No? Not time for wine yet? Fine. Water then." He chuckled. "You'll have to pay for it, you know."

She didn't care. When his fingers traced the line of her cheek, brushed the greasy strands of her hair, she didn't care. He poured water through her lips and it was the sweetest, softest, most wonderful thing she had ever tasted.

When she'd had a few gulps, he took the cup away and frowned with distaste. "You smell like the back end of a horse." He stood abruptly and left, taking the food with him, but returned with a small girl in tow. He left them alone and the girl went to Glenna's side. She flipped up the hem of Glenna's shift and Glenna instinctively reached to push it down.

"Never mind that," the girl muttered. "I'm only here to clean you." She glanced at Glenna, her expression full of regret. The girl looked older than she'd first seemed, only small. Underfed. The pale skin across her chest was mottled with bruises. "I'm sorry I couldn't help before. He keeps the keys, you see. I'm sorry."

"Who are ye?" Glenna managed.

"I'm Sarah. I work here," she whispered. "Before that I . . . well,

I know what's happening to you, because I've been in this same place. It will pass, though, when he tires of you. And then . . ." Her shoulders slumped as she let out a breath. "Well, don't you worry. You've enough on your mind for now."

Glenna gave up the fight and let Sarah do what she had to do. The sympathetic words hurt more than she'd expected, and while the girl swabbed her body clean, Glenna wept. She regretted the loss of the precious water as it slid down her cheeks, but couldn't stop the tears.

Sarah left with the chamber pot and Frank returned, bearing food. He started with water, then bread soaked in water, then small pieces of meat that tasted sweet on her tongue. She worked up the strength to sit and feed herself, and the food moved in her stomach, filling the empty spaces. Eventually she stopped eating, afraid she might get ill from too much at once, and shrank back against the wall.

He saw her summon her strength and stepped in before she could gain control.

"Glenna," he murmured. He stroked the side of her face. "I'm sorry I was gone so long. But I'm a busy man. Fortunately, my work is done for now. I can stay awhile."

A tear snaked down Glenna's cheek and her chin wobbled, but there was nothing she could do. She was weak and sick and half his size. He removed her shift while she said nothing at all, and she registered none of his compliments. She lay still as he moved over her, feeling him take greater and greater control. When he was done, he lay beside her and blew a long, satisfied sigh from under his moustache.

He sat up suddenly. "I almost forgot. I brought you a gift."

She closed her eyes and said nothing when he nudged her awake, dangling a pendant in front of her. A large pearl framed in gold hung on a delicate gold chain, like nothing Glenna had ever seen.

She frowned, trying to focus, but didn't reach for the gift. She didn't want anything from this man. Nothing but water . . . and freedom . . . and vengeance.

"I thought the pearl was right for you. The colour of your hair and all."

He struggled to hook it behind her neck but she said nothing. He stared at the little pendant, admiring the way it lay between her breasts.

Dougal would have known what to do at this moment. What would he have said? *Oh, Dougal. Help me!*

Frank continued to talk, apparently unconcerned whether she joined in the conversation. "My wife will never miss it. She has more trinkets than she knows what to do with. They look so much better on you." He ran his fingers over the pearl, then over her. She shuddered. What had she allowed to happen to her life? "I'll bring something else next time. I have something in mind."

Still smiling, Frank lay back down beside her and stared at the ceiling, apparently ready to chat. His voice was soft but energised. Like a boy, proud of his accomplishments. "You aren't the first, you know. But you are by far the most beautiful. Oh, if dear Julia ever knew!" He chuckled, pleased with himself, and rolled so he could face her, leaning on one elbow. His fingers explored the lines of her body and Glenna lay as if dead, despising the man more with every breath. "Her parents financed this tavern. They brought money from England and spent it on this place. And you know what? They've never once visited it." He frowned, shaking his head. "Imagine that? Pay for something and never see it? I can tell you, I paid for you and I damn well mean to see a lot of you."

Slowly Glenna emerged from the nightmare, sensing light. She could almost hear Dougal's sweet voice echoing within her mind. *Anythin' can be a weapon,* mo chridh.

She had nothing at hand. Nothing here but the man's gift and his words. She listened to him drone on about his wife, about the tavern, about his plans, and she started to wonder. Why this man would want to spill his secrets to her was a mystery, but in them might be weapons she could use. How far could she push this? How could she regain some of the power he had stolen from her? She decided to set a little bait. See if the slimy wee fish bit.

"I like jewellery that sparkles," she murmured.

His reaction was immediate. He leapt to his feet, surprised to hear her say anything, and encouraged by the words she chose. "Do you? Well, I did bring something else, though . . ." He frowned. "Your fingers are a lot smaller than Julia's . . ."

Glenna stretched out her hand, keeping her eyes closed. She felt the cool embrace of a ring as it slid onto her finger, then rotated and hung, heavy and loose. She brought her hand closer and examined the bright blue stone, then slipped the bauble from her finger to her thumb, where it sat more securely.

The man was an idiot. He talked of the gambling, of the women, of various nefarious ways money kept trickling into his pockets. While his in-laws congratulated themselves on owning a reputable, thriving business, Frank was paying them back, penny by penny, with ill-gotten gains.

When he had finished telling the day's stories, Frank got up, dressed, and locked Glenna in the room, leaving her alone to plan revenge. She slipped her shift over her head and went directly to his desk, from which she seized the paper and quill. She wrote everything she had just memorised. When she was done, she blew on her notes, wanting the words to dry quickly, then folded the paper and hid it under the sour-smelling mattress.

He returned a day later and she suffered in silence while he used her. The fact that she had to do this, that she was trapped in this disgusting position, made her sick. She hated him, and more than that, she hated herself for being so powerless. But not for long. No, not for long. Soon he would be sorry for everything. Very sorry.

Afterward, he presented her with pearl earrings to match the earlier necklace. All courtesy of poor, deluded Julia.

"Who were the other women? Before me, I mean," she asked, encouraging him.

She listened with disbelief as Frank obediently and proudly listed all his mistresses, ten in all over the past six years, all of whom had started out in this very room. Glenna filed everyone's name in her head and wrote them down later, noting he had only been married six years. How Julia would love to hear all this, she thought. How Julia's oblivious parents would enjoy taking the tavern and all its notoriety from him.

He left, but he would come back. There was no way to prevent him. But this would be the last time.

The prize Frank gave her after the fourth visit was a ring: a large, shining ruby set in the centre of a circle of diamonds. He had even had it sized so it fit her properly. She graced him with a bland smile that quivered on the edge of a sneer. She had to play the part if this was going to work.

"Frank, I want to get out o' this room."

He regarded her suspiciously at first, then nodded. He opened the door and called for Sarah, who arrived within moments with a new, relatively clean gown and blouse. He tossed it at Glenna, then watched her dress, even helped with the laces of her corset before lowering the blouse over her head.

"Not for long," he said.

She fought rage. "Just let me breathe some air outside o' this room, would ye?"

He led her into the tavern, which quietened when she stepped through the door. Her body prickled with humiliation, knowing every man in the place was aware of the situation. But she had to get past that, do what she needed to do. She glanced around, praying, and managed not to grin when her prayers were answered.

Sarah stood by the bar, holding a tray and waiting for drinks.

Frank's attention was distracted, though he still beamed beside her, showing off. None of the others had a woman like Glenna. It was degrading, but she fed his ego, fawning gently up against him.

"I'm thirsty, Frank. Can I get us drinks?"

"Sure," he said. She turned to go, but he grabbed her, twirling her around so her back was against his chest. He draped one arm over her shoulder, dangling his fingers over the rise of her breasts. The eyes of the men in front of them glazed a bit while she watched. Every nerve in her body wanted to scream, to lash out at these lecherous creatures, but it would have been in vain. Better to save her strength. "Go tell Sarah to bring a round for the boys, would you?" he said.

He let her go, and she strode to the bar, trying to ignore the comments that followed her. When she got to Sarah, the girl was watching with interest.

"He let you out already? That's fast," Sarah whispered, her lips barely moving.

"Help me, Sarah." The girl's eyes widened and she shook her head, but Glenna squeezed her hand and tucked her precious weapon within the girl's damp fingers. "Take this note and hide it. Somewhere he'll ne'er find it. It has everythin' I could get to ruin Frank. If anythin' happens to me, the note must go to his wife, Julia. When I go back to the table, you must go an' take the jewellery from under my bed. It belongs to Julia. Mind me, Sarah, ye canna sell it or wear it. It needs to be kept safe."

"Glenna?" Frank called.

She looked over her shoulder at Frank. "I'll be right there."

Sarah looked concerned, her eyes darting like a rabbit's. "I don't know."

"Sarah, do ye like . . . doin' what you do here?" She gave no answer, but Glenna hadn't expected one. "If ye do as I ask, ye and I will be safe from all of this. We will keep our jobs, but we will never again be touched by him or any other man in this place."

Sarah narrowed her eyes, then broke into a wide smile. It was a pretty smile, suddenly young, though a tooth was missing on either side. She spoke quickly. "Blackmail, is it? I understand now. Oh, Frank won't be happy about this. Yeah. I know a place in my room, a loose panel by the side of the fireplace. I'll hide it there tonight."

"After that ye will have to find an even safer place, for Frank will come lookin' for it. He'll want to kill both of us, so I've put a note in there, explainin' what it's all about. If we are killed, that letter will destroy him. Can you think of someone who might be able to help wi' that?"

Sarah looked down at the counter, going over something in her head. Then she nodded. "I know exactly the place and the person. Leave it to me, Glenna."

Frank allowed Glenna to spend a precious hour outside of the rank-smelling bedroom, then shuffled her back inside. He waited for her to walk to the bed, to sit in her forlorn condition and stare at him, but Glenna was well past that point. Instead, she strode to his desk and claimed his chair. Frank frowned down at her.

"What do you think you're doing?"

"Changin' the rules, Frank."

He flicked one thick eyebrow. "How's that?"

"Ye'll never touch me again," she said, her smile placid and confident.

He rolled his eyes. "Not that again. I thought we had moved on from there, Glenna. You are my property. I own you and I'll do as I like until I tire of you. Don't you understand that?"

"The game has changed, Frank. For I've somethin' that will change yer life. I've a few things, actually. Things yer dear wife will miss."

He said nothing, but she could see the anger rush into his tight cheeks.

"I also have the name of every lass ye've destroyed over the past six years. I'll find the girls, they'll understand what I've done, an' ye'll lose everythin', Frank. The tavern, yer wife, yer reputation . . . Ye did say reputation is the most important thing of all, did ye no'?"

"You won't get away with this," he hissed. "No one will believe you."

"Ah, but they will, for I've evidence." She blinked prettily, the thrill of the moment singing in her veins. If she weren't so weak, she'd have leapt to her feet and danced around the fool. He stared at her now, his eyes slightly unfocused as he tried to wriggle out of the situation. She stopped him. "Now ye'll be pleased to hear I have a solution for ye. I am no' goin' to yer wife or her parents or anyone else, yet. But dinna underestimate me. That will happen if ye deny my requests. Everythin' I need to destroy ye is in a very safe place."

He squinted at her. "Go on."

"I shall live here, upstairs, in my own room. I shall still work here, but only as a barmaid. Neither ye nor any other bastard in this place will ever touch me. An' that also goes for dear Sarah, who, as ye ken already, is one of the unfortunate lassies on my list." He flinched but didn't interrupt. "An' at the end of every week, we shall be paid wages." She smiled. "Do ye understand me, Frank?"

"I paid for you," he snarled. "I paid big for you. I should get something for all that."

She leaned toward him, feeling the hatred burn in her own eyes.

"What ye did to me was more than somethin', ye pitiful excuse for a man."

"You have to stay here. The service contract is for five more years," he said, grasping for anything with which he might regain control. "Escaped slaves hang."

"Ye'd want to keep me after all this?" She laughed. "What a fool ye be. But I see no cause to leave yet anyhow. Ye'll pay my room an' board, ye'll feed me, an' ye'll pay me at the end of every week."

In the end, he had no choice. She had cornered him neatly and he knew it.

There were many nights when she sat on her bed in her quiet bedroom upstairs and cried herself to sleep. This kind of life wasn't worth the price she'd paid. But she'd had no alternative. Memories of what Frank had done were scars she would carry forever, but she had survived. Now, if she were to believe Aline, she had to find the reason. Aline had said there was always a reason. Glenna wasn't about to allow Frank Hill to take that away from her.

CHAPTER 38

A Madman's Stories

Glenna puffed loose strands of hair from her brow as she leaned across the table, wiping away wet circles left by the empty glasses she now held on her tray. It had been a long day, the heat almost unbearable, the stink of unwashed men and alcohol sticking like sweat on the walls of the tavern. Tempers had been short since noon, and she'd stepped out of the room three times when fights broke out. Frank had tossed the ruffians into the street, but she'd seen a couple sneak back in later, desperate to wash away the dust in their throats.

She was tired. Her gown clung to her curves, but the men sitting at tables around her knew her well enough by now to know she wouldn't stand for their groping hands. Frank never interfered, but he didn't have to. Having freed herself from his clutches, she had impressed every man in the tavern with her temper. The others saw her in a different light and were hesitant to cross the little hellcat. Frank loomed always in the background, eyes dark with a turbulent confusion of lust and hatred. She had humiliated him, she knew. She had played a dangerous game, threatening to spill his secrets to his wife and her family, but it had been done to save her soul. Never could she have lived under the thumb of this repulsive man, and when he grudgingly paid her wages at the end of every week, she smiled politely and tried not to gloat.

Now he sat at the last of two occupied tables, staring at the cards in his hand and listening to the three other men at the table, none of which she'd seen before. She didn't like the look of one of them in particular. From his wide-eyed stare and toothy grin, she guessed he was probably quite mad. Frank set his cards down and leaned back, absorbed in the conversation while he absently walked a coin over the backs of his fingers, a habit she'd seen him do often. The money on the table seemed fairly evenly distributed, but she knew the game. The longer he could drag this out, the better chance Frank had of pulling one of his tricks. She'd never seen him lose, and no one had caught him cheating—yet. The crazy man sat across from him, doing the most talking, and when he slammed his empty cup on the table, Frank glanced up and nodded briefly at her. She went to fetch the man another beer, knowing from experience it was easier just to do things rather than bristle at every order. It simply wasn't worth the effort.

She waited at the bar while the cup was filled. "The others, too?" the bartender asked, gesturing with his chin toward the table.

"Hmm? Oh aye, I suppose so. Frank can sort it out later." She balanced the cups on her tray then headed back to the table. Frank frowned at the four drinks, knowing he'd only requested one, but said nothing as she set them in front of the men.

The man still hadn't stopped talking, and his voice carried throughout the tavern, like a dog yapping. He spoke in a rich Scottish brogue, and his matted beard sparkled with spit as he boasted of his exploits with the army, how they'd slaughtered Indians and French alike, sounding as if they'd single-handedly rescued the entire world. Glenna managed not to laugh. What was it about men and their exaggerations?

Frank was still frowning, and now the lines drawn between his eyebrows deepened with curiosity. He slid his cards into the centre of the table and cleared his throat. The other men seemed surprised to hear a voice other than the one that had been going on for the past five minutes.

"But you're Scottish, aren't you?"

"Bloody right I am," the man declared, spit gathering like froth in the corners of his mouth. "From Invergarden way. An' that's where my kin would be if we didna have to battle the bloody English all the time."

"And yet you're fighting . . . with the English army?"

For the first time, the man faltered, glancing down at the table for a split second. "Well . . . no. No' exactly." He looked up again, gaining momentum. "The English dogs saw they couldna defeat the French wi'out us Scots, aye? Bunch of lilly-livered worms, them. So they called the real warriors down from the Highlands an' gave us back our plaids an' pipes, let us live the way we should, but we had to fight the bloody battles here for them."

"Oh, come on, Hamish. An English army made up of Scots?"

"Aye. The Seventy-seventh Highlanders, we're called, an' a braver bunch of lads ye've never seen in yer life."

One of the other men at the table rolled his eyes and, with a sigh, laid his cards on the table. The other followed suit. It seemed none of them were going anywhere until Hamish had told his glorious story.

"Taught us to fight wi' their guns, their bayonets, then sent us out to defend their damn English honour. Honour! When has an

Englishman honour, I ask ye?" He shook his head and grinned, remembering. "But the men in the unit were braw fighters. Unafraid an' brimmin' wi' fight. Especially those bloody grenadiers, big tall fellows wi' more guts than brains."

The conversation was vaguely interesting to Glenna, though the thought of any self-respecting Scot volunteering to join an English army repulsed her. She liked the mental image of the plaids swinging again, the Highlanders snarling as they waited for a battle to begin. She remembered the sight and sounds of them so well when she tried, the smell of wool and sweat mixing with the battle lust. Glenna studied Hamish, sitting a little taller as he spoke of the Highlanders, his shallow chest puffed with pride. She imagined he might have been a soldier at one point, clean and disciplined, but at this point he looked like nothing more than a rat recently let out of a cage. She'd seen many of those in her colourful past.

Hamish's eyes narrowed and he looked at each man, assuring himself they were listening. "But there's two I didna trust as far as I could throw them. Aye, they were the biggest, and aye, the men would follow them to the gates of Hell, but the one, MacDonnell . . ." He sipped on his beer and a strange light filled his eyes. "I'll kill that man, I will."

"Why's that?"

"Oh, he was so much *better* than the rest of us, aye?" The dam opened and the mad fool spouted words that made no sense to Glenna. She circled behind him with his beer, then hustled past, nearly choking as she caught a whiff of his stink. "The way he looked at me, like I was no more than a slug under his boot. He always started it, comin' after me wi' threats, but the damn English only blamed me. He's the reason the army let me go, aye? They said they were concerned—they were *concerned* about my *stability*, no less. They know shite, those bloody captains. They should be worried about the black-maned, blue-eyed devil, that MacDonnell. He'll slice 'em all to bits while they sleep, he will. He an' his fellow, John. The rest of the men, they're all 'Aye, sir, Mr. MacDonnell. Oh aye, I'll jump for ye, Mr. Dougal. How high?' 'Tis enough to make a man ill, it is."

Glenna paused, her hand halting in midair after she'd placed the fourth cup on the table. MacDonnell was a common enough name in Scotland, as was Dougal. A big, dark devil named Dougal Mac-Donnell? Also common. Could it be . . . No. Surely not. And yet her heart quickened. She wanted to ask this lunatic for more, draw details from his saliva-speckled lips. But she didn't need to. The madness squawked continuously now, like a magpie demanding attention, his words fast and furious, leaving confused expressions on the other men's faces.

When he paused to swallow more beer, one of the others looked at Frank. "Are we gonna play cards or what?"

Frank held out one hand, placating him for the moment, then nodded at Hamish, encouraging him. Glenna could see why. Most of the time this place was either deader than a graveyard or roaring with fights. This was a story none of them had heard before, another kind of entertainment.

"I should be there, fightin' wi' the others, an' I would be if it wasna for bloody Dougal MacDonnell. The bastard shouldna even be there. Should be hangin' on the end of a rope by now. Naught but a common murderer, he is. If it weren't for his mate, Wallace, another animal what they scraped off Culloden, he'd be swingin' there now, meat for the corbies. Well, I'll kill him for them. I'll do what those bloody English didn't manage when they threw him off the cliff."

Glenna dropped her tray and it clattered to the floor, jerking every man's eyes to her. *Culloden? John Wallace? And the cliff?*

"Pardon me, sirs," she said, trying to control her voice. "Clumsy of me."

Frank said nothing, but Hamish's nostrils flared, and he regarded her through glassy eyes. "I'll tell ye what, I dinna mind clumsy under me."

Glenna smiled politely, divided between the natural urge to flee the disgusting man's innuendo and wanting to hear more about Dougal. *Could it be?* Frank chuckled quietly from his place at the table, but didn't help her out. Why should he? They were in a continuous state of war, he and Glenna.

"Very kind of ye, sir," she said sweetly. "Must be hearin' yer Scots that set me off. It's been a while since I've heard a sound like that. Takes me home, it does."

Hamish sat taller, looking surprised she'd even paid attention to him. "I'll take ye home," he offered.

"I couldna help overhearin' ye speak o' the army. What was it ye said it was called?"

"Seventy-seventh Highlanders. Under Montgomerie, we are."

She nodded, pressing her hands tight against the tray so as not to betray her trembling hands. Could it possibly be so easy? "An' where are they now, these Highlanders?"

Frank glanced at her, eyes narrowed with suspicion. She gave him a small shrug, wanting to reassure him there was nothing to worry about. She was only curious. They were her countrymen after all.

"Oh, no' far. I think maybe up Richmond way now. They were headed into Virginia when they sent me off. Some talk of the French, I think."

Glenna couldn't help herself. She blinked innocently, hoping to give Hamish the impression she believed every word he said. "An' this MacDonnell, he sounds a right bastard."

The man's eyes popped wide open. "Oh aye! A right bastard to be sure. I'm goin' to kill him."

"Aye, so ye've said."

"Soon as I've supped, I'm on my way. I've planned it all for a week now. The devil will ne'er ken what happened. He thinks he's the only one what can shoot a tail off a squirrel. He'll find out soon enough I can shoot, too."

"I'm sure ye can, sir."

Frank stood then. "Excuse me, sirs. Glenna, come with me. Deal me out of this hand, fellas. I'll be right back."

Glenna smiled demurely, trying desperately to look as if nothing were going on in her heart, in her head. But suddenly life had burst into colour. Energy buzzed through her, shooting from her toes to the tips of her long, blond hair, and it had everything to do with hope. *Dougal.*

Frank led her to the side of the room, then leaned down to peer into her eyes. "What's this all about?"

"What's what all about?"

"Talking with the customers, getting all chummy with the nasty old Scot."

"Jealous, Frank?"

Frank gnawed on his lower lip and Glenna could see the thoughts spinning through his eyes. How he hated her. How he wanted her. And he could do nothing about either emotion. He could, however, remind her of her place in the world.

"I still own you, bitch. I bought you fair and square, and you're stuck in this place whether you like it or not."

"Fair and square? *Fair and square?*" Now it was Glenna who leaned forward, spitting out her words, though she kept the volume low enough that only Frank could hear. "How can you say that? How can you say *any* of this is fair and square? *I shouldn't be here!*

I should be living my own life across the sea, in my own land, in my own home. I shouldna be waitin' on these horrible bastards here, or sayin' yes-sir, no-sir to yer every sick whim." She shuddered and the corner of his mouth twitched. "But I know well enough I canna leave. Dinna fash yerself o'er me. Where would I go? I ken ye'd shoot me down quick as ye could say my name."

He nodded. "Right you are. And I'd be within my rights." His stare was too intense, too inquisitive. Glenna fought to hold it with her own and barely managed before he spoke again. "Don't you start thinking about joining up with a whole army of Scots, hiding behind their skirts." An idea occurred and he hooted with laughter. "Those monsters would eat you for breakfast. You wouldn't be so high and mighty then, would you?"

She closed her eyes, wishing he would disappear, but of course he didn't. He was there when she opened them again, as he always was, watching and obsessing. "Leave me alone, Frank."

He nodded, appearing satisfied for the time being. He wanted her frustrated and she played the part, though in the back of her mind, plans were being put into place.

"Bring the table another round, would you, sweetheart?"

Crazy Hamish kept up his talking for another hour, and though he touched now and again on the subject of how he was planning to follow the army and kill Dougal, most of his words were inane. Still, she found herself wanting to stay close to him. This revolting stranger had been with Dougal, living beside him for months, maybe years. He was the only person on earth that she knew who had been with Dougal, for she now believed, with every beat of her heart, that it was her own Dougal of whom he spoke. He wasn't dead after all.

CHAPTER 39

Flight

In the back of her mind, Glenna had always dreamed of running away, but had never really imagined it happening. It was like she'd said in the tavern earlier: she knew Frank would kill her if she ran. But now, well, now everything had changed. Glenna didn't think twice about endangering her life if there was a chance she might find Dougal. If her heart was in her flight, not just her need to escape, then she wasn't as afraid.

Even though she'd doubted she'd ever find the courage, she'd put together an escape kit just in case. She'd managed to obtain a pair of young man's breeks, along with a tunic, an oversized coat, and a tricorne to top it all off. Unlike many women, Glenna was completely at home in a man's set of clothing. She'd lived half her life that way already. As she'd done so long ago, she'd sewn the waistband of the breeks into one long pocket, which held every penny she'd saved. Not a lot, but enough for a short journey, she imagined.

She'd shut down the bar two hours earlier and watched the drunken madman totter down the street, talking to himself, headed north. Did the man never get tired of hearing his own voice? She knew the road he was on, and her mind had been busy, putting together some kind of map to help her understand where she'd need to go. Now she waited, fidgeting, wanting to pace the narrow line of her room, but needing to keep silent. The planks of the building creaked on windy nights and the windows rattled in their frames, but there was barely a breeze tonight. When Glenna listened hard, she couldn't hear a sound in the entire place, and there was no noise outside, either. She sat leaning against the door of her room for an hour, waiting, listening.

She couldn't wait forever, or else she'd lose Hamish. An hour had to be enough. Without a sound, she tiptoed down the stairs into the main part of the tavern and slipped behind the bar. She tugged a set of keys from the box where the cash was kept, then snuck into Frank's office, the bedroom where he'd first introduced himself, so to speak. She jiggled the smallest key into the top drawer of the desk, and sighed with relief when it turned and lifted the lock. The room was dark, so she couldn't see inside the drawer, but her fingers closed around cool, smooth metal. She pulled Frank's pistol out and stuck both it and a load of shot into the back of her breeks.

Then she slipped silently into the street, clad as a boy, and started to run.

At first her head swam with exhilaration. She was out! She was free! And Dougal, Dougal would be there, so happy to see her! She headed down the same road as the former soldier, but ducked into the trees at the side as soon as she heard Hamish's drunken shuffle ahead of her. She slumped a little, knowing the rest of the journey would be slow, tracking this imbecile on his mission. All she wanted was to race blindly ahead, listening for Dougal and the others—how quiet could an entire army be? But there were too many variables, too many roads the strange man could take, so she had no choice but to follow him.

The following days flowed like molasses to her mind, though she almost lost him once when he hitched a ride on a wagon. Glenna had raced behind, hoping the ride would be cut short, but the driver seemed to be going exactly where Hamish wanted him to go. She watched, close to panic, as the rickety wagon disappeared down the road. Out of desperation, she ran to the nearest cottage and banged on the door. A bearded man opened it and frowned down at her.

"Excuse me, sir," she said, lowering her voice so she sounded more like a man. "I've a favour to ask. I'll pay ye for yer trouble. It's only I need to catch up to yon wagon that just headed up the road. If ye could find it in yer heart to loan me yer horse—"

"Loan you mah horse? Are you crazy, boy?"

She nodded. "It's important, sir. An' like I said, I can pay." She held out a few of her treasured pennies to show she was telling the truth.

The man squinted thoughtfully, his concern about her stealing the horse battling with his need for money. "Tell you what. I'll ride down there with you behind. When we catch up the wagon, you can pay me and you're on your own then."

"Oh, sir," she said, relief spilling out in her voice. "'Twould be such a blessin'."

He did as he'd said, letting her slide off the old chestnut as soon as the wagon appeared ahead of them. She paid him what she could, then dove into the trees so Hamish wouldn't see her. Not that he was looking, and she didn't think he'd recognise her anyway, but she hoped to keep hidden for as long as she could. They'd reached a broken piece of the road, its path pitted with holes that slowed the wagon's fragile wooden wheels, and Glenna had no trouble keeping up. In fact, she had to be careful she didn't overtake it. Eventually the wagon went one way and Hamish went the other, and they were back to his slow, dull walk.

Then she heard it: the distant crack of musket fire, the booming of artillery, and her stomach flipped. The familiar noises of war sent terror roaring through her heart, but the possibility that Dougal might be in the thick of that very battle was something for which she could hardly bear to hope. She became even warier now that Hamish slowed, cutting into the trees just ahead of her. But Glenna was a creature of the forest, as she had been in the Highlands. There was no tree or shrub she couldn't use to hide behind, and her feet were as quiet as those of the squirrels around her. Hamish appeared not to care about the noise he made, and she realised he was probably right. Who would hear him over all the gunfire?

Smoke hung in the air ahead, like a curtain she'd have to step through in order to see the show. Hamish didn't hesitate, but plunged through the swirling screen. She couldn't afford to lose him. He had led her all the way here, and now it was imperative she make sure he didn't accomplish what he'd set out to do. But first . . .

Her initial view of bright red coats, the colour always worn by the despised English, frightened her. Then she saw the swish of tartan beneath, and the red and white socks spattered with mud, and recognised her countrymen. So it was true. Scots fighting for the English. It made no sense to her, but her frown softened easily into a smile rich with anticipation. She would just have to ask Dougal all about it as they snuggled under a blanket sometime soon.

She stood behind a wall of Highlanders, as she had as a drummer boy so long before, only now she was a different person with a lifetime of experience behind her. As her eyes grew accustomed to the smoke, she scanned the soot-smudged faces of the soldiers, though it was hard to distinguish them in the heat of battle.

Then he was there. Glenna's mouth went bone dry and she almost forgot where she was. The rest of the battle noise was gone, sucked away as she watched him, the grace of his long fingers working the musket, loading, firing, shifting his aim, firing again. He looked up after a shot, checking, and she almost fell to her knees at the sight of that familiar, beloved profile, the sky blue eyes where she'd so often seen herself reflected. Barely able to breathe, she took a step toward him, then stopped, suddenly cold. If she'd found him so easily, so would Hamish. She ducked back, scouring the trees. Where was he? Like her, he'd been dressed in dull forest colours, not offering up a red target. While she primed her pistol, she studied every blade of grass, every rock, until she spotted him, squatting by a shrub only ten feet in front of her. He was staring at Dougal's broad back, a wide grin on his face.

Everything seemed to move very slowly after that. She saw Hamish get to his feet, saw him raise his pistol and extend his arm. He closed one eye to aim. The man's lips were moving, as they always were, quick and raging, spitting out his hatred for the man she loved.

"No!" she screamed, and fired, shooting Hamish through the side of his head.

The sound of a woman screaming turned the soldiers' heads and she looked back, meeting Dougal's eyes. He stared, frowning, looking unsure until she slid the tricorne off her head. Then his eyes widened and the broad red shoulders dropped, though his fingers still curled through the musket's trigger. He tilted his head to one side and mouthed "Glenna?" just as she was grabbed roughly from behind. The momentum spun her around until she faced the man she'd hoped never to see again.

"Goddamn crazy bitch," Frank roared, ripping the pistol from her hand. "What the hell did you just do?"

He practically lifted her by her arms, shoving her back against a tree while he shoved his shoulder hard against her, his mouth only an inch from her own. One hand hooked her throat, squeezing until stars flew in her vision.

"You just killed a soldier, my dear Glenna," he said, stuffing the pistol into the back of his own breeks. "For whatever reason, you just committed a capital offense. I don't think anyone in the world will blame me for what I'm gonna do to you now." He brought his other fist up under her ribs, knocking the wind out of her with one painful whoosh. "That's for the jewellery." The hand was gone from her throat and Glenna bent in half from the impact, gasping for air. Frank slammed his linked fists on the base of her spine, forcing her to her knees. "And that's for blackmailing me. Don't worry. I'll be going after Sarah next. And this . . ." She saw one booted foot pull back and braced for an impact she was helpless to avoid, but it never came. Instead she heard a grunt and the man's body toppled backward.

"Glenna?"

Dougal squatted beside her and touched her face carefully with his fingertips, as if uncertain she was real. She closed her eyes and tried to clear the whirling stars pinging around in the dark, tried to fight a surge of tears, wheezing in whatever breath she could find. When the ability finally came to her, she smiled and met Dougal's incredulous stare.

"Aye, Dougal, 'tis me," she said, her voice hoarse.

"But how—"

She pointed at Hamish, or what was left of him, crumpled a few feet beside them.

"Hamish?" He sounded incredulous. "Ye shot Hamish?"

The air was coming a little easier now, the stars dwindling out of her vision. "Had to. He was going to shoot you."

Cannon boomed nearby, shaking the earth, and Dougal dropped from a squat to his knees. He leaned closer, taking her face in his hands, drinking her in as she did the same. They didn't speak with words, but their eyes were full of each other, oblivious to the carnage going on around them. Tears spilled down her cheeks and he wiped them away, then kissed the place he'd just dried.

"God, Glenna," he whispered into her ear, and she shivered with joy.

"Ain't this sweet?" They both looked up and met the mouth of Frank's pistol barrel. "Sorry to interfere with what looks like a beautiful reunion, but this here bitch is mine. I paid for her. She ain't going nowheres with you or no one else."

Dougal looked at her, and her eyes told him everything, though she knew he'd never been able to read her thoughts, at least not in the way he could with men. Her chin wobbled uncontrollably, and in that instant she relived the rapes, the confinement, the misery.

"Is that right?" Dougal asked, rising slowly to his full height. Frank swallowed but held Dougal's ferocious glare. The pistol wavered, shifting from her to him.

Dougal didn't say a word, only stared at Frank, and Glenna felt an irrational terror that he was going to nod, agree that goods bought and paid for did, in fact, belong to the owner, and walk away. But no. That was only the past few years talking, what they had done to her, how they had destroyed the belief she had in herself and in Dougal. She watched the unblinking blue eyes bore into the smaller man, saw Frank squirm under the scrutiny, and with amazement she realised Dougal was seeing inside Frank's mind.

So now he knew. Now he saw Frank's story and much of her own. Moving faster than she could have imagined, he seized Frank's wrist and twisted it so the pistol dropped to the ground. Frank went with it, collapsing onto his knees with a cry. One twist more and she heard the bone in his wrist snap.

"Ye'd no right," Dougal growled, his voice soft and deadly. "No amount o' money or muscle could make this all right, Mr. Hill." Glenna stared, incredulous, knowing she'd never mentioned Frank's name to Dougal. She watched his power build before her eyes, a potent strength pulsing through and from him, a physical force that seemed to burn the air. It was almost as if he glowed from within, and Glenna felt an impossible urge to grab hold of him, share the magic she could almost see.

Frank was crying now, his broken wrist cradled in his other hand. But his pathetic, pleading expression meant nothing to the man before him. Dougal slid his short sword from his belt and held its point between Frank's red-rimmed eyes.

"I have seen yer crimes, Mr. Hill. Yer thoughts betray ye. If the world were fair, ye'd hang, only I can see too many people in yer wee town would let ye go. Ye've paid them well enough o'er the years." His eyes were like ice now, his face more ferocious than she'd ever seen. "I believe ye deserve to die slow, Mr. Hill, yer belly slit an' yer beatin' heart left to the forest beasts. But no' everyone gets what they deserve, do they?" He leaned close, his mouth only a couple of inches from Frank's tear-tracked face. "My Glenna deserved respect, as did the other girls ye destroyed."

Dougal's mouth tightened further. One of his hands gripped Frank's shoulder, holding him in place while the other thrust sharply forward, as if he punched Frank in the chest. But it wasn't Dougal's fist that plunged into Frank's heart. He yanked the blade back out and wiped the blood on his jacket, then shoved Frank's dying body backward with the heel of his boot.

"I've no time to watch ye die slow," he grumbled.

Out of habit, Glenna stood and reached for Frank's pistol, still lying on the ground by Dougal's feet. She had just closed her fingers around its handle when her arm exploded. She flew back at the impact and crumpled at the foot of a tree, then stared with disbelief at the blood gushing down the sleeve of her dark coat. Dougal was on his knees beside her again, his hand, already wet with Frank's blood, pressed hard against her wound. Another shot rang out, hitting a tree over their heads, and a vague thought came to her that a Frenchman's bullet had caught her. Their troops must be advancing closer, now that the Highlanders were without their lead grenadier.

"No, Glenna!" he yelled, all the strength of his hatred channeled into desperation.

She wanted to hold him, tell him the pain was nothing, assure him she'd be all right. After all, it couldn't be possible that after all this their time would be so short. But oh, it burned. He crushed her against his body when she started to shake. She didn't look up when another pair of boots came alongside, but the voice broke through. A voice she recognised from years before.

"Dougal? What's this? Who's the boy?" John Wallace, the man she'd thought dead so long before, from that awful day when he'd pulled the black slip of paper from the beaver skin hat, peered down at her, and his eyes widened with shock. "Aidan?"

"'Tis a long story, John. Even longer than yer own. This is Glenna. The English took her from me years ago and she's only now found me again. I canna let her die, John."

John pulled off his jacket and yanked his shirt over his head. He tore one stained white sleeve off at the seam and wrapped it tightly around her upper arm. "Clearly not."

She looked up at Dougal, her eyes almost crossing as she fought the pain.

His eyes filled with tears as he met her gaze. "Glenna is the reason I breathe, John."

Her eyes flicked to John, and she remembered Joseph. How both had died when she and Dougal had lived. John met her gaze and she saw sadness, such a deep sadness.

He nodded. "Then go, Dougal. Take her an' find a healer. But dinna let the bastards find ye. If the army catches up, ye'll have no need of yer breath anyway."

The men looked at each other over her head. "Thank ye, John. Keep ye well."

"Ye as well, my friend."

And they were up, Dougal cradling her in his arms as he tore through the brush, coming out on the roadside and not stopping to check for directions. His expression was set, his eyes focused somewhere else. Now she was here, in his arms, pressed against his warmth, and yet she craved his voice, his touch, his smile. She breathed in his stink of battle-weary uniform and sweat and lost the fight to stay conscious.

CHAPTER 40

Leaving the World Behind

Dougal ran farther than he'd ever run, barely noticing her precious weight as it stole the strength from his arms. It didn't matter. His arms could fall off if they wanted, just so long as he saved her.

Glenna! He glanced down at her grimy face, the angel eyes closed now, but she still breathed. He shifted her so her breath stroked his neck like a feather, tickling and reassuring and filling him with a strength he'd never known before. *Hang on, Glenna,* he thought, unable to speak through his straining lungs. He heard the promising shush of running water ahead and ran straight for it. When at last he reached a stream, he laid her gently beside it, then collapsed beside her on all fours, breathing hard. She lay still, her frail figure almost swallowed up in the man's coat she wore. Sweat dripped from his brow, landing in the grass beside her, and he crawled to the water to flush his face and cool his burning throat. Then he crawled back and stared at her unconscious body a moment longer, swallowing hard with disbelief. *She was here. She'd found him.* So there had been a reason for him to survive all along.

His fingers pried open the bits of sleeve around the injury and he nodded, fairly confident the bleeding had almost stopped. His trembling fingers fumbled with the knot John had tied, then gently removed both the tourniquet and her coat. She moaned as he moved her, but the little sound only encouraged him. He would have been more concerned if she hadn't objected to the pain.

The sleeve of the linen tunic beneath was almost black with her blood, but he was right. The bleeding had stopped for now. He cupped his hands and dipped them into the stream, then poured the cool water on the messy wound. She jerked awake at the sudden cold, but he spoke softly, reassuring her, then brought more water. He cleaned her arm as well as he could, inspecting it as he went along, murmuring sweet words, though she remained only slightly alert. She had bled a lot, but it didn't look as if anything major had been struck. He was fairly sure the bullet had passed straight through, which was good. Still, she would need help from someone far more experienced than he.

When she was cleaner, he rinsed out John's sleeve and tied it back around her arm, though this time it was a bandage rather than a tourniquet. He covered her with the black coat, then his own, then curled around her on the ground, holding her close. When night fell, he stayed awake as long as he could, wanting to know if she cried out, needing to know if they'd been discovered, but in the morning they were still alone, and colour had flowed back into her lips.

He shifted onto his elbow and gazed down at her, remembering every freckle and line he'd known so well, spotting ones he'd never seen before and wanting to know when they'd appeared. She was lean, but other than her arm, she seemed healthy, despite . . . He closed his eyes, not wanting to relive what he'd seen in Frank's thoughts. What she'd survived threatened to kill him. He wished he could have done much worse than kill Frank Hill.

God, Glenna. How can ye be here? How did ye find me? Do ye ken how my soul has cried for ye every day, every night?

Very gently he slid his fingers down a lock of her hair, playing with a knot that had tied itself near one small ear. Her eyes blinked open and Dougal almost cried, seeing their familiar blue.

"Dougal," she whispered. "Oh, how I missed ye."

He did cry then, a slow, fat tear creeping down one of his smoke-smudged cheeks and dropping onto the grass. She did, too, her face tortured with emotions as she reached up with her good hand and touched his face. He wanted to say so many things, but he couldn't speak. There was nothing in his mind but her, no words forming, no way to tell her how he felt, how he couldn't breathe, how all that mattered was her. She seemed all right with that, though. She ran those little fingers over his short beard, over the creases cut deeply around his eyes, over a scar he'd picked up a few weeks past from his own brush with a bullet. Her other arm brushed accidentally against him and she gasped slightly, reminded of the wound, but he'd already checked. There was no more bleeding and her arm was warm, not hot.

"Ye will be fine, *mo ghràidh*," he managed.

She nodded. "Kiss me?"

"Oh, Glenna," he said, finally smiling and riding a wave of joy when she answered that smile. "I thought ye'd never ask."

He touched her lips with his, so soft the kiss was barely there, and almost panicked, thinking the feel of her was unfamiliar. But she hooked her hand behind his neck and pulled him closer, pressing her mouth against his, and he lost himself, falling back into the magic of her, the sweet, wonderful Glenna who was his everything. When at last they drew apart, they were both flushed and her quick breaths almost stole what remained of his self-control. He needed to love her, to sink into her warmth and feel her around him, to hear her sweet cry as she moved with him and beneath him, but not here. Not now.

"What will we do, Dougal, now that we're both outlaws again?" she asked, twisting the side of her mouth into a curl he'd never forgotten. "We've both just killed men an' ye just deserted the king's army."

He'd wondered that himself, though his first priority had been to ensure her safety. He'd lain awake for hours the night before, curled against her as he thought it over, trying to figure out where they could hide, where they could live in peace again. And then his brother's voice had come to him, as clear as the lonely call of a wolf in the next valley. *Dougal. Come home.*

He'd smiled in the dark, his cheek pressing against the back of her head, feeling happier than he'd ever thought possible. Now he lay with her in the early sunlight, starting a new day. Dougal kissed her again, then set his cheek against hers and nuzzled into the messy pile of soft blond hair that cushioned her head, making her giggle with his breath on her ear. He chuckled and felt her curl instinctively against him, wanting him, needing him as he needed her.

"Ye needna worry about a thing, my love. We've a home an' family waitin' for us."

She sighed, relaxing. "Never leave me, Dougal."

"No. Never again."

An owl hooted from nearby, unconcerned but vocal, his calls clear and haunting. He did it again, then stopped, leaving a vacuum of sound. Dougal's fingers pressed against Glenna, sensing another rhythm. It beat slowly, calm and determined. He pressed his ear against her body and sank into the sound of her heart, the gentle, soothing assurance that she was there, she was there.

TURN THE PAGE FOR A SPECIAL EXCERPT
FROM GENEVIEVE GRAHAM'S . . .

Under the Same Sky

CHAPTER 1

A Dubious Gift

He has always been there. That fact is as important to me as my own heartbeat.

I first saw him when we were children: a young boy with eyes as dark as rain-soaked mud, staring at me from under a mane of chestnut hair. I kept him secret, invisible to everyone but me. He should have been invisible to me as well, because he was never really there, on the same windblown land, under the same sky. We never stood together, never touched as other people did. Our eyes met, and our thoughts, but our bodies were like opposite banks of a river.

When I was little, I thought of him as just another child. One with a slow smile and gentle thoughts that soothed me, as if he held my hand. When he didn't fade with my childhood years, I began to wonder if he were a spirit, communicating through my dreams. In my heart, I knew he was more. His world was the same as mine. He was as human as I.

I was born in the year of Our Lord 1730 on a patch of grassland in South Carolina. Our pine-walled house, dried to an ashy gray, stood alone, like an island in a sea of grass. Its only neighbours were a couple of rocky hills that spilled mud down their sides when it rained. They stood about a five-minute run from our house, just close enough to remind us they were there. The house barely stayed upright during the mildest of storms, and we had no neighbours to whom we might run if it ever collapsed. When winter struck, the wind sought out gaps in the walls, shrieking around bits of cloth we stuffed into the holes. The cold pierced our skin as it had the walls, and we wrapped our bodies in dried pelts that reeked of tanned leather. Our barn offered even weaker shelter to one aged horse and a few poorly feathered chickens who, fortunately, were good layers. My father owned a rifle, and he occasionally chanced upon a prize from the nearby forest. He also ran a tangled line of traps that provided most of our meals. Beyond that, we had little. What we did have we mended many, many times.

I was never a regular child, spending my days with nothing but play and chores on my mind. How could I be? My dreams showed me what would happen an hour, a day, a year before it did. I had always dreamed. Not symbolic imaginings of flying or falling, but dreams that showed me where my life would eventually go.

I could also see what wasn't visible, and hear what made no sound. When I was a toddler, my mother encouraged my odd abilities through games. She would pry a toy from my grip and hide it somewhere, then return and say:

"Go, Maggie. Go find your toy."

I ran to the target and came back every time, prize in hand.

Mother said I had "the Sight." I never told her there was more. I never told her about the boy I could see, who spoke to me without words. I wanted to keep him safe within secrecy, as if sharing him might make him disappear.

My dreams introduced me to people I had never seen, and took me to places I could never have known existed. Most nights they appeared and vanished, leaving vague memories in the back of my mind. Other nights I awoke bathed in sweat, drowning in images I didn't understand: hands flexing into fists, bristled fibres of rope chafing my skin, the thunder of horses' hooves. And blood. So much blood.

Mother didn't experience dreams like mine, but she knew I had them. Their existence terrified her. Mother was a small woman of few words. When she saw me awake from the dreams, my head still fuzzy with half memories, her face paled and she looked away, helpless and afraid.

Her mother, my grandmother, had had the Sight. Mother both respected and feared its power. My grandmother saw her own death a week before it happened. She felt the hands as they tied her to a stake, smelled the smoke as the tinder beneath her bare feet caught fire, and heard the jeering of the crowd as they watched her burn as a witch.

Mother told me the story only once. That didn't mean it couldn't repeat itself.

Mother did the best she could. Many nights I awoke in her arms, not remembering her arrival, only knowing she came when my screams jolted her from sleep. She held me, rocked me, sang lullabies that ran through my body like blood. But her songs held no answers, offered no way to chase the images from my mind. She did what she could as my mother, but I faced the dreams on my own.

Except when I was with the boy no one could see. Sometimes he would brush against my thoughts like a feather falling from a passing bird. Sometimes we conversed without words. We could just *be*, and we understood.

As an infant, I lived with my mother and father and our decrepit horse. My sister Adelaide was born two years after I was. When I first saw her, wrapped like a pea in a faded gray pod, I stroked her little cheek with my finger and loved her without question. We were best friends before the newborn clouds faded from her eyes. Two years later, she moved out of her crib and my bed became ours.

Our brother was born that year. He died before he drew his first breath. We named him Reuben and buried him next to the barn.

Little Ruth arrived on a cloudless day in March when I was six. Ruth Mary Johnson. She was soft and fair and filled with light. Even my father, a man with little patience and less affection, gentled at the sight of her.

Neither one of my sisters had the Sight. Like my mother, they were slender and delicate, like fair-skinned deer. My mother's skin was always so pale, even under the baking sun, she looked almost transparent. The only way to bring colour to her cheeks was to make her laugh, and my sisters and I did our best to paint them pink. I took after my father, with his brown hair and plain face, though my hands weren't as quick to form fists as his. My arms and back were built for lifting.

By the time I turned seven, my dreams had become more vivid, and more useful to the family. I was able to catch Ruth before she tripped down a hill, able to find a scrap of cloth my mother sought. One winter I dreamed of a corn harvest, and my mother, daring to believe, planted a garden of it that spring. Her gardens never provided much food, because the ground around our home was either cracked by drought or flooded by heavy rains that stirred the dust to mud. That summer, though, the corn grew high.

Usually my dreams came when I slept, but sometimes they appeared when I sat quietly on my own. They weren't always clear. Most of the time they had faded into wisps of thought by the time I came back into focus, but they never fully disappeared.

My mother and I never talked about my dreams. Neither of us acknowledged them out loud.

Just like we never talked about my father's death.

It happened on the night of my seventeenth birthday.

I dreamed of a wheel from our wagon, its spokes blurred to a quick gray. Our ancient gelding pulled the bumping wagon over a moonlit ridge as my father returned from a late trip to town.

He slumped on the wagon bench, his weary body jiggling over every bump. I saw him lift his chin and glance toward the sky. Low-lying storm clouds glowed in the light of the full harvest moon. Everything around the wagon took on a strange orange tinge: the sparse patches of spring grass, the heaps of boulders casting pointed shadows in the dark. Tufts of salted brown hair peeked from under my father's hat, and he tugged the brim lower on his forehead. My father was not a patient man. He clucked to the horse and snapped the reins over the animal's back. In response, the gelding tossed his head and picked up speed just as they reached the peak of a long hill. My father should have known better. The pitch was too steep. Once the wagon started racing down the hill, the horse couldn't slow. The wheels spun out of control, bouncing off rocks and jolting my father so he barely stayed in his seat. He leaned back, lying almost flat as he strained against the reins, but couldn't slow the panicked horse.

The wagon clattered downhill, too fast to avoid a boulder in its path, and the front wheel smashed into splinters. Jerking in reaction, the wagon staves twisted from the horse's harness, ricocheted off a solitary oak, and hit the ground with a sickening crack. The horse screamed and ran faster still. My father struggled to loosen the reins tangled around his wrists, but couldn't do it fast enough. He was yanked from his seat and tossed into the air like a sack of flour. He hit the ground. Hard. His body crashed against rocks and shrubs as he struggled to free himself from the reins, tearing his clothes and scraping long gashes in his skin. The horse raced down the hill, eyes white with terror, chased by the screams and the body that thumped behind him like an anchor.

After a while, the screaming stopped. The horse checked its wild run and trotted to a stop, sides heaving, the insides of his back legs wet with white foam. His nostrils flared, and he bobbed his head nervously at the scent of fresh blood. But he sensed no imminent danger. He dropped his head to a patch of grass and began to graze. My father's lifeless body rolled to rest a few feet away.

The dream ended and I sat up, gasping, the neckline of my shift soaked with sweat. I twisted toward the window, but all was silent, silver under the moon. I threw back the covers and stood, shaking, on the cold floor.

I knew where to find my father's body. Not far—the horse had raced past a familiar oak my sisters and I often climbed.

I woke my mother and we ran without a word along the dimly lit path, faded nightgowns flapping around our ankles.

My father's body was little more than a heap of bloodstained rags. The horse stood nearby, chewing, glancing at us before dropping his head to the grass again. Scraps of cloth fluttered along the pathway the wagon had taken, bits of clothing caught on rocks. My father's tired gray hat lay at the top of the hill.

I stared at what was left of him and wasn't sure how I felt. He hadn't been a kind man. The only thing he had ever given us was beatings.

Still, I should have been lost in grief beside my mother, but my mind was on something else. My dreams had changed. For the first time, they had occurred simultaneously with the event. My dreams were no longer limited to vague messages forecasting the future.

Burying a man in hard ground is difficult work. It took two full days for Adelaide and me to manage a trench large enough for his mangled body. Even then, we had to bend his knees a bit so he fit into the hole. My mother read from her Bible, then nodded at me to shovel the earth onto his body.

Our father had never spent much time with us when he was alive. Even so, the house seemed eerily quiet after his death. It was strange not hearing his heavy footsteps, not hearing him gripe about the sorry state of his life. We mourned, but not terribly. When he left the living, my father took with him the stale reek of alcohol, a sullen expression, and a pair of overused fists.

My mother, my sisters, and I were forced to take on my father's duties, which included driving the wagon to town for buying and selling. The ride took over two hours each way, but once we arrived, we forgot every bump. My sisters and I never tired of the activity in town. The painted building fronts with fine glass windows, the people who walked the treeless street, kicking up dust as they visited the stores. Dirty children watched like sparrows on perches while fancy ladies strolled the boardwalks under parasols, protecting their faces from the sun, tucking their hands into the arms of stiff-backed men in suits and hats. Sometimes they were shadowed by people whose eyes gleamed white out of sullen black faces. My mother told us they were from Africa, brought to America as slaves.

The town of Saxe Gotha boasted more than two skin colours. Fierce tattoos and feathers enhanced the bronze skin and black hair of men who moved with the casual grace of cats. They avoided the plank walkways, preferring the dust of the road under their feet.

My father had told us stories about Indians and their bloodthirsty ways. We had stared open-mouthed as he regaled us with violent tales. So when I saw the Indians in town, they both frightened and intrigued me, but I never saw them attack anyone. They were in town for the same reason we were: to trade. An uneasy peace existed between them and the white men while business was conducted. They brought deerskins and beaded jewellery and left with weapons, tools, and rum. No one spoke to them on the street, and they offered no conversation. Business complete, they leapt onto the bare backs of their horses and disappeared into the shadows of the trees beyond the town.

I felt an odd connection to these men. When my mother led my sisters and me into the local shop to trade eggs or small hides for blankets or whatever else we needed, the other customers avoided us as if they were afraid our poverty might touch them. At the end of our day, we climbed onto our clumsily rebuilt wagon, pulled by the only horse we'd ever owned, and were gone.

We crossed paths with the Indians, but never came close enough to make contact. And yet their images began to appear in my dreams, to emerge from the trees and surround me with purpose, the tight skins of their drums resonating with the heartbeat of the earth.

CHAPTER 2

Battle Dream

There was so much blood. My senses reeled with the unfamiliar heat of it, the stench, the sticky weight of it.

It was more than dream. It had to be. The images were real, but hadn't come from my own thoughts. It wasn't my bloodstained hand that gripped the slick hilt of a sword.

But I knew whose it was. He was perhaps twenty, two years older than I, with deep brown eyes. I had seen him my entire life. We had grown together since I was a little girl, in dreams as clear as waking days.

Usually when I saw him, he was at peace. Not this time. His dark hair was pulled back from his sweat-streaked face, tied into a tail. His teeth were bared. He was weak with injuries and exhaustion, disheartened by the sight of an endless tide of red coats pushing toward him through a field of smoke. Muskets and cannons boomed in their wake.

Every one of his muscles ached. I rolled over in my bed, feeling the tension between my shoulders though I was cradled within my mattress. His head thrummed, echoing the drums in the field, the crack of guns, and his racing heartbeat.

I felt what he felt, but my body was miles away. My eyes burned with gritty tears. My limbs were heavy, weighted down by defeat. The stink of sulphur singed my nostrils, and my feet squelched through ice-cold muck while my body slept in my warm, safe bedroom, the air sweet with baking bread.

The sensations roaring through my veins were unlike anything I'd felt before. Fear forced the blood through my veins at an exhilarating speed, but I had to control the panic. He was in grave danger. He needed more than encouragement from me. He needed me to be a part of him. My senses were alive, my body untouched. I gave him all I had, despite the fact I couldn't touch him. Where he felt pain, I brought a healing touch. Where there was dizziness, I gave him strength.

A grunt alerted me to someone approaching from behind. In my mind I thrust out an arm, and the body I inhabited followed. He jumped, reacting to my unexpected presence, and I felt his sense of surprise. But of course I was there. I would never let him die. He took the strength I offered and turned it to rage. He roared, fighting for his life, twisting and moving with the violent grace of a wolf. His sword blocked a strike, although the smoke was so thick I almost didn't see it happen. Steel sliced through the air on his other side, and I turned to foil its attack, knowing he would turn with me. Again and again he blocked killing blows and struck out, cutting through the attacking soldiers. His strength was returning, his confidence back in place. I felt a surge of power as it filled his body and mind.

All the silent communication from our childhood had brought us to this point. I would never leave him. I would be wherever, whatever he needed me to be, if only in his thoughts. I would give him courage and strength and love. And he would give me the same whenever my mind called to him.

Close enough that our minds were like one, far enough that we never felt each other's touch. We were what we had always been.

CHAPTER 3

Beyond the House

For nearly two years I spent my days looking forward to falling asleep. For me, the darkness was full of life.

The dreams that comforted me the most were the ones featuring him, the boy from my childhood, now grown into a man about the same age as I. He was tall with a solid build and ruddy complexion. Dark hair fell in loose waves to just past his shoulders, and sometimes a short beard framed lips that curled slightly at the edges. When we saw each other in dreams, his smile felt so warm I thought I might burst into flame. But it was his fathomless brown eyes that spoke to me the most.

He usually visited when I slept, but if I could find a quiet place and relax, I might see him under the light of the sun. He appeared in my thoughts as if to watch me, as intrigued by me as I was by him. Sometimes I sensed his presence, but couldn't see him. Occasionally the spectre of a wolf loped through my thoughts, but somehow I knew the spirit of a man lived within its coarse dark coat. The eyes were the same: unflinching, deep wells of intelligence. So, without any other name to give him, I took to calling him Wolf.

I had dreams where I walked without him, seeing images I didn't try to understand: colours that swirled and left me breathless, streams of voices shining silver as they passed, featureless faces shadowed by unfamiliar trees.

Then something changed. The dreams went dark.

Nightmares invaded my sleep the summer after I turned seventeen. It was the hottest summer anyone could remember. Weeks passed with no rain, and the air grew fragile with need. Dead grass lay flat on the cracked earth with no hope of resurrection. Cicadas screeched from the faraway forest, a constant trill from dawn until dusk. And at night apparitions stole my sleep—bulky shadows creeping closer or retreating at their whim, like creatures hunting.

Everyone has nightmares, but mine were different. They showed me my future. Except they were unclear. All I knew was something horrible was coming. Something I couldn't see, but knew. I could do nothing but wait.

I found it hard to fall asleep in the heat, but I didn't mind. When sleep finally claimed me, I wished it hadn't come. My nightmares became darker every night, oppressive with growing urgency. Their menace accompanied me constantly, even creeping into my waking hours.

When the need for waiting came to an end, I knew. On the morning of that day, sunshine flooded the walls of the bedroom I shared with my sisters, but I saw only blackness. Fighting dizziness and nausea, I rose from our bed, needing to escape the grasp of the dreams. My legs were weak, and I clung to the yellowed wall. I stared at my sleeping sisters for so long they awoke and returned my stare.

"What is it?" Adelaide whispered.

My mouth opened and closed, but words were trapped in my throat.

"Get Mama," Adelaide said to Ruth, keeping her eyes on me.

Ruth ran to our mother's room, next to ours. Mother came and stood with me, letting me cling to her as if I were a small child. Slightly steadied by her presence, I dressed in the same dress I wore every day. I only had one other, and I kept it folded in our wardrobe, saving it until this one was too dirty to wear. On the table by our bedroom door sat a large tin bowl and a small ewer half full of precious well water. I dipped in a cloth and used it to scrub my teeth, then wet down my hair with my fingers and tied a neat blue ribbon around my braid. My mother had given me the ribbon a week before, in celebration of Adelaide's fifteenth birthday. Blue for me, pink for Adelaide, and yellow for Ruth. To distract myself from the pounding fear in my head, I kept busy, mending torn clothing and cleaning the house. I wove a thin bracelet for Adelaide out of the dry grass that brushed our house's walls, and pieced together a little dress for the black-eyed rag doll Ruth carried everywhere.

The day seethed with heat, trembling in distorted waves over the baked grass. There wasn't even a hint of breeze. The late afternoon sun bubbled low on the horizon, and its glare painted black silhouettes of our small barn and listing fence posts.

From out of the silence came the sounds of horses' hooves, heavy on the dried earth, coming toward our house.

My mother had never been a hunter, but I had seen her use our father's rifle against coyotes that pestered our hens. She had never hit one while I'd been watching, but the crack of a shot scattered the predators and urged them to seek easier meals. At the sounds of the horses, she grabbed the rifle from where it hung on the wall. My mother, my sisters, and I crowded through the doorway and stood on either side of its crooked frame, squinting into the light and watching the black profiles of men on horseback as they rode toward us. She held the rifle across her body like a shield, resting the end of its barrel on our faded wooden doorstep.

Before their faces came into view, I knew who they were. I started to shake. Adelaide took my hand and clung to it.

Fiction
Graham, Genevieve
Sound of The Heart

Fiction
Graham, Genevieve
Sound of The Heart

DATE	ISSUED TO